Two brand-new stories in every volume... twice a month!

Duets Vol. #39

"Colleen Collins is a real find," says *Under the Covers*, and there's no doubt Colleen is one of the funniest authors around. Joining her in this volume is talented Darlene Gardner, an Intimate Moments writer making her Duets debut with a hilarious story!

Duets Vol. #40

According to *Romantic Times*, Cara Summers "thrills us with her fresh, exciting voice... rich characterization and spicy adventure." Teaming up with Cara in this humorous Christmas volume is talented Lori Wilde, who has more than ten books to her credit.

Be sure to pick up both Duets volumes today!

She's Got Mail!

Ben tapped Rosie on the shoulder. "Take a seat."

Rosie looked around for the man she was to meet. The poor guy desperately needed a man-to-man talk with magazine columnist Mr. Real. Only he had no idea *Mr.* Real was really a *Ms.*

"The guy I'm meeting is late, too," Ben said. "Do you want a coffee?"

"That would be great." Rosie smiled in appreciation as she watched Ben walk away. He had a self-assured, confident gait. Confidence—she liked that in a man. Her gaze dropped. And he had one terrific butt—she liked that in a man, too!

A few minutes later Ben arrived with two cups of coffee. "I'm meeting someone from a local magazine. *Real Men.* Do you know it?" he asked.

Rosie nodded absently, but her heart was racing. Slowly pieces of a puzzle were starting to form a picture in her mind. She and Ben were both meeting someone at the same time, in the same place. He was meeting someone from *her* magazine. Ohmigod! Ben was there to meet *her!*

For more, turn to page 9

Forget Me? <u>Not</u>

"If Reid was so wonderful, suppose you explain why you like me better," Zach teased.

He was toying with Amanda again. She understood that, but it didn't make it any more palatable.

Once, just once, she'd like to turn Zach topsy-turvy and see how *he* liked it. She thought of Zach in the parking lot at the the go-kart track, earnestly informing her that he wasn't about commitment. That all he was about was having a good time. A devilish idea struck her, and she didn't even try to extinguish it. It was time she got back at Zach.

"I'm not sure if I do like you better," she lied. "But I certainly couldn't go ahead with my wedding to Reid, considering that I might be pregnant by you."

"Pregnant?" Zach uttered the single word. Then his gorgeous mouth dropped open, those incredible blue eyes widened and his smooth skin paled beneath his tan.

For the first time since Amanda had met him, Zach Castelli was speechless.

For more, turn to page 197

If you purchased this book without a cover you should be aware that this book is stolen property. It was reported as "unsold and destroyed" to the publisher, and neither the author nor the publisher has received any payment for this "stripped book."

HARLEQUIN DUETS

ISBN 0-373-44105-3

SHE'S GOT MAIL!
Copyright © 2000 by Colleen Collins

FORGET ME? *NOT*
Copyright © 2000 by Darlene Hrobak Gardner

All rights reserved. Except for use in any review, the reproduction or utilization of this work in whole or in part in any form by any electronic, mechanical or other means, now known or hereafter invented, including xerography, photocopying and recording, or in any information storage or retrieval system, is forbidden without the written permission of the publisher, Harlequin Enterprises Limited, 225 Duncan Mill Road, Don Mills, Ontario, Canada M3B 3K9.

All characters in this book have no existence outside the imagination of the author and have no relation whatsoever to anyone bearing the same name or names. They are not even distantly inspired by any individual known or unknown to the author, and all incidents are pure invention.

This edition published by arrangement with Harlequin Books S.A.

® and TM are trademarks of the publisher. Trademarks indicated with ® are registered in the United States Patent and Trademark Office, the Canadian Trade Marks Office and in other countries.

Visit us at www.eHarlequin.com

Printed in U.S.A.

She's Got Mail!

COLLEEN COLLINS

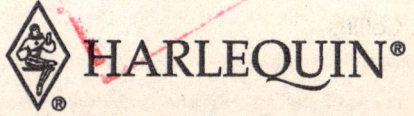

HARLEQUIN®

TORONTO • NEW YORK • LONDON
AMSTERDAM • PARIS • SYDNEY • HAMBURG
STOCKHOLM • ATHENS • TOKYO • MILAN • MADRID
PRAGUE • WARSAW • BUDAPEST • AUCKLAND

Dear Reader,

I've always loved those classic films that feature the theme of mistaken identity, especially when a man—by necessity—has to be disguised as a woman. (Remember Jack Lemmon and Tony Curtis in *Some Like It Hot*, or Dustin Hoffman in *Tootsie?*) The fun heats up when the guy becomes hopelessly smitten with a beautiful woman. But how's he supposed to win his lady love when he's busy being the girl's best friend? *Female* friend, that is. Being a Duets author, I couldn't help wondering what would happen if I turned this scenario around.

In *She's Got Mail!*, ambitious magazine writer Rosie Myers has to fill in for *Real Men* magazine's "A Real Man Answers Real Questions" column. The catch? She has to pretend to be a *real* man. So when she starts to get letters from the man of her dreams, she's in trouble. Because Ben Taylor thinks he's getting man-to-man advice—from the woman who's turning his world upside down!

I hope you have as much fun reading this story as I did writing it. I'd love to hear what you think. Write to me at P.O. Box 12159, Denver, CO 80212.

Enjoy,

Colleen Collins

For my sister, Judy Collins.
This one's for you, Doots!

1

ROSALIND "ROSIE" MYERS'S mother always swore Rosie would be late to her own funeral. Rosie tried not to think such morbid thoughts as she skidded her Dodge Neon around a corner, bounced the front wheel over a curb, and careened down an alley.

Alanis Morissette might be wailing a woeful tune over the car radio, but Rosie felt calm. Thanks to her newly rented parking space—located in a primo spot next to the back entrance of her Chicago office building—she'd be on time to work this morning. Worst case scenario, she'd have to speed-walk to her desk. But she'd be there, copyediting, mere minutes after eight this fine June morning. Which should please her manager, Teresa, who didn't care about the funeral, but just wanted Rosie to be punctual.

Brushing crumbs from her breakfast, a nutri-quasi-Twinkie bar she'd chomped between Michigan Avenue and State Street, Rosie checked the plastic digital watch face she'd taped to the console.

It was already mere minutes after eight.

Okay, maybe she'd be running, not speed-walking, to her desk, but she'd be gripping her pencil and inserting commas by a quarter after, at the latest.

Whomp. The car lurched over a speed bump, the back fender scraping its adieu. Cringing, Rosie listened for any telltale clanging behind her. None. Good! Her budget didn't allow for another muffler pipe replacement.

Ahead, to the right, she spied the familiar concrete steps that led up to the back entrance of the posh Loop office building. Directly behind those steps was her coveted parking space. Like a little home away from home.

Home. Her insides twinged as she flashed on the family farm in Colby, Kansas, where she'd lived all of her life before moving to Chicago seven months ago. Through the crack in her windshield, she peered at the gray Chicago air and wondered where along the way the blue skies of Kansas turned dirty. Or at what point the breezes that rustled through wheat fields became winds whistling down streets filled with cars and pedestrians.

She passed the steps and turned into her space....

Screech.

And slammed on the brakes.

Or at what point some jerk pinched her parking space!

Blinking, she gripped the wheel, amazed she'd managed to miss rear-ending a sleek, black BMW that had taken up residence in her space. *Her* space! Shaking from the near accident and the gall of the intruder, Rosie shoved the gear into reverse and backed up a few feet. After setting the brake, she jumped out of the car.

Splash!

Her loafer-clad foot landed solidly in a pothole filled with dirty water. She looked down at the splotches of dark water on her white leggings. Some of the mud had also splashed onto the bottom of her brown corduroy skirt. Her co-workers would think she'd slogged through trenches to make it into work. Although she doubted any of the editorial staff at *Real Men* magazine would believe *that* excuse for her tardiness, especially Teresa. Now she'd have to park blocks away. Rather than *mere* minutes late, she'd be *mega* minutes late.

She glared at the splotchless BMW. Sidestepping the pothole, she moved closer—her feet making squishing sounds as she walked—to the offensive automobile and scrutinized the license plate. ILITIG8.

I litigate. "I'll just bet you do," she muttered, eyeing the upscale car.

Her eyes narrowed as she peered up at the bank of square windows along the third floor of her brick office building. *Real Men* magazine, her company, took the bottom two floors of this building. On the third floor were some stockbrokers, accountants, and if memory served her correctly, *one* lawyer.

"Now I've got you," she said, pleased with her impromptu sleuthing. She was going to be substantially late to work now because it would take forever and a day to find a parking space. *If I'm going to be mega-late anyway, after walking back, I'll take a few extra minutes and pay a visit to the third floor before heading to my desk.*

Honk!

Rosie turned and glared at a square yellow truck stopped behind her Dodge. A burly arm, covered with hair and tattoos, waved at her in a very unceremonious fashion.

"You own this alley, lady?" The truck driver's voice sounded hairier than his arm.

Men. Couldn't deal with a little inconvenience. Rosie brushed back a curl that had toppled over her right eye. "As a matter of fact, I do!" she retorted, seizing the opportunity to vent. Falling back on the coping mechanism that started in her teenage years when she had to deal with her four strong-willed, overprotective older brothers, she adopted the personality type of one of the Greek goddesses to give her strength.

Although she was much better at running, she sashayed back to her Dodge with the grace of Artemis, a perfect choice for an alley goddess. After settling into the driver's seat and easing the car down the lane, Rosie twiddled her fingers in a goodbye wave to the fuming trucker.

"GOOD MORNING!" A hand, wriggling bright orange-tipped fingernails, snaked around Benjamin Taylor's office door.

Ben gripped his cup of coffee as his ex-wife's head followed the hand. Meredith's lips were the same color as her fingertips. He momentarily wondered if that was a real lipstick color...or if she'd been kissing those plastic pylons the city put on the streets. New lipstick. New nails. Maybe she'd just broken up with her latest boyfriend, Dexter-Something, and was turning to cones for attention and affection.

Or turning to her ex-husband, easygoing, always-there-for-you Ben.

"No good morning?" Meredith put on her best pout, which—to Ben's still blurry precoffee vision—looked as though she'd condensed her cone-orange lips into a circle of glowing lava.

"Morning," he barked, then quickly took a sip of hot coffee. *Please, God, don't let those lava lips feel the need to plant a kiss somewhere.*

"That's better," she simpered. The rest of Meredith appeared in the doorway. He tried not to squint at the visual blast of bold orange, green and blue that comprised some satin kimono-robe-thing she was wearing. Typically when she dropped a boyfriend, or vice versa, Meredith also dropped her old look. The facts were stacking up that this new oriental theme was the result of a recent breakup with Hex...Lex...whatever his name was.

She eyed a lamp in the corner. "I saw the most to-die-for coatrack—black lacquer, faux mother-of-pearl inlay—that would look *perfect* there...."

Ben stiffened. Typically, when she took on a new theme, so did Ben's office. That's what happened when one's ex-wife was an interior decorator who had enough money to indulge these whims. New themes weren't a bad thing, except when the jobs were left incomplete. History had proven that she'd start redoing some wall or chair—or coatrack—in a to-die-for style, fall madly in love with some new man, and leave Ben's office in midtheme.

Ben had long ago decided that just as archeologists interpreted the lives of cavemen from the wall drawings, someone would someday track the love life of Meredith Taylor from the various decorating themes in Ben's office.

"That lamp stays," Ben warned.

It still irked him that she'd kept his last name. You'd think an ex-wife who'd been remarried and divorced since your divorce would keep husband number two's last name. Or revert to her old, original name or use *any* name other than the name the two of you shared during a short, fitful marriage that, at best, was a millisecond of insanity in an eternal universe.

"All right, lamp stays." She blinked her overmascaraed eyes at him. "You've never spoken to me in that tone of voice."

His outburst had surprised even him. But one look at

Meredith's eyes told him to tread carefully—this was a brokenhearted woman on the redecorating rebound. "I plead not enough coffee."

She arched one eyebrow. "Darling, sometimes you say the oddest things."

"Lawyer talk." Yep, she'd definitely broken up with Dexter-Whatever. She never called Ben darling when she was involved with someone.

"Like my hair?" she asked, gesturing toward it with those orange-tipped appendages.

He wondered when the hair question would raise its head. He tried not to frown as he checked out the hodge-podge of curls and what was sticking out... "What are those? Pick-Up Sticks?"

"Darling, they're chopsticks!"

Chopsticks? "It's so...Dharma." The way bits of her hair stuck out, it also looked like a bird's nest gone amok. But he had enough sense to keep that thought to himself.

Whether she was going through an oriental theme or a bird theme, he noted the slight stoop to her shoulders and the dark circles under her eyes. Despite their tumultuous divorce, and the fact she always returned to Ben like a swallow to Capistrano, he didn't have the heart to hurt her feelings further. It was so obvious that Meredith was in mourning.

"No, really, your hair looks...nice," he murmured, making a mental note not to have Chinese for lunch.

"Nice—?" Her green eyes took on an expectant gleam that said, "Only one word? *Nice?*"

"Nice...and brown," he amended.

Too little, too late. The gleam took on a sinister edge. She opened her mouth to say something, but was cut off by a second high-pitched female voice.

"Mer-e-dith!" Heather, whose idea of year-around fashion, rain or shine, was a skimpy shift dress, wrapped her slim brown arms around his ex-wife's shoulders. They gave each other air kisses. Heather pulled back and appraised Meredith's new look. "You look cool! Dig your hair, too! That let-it-go look is *so* in these days."

So much for the oriental versus bird themes. It was a let-it-go theme. Dread chilled Ben's veins as he imagined Meredith redecorating his office—or part of it—in a let-it-go style. He gave his head a shake, trying to dislodge the images of chopsticks and bird's nests adorning a corner wall.

Meredith smiled demurely, obviously mollified by the avalanche of Heather's unsolicited compliments—a far better coup than Ben's two-word response. She lightly fondled one of the chopsticks. "Thank you. Felt like trying something new."

Heather's blue eyes softened. "Broke up with Dexter, huh?"

Meredith's cone lips quivered. She sniffled, loudly, before collapsing into Heather's arms. Heather, her long blond hair spilling down the gaudy kimono, shot Ben a look. "Don't you have anything to say?" she asked edgily.

"You're late."

Heather flashed him an impatient look. "Not to me, to Meredith."

"Her hair looks nice and brown. But it's almost nine and you're late."

Heather huffed something under her breath and continued cradling the distraught Meredith, who was blubbering about Dexter wanting ice cream back.

Ice cream?

Ben watched the two of them, his ex-wife and ex-fiancé, and realized he almost had enough exes to play tic-tac-toe. But at thirty-six, he was not in the market for another ex. Or even another current. If anything, he yearned for basic male companionship. Hell, a night of beer and bowling with the boys would suffice. Although, truth be told, he preferred wine, and chess—pastimes he once shared with his best buddy Matt before Matt fell in love and moved to California.

Since then, the closest Ben ever came to a man-to-man conversation, in a roundabout way, was when Heather would read out loud the "A Real Man Answers Real Questions" column from her favorite magazine, *Real Men*, where men would ask about everything from the best fishing lines to the best pickup lines. When clients weren't around, and Heather was out to lunch, Ben sometimes read the questions and answers himself, but he'd rather be caught dead than be seen reading a magazine whose covers were plastered with buffed males grinning smugly over articles like "Australia's Great Barrier Hunks" and "Chicago's Hottest Firefighters."

When clients were present, he insisted Heather hide the magazine. After all, Ben specialized in employment law—he didn't need an adversary spying magazines plastered with naked, sweaty males and accusing Ben of gender bias or sexual harassment.

Heather also read those Venus and Mars books, but Ben didn't care if she left those on her desk. The covers were sensible. No naked bodies. Gender-fair titles—Venus for women, Mars for men. Sometimes Ben stared at those books, with titles ranging from Mars and Venus on a date to Mars and Venus in the bedroom, and he wondered if there'd ever be a book for men who had somehow landed on Venus but wanted to move to Mars. Because that's how Ben's personal life felt. Trapped on Venus, a world filled with former lovers and wives.

Heather, still cradling the weeping mound of kimono and chopsticks, mouthed, "She's hurting."

Ben mouthed back, "So am I. I need another planet."

Two years ago, he'd met Heather at a local bagel shop. The boy behind the counter, enthralled with her beach babe look, waited slavishly on her while a disgruntled Ben bided his time. But when Heather turned those baby blues on him, and gave that head of shimmering blond hair a shake, he had the irrational wish to be her bagel slave, too.

Within a month, they were engaged and she was the receptionist in his one-man legal firm. But the beach babe was really an ice princess at heart. Six months later, he felt as though he were living with a frozen bagel. When they broke up, he helped her find another apartment, but when she had difficulty landing another job, he told her she could stay. He reasoned that she knew his clients and understood his work style. Besides her penchant for shifts, she was fine at her job.

He just hadn't anticipated that his two exes would meld into one giant Super-Ex.

"Say something to her," mouthed Heather over Meredith's heaving shoulder.

He was a lawyer, dammit, not a heartbreak counselor. But if he had an Achilles heel, it was his heart. He couldn't stand to purposely hurt someone, especially a female someone. It was undoubtedly the direct result of growing up as the man of the house and being protective of his mom and sis, a habit that spilled over into his other relationships with women.

He blew out an expanse of air. *Say something.* "Sorry he wanted that ice cream back."

Meredith spun around so fast, he thought he was watching a remake of *The Exorcist.* "Ring!" she squealed. Her voice rose so high, he swore he heard the distant barking of dogs. "He wanted the *ring* back, not the ice cream!"

Heather, swishing back her straight blond hair with a shake of her head, glared at him accusingly. "How could you be so insensitive?"

Meredith, obviously on a self-pitying roll, added, "You never cared for me when we were married, either!"

As he stared at those two furious faces, scrunched into seething looks he'd seen a zillion times before, a third face appeared behind them. A heart-shaped face topped with a wild mop of brown curls, one of which spiraled down her forehead, like the little girl who, when she was good, was very, very good but when she was bad...

"Are you Benjamin Taylor, P.C.?" the good-bad girl asked.

No, I'm the insensitive, uncaring ex-husband-fiancé lout who doesn't know the difference between an ice cream and a ring. "Yes."

"I litigate?" she asked.

He paused. "I don't know. Do you?"

He swore her curls quivered as her brown eyes narrowed. "Your license plate," she said tightly. "Is it I-L-I-T-I-G-8?"

"Did somebody hit my car?" He shot out of his seat.

"No, but you were *almost* rear-ended," she said, her voice dropping to an ominous register. "By me." She leaned forward, her small point of a chin leading the way.

"You stole my parking spot, you...you...thieving BMW litigating lummox."

Litigating lummox?

Meredith and Heather glanced at the angry woman, then, as though by osmosis, seemed to absorb her animosity. Turning back, they intensified their glares at Ben, which created a triad of furious females blocking his doorway. What was it with women? If one went to the bathroom, they all went. If one hated you, they all did. Ben hadn't even finished his morning cup of coffee, and he'd already pissed off three women...and one of whom he'd never seen before in his life!

It was the beginning of another glorious day in the life of Benjamin Taylor.

But *confrontation* was a lawyer's middle name. Twisting the corners of his mouth into a professional smile, he said courteously, "Won't you come in so we can discuss this?"

"Why should I—?"

"Not you, Heather. Our *guest*." He cast his ex-fiancée, who knew when to back off, a warning look. With a shake of her head, she pivoted neatly on those oversize platform shoes and clomped back to her desk.

Ben crossed to the door. In an aside to Meredith, he whispered, "I'm sorry I misunderstood about the ring.... Why don't you check out the couch?" He darted his gaze to the piece of furniture against the far wall in the reception area. A moment of peace was worth the couch sacrifice.

With the merest hint of a sniffle, Meredith swiveled and made a beeline to the object.

He turned his full attention to the curly-haired good girl. Bad girl. Mad girl. She wore an ill-fitting white blouse semitucked into a knee-length brown skirt, both of which reminded him of those chocolate-and-vanilla ice-cream bars he relished as a kid. But he didn't dare voice that, now that he knew the evil connotation of the word *ice cream*. Ben gestured her inside. "Please come in, Miss—?"

"Myers. Rosie Myers."

So it was Miss, not Mrs. Not that he cared. Maybe it was that wayward curl that intrigued him. Or the flash of lightning in those hazel eyes—which were now checking out the room as though a pervert had just invited her into the back seat of his car. "It's a law office," he said, "not a torture chamber. Please, have a seat."

She shifted her gaze to his, giving him a we-are-not-amused look, before crossing to one of two wooden guest chairs, silhouettes of harps cut into their backs.

As she walked by, Ben noticed a spatter of mud in her hairline. And a chunk of mud on the toe of one of her sensible brown loafers. So it wasn't a surprise she also wore mud-splattered tights. Didn't she say she'd almost rear-ended his car? How? By running into it with her body? "Care for coffee? Tea?"

Rosie picked the chair farthest from Ben's rectangular pine desk. "I'd kill for a coffee."

He gave her a double take, hoping he didn't have a homicidal rear-ending caffeine freak on his hands. "Heather, would you mind bringing—"

"I'm still helping Meredith!" she answered curtly from the other room.

With what? A stuck chopstick? Looking back at Rosie, he asked wearily, "Sugar? Cream?"

"Three teaspoons sugar. Plenty of milk."

"That's a milkshake, not a coffee," Ben murmured as he headed to the coffee station in the reception area.

Rosie sat stiffly in the harp chair and checked out the inner sanctum of ILITIG8. She was already so late for work, what was another ten minutes? She hated disappointing Teresa, though, who was pretty cool when it came to bending rules. Unfortunately, Rosie had bent the tardy rule so far, she'd broken it, so Teresa had had to lay down the law: get into work on time or go on probation.

Although probation was not high on Rosie's wish list, after stomping in a puddle, exchanging greetings with a trucker, and hiking six blocks into work, she *needed* a few extra minutes. And needed a few more to negotiate a parking space with a lawyer.

Considering what faced her, she also needed that free cup of coffee.

She scanned the room. Looked as though an interior decorator had had a breakdown in here. On one wall were several paintings of landscapes. Rosie fought a surge of homesickness as she scanned the images of rolling earth and sky, the type of world in which she'd spent most of her twenty-six years. She quickly shifted her gaze to another wall, where an arrangement of round brass thingamajigs, covered with beads and feathers, hung. One of the round thingamajigs, on closer inspection, was a clock whose face was embedded in an old chrome steering wheel.

"Here's your coffee," Ben said pleasantly, handing her a steaming mug. He headed around the pine desk and sat in a high-backed swivel chair.

He had an ease about him, which surprised Rosie. And he wasn't dressed in a stuffy suit—the way lawyers in the movies dressed—but in slacks and a light pullover. The sweater's blue-and-smoke diamond pattern complemented his brown hair, a café au lait color, and his blue eyes. Maybe his office hadn't settled on a style, but he definitely had one. And although she'd tried to ignore it, his style had a sexy edge. A slow, feverish heat tickled her insides.

"Thank you," she croaked, wishing her voice would behave. Forget the voice—she wished her body would behave! She quickly diverted her attention to the graphic on the cup and stared at James Dean, a cigarette dangling from his lips, slouched in front of the marquee *Rebel Without a Cause*. Did Ben Taylor think the image of some studly movie star would mollify her? At the very least, he should have picked her a cup that didn't have cars drag racing in the background. If she looked closely enough, she'd probably find one of the cars sneaking up on a parking space, too.

"My, uh, interior decorator got me these," he explained, catching her reaction. "It's a set of mugs called the Golden Age of Hollywood...from my, uh, decorator's Tinseltown theme era. I prefer to use my china for guests, but it appears my receptionist took them home for a party...." His voice trailed off as he cast a tired gaze around the room, stopping on a framed poster of Jimmy Stewart under the title *Mr. Smith Goes to Washington*.

He seemed preoccupied with Jimmy Stewart, so Rosie took a sip of James Dean, nearly groaning as the sweet hot liquid warmed her mouth. That was one of the problems of being perpetually late. She never had the time to savor something as toe-tinglingly delightful as a great cup of java. She closed her eyes, inhaling the roasted scent, savoring the moment. "This is delicious," she murmured.

When she opened her eyes, Ben was staring at her with a twinkle in his. "Appreciate your enjoyment," he said, his voice dropping to a husky register.

Their gazes locked for a long moment. Rosie's heart hammered so hard, she swore the sound must be echoing off the walls. She gripped the cup, not wanting it to slip out of her suddenly moist palms. Minutes ago, he'd simply been ILITIG8. Now he was a powerful, exciting presence that unnerved her body and ignited her libido.

She wanted to kick herself. She wasn't here to enjoy herself, but to be angry. To demand her rights! "Is that what you lawyers do?" she began, breaking the charged silence. At least her voice was behaving better—it wasn't croaking anymore. "Do you wear people down with coffee and movie stars so they forget what they're fighting for?"

"Movie stars?" He looked perplexed. "What are *they* fighting for?"

She casually wiped one moistened palm against her skirt. "You stole my parking space."

"*Stole* it?" he repeated. He motioned in the general direction of north. "The space behind the stairs, next to the back entrance?"

She leveled him her sternest look. "Right."

"Wrong." Cocking an eyebrow, he took a swig from his mug, decorated with a sloe-eyed Marlene Dietrich in a top hat. Lowering his drink, she swore he flinched when he looked at the movie title over Marlene's head, *Blonde Venus*. He plunked down the mug, too hard, and opened his desk drawer. "Yesterday I paid the monthly rental fee for the space my car is currently occupying."

She blinked, surprised. "Yesterday? So did I."

"Perhaps you paid for another parking space," he suggested, rummaging through the drawer.

"No, that's my space."

He held up a piece of paper. "Here's my receipt. Do you have yours?"

"Somewhere. At home." Probably in the pile of paper on the edge of her dresser. Or maybe in the pile of paper in the fruit basket that hung in her kitchen. "Yes," she said. *In some pile.*

He handed her the piece of paper. "I believe this has all the pertinent information."

Pertinent. Trust a lawyer to not simply say "information." As though "*pertinent* information" gave it an extra distinction. She read the handwritten receipt, upon which was typed his name, yesterday's date and the number C1001.

"C1001. Maybe that's another pertinent space," she said, handing back the paper.

He gave her an odd look before responding. "According to their chart, the Cs are the spaces behind the stairs."

This was getting nowhere. She didn't have her receipt. She didn't know C spaces from Z ones. And she *really* didn't want to do the six-block trek again tomorrow morning. She wanted back her space, free and clear, today. For that matter, she wanted back her common sense—to not let some Michael J. Fox look-alike with a killer Harrison Ford grin get the better of her. She cleared her throat. "The building office has copies of our receipts. I suggest we discuss this with them at lunchtime. Shall we meet there at...noon?"

He opened his appointment book. A few strands of his straight hair, parted neatly on the side, fell forward as he bent his head to scan a page. Looking up, he said pleasantly, "Noon's fine."

"Noon, then," she said. He had a receipt, an appointment book, two secretaries it appeared, matching mugs, a BMW, and a sweater with the same cornsilk blue as his eyes. Rosie, the mud-sloshed misfit, felt as though she had nothing, not even the space she came in here to get. To make up for it she irrationally vowed to have the last word, before she left.

She downed another gulp of coffee, which she'd barely swallowed when she realized Ben was standing. She meant to set her cup on the carved coffee table next to her chair, but the bottom of the mug hit the table edge, causing the coffee to splatter onto her stockings and the carpet.

Ben lunged forward, grasping the cup the same time as she stabilized it. They hunched together in the center of the room, like two coffee cup worshipers, Ben's hands encircling hers. Rosie tried not to notice the warmth of his fingers. Or the musky scent of his cologne. Or the rising heat within her that had nothing to do with the hot coffee.

"You spilled coffee on your tights," Ben murmured, the tender roughness in his voice sending a delicious shiver down her spine.

Belatedly, she felt the warm liquid on her legs. Looking down, though, it was difficult to decipher which splotches were mud and which were coffee. She sure knew how to make an impression.

Ignoring her tights, she straightened. "See you at noon."

Ben, dropping his hands, stood with her. He had to be six feet to her five-three. "That's right. Noon."

"Yes, noon." She turned and headed toward the reception area.

"I'll be in the building office at noon," he called out.

Rosie stopped. He had to get in the last word, didn't he? Looking over her shoulder, she said, "Yes. *Noon.*" There. He wouldn't dare out-noon her again.

"I was talking to Heather."

"Oh." Rosie did a modified speed-walk through the reception area, passed the two women who were staring at the couch, and went out the door. Only when Rosie was in the hallway did she realize she was still clutching James Dean.

2

"MR. REAL RAN OFF with a woman named Boom Boom?" asked an incredulous Rosie, who had barely sat down before her best pal, Pam, rushed into the editorial department to tell her the office gossip.

As Pam leaned closer, Rosie caught the familiar scent of her friend's patchouli perfume. "Hold on," Pam whispered, "it gets better. Boom Boom is a bongo-playing stripper." Pam mimed playing bongos, a mischievous twinkle in her chocolate-brown eyes. At the end of her impromptu performance, she said, "I was dying to tell you the moment I heard, but you were awfully late...." She raised her eyebrows expectantly.

"Had to park six blocks away. Has Teresa been looking for me?"

"Nope. She got pulled into a powwow. Bigwigs are brainstorming how to replace Mr. Real overnight."

Rosie's mind reeled as the facts fully sank in. She didn't know what was more shocking—that the graying, habit-driven *Real Men* magazine columnist known as Mr. Real had thrown his career into the air, or that Boom Boom could bongo while boom-booming. Back in Colby, the most scandalous occurrence of the past ten years was when Bobby-Joe Reed mooned ol' Mrs. Ferguson, who hadn't been able to talk for weeks afterward—a condition her doctor called post-traumatic stress.

Perched on the edge of Rosie's desk, Pam kicked one sandaled foot back and forth. "Six blocks away? Thought you rented a parking spot yesterday."

"A lawyer filched it," Rosie murmured, focusing on the sleek oak desk in the corner. That's where William Clarington, aka Mr. Real, had plied his trade writing the immensely popular "A Real Man Answers Real Questions" column.

As she'd speed-walked to her desk a few minutes ago, she'd wondered where William, *never* Bill, was. Every morning he arrived promptly at 8:10, carrying a latte and a bran muffin to his desk. Slightly stooped, with a pencil-thin mustache William referred to as his "cookie duster," it astounded Rosie that he even *knew* anyone named Boom Boom, much less ran away with her. The thought of them jetting off to some exotic locale, where they were probably feverishly playing bongos and dusting cookies, unleashed within Rosie an unexpected, wild rush of yearning.

"What're you thinking about, Rosie?" Pam asked.

Rosie met Pam's concerned gaze. "The wildest thing I've ever done is fly to Chicago. Prior to that, I once tipped a cow."

"I hope not more than fifteen percent. Cows are notorious for bad service."

"No, in Kansas 'tipping a cow' is literally tipping it." Rosie made a pushing motion with her hands.

Pam stared at Rosie's hands. "If that's what you did for fun," she said with a chuckle, "good thing you moved to Chicago, and better yet, became pals with me." Pam was city savvy and had helped Rosie survive the culture shock of moving from a small-town farm to a metropolis apartment. Pam leaned over and helped herself to a tissue on a neighboring desk. "Please don't tell me you were tipping this morning, though."

"Why?"

"Because you have mud on your forehead." She brushed at Rosie's right temple. "All gone."

Rosie groaned. "I had *mud* on my face?"

"Better than egg." Pam tossed the tissue into the metal trash can next to Rosie's desk.

Rosie dropped her head into her hands. In a woebegone voice, she said, "I strode, full steam, into a lawyer's office and called him a *thief*. If I'd known my face was covered with a mud pack—"

"Mud speck—"

"I'd have wiped it off!" She rolled her eyes. "*Mud* on my face. No wonder he gave me those odd looks." And she'd hoped those had been looks of heated interest. Maybe if she dated more often, she'd know the difference between a heated look and an odd one.

Pam's gaze dropped. "Dirt on your legs, too. Good lord, girl! What'd you do before work? Practice mud wrestling?"

"Mud sloshing. That's when you step grandly into a pothole filled with mud and gunk. After that, I argued with a trucker, confronted a lawyer and stole a coffee mug."

Pam nodded slowly, fighting a smile. "Okay, I'll accept everything but the theft. Stooping a little low, aren't we, to steal a coffee mug?"

"I accidentally walked away with it, but I was so flustered at the time...." She sighed. Nothing had gone right with Benjamin Taylor, P.C. She'd felt so in control—so self-righteous—when she'd barged into his office. But she'd left with a seriously unbalanced libido, receiptless, and worse, after accusing him of being a thief, a thief herself. "You'd think," she said, looking at the family portrait that sat on her desk, "that after growing up with four brothers, I'd know how to handle a man."

"Honey, we *all* know how to handle a man. Worrying about that right now, however, is *not* the proper channel for your energy." With a wink, Pam picked up a miniature windup dinosaur, dressed in a cheerleader skirt and holding tiny pom-poms, from Rosie's desk. It had been a going-away gift from one of her brothers, who'd said to remember he was always with her in spirit, cheering her on in her new life. Winding the toy, Pam shot Rosie a knowing look. "Wonder who's going to fill in for Mr. Real?"

Rosie got Pam's drift. They were both assistants at *Real Men* magazine—Pam in Marketing, Rosie in Editorial—jobs that were one step above the mail room. They'd made pacts to escape "assistant gulch" before the end of the calendar year, which meant they needed to move fast on any job opportunities.

"My last, uh, volunteer efforts didn't go so well," she reminded Pam. "I think I need a dose of your big-city, big-office wisdom. Want to come over to dinner tonight? I think I have some leftovers."

"Sure. We'll brainstorm while eating. And as to your past volunteer efforts—" Pam made a no-big-deal gesture, her beaded bracelet jangling with the movement "—you were green. Didn't know the ropes. That was months ago, anyway. Nobody's going to remember." She arched one eyebrow. "By the way, have I mentioned you're looking thinner?"

It was a line they tossed at each other when one or the other needed an ego boost. It was silly, but it always coaxed a smile. Grinning, Rosie checked her leather-banded watch, a going-away gift from another brother, the misguided one attending law school. "Paige is probably still in that powwow...."

"Paige? Our indomitable managing editor? Now *there's* a woman who knows how to channel her energy properly." Still clutching the dinosaur, Pam lifted the telephone receiver. "Jerome's extension is four-three-three. I'll dial." She tapped in the number for Jerome, Paige's assistant.

Before a stunned Rosie could say "I'm still in mud-and-mug recovery," Pam was handing her the receiver. Swallowing hard, Rosie accepted it. Raising it to her ear, she said cautiously, "Jerome?"

"Yeah."

He always copped a tough-guy attitude when Paige was out of the office. Like a Johnny Depp wanna-be. But when Paige was in, he became Mr. Sweet-and-Light himself, a young Prince Harry. It was like dealing with Jekyll and Hyde—except with Jerome, it was Johnny and Harry.

"This is Ro—" She cleared the frog from her suddenly clogged throat. "Rosie—Rosalind—Myers. I'd like to set up a meeting with Ms. Leighton today."

"She's booked."

It was obvious he hadn't even checked her appointment book—or computer form or whatever medium Superwoman used to schedule her life. Rosie exaggerated a sneer to Pam, indicating Jerome was being less than cooperative. Pam held up the dinosaur and made it dance in the air, cheering Rosie on.

"Perhaps she has a few minutes available between appointments?" Rosie suggested, sweetening her voice with even more sugar than she'd put in her coffee.

"Nah."

Rosie made a "gr-r-r" face to Pam, who picked up a stray quarter on the desk and waved it.

"Can I give you a quarter?" Rosie said into the receiver.

Pam mouthed a big "no" and mimicked eating.

Smiling, Rosie nodded vigorously. "Can I give you some food?"

Shuddering dramatically, Pam grabbed a ballpoint pen off Rosie's desk and scribbled "lunch" at the top of Rosie's week-at-a-glance calendar.

"I meant lunch," Rosie quickly corrected "Can I treat you to lunch?"

Pam punched the air with a big thumbs-up.

"You're in luck," Jerome answered, his voice oozing sweetness and light. "She just got out of a meeting. If you hurry, you can catch her before she leaves for her ten o'clock. And I like Focaccio's."

"Great," answered Rosie. "I'll be right there. And we'll set up a lunch at Furca—Forcha—whatever. Bye." She quickly hung up the phone.

"You got an appointment with She Who Rules?" asked an elated Pam.

Rosie brushed a curl out of her eyes. "Yes. And in the too near future, I'm buying lunch for He Who Blackmails."

"I knew that'd work with Jerome. But it's a small price, girlfriend. Wish I wasn't tied up with meetings the rest of the day—I'll be dying to know how your Paige encounter went. Tonight, over dinner, you'll have to spill all."

"Deal." Rosie stood, smoothing her hands over her skirt. "How do I look?"

"Take off those stockings in the ladies' room. Otherwise, you look...like Mr. Real." With a wink, Pam set down the dinosaur, which rattled a path across the desk, the pom-poms rising and falling.

ROSIE STOPPED at the women's bathroom down the hallway from Paige Leighton's office. Slipping inside, she scrambled out of her splattered leggings and started to stuff them into her skirt pocket, then changed her mind. She didn't want to look as though had a lump on her thigh—not in the elegant Paige Leighton's inner sanctum. Rosie tossed the hose behind the trash can to retrieve later. *I really should carry a purse instead of relying on pockets.*

She closed her eyes and told herself to relax, to *breathe.* Opening her eyes, she checked her reflection in the mirror. She had an eerie blueish glow, which she hoped was due to the fluorescent lights. Maybe her mother was right—maybe she should wear makeup.

Poking at the chaos of curls that framed her face, she scrutinized her overall presence. To combat the blue and the anxiousness in her eyes, it was time to adopt a goddess. *I'll stick with Artemis.* Goddess of the Hunt, Artemis always aimed for her target, knowing her arrows unerringly reached their mark.

Like me, aiming to be Mr. Real.

She didn't have to strain any brain cells to know they wanted a man in the job. After all, it would be false advertising if the "A Real Man Answers Real Questions" column was written by a woman. But an interim Mr. Real would be a coup—an opportunity for her to escape the gulch and prove she could write. Otherwise, she'd be stuck proofing and copyediting until her brown curls grew gray, her last dying moment spent crossing out an errant comma.

She checked her watch. Goddess time!

A few moments later, Rosie passed Jerome, who smiled slyly at her as she walked into Paige's office. He'd always made her uncomfortable the way he eyeballed women. Worse, she'd soon have to sit across from those eyeballs at lunch. That Focha-whatever place would probably cost Rosie a month's worth of her favorite nutriquasi Twinkie bars.

Her footsteps slowed as she stepped onto the plush egg-white carpeting that cushioned the floor of the vast office. Paige, who could be a stand-in for Lauren Bacall, sat behind a metal-and-glass desk. Seeing Rosie, she pulled off her reading glasses and set them aside. Folding her hands in front of her, she smiled without crinkling her eyes. "Jerome told me you had something important to discuss. I have only a few minutes...."

A few? Rosie dove in. "The 'A Real Man Answers Real Questions' column is currently without a columnist."

Paige blinked, then nodded, not one iota of emotion flickering across her powdered face. "And—?"

"I would like the...opportunity to be the interim columnist until you find another Mr. Real." Her brother the salesman always said to hit hard and hit fast when you wanted something. Well, thanks to Artemis, she'd just done that. Rosie eased in a slow breath, waiting for Paige's reaction.

"Rosie," Paige began, elongating the *O* in Rosie. "Didn't you have several previous 'opportunities'?" One shapely eyebrow raised slightly, emphasizing the question in her voice.

"Uh, yes." Ugh. So even Paige Leighton, the managing editor high priestess, had heard about those first two writing assignments that Rosie had mangled.

"I seem to recall," Paige continued, "that Sophia Weston needed an article on 'Women Who Need to Please' and you wrote about..."

Rosie cringed inwardly. *Persephone, the goddess of the underworld who expresses a woman's tendency toward passivity and a need to please.* Rosie had thought, at the time, she was being brilliant. But Sophia Weston, senior features editor, was so irked, Rosie worried for two solid days that *she* would be the next goddess of the underworld for her rampant creativity. Rosie forced a smile. "I misinterpreted Ms. Weston's guidelines."

Paige tapped one pink-polished nail against the glass desk. "And I believe there was another incident?"

Incident? When had writing assignments become incidents? "Well, yes, there was a second, *small* writing assignment. Very small." She debated whether to call it infinitesimal, but decided that might be pushing it. "Ad copy."

"Bridal ad, I believe."

Sheesh. Paige might be old enough to have dated Humphrey Bogart, but she had a young memory. What did she do? Binge on ginkgo biloba? "Yes," Rosie admitted. "It was a bridal ad."

"One of our best advertisers, as I recall. Seemed they found a rather...unsightly typo?"

"Hera," Rosie admitted. She might as well hit hard and hit fast with the truth, too, and put a stop to this trip down memory lane. "I changed 'Her beauty' to 'Hera beauty.'"

"Right. *Hera* beauty. I remember now." Paige leaned

forward, her gray-blue eyes nearly matching her mauve earrings. "How did that happen?"

Double ugh. Now she had to explain the "Hera Incident." "I thought it would...enhance the ad to use the name Hera, the goddess of marriage." And, oh boy, did she enhance it. Only because the head of sales had pacified the irate customer by offering free ad space for six months was Rosie able to keep her job.

"Oh-h-h."

Rosie wondered if Paige always elongated her *O*'s.

Paige tapped her fingernail again. "You seem to have a thing for goddesses."

If Rosie admitted that at this very moment she was Artemis, she could kiss off being Mr. Real. Instead, she offered a half smile, not wanting to explain how she *had* to be a goddess to survive her four brothers' antics.

"Mr. Real isn't a goddess," Paige said drolly.

"No, he's not." *But he'd make a great Athena.*

"And this is a job for a seasoned writer. Which you're not. And for someone with a good track record. Which you don't have."

Think Artemis. Be strong. "I am a seasoned writer," Rosie began, hoping Paige Leighton didn't hear the quaver in her voice. "I worked for two years on the high school newspaper, the last year as its editor. After that, I graduated from college with a degree in journalism. I worked on the town paper, starting as gofer and working my way up to copy editor, then reporter. That's ten years of writing—if that's not seasoned, I'd like to know what you view as bland."

That last comment sneaked out. This was Paige Leighton she was talking to. Rosie had to watch her tongue, something her mother had warned her of repeatedly.

Rosie quickly pushed ahead. "And it's true I made those four paws—" From the look on Paige's face, Rosie knew she'd butchered that French term. Darn. Why did she attempt to speak French when at best she knew a few sentences in Spanish? Because Paige was cultured classy, and owned that summer home in Provence.

"Four what?"

"Mistakes," Rosie explained softly, wishing she'd dated that high school foreign exchange student, Guillaume, when she'd had the chance. She might have learned a few key French phrases. But no. Competitive Rosie opted to beat him at tennis instead of getting to know him over dinner.

"Oh." Paige nodded slightly. "Faux pas."

"Right. That's what I meant." Now that she'd bludgeoned French, Rosie decided to go for the hard-core truth—in English. "I wanted desperately to prove myself, and fell back on a favorite theme, goddesses," she admitted quickly. "I know I blew those jobs. But after that, I dug in and studied the magazine, the readership and the corporate expectations. *Real Men* has a circulation that rivals larger, more established magazines such as *Architectural Digest*. Eighty-five percent of our readership is women, most of whom are in their late twenties, which is my age bracket. Which means I'm better qualified to write for that particular audience."

Rosie let that sink in before continuing. She had definitely overstayed her "few minutes" but Paige hadn't kicked her out...yet.

"Of course, there's the small issue that I'm not a man—"

Paige arched one eyebrow in response.

"—but I sat only ten feet from William Clarington

these past seven months. I heard everything he said, proofed much of what he wrote, both of which give me an edge to fill in for him until, of course, the magazine hires a man." If Rosie wasn't mistaken, Paige looked interested.

Paige stood, smoothed her silk jacket, then walked around the desk. Leaning back against it, she crossed her arms and leveled Rosie a look. "You're hungry. I like that. And you put your nose to the grindstone and learned from your past mistakes. Like that even better. I'll make a deal with you. You can be the interim Mr. Real on two conditions. One, not a *single* goddesslike word can touch that column, you understand?"

Rosie nodded.

"Two. It's *imperative* the column's tone sound like William, Mr. Real. We don't want our readers—especially the growing number of men who write to Mr. Real—to ever suspect that he's a woman. I think maybe you can pull off playing Mr. Real for a few weeks...if you agree to those two terms."

Agree? She'd name her firstborn Paige if that's what it took. "Yes," Rosie whispered, not trusting her voice to behave.

Paige gave her a small smile as she headed back around the desk to her chair. Sitting down, she put her reading glasses back on. "Your few minutes are up."

Rosie floated across the carpeting, past Jerome and down the hallway. She'd talked her way into being the interim Mr. Real! Goodbye gulchdom, hello writerville.

BEN SAT in the building office foyer, wondering if Rosie Myers remembered they'd agreed to meet here at noon, which was ten minutes ago. Except for the piped-in Muzak, he didn't mind waiting. It was a relief to escape his office, where Meredith had spent the rest of the morning analyzing his couch, which should be a first in Freudian psychology.

Although considering Rosie was late, he should have asked her where she worked or how he might reach her. All he knew was her name, that she had an abnormal desire to possess his parking space, and that she favored the mud-splattered look.

He smiled, recalling the little spot of mud nestled in her hairline. Most women fretted if a hair was out of place or if their lipstick wasn't on straight. At the other end of the spectrum was Rosie, who looked as though she'd just polished off a mud pie.

At that moment, Rosie charged into the foyer. Seeing Ben, she halted and heaved a few deep breaths. "Sorry I'm...late," she said between pants. "I lost...track of time."

She wet her lips, making him wonder if that was a nervous gesture because she was late—or if it was because of him. "That's all right. I enjoyed the reprieve from Super-Ex."

Frowning, Rosie swiped a curl off her forehead. "Super what?"

"Never mind," he said, flipping his wrist to check the time. "The building manager has been waiting at least fifteen minutes. Shall we?" He gestured toward an open wooden door, upon which was stenciled in white block letters Archibald Potter, Building Manager.

Nodding, Rosie did a quick adjustment to her blouse, which was once again partially tucked into her skirt waistband. She must live alone, Ben surmised, because no one with a heart would let her leave the house looking as though she'd dressed in front of a wind machine.

After rectifying her wayward blouse, Rosie cocked her head and frowned. "Is that an orchestra playing the Rolling Stones?"

Ben glanced at one of the speakers embedded into the ceiling. "Unfortunately, yes."

"'Let's Spend the Night Together'?"

"Okay, but first let's talk to Mr. Potter." Ben avoided her eyes as he motioned her toward the office door. He shouldn't have said that, but the urge to ruffle Ms. Mud Pie was too great.

She huffed indignantly, although he noticed circles of pink staining her cheeks. So she liked the idea of spending the night together?

"I meant the song title!" As she sailed passed him, he noticed the mud along her hairline had been removed. Also gone were the stockings that looked like a Rorschach test.

As they entered Mr. Potter's office, Ben mused how Meredith would have a field day in here. It had no style, unless there was such a thing as a price-saver-office-supply theme. The room's furnishings consisted of a fake ficus tree, a Write 'N Wipe calendar scribbled with illegible notes, two folding chairs, and a metal desk with a faux wood front. Behind the desk sat a spectacled Mr. Potter, wearing a white button-down shirt with the sleeves rolled up. Besides the emerald-green leaves on the ficus, the only other piece of color in the room was Mr. Potter's flaming red hair.

"Hello, hello," Mr. Potter said, motioning them toward the folding chairs. "I told Mr. Taylor to bring you in when you arrived," he said to Rosie.

They all three sat at once, the creaking of the chairs sounding like a metallic chorus.

When the creaking stopped, Mr. Potter pushed the bridge of his frames up his nose. Placing his elbows on his desk, he steepled his fingers and looked at them. "Mr. Taylor said there's some issue over a parking space?"

"Yes," Rosie answered matter-of-factly. "He stole mine."

She makes cutting to the chase seem like a detour, thought Ben. But he kept his mouth closed because Rosie was off and running, explaining the entire ILITIG8, rear-ending adventure to an astonished-looking Mr. Potter, who probably heard few such colorful stories in his beige life.

Sitting close enough to rub elbows, Ben had his first real opportunity to look more closely at his parking-space nemesis. She had a clear, glowing complexion—the kind that looked as though it had been scrubbed with soap and water. Impossible. Didn't all women buy expensive creams and bottles of gooey stuff to slather on their faces? It was a throwback to another era for a woman to simply wash her face and call it clean.

Simple. Efficient. He liked that.

Plus, the fresh pink of Rosie's skin nicely set off the dark mound of curls that framed her face like a wiry halo. Halo? He almost laughed out loud at the thought of the parking space fanatic being an angel. Maybe a recent fall to earth accounted for all those muddy slosh marks he'd seen earlier.

He tuned in to the Earth Angel's animated monologue.

"Then, after trudging eight long city blocks from the *only* other parking spot I could find, I visited Mr. Taylor in his office—"

"Eight?" Ben interrupted. "I don't recall your saying 'eight' before." Earth Angel might simply wash her face with soap and water, but it appeared she got elaborate when it came to words.

She smiled demurely. "You're right. It was actually ten...."

And she was off and running again. Quite the storyteller. But rather than correct her, Ben leaned back in his chair. He'd wait until she wound down—after all, *he* had a receipt.

From behind his desk this morning, he'd have thought she wore makeup. This close, he saw the most she wore was a dab of lipstick. Her lashes, thick and dark, complemented her mink-brown hair and hazel eyes. And beneath that pug nose were lips that naturally puckered, as though ready for a kiss. Reminded him of his favorite Manet oil, *Portrait of a Woman*. A painting of an alluring, dark-haired woman with luscious lips poised for a smile...or a kiss.

Amazing. Rosie's lips kept their delicious shape even when she talked, which at this moment she was doing at quite a clip. He imagined how those lips would feel against his. Pliant, soft. She'd taste sweet and hot, like sugar and coffee....

"Mr. Taylor?" Even through Mr. Potter's thick lenses, Ben caught a beady-eyed look that was half confused, half annoyed. It reminded Ben of the innumerable times in school he'd been caught fantasizing about some girl, the teacher looking at him in much the same way as Mr. Potter was now. And Ben would have to rapidly piece together whatever the heck was under discussion—or simply wing it. Fortunately, he was brilliant at winging it. No wonder he ended up a lawyer.

And considering his appreciation of women's beauty, no wonder he ended up on Venus.

"Mr. Taylor?" Mr. Potter was looking more and more confused. "Is that true? You stole her parking space?"

Her parking space? She'd obviously done an outstanding job presenting her side of the argument. "*My* space," Ben corrected. "I rented it yesterday and have the receipt with me." He fished in his pants pocket, feeling mildly idiotic that he'd let a pair of lips sidetrack him from the topic under discussion. "Here it is," he said, trying to sound extraordinarily professional as he handed over the slip of paper.

Mr. Potter read it, nodded to himself, then gave that confused look to Rosie. "C1001. That's the space we're talking about...and it clearly says right here that it's Mr. Taylor's space."

Her face flushed. "That's impossible." She tapped her loafered foot against the floor. "Could you please look up my transaction from yesterday? I left my receipt at home."

Mr. Potter swiveled, typed something on his keyboard, then scrutinized the computer screen. He made a tuneless humming sound, probably one of his side effects from listening to Muzak all day long. "Well, well," he finally said in a surprised tone. "Looks as though you were also rented C1001."

"The space next to the stairs in the back of the building," Rosie clarified.

"The same." Mr. Potter leaned a little closer to the computer screen as though his eyeglasses couldn't be trusted one hundred percent. "Yes, you were definitely rented C1001." He leaned back and blinked at the two of them. "Appears my office assistant rented the same space to both of you."

"Isn't that illegal?" Rosie shot a meaningful glance at Ben as though it were time for him to metamorphose into Super Lawyer. Interesting how she expected him to jump to her defense after trying to put him on the defensive.

But he also liked her needing him. Had *always* liked it when an attractive woman needed him. He'd never leave Venus if he didn't come to his senses. "Perhaps," Ben said, "it should belong to whoever paid for it first."

Mr. Potter stuck out his bottom lip, thought for a moment, then shook his head no. "Sometimes my assistant will go into a file and add missing information, which changes its time stamp."

"Meaning, the time stamp on a file doesn't necessarily reflect the actual time of transaction," Ben said.

"Yes, yes. Correct." Mr. Potter typed something on his keyboard, after which the screen blipped to gray. "I am sorry. This is clearly our error. Unfortunately, there are no other available spaces to rent at this time."

"You need to fix this," Rosie said, scooting forward to the edge of her seat.

Mr. Potter steepled his fingers again. After a moment's reflection, he said, "I'm not Judge Judy. I can't just say one of you is right, the other wrong. Someone needs to back out of the space, so to speak."

"I think Mr. Taylor should back out," Rosie suggested.

Ben, still taken aback at the Judge Judy reference, gave her a belated double take. "Why?"

"Because I *need* that space. It ensures that I'm on time."

"So if your car were parked in that space, you would have been on time to this meeting?"

She huffed something unintelligible. "In the *mornings* it helps me get into work on time. You own your business, so you can come and go as you please. I, on the other hand, *must* be to work by a certain time, so I *need* to park close to my office."

This mumbo jumbo logic was rubbing him all the wrong way, reminding him of variations of every conversation he'd had with his exes, even *before* they were exes. Good ol' reliable, dependable Ben should give or abstain or forgo so the woman could have whatever she needed—or thought she needed. Well, he was tired of being the caretaker for planet Venus, which now had a new member, a Miss Rosie Myers.

"I also require that space, for both myself and my clients. Do you have clients?" She opened those luscious lips to say something, but Ben kept talking. "My clients get irritated if they can't park nearby. And if I lose my clients, I lose my business. So if that space means either you'll be *on time* for work or I *lose* my business, I should retain the space." He folded his arms for effect.

She did the same. They stared each other down. If Ben wasn't so peeved at her bullheadedness, he would have found it amusing that they were both folding their arms while sitting in folding chairs. But he kept his mouth shut and calmly met her furious stare.

Without breaking eye contact with Ben, Rosie said evenly, "Mr. Potter, you're going to *have* to be Judge Judy. Make a choice."

With a weary sigh, Mr. Potter stood and retrieved a blue polyester jacket that had been hanging on the back of his chair. "I have a bathroom flooding on the third floor and a renter who, despite my degree in business management, thinks I'm a plumber. There's an accountant on the same floor who swears the frigid air-conditioning has blasted away potential customers and frozen two of his prize tropical fish. Although I send in building maintenance people every day to adjust the temperature, the accountant thinks I'm also an air-conditioning specialist."

As he shrugged into the jacket, he continued, "And then I have you two who view me as a middle-aged jurist with an attitude." After adjusting the lapels, he leveled them a vexed look. "Okay, here's my verdict. Neither of you gets the space."

Both of their mouths dropped open.

"You can't do that!" Rosie exclaimed, unfolding her arms.

"Watch me." Mr. Potter reached for the keyboard.

"Wait a moment," said Ben, trying to sound incensed, but secretly admiring the mild-mannered Mr. Potter for playing tyrant. Definitely a Mars man. Ben glanced at Rosie. "Let's share the space until another one's available. I'm sure Mr. Potter would agree to refund each of us half the rental fee, especially considering this mishap was the fault of the building office."

Mr. Potter, obviously not wanting to tangle with a lawyer, nodded.

"How do we share the space?" Rosie asked edgily.

"Take alternate days?" Ben suggested.

She cast a sidelong glance at Mr. Potter. "Sounds fair," she said sweetly, as a curl tumbled over the center of her forehead, reminding Ben again of the little girl who when she was good was very, very good, but when she was bad... But surely she had no intention of being "bad" over sharing a space, did she?

Rosie glanced at her watch. "I need to get ready for a meeting, so I must be going." She turned a pair of dewy hazel eyes on Ben. "Shall we discuss the particulars of sharing this space later today?"

She was being too agreeable. Too sweet. He didn't trust her for a millisecond. "I have to be in court the rest of this afternoon."

"Tomorrow morning?" When he nodded in agreement, she added, "Good. I'll drop by in the morning after I park. See you at seven-forty-five?" She stood.

He stood with her. "After you park—?"

Her eyes narrowed slightly. "You got the space today, so I get it tomorrow. Alternate days, right?"

"Uh, right."

"Good, good," said Mr. Potter, waving them toward the door. "Situation resolved. You'll both have partial refunds by the end of the week."

After all three of them exited the office, Mr. Potter locked his office door. "Have a nice day," he said blandly, his voice like human Muzak. Without another glance in their direction, he strode away purposefully. Ben figured Mr. Potter was on his way to stem a flood, thaw frozen fish, or maybe settle a TV court case.

Alone, Ben and Rosie stood awkwardly in the foyer. "Tomorrow morning," said Ben, rocking back slightly on his heels. "Seven-forty-five, no later. I have a client showing up at eight."

"Seven-forty-five," she verified before walking away.

"Not seven-fifty-five," he called out after her. "Seven-*forty*-five." She'd been late for this meeting—he couldn't afford that also happening tomorrow morning.

"I know the difference between forty and fifty," she yelled before disappearing around a corner.

Difference. There was definitely that between Rosie and the other women he'd known. She didn't wear makeup, but seemed to have an affinity for mud. Didn't dress under normal conditions, but in front of a wind machine. Yet despite those quirks, her natural, fresh beauty shone through. He had the sense nothing could dull her inner sparkle and fire—just as nothing could dull the brilliance of an exquisite diamond.

Inner sparkle and fire? Diamond?

Forget the gem analogies—this lady is ruthless in battle. But this time around, so was Ben. After years of giving in and taking care of women, he was drawing a line in the sand—or in the asphalt—when it came to that damn parking space. No matter what "timely" excuses Rosie Myers used, she was not going to get that space every day, which he had a sneaking suspicion she'd bargain for. Or take.

The Muzak swelled into a heartrending love song.

Love.

Venus.

It was time for Ben to make a planetary move.

3

"HELLO," Ben mumbled as he entered the reception area of his office. He was wiped, burned out, after a long, tedious afternoon in court. Meredith, back from some shopping expedition as indicated by an assortment of nearby bags, was busy measuring the alcove where the couch sat. She barely nodded a greeting. Heather, a phone nestled in the crook of her neck, talked while holding a hand mirror with one hand and applying lip gloss with the other. She waved the tube of gloss in Ben's direction.

"I'm fine, thanks," he muttered, trudging into his office. This was how he'd felt when he'd lived with each of these women. Barely more than a passing blip on the screens of their wall-measuring, lip-glossing lives. Sinking into the chair behind his desk, he looked wearily through the open door at his ex-wife as she measured a side wall with obsessive precision. *That must be what happened to Dexter. He didn't measure up.* Sometimes Ben wondered if Meredith wasn't looking for a great catch, but a man she could redo. A man who was...

"Outdated, lumpy and gauche," announced Meredith, straightening. The metallic measuring tape flew back into its container with a zinging sound.

Yep, that was the kind. Someone she could redecorate for the rest of his lumpy, gauche life.

"He's always going for that yucky blue color, too," chimed in Heather.

Super-Ex is back to their favorite topic. Me. "Heather," Ben called out, forcing himself to sound pleasant, "please refrain from discussing me while you're still on the phone."

She made a huffing noise that sounded oddly muted. Probably from lip gloss overdose. "It's my friend, Carla Wright, not one of your clients."

So speaketh Princess Bagel. "Carla or not, you're at work. I'd like my reputation to remain solid whoever might overhear." Solid? As if there was anything stable about life in Super-Ex-Ville. Absently, he played with a piece of blank paper lying on the desk.

"Gotta go, Carla," Heather said with great fanfare, followed by a crisp click as she hung up the phone. "Better, Benny?"

Benny—he cringed—the nickname she'd bestowed on him soon after their fateful bagel meeting. Solid Benny rubbed his eyes with his thumb and forefinger, making a mental note to correct his will to read that Heather Krementz had zero rights when it came to any words engraved on his headstone. The last thing he wanted was Benny Taylor chiseled into a slab of granite. With his luck, the instructions would be misunderstood—probably because Heather was applying lip gloss while talking—and the engraver would accidentally write Bunny Taylor.

No, worse. With his luck, Meredith would insist she pick out the stone—which would reflect some recent boyfriend phase. So Ben would end up as Bunny Taylor on a slab that resembled a hockey puck or a Cuisinart.

"Better, Ben-n-ny?" repeated Heather.

"Better," he mumbled, grabbing the nearest pen. He scribbled the day's date at the top of the paper, then held the pen midair, pondering how to best reword his will.

"That yucky blue is called French blue," Meredith

said, referring to Heather's previous comment. "It's that blue-gray hue that positively dominates the landscape in Provence."

His pen poised midair, Ben squeezed shut his eyes and hoped fervently Meredith wouldn't launch into a story about their honeymoon ten years ago....

"On our honeymoon," Meredith said, raising her voice, "Benjamin fell in love with French blue. He bought shirts, tablecloths, even a ceramic *fish* in that color."

Ben opened his eyes and gazed longingly at the "yucky blue" ceramic fish on his desk. He wished he could become that fish and swim out of here, away from the ex reunion. Forget the will. He didn't have time to think and contemplate. He needed to vent. On the paper, he scrawled, "I'm swimming in a yucky blue sea of exes...an ex-wife, an ex-fiancée...."

"He bought sheets in that color, too!" Heather chimed in. "It was like sleeping on Windex!"

He crossed out "yucky" and wrote above it "Windex."

"Heather," Meredith said, "first thing tomorrow morning, I'll make arrangements for moving personnel to retrieve this couch. While they're doing that, they can also pick up that coatrack in Benjamin's office—"

"The coatrack stays!" Ben surged from his chair, stabbing the air with his pen, like some kind of deranged scribe hailing a taxi.

Meredith turned, those orange-cone lips forming a surprised "Oh!" as in "Oh, what reactionary behavior have we here?" A moment later, Heather peered into his office, her glossed lips forming a surprised "What?" as in "What?"

He knew them so well, he could decode their thoughts from a single spoken word.

He kept his pen poised, defying them to interrupt. After a quick glance at his wristwatch, he announced, "It's four-thirty." When they both stared back, expressionless, he leveled a look at Heather. "Although you were late this morning, no need to make up the time tonight. See you tomorrow." He swerved his gaze to Meredith. "The couch is yours, but the coatrack is mine." Yours, mine. It felt like their property settlement all over again—except that had been more like yours, yours, yours. "If those moving people move it even an inch, I'll sue them." He *never* threatened anyone—even during intense legal negotiations—but suddenly, Benjamin Lewis Taylor swore he'd snap if that coatrack moved a millimeter. Deep down, he knew his reaction was over more than just an old rack, but if Meredith could transfer her feelings to furniture, then dammit, so could he.

He sat back down and rolled his shoulders dramatically, mainly because he knew they were both still staring at him and a dramatic shoulder roll looked authoritative. Poising his pen over the paper, he wondered how many other men had to dismiss their exes. For that matter, how many men kept their exes?

It was awfully quiet in Ex-Ville. He slid his gaze toward the door.

They remained frozen, obviously taken aback at Ben-Benny-Benjamin's outburst. Or maybe he'd stunned them with his shoulder roll. He tapped the face of his watch, indicating the time. Heather, with a toss of her head, clomped away in her platform shoes. Meredith, however, took several steps toward Ben's door, stopped and cocked one imperious eyebrow. Like a geisha with a bad attitude. "The coatrack is dead, Benjamin," she said in that low monotone she reserved for serious confrontations. "Let's give it a burial and move on."

Only Meredith gave interior decorating a life-and-death twist. "The coatrack lives," Ben countered, dropping his voice a register. "So does the couch, but I sacrificed it to you in your hour of decorating need."

Meredith's green eyes glinted. "And what is that supposed to mean?"

"Hour of decorating need or that the couch lives?"

Those glinting green eyes narrowed until all the glint was gone. "The hour comment."

He leaned back in his chair and crossed his arms. "You need to decorate my office—or, more specifically some section of it—whenever a boyfriend era ends." He scanned his office. "Let's see...the cow-dotted landscapes were from your Cowboy Curtiss era—"

"Why do you always add the 'Cowboy' part? He was a master chef at a dude ranch—"

"The harp-shaped chairs were from your Antoine—or was it Beauchamp?—era, the fellow interior decorator." Ben gestured toward another wall. "The Jimmy Stewart poster and matching Tinseltown cups were from your Rocky era—"

"Rock. No *Y*. Just Rock."

"And those copper plates with the feathers and beads sticking out...what was his name? Thunder? Lightning?"

Meredith pursed her lips before speaking. "Storm."

"Yep. He's the one who should have had a *y* tacked onto his name because that relationship was *storm-y*. You didn't care about the couch then. Remember? You had a desperate need to tear down a few walls." Ben shuddered. "Fortunately, building management denied you a permit."

Meredith brushed something off her kimono skirt. Putting on her noblest voice, she said, "I'm doing you a favor by removing that couch. Plus, French blue is passé."

"So is Geisha orange."

One of her chopsticks quivered.

Now he'd done it. Her face crumpled into that pitiful look of hurt he'd seen at the crash-and-burn ending of each boyfriend era. Now Ben felt like a cad. He'd glibly pointed out her past disastrous relationships. Mocked her decorator-recovery program. As recompense, he toyed with sacrificing the coatrack...but stopped himself.

That's what I always do. He would offer some piece of his life to smooth things over. What would he do when he ran out of furniture? Offer a leg? An arm? A spark of anger flared within him. Yes, Meredith was hurting...but she needed to find a way through her hurt without literally dismantling Ben's life. "Why can't you swipe other people's furniture?" he asked.

They stared each other down so long, Ben swore he'd lost feeling in his right eyelid. But he was tired of backing down. *Refused* to back down. Suddenly, he was ready to fight to the death over that couch.

Was that a tear in Meredith's eye? Was her chin trembling?

He felt yanked back to his years growing up, being the built-in caretaker and mediator for his kid sister and mother. Good ol' peacemaker Ben who could never stand to see a woman cry. Okay, he'd go the compromise route. "Let's...re-cover the couch rather than replace it."

Meredith sniffled. "It's lumpy."

"We'll put it on a diet."

Her orange-cone lips trembled as she smiled. He'd always liked it when she let down her guard. She looked younger, more relaxed. Ben would bet his coatrack that Dexter hadn't seen enough of that smile.

"I'll bring some swatches by tomorrow," she said softly. "Some colors that will look darling, darling."

She left so quickly, he still wasn't sure which "darling" was the couch, which was him. As the main office door clicked shut, Ben breathed a mind-leveling sigh. Alone. Finally. No ex-wife. No ex-fiancée. Just he and several decorating themes...and the couch for which he'd been willing to fight to the death.

Although he'd never have gone to such an extreme, it felt good to feel passionate about something again. Even a couch! He hadn't experienced a passion for anything—or anyone—in a long time. Forget passion. He couldn't remember when he'd last had *fun*. Had to have been with his best pal, Matt, full-time lawyer and part-time rake, who fell hard for a beekeeper from Northern California. Almost a year ago, Matt quit his law firm and moved to California to help his wife-to-be with her bee farm. Matt had joked he'd gone from an A-type personality to a B-type.

It was funny, but also true. Matt turned from an uptight lawyer to a laid-back guy. Meanwhile, Ben remained in Chicago, an uptight lawyer who spent his days in court or in his office, Ex-ville. His only male bonding these days was with his dog, Max. But sharing a drink and swapping tales with a Brittany spaniel didn't cut it. Plus, the conversations were awfully one-sided.

What were Ben's options? He could hang out at the local bar, a watering hole for lawyers. But after a day of negotiating and mediating, it set his teeth on edge to hear more lawyer talk. Other options? Go to a strip club? Not Ben's style. Take up fly fishing? He preferred chess.

"If I want male camaraderie, I first need to escape

Venus and move to Mars," he muttered, thinking again of those Venus-Mars books Heather was always reading. That author was making a mint telling women how to be Venus and men how to be Mars. Too bad Ben couldn't drop him a line and get some shortcut directions to the manly planet.

Writing a big-buck author was far-fetched. But what about that columnist? The one in *Real Men* magazine, the periodical he made Heather hide. Ben tapped his fingers along the edge of his desk. *Sure, buddy. What kind of man writes to "Mr. Real"?*

From what Heather had read to him, men from all walks of life. Carpenters. Doctors. "Mr. Real" sounded sophisticated, but also gave some get-down, get-real advice on everything from predatory pricing to predatory dating.

Ben moved his fingers to his computer keyboard. It would be easy to search the net for *Real Men* magazine, find their e-mail address, type a note to Mr. Real. No. Heather had access to his e-mail, which was essential to his business. When he was off-site, he could call her, have her check his messages, write back to whomever. No, e-mailing Mr. Real was out of the question. Heather would read it, tell Meredith, and he'd never hear the end of it.

He glanced at the piece of paper he'd scrawled on earlier. *I'm swimming in a Windex-blue sea of exes...an ex-wife, an ex-fiancée.*

Hmm. Sounded like the beginning of a note to Mr. Real.

"WHERE'S MR. REAL?" Seth, one of the mailroom gulchers, waved an envelope over William Clarington's desk.

"Blue?" Rosie blurted, checking out Seth's short-cropped hair. "I had just gotten accustomed to medicine red."

"Medicine-cabinet red," Seth corrected. Two weeks ago Seth had dyed his short-cropped blond hair a neon-like red, which he claimed was labeled Medicine-Cabinet Red on the bottle.

"Let me guess," Rosie mused. "Blueberry-Box Blue?"

"Squad-car Blue." He ran his fingers through his hair. "The flashing blue light on top of the cop car?"

"Very...urban."

"And distinctive. Yellow blends. Blue commands attention."

Rosie figured if she took a picture of Seth outside, his blue hair would blend right in with the sky and he'd look bald—defeating the whole commanding blue-hair experience. "Interesting policelike hue," she murmured, not sure how one complimented someone with Squad-Car Blue hair.

"So, where's the dude?" When she didn't answer, Seth elaborated, "Mr. Real?"

Rosie sat a little straighter. "You're talking to him."

Seth scratched his blue head. "You're the copy editor who sits—" he looked around, then waved the letter at her desk "—over there."

Rosie swiped at a curl that toppled over her forehead. "I've been promoted. Well, for a few weeks. Until they hire a new Mr. Real, I'm...the dude."

"Whoa!" Seth took a step back, tilting his head as though to see her better. "You? Mr. Real? Men ain't gonna like this."

"Men ain't gonna know."

Seth cocked an eyebrow, which looked oddly blond

with his blue hair. "How they *not* gonna know? Girls write different than guys."

"Oh, really? Do tell." Rosie leaned back in Mr. Real's ergonomic desk chair and crossed her arms.

Seth seemed stymied for a moment. He scratched his T-shirt, decorated with a picture of a red-white-and-blue cow. Along its flank was painted the skyline of Chicago. Underneath, the words Chi-Cow-Go. Cute.

Seth stopped scratching. "Chicks—ladies write more flowery. You know, they use words like *pink* and *pretty*."

"I'll avoid all *P* words. What else?"

"And they gush on and on." Seth made a rolling motion with his hand as though she might not understand what *gush* meant. "And they use too many words. Sometimes big ones."

"I'll work on the gushing. Never hurts to trim prose. But I can't promise not to use big words. After all, I'm a seasoned writer." Rosie smiled, liking the sound of those words as they rolled off her tongue. "Anyway, I've sat so close to William for the past seven months, I've heard nine-tenths of his conversations. I've proofread hundreds of his articles. I know how he talks, how he writes. For the next two weeks, no one could possibly guess it's a woman behind the man's words." Actually, a goddess behind the woman behind the man's words. Rosie wasn't sure yet if she'd don Athena or Artemis for the next two weeks—which she could do as long as no goddesslike words slipped into her Mr. Real answers.

"What if some dude sees you?" Seth had moved closer to her desk and was fiddling with a pile of thick, gold paper clips, remnants of William Clarington's former life.

"What dude is going to march into the offices of *Real Men* magazine, sneak past the front office receptionist, and know where to find William's former desk? Such a dude would need some serious built-in radar." Rosie leaned forward. "And no one within the magazine offices would blab because blabbing means that person would spend eternity in the gulch." That last point cinched any blue-haired men gabbing to the wrong dudes.

"The gulch sucks." Seth made a face.

"Tell me about it. This is my chance to prove myself. Make the great leap to life beyond the gulch."

Seth stopped playing with the paper clips and held his hand up, palm toward her. It took Rosie a moment to realize he was giving her a high five. She stood and slapped the palm of her hand against his.

"You're a cool chick," Seth said. "I mean, uh, you're a cool woman to be impersonating a dude. This is sorta like that Robin Williams flick."

"*Mrs. Doubtfire?*"

"Yeah."

Rosie tried to dismiss the image of Mrs. Doubtfire beating out a fire on her breasts. There would be no crises for the next two weeks, whether Rosie was a dude or a woman...or a goddess. "I get to wear my own clothes, fortunately."

"Cool." He tossed the letter onto the desk. "Can I have one of those?" He pointed to the gold paper clips.

Mr. Real was gone. Forever. Why not? "Sure."

Seth picked up a clip and attached it to his belt. He adjusted it one way, then another. Seemingly pleased with the impromptu accessory, he walked away with his signature swagger. "Good luck, Mr. Real," he called over his shoulder.

Rosie watched him leave, wondering what her oldest brother, Dillon, who'd never left the family farm in Colby, would say if he saw a man with blue hair. *Noth-*

ing. He'd be speechless, thinking Seth was from another planet.

"Planet Chi-Cow-Go," she murmured, chuckling to herself as she picked up the envelope and read "To Mr. Real" printed in black ink on the outside. Her eyes were tired of perusing William's computer screen, reading the gazillion e-mails addressed to realman@realmag.com. No wonder the real Mr. Real ran off with Boom Boom the bongo player. After telling hundreds of men how to live their lives, Mr. Real probably decided to get his *own.*

She flashed on William and Boom Boom cavorting in the Bahamas or some other tropical paradise. Rosie sighed as images filled her head. Brilliant sunsets. Crashing waves. Two naked, sand-coated bodies writhing on a beach. But these bodies weren't William and Boom Boom...

...they were Ben and Rosie.

Me and Ben? Writhing nakedly? She shut her eyes, her tummy clutching in anticipation of such a sensual encounter. The exploration of each other's bodies, the discovery of each other's pleasures...their inner world more fiery and exotic than the outside one.

She opened her eyes. "It's this desk," she whispered hoarsely, running her fingers over the smooth polished oak. "I'm picking up Boom Boom vibes. Better to pick up the letter opener." Rosie snatched the silver opener and glanced at the words engraved on its handle: Old Men Ought to Be Explorers.—T. S. Eliot.

Why would someone engrave that on a letter opener? Perhaps a gift from Boom Boom? Rosie's mind reeled with images of a bongo-playing stripper quoting T. S. Eliot. *What a killer combo. Great beater, great reader.*

Okay, she got what William saw in Boom Boom, but what did a stripper see in an uptight, persnickety columnist who ate a bran muffin at 8:10 sharp every morning?

Old men ought to be explorers. Maybe Mr. Real wasn't as old or unadventurous as Rosie had labeled him. Maybe Boom saw the real Mr. Real—saw that he was, at heart, a globe-trotting tiger. An old fantasy resurrected in Rosie's mind, one where she was Isak Dinesen, the writer Meryl Streep had portrayed in the movie *Out of Africa.* Isak was a woman ahead of her time. A multifaceted adventurer who ran a farm in Africa, maintained a long-term, torrid love affair and wrote memorable stories.

With more flair than she knew she had, Rosie blithely zipped open the envelope, the tip of the blade barely missing her other hand. She paused, staring at the reflection of fluorescent light off the gleaming silver blade. "Stay focused, Rosie," she whispered. "If you cut off your pinkie, you won't be able to write back to Mr. Real's readers." That's when she knew which goddess she needed for this job. *Wise, coolheaded Athena.* Rosie cooly laid the silver opener aside and eased the letter from its envelope.

The date at the top of the letter had been so hurriedly scrawled, it was difficult to decipher it was today's date. Rosie glanced at the rest of the letter. No, the guy just had horrendous handwriting. Or maybe he wrote it in a frenzied hurry?

Thinking back to the crazed speed at which she drove into work most days, Rosie could relate to that. Already empathizing, Rosie read on.

"Mr. Real, I'm swimming in a Windex-blue sea of exes...an ex-wife, an ex-fiancée."

Rosie paused, wondering why the word *blue* seemed to predominate the past few minutes of her life. Maybe there was some cosmic, mythical meaning behind this color? Nah. More likely, this man was simply blue. Depressed. She looked down at the scrawling handwriting and its terse loops and dips. Or angry? She continued reading.

> Why are women so needy? Growing up, I was the built-in mediator, cook and limo service for my mother and sister. That was sixteen years ago, but not a damn thing has changed. These days, I'm still a nice guy to an ex-fiancée who wants me to be her caretaker and an ex-wife who has a deranged need to redecorate my office with busted love affair themes. And get this—some strange woman also wants my space!
>
> My ex-fiancée has access to my e-mail, so respond to the P.O. box on the envelope.
> Signed,
> Wishing to move from Venus to Mars

He liked the Roman gods and goddesses while she stuck with the Greeks. But, hey, same thing. "He's obviously one very together, insightful male," Rosie murmured. "If anyone ever needed a goddess's guidance, it's this lucky man."

Rosie quickly looked up. Good. No one heard that last comment.

4

AT 8:30 P.M., after a business dinner meeting, Ben eased his BMW up the driveway of his house in the outskirts of Chicago. Home sweet ranch-style home. The one place in the world where he could walk in and—except for his dog, Max—be alone. No ex-fiancées. No ex-wives. And no space nabbers nabbing his space.

He punched a button above the rearview mirror. The electric garage door opened and he drove inside. The back of the garage was lined with tool-filled shelves. Mixed in with the saws, drills and toolboxes were remnants of abandoned hobbies: a baseball mitt, a pair of in-line skates, a battered trumpet case.

He got out and pressed the button on a side wall. As the garage door creaked closed, he looked up at the ceiling from which hung a kayak, an abandoned hobby he'd often dreamed of resurrecting. At one time—Nine years ago? Ten?—he'd loved kayaking down rivers. Feeling the heat of the sun on his skin. Hearing the slap of water against the hull—a hull now covered with dust. He'd even fantasized about kayaking in some exotic locale— like New Guinea or Africa—and taking photographs. Fitting a key into the door lock, he wondered where unused dreams went. Milwaukee?

The door opened into his kitchen, which was filled with the soothing strains of classical music. He always left the radio playing for his dog. Late afternoon, various lights also turned on automatically. "Max?" he called out, looking across the kitchen at the nearly closed sliding door that led into the living room. Through the narrow opening, his Brittany spaniel would stick its nose, nudging and sniffing the air, anxious to greet his master.

But tonight, no nose greeted Ben.

"Max?" he called again, checking the blinking light on the phone. Clients. More legal problems, questions, issues. They could wait. Right now he needed to unwind, chat with Max, do *anything* but play lawyer.

Still no nose.

Ben crossed the linoleum floor and slid open the door. "Maxwell?"

But instead of the scrabble of dog toenails on the living room hardwood floor, he heard the sharp *click click* of high heels.

"Not Maxwell, darling. Meredith." His ex-wife halted in the living room, center stage, and smiled so broadly, the white rectangles of her teeth looked eerily like the white wood-paneled blinds behind her.

"How'd you get in?" Ben looked around. In her deranged postaffair state, maybe she'd cut a hole in a window with that mega-ice-cream-diamond ring Dexter wanted back.

"No hello?" Those blindingly white teeth disappeared behind a pout.

"Hello," he snapped, scanning the room. "Did you break in to steal another couch?"

Meredith threw her head back and laughed. Ben flinched as one of her hairdo chopsticks came precariously close to getting tangled in his ficus tree. As he debated whether to make a mad lunge to save the tree, she raised her head and propped her hands on her kimono-clad hips. "Darling, darling. I'm not stealing a couch. Or a chair. Or any coatracks." She opened her arms so wide, he feared she'd break into a song from *The Sound of Music*. "I'm—" she paused dramatically "—re-modeling your bathroom!"

He stared at her so long, he felt that same eyelid start to go numb.

"Say something!" Meredith gushed, her arms still open.

"You broke into my house to remodel my bathroom?" This had to be a first. A thief who doesn't steal, but remodels.

She dropped her arms, which fell with a soft *fwop* against the silky kimono getup. "I didn't *break* in," she said peevishly. "I used the key hidden under the brick."

"The brick?"

"The third one—the loose one—on the outside of the brick patio. We wrapped the house keys in a plastic bag and stuck it under there...remember?"

He'd almost forgotten. Which was easy to do considering his backyard patio was a sea of bricks. A big, round brickred sea. Something Meredith had had installed as a good-will gift after their ill-willed divorce...the divorce where she got to keep the house, the car, the antiques. But worst of all, she'd insisted—and pleaded and cried—that she wanted to keep their golden retriever, Bogie.

That was a painful trot down memory lane.

Ben had only been bitter over losing Bogie. That dog had been his pal, his kayaking buddy, his confidante. Newly single and worse, Bogie-less, Ben had crashed on his friend Matt's couch for several months until Ben found this small, affordable ranch home in suburban Chicago. Meredith, knowing Ben loved the massive brick fireplace at their old home, took it upon herself to bestow him with a brick patio. He had thought it a gracious gift until Ben discovered Meredith had just broken up with a bricklayer.

He still wondered what their sex life had been like.

At that moment, Max trotted into the living room, his short tail wagging double time. Max rarely got anxious. Had to be Meredith's impromptu visit.

"How'd you think I got in?" she said, obviously more miffed that she'd been accused of breaking in than dismantling someone's bathroom.

"Through the doggy door."

"Doggy—? Hardly!" Meredith smoothed her hand over her dress. "My hips would get stuck."

An image that filled Ben with a moment of deliciously perverse pleasure. Meredith, stuck in the doggy door. He'd take his sweet time calling for help. Feign deafness to her calls for assistance as he popped open a beer, sat in his favorite chair and, with Max leaning against him, read the paper for, oh, thirty, forty minutes before calling the fire department.

"What are you thinking about?" Meredith said testily.

"Doggy doors. Fire departments." Time to stop dawdling in day dreams and put a stopper on Meredith's newest redecorating urge. He'd deal with little issues like breaking and entering later. "Leave my bathroom alone, Meredith," he said in his best he-man no-nonsense tone. "A bathroom is a man's castle."

Max's tail thumped against the floor, like an exclamation point to Ben's statement.

Meredith dipped her head, barely missing the ficus tree again. "Well, as of today, your castle needs a new commode."

He had to ponder that for a moment. "Toilet? Why? What happened—"

"And your castle also needs a new shower," she said speedily, ignoring his question. "That blue-and-gold-speckled tile and grimy sliding-door look is passé."

"To hell with passé. What happened to my toilet?"

"Well," Meredith raised her eyebrows so high, they nearly blended in with her hairline. "After the moving men undid the bolts—"

"What were moving men doing in my bathroom?"

"How was I supposed to get a plumber at this hour?"

This logic was giving him a headache. He raised a warning finger when she started to speak. "Forget whoever was in my bathroom, just explain why they removed—" Forget asking. He made a beeline for his castle. The scrabbling of Max's nails and the clicking of Meredith's heels followed him down the hallway.

Right before he reached the bathroom, Meredith said, "I forgot to mention something. After that little explosion, we had to turn off the water...."

ROSIE, more than a little cranky from having to double-park her Neon in a spot barely large enough for a cow, shoved open her apartment door. After stepping inside, she closed the door, turned the lock and shoved the bolt. "Home Sweet Fortress," she murmured. Back in Colby, they never locked doors. But in Chicago, she'd been counseled by her friend Pam to always lock her door. Any door. Car, apartment, whatever. "You get in and you lock it," Pam had lectured with a dead-on And-I'm-not-kidding-around look.

Rosie tossed her keys into an upside down helmet on a coffee table. It had been her dad's, from when he served in Vietnam. Years ago, he'd given her brothers mementos from that war—but nothing to her. She'd complained. Said even if she was a girl, she too wanted something that held meaning for him, something that got him through the war and back home. A few days later, he quietly walked into her bedroom and handed her his helmet. Obviously, he'd worn it, but she never knew he'd also used it as a food and water bowl for a German Shepherd war dog, an animal that had once saved his life.

Rosie now stared at the helmet, taking a moment to remember her dad's stories. The husky timbre of his voice. The way he'd squint one eye when he wanted to drive home a point. The way he'd lightly tap her on the head, an unspoken I-love-you gesture. Typically, she tossed the keys into the helmet, which jangled and clattered as they hit bottom. If she didn't toss the keys into the hat first thing upon getting home, she'd never find them again in the morning. But tonight, she gently placed them inside before settling onto the futon love seat and stretching out her five-three frame.

Silence.

This was always the toughest part of the day. These first few minutes of stony quiet after coming home. Because no matter how hard she listened, she wouldn't hear her family's voices, watch their comings and goings. At this point in the day, her heart always shrank a little as she yearned for how it used to be. She'd slam open the screen door, hear her mom's voice, "Don't slam..." Rosie, tossing a coat or book on a side table, would apologize for the slamming while waving hello to her dad. He'd be in his overalls, sitting in his favorite armchair, reading the paper while watching the news. Sometimes he'd catch a discrepancy in what he read and what he heard and loudly announce the difference, whether anyone was around to hear or not.

Scents of chicken or beef wafted from the kitchen, where her mother was making dinner. The meals were basic fare. Chicken and potatoes. Meat loaf and potatoes. Spam and potatoes. But every few weeks the dreaded meal appeared on the table. Everything Stew. A combination of chicken, meatloaf, Spam, potatoes and anything else that caught Mom's eye. Once a piece of apple pie slid accidentally into the stew—which her mother proudly announced at the dinner table as though whoever bit into a piece of apple got a prize.

Rosie never dreamed she'd miss Everything Stew. But what she'd give right now to be sitting at the thick oak table, seeing the cast-iron pot appear, and suppressing her groan along with her father and her brothers. They'd exchange glances as they picked at the stew's contents, watching as one or the other identified a fragment of a former meal.

Br-ring. Br-ring.

Jerked out of stew memories, Rosie listened for the source of the sound. Was it buried under that pile of magazines? Wedged under that pillow?

Br-ring. Br-ring.

"I've got to remember to put the phone in the same spot," she muttered, tossing aside a pillow. Nothing. If the phone fit, she'd have kept it in the helmet along with her keys—then she'd never be in this predicament again! Shoving aside some magazines, her fingers hit something hard. The receiver! She yanked it to her ear. "Hello?"

"Rosie Posey?"

Recognizing her oldest brother's voice, Rosie grinned. "Dillon!" She fell back onto the couch. "What's up?"

"How's our big-city girl?"

"Missing Mom's Everything Stew."

"Is food that awful in Chicago?"

"No." Rosie giggled. "Just got a bad case of the lonelies."

"Mom's Everything Stew could give you a bad case of something else. Li'l sis, if you miss it that much, we'll gladly send you a batch. The *entire* batch."

Rosie laughed. "*No* thanks. It was a weak moment, not a special request. So what's up? Usually you call on Saturday mornings." *Every* Saturday morning, to be exact. Seven-thirty sharp. Rosie had an inkling it was her brother's way to ensure she was safe. Not staying out too late—or worse, not coming home. Actually, it wasn't just Dillon who called. All *four* of her brothers called, each taking a turn as though she wouldn't catch on they were keeping tabs that way. But she didn't mind. Such overprotectiveness meant they loved her. Wanted to watch over her. After all, she was the baby sister in a family of four boys.

"Thought you'd like a friendly reminder that this Sunday is Father's Day," Dillon said. "Pops checked the mailbox at lunch, then again before dinner."

Dillon didn't need to explain further. Her dad was looking for a card from Rosie. Her father was a big, rough-handed farmer with an even bigger, sensitive heart. More than once she'd caught her father brushing aside a tear while watching a sunset or listening to the church choir.

"It'll be in the mail tomorrow. Promise."

"That's my Rosie Posey. How's everythin' going?"

She sighed, suddenly feeling the weight of the workday. "Busy. Got a promotion. Temporary, but at least I get to write for a while."

"Write? You're one of them magazine writers now?" Dillon, unlike her other brothers, had never pursued an education beyond high school. He loved the farm, which everyone knew he'd take over when her father couldn't manage the land or care for the stock any longer. As her other brothers had their own careers, no one minded that Dillon would take over the family farm.

"Yes, I'm one of the magazine writers." A minor exaggeration. But it didn't seem necessary to admit she was actually the columnist filling in for Mr. Real.

"Writing articles about big-city life?"

"Sort of." Didn't seem necessary, either, to admit she was writing man-to-man advice on how to fend off ex-wives and ex-fiancées and space-nabbing women. Remembering her own space-nabbing adventure this morning, she stared at the splotches of dried mud on her skirt. *That litigating lummox.*

"Life treating you good?"

"Except for a certain guy, yes."

There was a long pause on the other end. "What guy?"

She brushed at a stubborn splotch of dirt. "A jerk." She'd only worn this skirt once, but now she'd have to take it back to the dry cleaners. Forget that he heated her imagination with fantasies of naked writhing; that jerk was costing her money!

"Jerk?"

"Yes, a jerk who's trying to invade my space."

"What happened?" Dillon asked gravely. "He still botherin' you?"

"He's going to bother me until he gets his way, that space-barging, space-stealing—" she was running out of space words "—mud-splattering jerko." She glanced up at the clock and gasped. "It's almost seven! Damn—" She squeezed shut her eyes. "I mean, darn. I forgot about Pam coming over. I told her I'd fix dinner and I haven't done a thing." There was some leftover chicken, a jar of pickles, and a half-eaten piece of cherry pie in the fridge.

Suddenly she understood the reasoning behind her mother's Everything Stew.

"Invaded your space? Bothering you until he gets his way?"

"Dillon, gotta go! A card will be in the mail to Dad tomorrow. I love you!"

She waited for his murmured "Love you, too" before she hung up.

THE SOOTHING STRAINS of a violin woke Ben up from a dream filled with moving men dressed like geishas, who were carrying orange cones, couches and commodes. He blinked sleepily at the clock radio and turned up the volume. Brandenburg Concerto no. 1. He smiled to himself. Was there a better way than Bach to get up in the morning? For a fleeting moment, he thought about waking up with Rosie, her warm body nestled against his. Those sleepy hazel eyes blinking at him, those luscious lips whispering, "Good morning."

That *definitely* beat Bach as a better way to wake up.

Trying to ignore the hard jolt that seized his groin, Ben slid out of bed. He had to get up, get to work, not fantasize about that territorial, strong-willed—okay, and titillatingly attractive—woman. He headed across the carpeting to the bathroom, flipped the light switch and halted.

Something was different.

He rubbed his eyes, then scanned the white walls, white porcelain sink, the white—

"She stole my commode!" he barked, staring at the hole in the floor left by Meredith the Bathroom Marauder. His gaze swerved to the left. "And the shower door!" Shuffling from one foot to another on the cold tile floor, he recalled the cold facts from the night before.

He'd marched into the bathroom and first noticed the water. On the walls, the floor. While Max thumped his tail madly, Meredith had hurriedly explained something about the movers unbolting the commode, but forgetting to dismantle the main water pipe. With water spewing everywhere, they'd had to turn off the main water valve to the house.

But Meredith had promised everything would be better than new. She promised a plumber would fix the main pipe today. She'd left a case of bottled water. And she'd promised to show Ben some pictures of new commodes.

He hadn't asked—hadn't wanted to know—further particulars. It had been one hell of a day. He'd told Meredith, her orange-cone lips quivering, to fix things ASAP. Then he'd fixed Max's dinner, fixed himself a Scotch on the rocks, then gone to bed, setting the alarm thirty minutes early so he could get to work early and shower, shave and dress in the exercise club located in his work building's basement.

He glanced at a wall clock. Six-thirty. He had to step on it. After throwing on a pair of sweats and tennis shoes, Ben conversed with his dog while fixing his food. "Your master's first wife—and God help me, *last*—wasn't satisfied re-covering my office couch," Ben grumbled, setting the dog's bowl on the floor. "No, that woman had a demented need to tear apart my bathroom as well." Ben gave Max a male-bonding pat on the head. "Take my advice, buddy. Don't get married. And if you do, marry a dog who doesn't need to control or redecorate you. This is your castle. Stand up for your rights."

Max licked Ben's face before chowing down.

Ben ran back upstairs and grabbed his workout bag—which he'd packed the night before with work clothes and bathroom supplies—then raced through the kitchen, stopping only to turn on the kitchen radio to keep Max company. Moments later, Ben backed out the driveway while wisps of orange and pink threaded the eastern sky. He could be at work by seven-fifteen, park, shower and dress, then move his car before Rosie showed up.

Twenty minutes later Ben careened down Clark before swerving sharply down an alley. After his car sailed over a bump, Ben cut the wheel sharply to the right...

"Wha-a-a-?" He slammed on the brakes, his front bumper nearly kissing the rear end of a tacky green economy car. Gripping the steering wheel, Ben glared through the windshield at the offending vehicle.

"What in the hell is this car doing here?" he yelled. How many people was Archibald Potter renting that space to?

Seething, Ben quickly went over the facts. At yesterday's meeting, Potter had checked his computer records. The space had been rented to only two people. Which meant...

"That tacky green Neon belongs to Rosie," Ben muttered ominously. Forget the earlier waking-up-in-bed fantasies, this was *reality!* "What is it with the women in my life? They're either redecorating or invading my space!"

Ben slammed the gear into park and hopped out of the car.

Splash.

He blew out an exasperated breath before looking down. His sockless, sneaker-clad feet were standing in a pothole of muddy water. "Now I know where her mud-splattered look came from." He stepped out of the hole. "But before I repark, a man's gotta do what a man's gotta do." He sloshed his way to the back doors of the building.

Minutes later, Ben returned to his car to find a square yellow truck halted behind his BMW. Even in the early-morning haze, he could clearly see the scowl on the truck driver's face.

"Hey!" the guy yelled out his window, jabbing a cigarette at Ben. "Just 'cause you drive a Beemer, you think you can block traffic?"

Ben shrugged. "I had to use the men's room."

"What?"

Ben didn't want to repeat the reason—the last thing he wanted was his entire office building to hear him yelling that he'd had to take a leak. But the slovenly, burly truck driver looked as though he'd kill if he didn't get a valid excuse. Ben cleared his throat. Raising his voice, he repeated, "I had to use the men's room."

The driver blinked with great exaggeration. "How unusual—like the rest of us don't." He took an angry puff off a cigarette, letting the smoke stream out of his nostrils while he continued talking. "Other guys take leaks without causing traffic jams. You're costing me time and money!"

"You're right," Ben answered, putting on his best mediating voice while putting his hand on the door handle. "I'm leaving."

"Make it snappy!"

That did it. Ben, always the peacemaker, the good guy, snapped on the "snappy" comment. Enough was enough. If he wanted to park crooked—all right, and also block an alley—for ten lousy minutes, well by damn, he'd park crooked and not have to explain he was in the men's room.

His face growing hot, he turned slowly and faced down the driver. "I said, 'you're right.' So what's the beef, Dog Breath?"

Ben's mind raced. In horror, he wondered where he'd come up with the death wish to insult a guy who was twice—maybe three times—his size. And worse, he called him Dog Breath, a label he never used with anyone, even his dog Max. As these thoughts crowded Ben's mind, Dog Breath threw open his door, jumped to the ground and marched right at him.

Ben prayed the mud hole—strategically placed between him and the trucker—would hinder the one-man death march.

No such luck.

Dog Breath stepped in and out of the hole as though it were a mere dent in the road. The death march continued, unabated. Next thing Ben knew, a big jowly face was inches from his own. He fought the urge to cough at the stench of cigarette smoke.

"My beef, Mr. Beemer, is that people like you think they own the road."

Holding his breath, Ben stared at the man's chest, which was a blur of plaid. He raised his gaze to the man's beady eyes, which were difficult to see through the folds of fat. But Ben didn't want to back down. Hell, he'd backed down long enough...to Meredith, to Heather, to Ms. Parking Space.

"If I'm costing you time and money," Ben said, "why are you arguing with me, preventing me from getting in my car and moving out of your way?"

Dog Breath snatched a handful of Ben's sweatshirt and jerked him closer. "I'm not arguin'," he growled.

Ben would have growled back, but the tightly pulled sweatshirt was like a noose around his throat. "Physical violence," he rasped, "never solved anything."

"Oh yeah?"

"I'm a lawyer."

"All da better."

The last thing Ben remembered was a chicken-size fist obliterating his vision.

ROSIE STARED at the flaxen-haired receptionist, who was studiously applying mascara with one hand while holding a small hand mirror with the other.

"If Benny said he'd meet you at seven-forty-five," the receptionist said, her eyes never wavering from the hand mirror, "he'll be here any minute. He's very punctured."

Rosie paused. "You mean punctual?"

"Yes," the woman answered absently, adroitly twirling the mascara wand along her lashes.

Makeup. Rosie never understood why women took such pains to slather on that stuff. Rather than stare at the eyelash-thickening procedure, she checked out a painting over the receptionist's head. It was a tropical beach under moonlight. Rosie eyed the pearly crest of waves along a dark beach, the spiked silhouette of palm trees, the man-in-the-moon face which was also...a clock? Rosie leaned forward. The moon was definitely a clock. What kind of office had a tropical painting with a clock for a moon? *Lawyers. No sense of decor.*

Rosie compared moon-time with her wristwatch. Both read 7:55. She crossed her arms under her chest. Okay, so she wasn't exactly always on time herself, but hadn't Mr. ILITIG8 said, "Not seven-fifty-five—seven-forty-five"?

Uh-huh. Real punctured.

The clattering of a dropped hand mirror interrupted Rosie's thoughts.

"Benny!" The receptionist stood up, her voice rising with her. "Did you get mugged?"

Rosie turned to look.

If she'd run into this man on the street, she'd never have recognized him as the nattily dressed lawyer she'd met yesterday. Today he wore a soiled gray sweat suit that looked oddly stretched out around the neckline. His tennis shoes were caked with mud. His hair, which yesterday had been neatly parted on the side, stuck out in tufts that reminded her of the baby chickens back home. One hand clutched the handle of a workout bag—the other held a wadded white napkin to his chin.

Ben started to speak, but his voice was muffled behind the napkin. He moved it from his lips. "I wasn't mugged," he said gruffly, "I was slugged."

"Is that a Starbucks napkin?" the receptionist asked, making Rosie wonder if this woman was more caught up with brands than injuries. "That's why I prefer decaffeinated," the receptionist said, jabbing her wand into the air for emphasis. "Too much caffeine makes people do weird things."

Ben heaved a weighted sigh. "Heather, it has nothing to do with caffeine. A kindly convenience store cashier offered me this napkin filled with ice."

"Wow," Rosie said softly. "You can get everything at convenience stories these days. Even medical help."

Ben flashed her a disbelieving look. In a low growl, he said, "It's you."

She straightened. "We had an appointment at seven-forty-five." When his blue eyes narrowed, she bit her tongue, wishing she hadn't blurted the appointment thing. The man obviously had a very good reason for being late.

"Sorry," he said, sounding about as unsorry as anyone she'd ever met. "I would have been here on time, showered, dressed appropriately, and *un*slugged if *somebody* had gotten into work at a *reasonable* time, not some nocturnal predawn hour. Otherwise, I could have briefly used the *shared* space." He clenched his jaw muscle, then winced. Adjusting the napkin, he glanced at Heather. "You're early."

"I was late yesterday, so I'm early today," she said, adjusting a strap on her shift before sitting back down. "Making up for that hour."

"Making up, all right," he murmured, glancing at the mascara wand. "I'd love a Scotch," Ben said to no one in particular, "but all I need is early-morning booze breath to complete this gone-to-hell look. After picking myself up from the alley asphalt, I had to park four blocks away. Do you believe on the way back, somebody mistook me for a vagrant and slipped me a quarter?" He gave his head a shake, then winced again. "But all's not lost. Maybe Meredith can use this down-and-dirty, slugged look as a new theme when she breaks up with her next boyfriend." He headed toward his office. "Would you be a pal and get me a cup of coffee? Black." He disappeared through the doorway. "Like my heart."

"Oh, I almost forgot! Your eight o'clock will be a few minutes late!" The receptionist brushed her hair back with her mascara-wand-free hand. "I've never seen him like this!" she whispered urgently to Rosie. "Even the time that Christmas tree fell on him and we had to call 911."

"Christmas tree?" Rosie repeated, blinking. But the receptionist was engrossed in putting away the mascara and digging around in a little polka-dot bag from which she extracted various tubes and bottles. "I'll get the coffee," Rosie murmured, unsure who exactly Ben had called "pal," considering he seemed a bit peeved with both of them.

Okay, maybe a little *extra* peeved with Rosie, but considering they had to negotiate sharing the parking space, she decided it was best if she were his pal. That's what Athena, the goddess who joined men as an equal, would do. Yes! Athena was the perfect goddess persona to adopt for this encounter.

Rosie-Athena headed to an arrangement of coffee stuff on a corner metal table. Reaching it, she scanned the pot, sugar and cream containers, and the collection of Hollywood mugs. Rosie felt a mild surge of guilt as she recalled that the James Dean cup still sat on her desk. Well, she'd return it later. For now, should she pick the mug with the movie title *Singin' in the Rain*? No. There might be sunshine outside, but Ben looked as though he were having a rainy day. And he definitely didn't look as though he wanted to sing. Nix that one.

Blonde Venus? No. He'd visibly flinched when he'd glanced at that yesterday. *My Fair Lady*? Hmm. *Some Like it Hot*? Hot coffee. He'd like it. Yes!

Rosie poured the steaming liquid into the cup, checking out its picture of Marilyn Monroe wearing some clingy dress and playing a ukulele. Did Benjamin Taylor like that kind of big-breasted, blond-bombshell type? An uncomfortable feeling skittered around Rosie's stomach. Maybe she'd quaffed her nutri-quasi-Twinkie bar too quickly. Still staring at Marilyn's red lips, fluffy blond hair and killer curves, Rosie realized the skittering wasn't indigestion—it was...*emotion*.

Jealousy?

Impossible. *So what if Benjamin Taylor is impossibly cute, even with that chicken-tuft hair and a swollen jaw, how can I possibly be jealous about a slugged lawyer and a dead movie star?* Even as these thoughts tumbled through her mind, some internal voice offered an answer. *Because Marilyn Monroe represents everything you aren't—she's sensual, sexy, and has a body that could stop a herd of stampeding cattle.*

Rosie put the pot aside and grabbed the *My Fair Lady* mug for herself. Audrey Hepburn—as Eliza Doolittle—wore an ill-fitting jacket, a wrinkled skirt and a smudge of soot on her nose. *Is that how I look to men?* Rosie tried to forget the clump of mud that had stuck to her forehead yesterday. She turned the mug and stared at another picture of Audrey Hepburn as the suave, refurbished Eliza Doolittle—an elegant, classy lady who eventually wooed her man.

Rosie stared longingly at the image. *Maybe if Mom hadn't been so busy helping run a farm and raising five kids—four of them boys—I might have learned the secrets of being feminine and elegant.* Rosie slid a glance at the receptionist, who was carefully outlining her lips with some sort of pink-leaded pencil. *I could never draw a straight line, much less outline my mouth. I'd slip, skid off my top lip and end up drawing a big wobbly circle around my nose.*

As Rosie poured coffee into the *My Fair Lady* mug, a yearning filled her. A yearning to be a new Rosie. Not a lip-lining, movie-star Rosie. But an adventurous Rosie whose dreams were bigger than the gulch, bigger than *Real Men* magazine. Isn't that what Boom Boom and Mr. Real had done? Escaped from humdrum to bongo drum?

Picking up the mugs, Rosie grinned. Too bad there wasn't a goddess named Boom Boom, who inspired women to bongo their way from a mediocre life to an exciting one. Rosie paused. Just as she stirred sugar and milk into her coffee, why couldn't she also stir a little Boom Boom into her Athena?

With an extra oomph to her step, Rosie strutted into Ben's office.

5

"I DIDN'T ASK YOU to bring the coffee," Ben grumbled, pressing the ice-filled napkin to his jaw. He warily watched Rosie place a steaming mug in front of him.

"I'm not your pal?" she asked sweetly.

Too sweetly. Either she overdosed on sugar in her own coffee, or she wanted something. Like to take over the parking space. Just the way Meredith was taking over his bathroom. Nice, mediating, peacemaking Ben had had it. "You're a thief."

"Okay, you've had a bad morning. But I'm not a thief. I didn't steal that spot—today's my day."

Now what was she trying to do? Pacify him? Oh, she was one to take the high road. Yesterday, when she'd been the mud-splotched one, different story. He opened his mouth to say as much, but when she crossed her legs, all he could focus on were a pair of shapely calves that tapered to a pair of slim ankles. Those were the kind of killer legs that would look fantastic in a pair of... "Loafers?"

"What?"

She wore a pair of scuffed brown loafers. His gaze shot back to her face as though he hadn't done the leg-loafer tour. But his mind reeled that a woman with supermodel legs dressed like a spinster librarian. The combination was startling. Titillating. After being married to a woman who changed styles more often than Cher, it was stimulating—mentally *and* physically—to meet a woman who exuded practicality and sensuality.

"What are you thinking about?" Rosie asked.

"Cher?"

Rosie frowned. "Share...the parking space?"

Now he frowned. "She's a parking space?"

"How hard did that guy hit you? Maybe you should see a doctor. I could drive you—my car's nearby."

Nearby. If his jaw didn't hurt so damn bad, he'd growl. "What'd you do," he asked menacingly, "park there all night? Sleep in the car? That's against the law, you know."

"Hardly! I got here early, that's all."

"How early—3:00 a.m.?"

She sputtered something unintelligible before speaking up. "A little before seven, if you must know. Didn't realize there were time constraints on *my* parking day." She took a swig of coffee, but kept the mug at her lips like a barrier behind which to observe him.

"Yes," he said matter-of-factly, "Tomorrow *is* my day."

"That's right," she responded eagerly, emerging from behind the cup. A dark, spirally curl toppled over her forehead. "Today was my day, tomorrow's your day."

Women had toyed with his affections, stolen his objects, and he was determined to hold on to something, *anything*, even if it was the simple fact that tomorrow was *his* day. *His.* He had the urge to say as much again, but when he opened his mouth, a pain shot through his jaw. And this damn napkin was turning into a soggy mess. He tossed it into a nearby trash can where it landed with a soggy *whomp*.

"Your jaw!" Rosie eyes glistened with concern as she stared at him. "It's swollen and red!"

"You should see the other guy," he mumbled.

"He's in worse shape?"

"Oh, yeah. When I fell to the ground, I think my right foot brushed against his. Doctor thinks he'll walk again, though."

"Really?"

Ben stared into those big, hazel eyes. He couldn't remember the last time he'd seen such an untainted look. What kind of woman grew to be Rosie's age and retained such innocence? "No," Ben said, determined to hold on to his anger, "the other guy is fine. I was kidding."

"Oh." She swiped the curl off her brow. "Then why did he slug you?"

"He doesn't seem to like lawyers."

"Who does?" Rosie pursed her lips. "I mean—"

Ben raised his hand. "Please. My morning has been difficult enough without digressing into why people hate lawyers. Let's finalize our parking space agreement. Alternate days, right?"

Rosie nodded.

"I'll put that in writing."

"A legal agreement?" She frowned.

"It's to protect you, too, of course."

Rosie felt her fury sparking, but stuffed it back down. After all, Athena wouldn't react angrily: Athena would negotiate with the man as an equal. "What if I have to run into work early one morning—like you did today—and I zip into our parking spot for, say, ten minutes? Will you sue me?"

Ben took a sip of coffee, his blue eyes focused intently on her face. They were warming from frosty blue to a kind of summer-sky blue, the color of Kansas skies on an easygoing summer day.

Taking advantage of his moment of reflection, Rosie

charged ahead. "You know, this morning was a fluke. I had to get in extra early because I was mega-late yesterday. And I knew I'd be meeting with you at sevenish, so I also wanted to make sure we'd have enough time to chat." *Chat?* Men didn't say *chat*. Especially lawyers, she bet. "I mean, time to talk. Discuss. Negotiate."

Ben set down his cup. "More parking spaces will eventually be available."

The last word—*negotiate*—must have done the trick. Eager she was on his good side, Rosie rushed on, "Right! Probably soon, too. Maybe in a week or so." She had no idea what she was talking about, but he wasn't glaring at her, which was enough encouragement for her to continue. "Kind of silly to write up some petty legal document when there'll be no need to share that space in a week or so. Maybe even a day or so."

Ben started to respond when Heather poked her head in the door. "Your eight o'clock's here. Well, technically, your 8:10 now." She disappeared.

"Great," Ben murmured. "New client and I look like a bum."

"Not true," offered Rosie. "You only look a little rough around the edges. A little dangerous." The last just slipped out, but it was true. The man had looked cleancut and professional yesterday, but she almost preferred his look today. Unshaven. Rumpled. *Dangerous*. Her heart thumped erratically. "Looking dangerous is good for a lawyer, right?" she said, trying to cover her slip.

He gave her a look that escalated her heartbeats from mere thumping to wild boom-booming. When he raked a hand through his hair, she felt her own scalp prickle. God, what would it be like to be touched by a rumpled, dangerous man like Ben? To writhe nakedly in some exotic locale?

"Let's skip the agreement and just mark the schedule on our calendars."

"Yes," she said, a bit too breathlessly. She was losing it. Rosie Myers, who could beat guys at Ping-Pong, sprints and the long jump was losing it, big time, in front of Benjamin Taylor.

"And as we discussed, tomorrow's *my* day."

Yes sir! Nothing like a little bossiness to put a damper on a heat rush. Sheesh, this guy was more territorial than ol' Mr. Harrison, the pharmacist who gave his own tickets to people who parked in front of his drug store. Even though the police continually warned Mr. Harrison that the street was city property, he still gave tickets, griping that he had parking rights in front of his business. Because of his age, everybody in town put up with cranky Mr. Harrison. Some people even paid their tickets.

"You know," Rosie said, rising. "I could give you my phone number so if you ever needed a quick ten minutes, even an hour, you could call me."

Ben set his cup down so hard, a ceramic blue fish on his desk shook. "I, uh, don't think that will, uh, be necessary." But his head-to-toe devouring look said something else—that maybe he'd like that?

Or maybe she'd imagined that look, just as she'd imagined too many other things with Benjamin Taylor. "No—no," she stammered, trying to clarify, "I meant if you ever needed a quick ten minutes in the parking space. For *parking*. Not for..." She suddenly felt as though she were running a fever. Hot. Too hot. She'd never invoke this new Boom Boom goddess again. "To-tomorrow's your day." Not waiting for any response, Rosie speedwalked out of his office, past his eight o'clock—some guy dressed in a three-piece suit—and out the door.

Only when she was outside did she realize she had

stolen another mug. *My Fair Lady*. Feeling anything but, she jogged toward the elevators.

"BENNY, you look so-o-o much better!" Heather cooed, cradling the phone in the crook of her neck while filing her nails. "I'd hardly know you'd been slugged except for your red jaw!"

Ben, showered and dressed in slacks and a shirt, halted in the doorway and closed his eyes. "Not while you're on the phone, Heather," he admonished quietly.

"Not what?"

He opened his eyes. "Don't say such...personal things to me. I'd prefer my reputation at work to remain professional." He was one to talk. He'd interviewed his 8:10 appointment dressed in a wrinkled, muddied sweat suit.

Heather stopped filing. Waving the receiver, she said, "It's Carla, not one of your clients!"

How long had they been having this discussion? A hundred, a thousand times? Maybe he should quit fighting it. Save his energy for commode filchers and parking space thieves. "Tell Carla hello," he mumbled, crossing to his office. Stepping into his inner sanctum, he tossed his workout bag into the corner before sitting behind his desk. To the right was a stack of folders, each holding relevant papers for a case in progress. He reached for the top folder when a white envelope in the center of his desk caught his eye.

On its front, in black ink, was boldly printed "To: Wishing to Move from Venus to Mars."

Mr. Real wrote back! Finally! Ben wasn't alone in a world of women. Ben ripped open the envelope, wadded and tossed it into the trash can. Pulling out the letter, he began reading: "Mr. Mars:"

Ben had liked that in all of Mr. Real's responses. The guy had class. No matter the tone of the writer—and some got heated—or how the writer had signed his name, Mr. Real always called everyone Mr., Mrs., or Ms. Not only was he a man's man, but a gentleman. Ben read on: "You ask why women are so needy? My conjecture is that you still seek those same types of relationships with other women."

"Get down, Mr. Real!" Ben whispered to himself. *This guy isn't just a columnist, he's a shrink.* Leaning back in his chair, Ben continued reading: "Other types of women exist in the world: independent, adventurous, a man's equal. Too many men look for the superficial and miss the substance."

Ben pondered that last sentence for a moment. A woman being a man's equal? He wasn't born yesterday. He knew all about Gloria Steinem and the women's movement. It's just that Ben had never experienced a relationship with a woman who was his equal, who *wanted* to be his equal. He'd always taken care of women, been absorbed into their problems, issues. "No wonder I became a lawyer," he murmured, reading on. "For whatever reasons in your background, it's evident you're feeling trapped. Let's investigate that. You say you're a nice guy. That you have a couple of manipulative exes and a strange woman who wants your space. My question to you: What is your space? Your world, your home, your office?"

Ben looked around at the variety of decorating themes in his office. This wasn't a space—it was a high-end flea market. Shaking his head, he went back to the letter. "Right now, you're wanting to move from planet to planet. I'm impressed. That's one big move. I suggest you first pick a different space—a vital space. If you can't share it, then place your stakes. As with most things in life, it's best to start small, then think big. After all, every journey begins with a single step. Respectfully yours, Mr. Real"

"You should have seen my journey this morning," Ben muttered, thinking of the hundreds of steps he took along those long blocks into work. He probably could have handled it if he hadn't been slipped that quarter. Forget the insult—what could a quarter buy in today's world? Ben made a mental note to give a dollar to the next homeless person he met.

But back to the letter. Share a space... He already did! His bathroom, his office. But find a space to mark his territory? Good thinking. A small, first step. Ben tapped his fingers against the desk. Small space. Small.

The parking space! Which was definitely small compared to Mars and Venus. He nodded to himself. He'd build from there—like, next claim his office, then his bathroom. Soon he'd be claiming his right to take on the world, to dust off his kayak and discover regions unknown.

A warmth flooded his veins, a feeling he hadn't known in years. Satisfaction? Anticipation? If he didn't know better, it was almost like falling in love, something he hadn't experienced in a long, long time. Of course, this wasn't really falling in love—it was luxuriating in a moment of euphoria. One small step for Benkind, one giant step...

"To Mars!" he said out loud. "I'm building a new life!"

"What?" called out Heather from the other room. The *thunk thunk* of footsteps preceded a waterfall of blond hair as she peeked into his office. "You're building something? In here?"

Ben looked at her platform shoes. Talk about building—Heather built an extra inch or three to her height when she wore those leg-tottering shoes. "I'm not building anything. I was just experiencing a moment of exuberance."

She looked around the office. "Alone?" Flashing him a perplexed look, she added, "I've been worried about you lately, Benny."

That confession took Ben by surprise. "You're worried about...me?"

"Yeah." She sidled into the doorway. Today she wore a shift covered with purple butterflies and pink flowers. Heather missed her calling as a flower child. "You seem—" she tilted her head as she scrutinized him "—more preoccupied lately."

"Preoccupied?"

"Yeah. Like the couch. When Meredith has needed to redecorate before, you've let her do her thing. But this time, you got preoccupied with it!"

Preoccupied? Heather wasn't worried about his well-being, she was worried about him setting a few boundaries. Unheard of before now. "What you two fail to understand is that it's *my* couch. I love that couch. And Meredith needs to learn she can't come back to me every time one of her love affairs goes bust. She has to learn that she has a strong heart, that she'll be okay without re-covering or redecorating or stealing toilets."

He meant to vent, but instead his on-the-fly analysis hit home. Meredith did have a strong heart. Damn it, she lived. She experienced life. Which meant she wasn't afraid to love deeply, crash and burn, then pick herself up and love again.

Of course, during the picking-herself-up phase, a corner of his life got redecorated. Nevertheless, Ben had to hand it to Meredith—she had more guts to delve into life than he did.

After a long pause, Heather said, "See? You're preoccupied again."

"Maybe it's time for me to be preoccupied," Ben said quietly. "Time for me to figure out who Benjamin Taylor is, what I want."

A second head appeared in the doorway. "Darling, what you want is to see some new commode samples!"

Ben flinched. What had Meredith done to her hair? Instead of chopsticks, she had small, bright, silver things sticking out of another wild bird's nest number. For a mind-numbing moment, he wondered if she had stuck commode handles into her hair.

"You—" he tried not to stare at her hair "—you didn't drag a bunch of toilets in here, did you?"

Meredith gave him an are-you-crazy look. "Do I look that strong?"

If you put your mind to it, you could drag in a herd of water buffalo. He offered a small prayer that Meredith's next affair wasn't with a safari tour guide. "Well, you have been lifting weights," he muttered, eyeing the sheets she held in her hand. Photos of commodes? And he thought yesterday morning had started off strangely.

Meredith stepped jauntily into his office. Today she wore a red dress with a satin jacket embroidered with birds and bonsai trees. Good thing her business was lucrative, otherwise she couldn't afford a new wardrobe every postaffair. Or afford these ex-husband redecorating binges. "Oh, you noticed," she said, flexing one arm. "I've been working with a personal trainer—"

"Show me the pictures." Ben didn't need to see his ex-wife flex. He needed a commode and shower door, pronto.

The room filled with an incenselike scent as she walked into the room. Of course. New look, new perfume. "You'll adore these commodes," Meredith said. "Very European. Custom-mixed porcelain. This one is called the Renaldo. Notice the flowing, neo-Italian lines...."

It was too much. Truckers. Incense. A commode named Renaldo. "Meredith," Ben barked, "if you put neo anything in my bathroom, I will throttle you with my bare hands!" He gripped the edge of the desk, resisting the urge to press one of those handles in her hair. "Just fix the pipe so I can turn on my water. And get me a square, white toilet. End of discussion." To her stunned expression, he added, "And please close the door behind you. I need to make an important phone call."

"NICE MUGS."

Rosie looked up. Jerome slouched against her desk, wearing a pair of jeans, a white Gap T-shirt and a whiskey-colored leather jacket. *Paige must be out of town.* Jerome only dressed like Johnny Depp when his boss was out of the office. "What?" Rosie asked.

Jerome looked at the two coffee mugs, *Rebel Without a Cause* and *My Fair Lady,* on her desk. "Nice..." his dark-eyed gaze traveled up Rosie's torso, lingering where they shouldn't before meeting her eyes "...mugs."

He could be such a scum. She'd witnessed his smarmy come-ons with others, but with her? He liked the type who giggled and walked provocatively in high heels. Rosie was the type who spoke her mind and speed-walked in loafers. Contemplating his motivations, she avoided Jerome's gaze as she rearranged the mugs around her wind-up dinosaur with pom-poms. Suddenly it made sense to separate the rebel from the lady.

Which meant she'd act as though he hadn't made that stupid mug comment.

Seemingly absorbed in her dinosaur-rearranging task, Rosie said nonchalantly, "Thanks for setting up that meeting with Paige."

"You owe me lunch."

"Yes, I owe you lunch." *And nothing else.*

"Focaccio's," Jerome said, hitting the first syllable so hard, Rosie knocked over the dinosaur. One corner of Jerome's mouth twisted into a lascivious grin.

Rosie clutched the dinosaur tightly. "We're still talking about lunch, right?"

"Focaccio's," Jerome repeated in a husky whisper, "is a restaurant."

"I know that." He was pronouncing it differently this time. What a sneak.

"When we goin'?"

"When I get my paycheck." She didn't have to say *which* paycheck. Maybe it would be the paycheck she received in a year. Or two.

"Oh, right, I almost forgot." Jerome reslouched so his *other* hip leaned against the desk. "You gulchers live paycheck to paycheck."

She sensed danger. Just the way her farm animals back home sometimes sensed danger when no obvious threat was nearby, she sensed Jerome sneaking up for some type of surprise attack. "I'm no longer a gulcher," she said, keeping her voice level. "Now I'm Mr. Real."

Jerome looked surprised, then broke out in laughter. "Mr. Real," he finally said, the words choked out as though it were a struggle for him to be serious. "That's rich." He reached over and stroked her clenched fingers, wound tightly around the dinosaur. "You're filling in for Mr. Real only because of me, baby."

Baby? A nauseating spurt of adrenaline shot through her. She eased her hand away. "You got me in to see Paige. I did the rest."

"But you never would have had that opportunity if I hadn't opened the door."

Rosie was squeezing the dinosaur so tightly, she was sure she'd have a permanent imprint of a little dinosaur face on her palm. "So you opened the door...." she said calmly, determined to not let her voice shake as her hands were doing.

He leaned so close, she could see the lusty glint in his dark eyes. Smell his sweat. "I could open it again," he said, his words thick with insinuation. "Help you get another opportunity."

Through clenched teeth, she said, "Are you propositioning me?" Even after years of being told, "Watch your tongue," Rosie couldn't take this macho act any longer. He'd already blackmailed her for lunch—now he was blackmailing her for more.

Jerome stepped back, fast, and adjusted the lapel of his leather jacket so the collar stood up. In his best Johnny Depp "I'm cool" voice, he said, "I never said anything like *that.*"

"No, you implied it."

He cocked an eyebrow. "I came here to deliver a message from Paige," he said, suddenly all business. "She wants stats on your Mr. Real answers. Number received. Number answered. Quality of responses. Quality of feedback."

Sheesh. When Jerome got serious—or miffed?—he

turned from a bad boy into a tough guy. She shouldn't have accused him of propositioning her. What if he said some negative things to Paige about Rosie? *There goes my great escape from the gulch.* "I've only been Mr. Real for a day," she said, forcing herself to sound light, professional. "When does she want these stats?"

"Tomorrow morning. First thing."

"First thing?" She opened her cramping fingers, giving the dinosaur some breathing room. "How first is 'first thing?'"

"Let's see...I have two openings. Ten or seven-thirty."

"Ten would be good," Rosie offered. That'd give her more time to pull together statistics, print off a few of the questions and answers as examples, forecast estimates based on the number of outstanding questions in William's inbox....

"Sorry," Jerome said. "Ten's taken. Your slot is seven-thirty. She can squeeze you in between a breakfast meeting and a senior management staff meeting. Don't be late. If there's anything Paige hates, it's when people are late to meetings. She calls it passive-aggressive insubordination."

Paige called it all that? "Seven-thirty," Rosie repeated, deciding she'd be here early just in case Jerome had given her the wrong time. The last thing she needed to do was saunter into Paige's office at seven-thirty and discover the meeting had been for seven.

Jerome nodded sharply, then pivoted to walk away. He stopped midpivot and looked over his shoulder. Narrowing his eyes, he said, "Didn't know Mr. Real had mugs."

She opened her mouth to say something—but watched

her tongue. Jerome, obviously pleased that he'd gotten the upper hand, walked away with a territorial strut.

Rosie was still staring at the back of that whiskey-colored jacket, wondering how a coffee stain would look on it, when the scent of patchouli perfume announced Pam's arrival. She half sat on the edge of Mr. Real's desk. "I think he likes you," she said slyly, watching Jerome turn a corner.

"Spare me," Rosie muttered.

"I'm serious."

"So am I."

Pam picked up one of the gold paper clips. "Girlfriend, you haven't had a date since you landed in the Windy City. Seven long months. Jerome's hot stuff. He dated Tina in Accounting."

"Did he blackmail her, too?"

Pam paused, studying her friend's face. "Are we talking about the lunch thing? Not such a high price considering he got you an appointment with Paige. Which led to this job."

Rosie sighed. "Jerome doesn't just want lunch. He wants dessert, too."

"So buy the guy an ice cream cone afterward!"

"We're not talking ice cream." Rosie flashed her friend a look. "We're talking something hotter." Rosie extracted the dinosaur from her cramped fingers and set it between the *Rebel Without a Cause* and *My Fair Lady* mugs. "If I wasn't angry at being so grossly propositioned, I'd laugh at the irony. I have a man propositioning me so I can keep my job as a man!"

Pam turned serious. "If he propositioned you outright, you should go to HR."

Human Resources. And how would Rosie prove Jerome had propositioned her? That he'd complimented her coffee cups then offered to open the door? Called her "baby"? "It wasn't outright. It was...implied."

Pam crossed her arms. "And knowing you, my sweet country friend, you said it like it is."

"Oh, you mean when I asked him if he was propositioning me?" Rosie shook her head. "Dumb move. What am I going to do?"

Pam checked out the vicinity to ensure no one would overhear. "Girlfriend," she said softly, "only because I want to see you escape the gulch, I recommend you do some damage control." She held up her index finger. "Damage control number one. Apologize for misinterpreting Stud Boy—"

"I didn't misinterpret—"

"Pretend!" Pam wagged her index finger at Rosie. "You pretend you're those goddesses, so pretend you misinterpreted his motives. Anyway, if you don't apologize, who knows what he'll say to Paige."

Rosie heaved a sigh. "I'll apologize," she said tightly.

Pam held up two fingers. "Second, take him to lunch as you promised."

"He's going to want dessert."

"Are we back to that old song?" Pam nudged her friend playfully. "You can handle that Johnny Depp wanna-be." She looked thoughtfully at Rosie for a moment. "Or...perhaps you're not so experienced with handling men..."

Rosie felt her cheeks go warm. She and Pam were close, but they'd never talked about personal details of their lives. "I've had some experience with men," Rosie said softly. And she wasn't a virgin. Pretty darn close, though. If there hadn't been that night with her high school boyfriend, Orville, before he'd left for college, she'd still technically be a virgin.

"So you're experienced. You're able to handle a man. Just do lunch, don't do him."

"Pam!"

"Hey, what good's a best girlfriend if she doesn't tell it like it is?" Pam's chocolate-brown eyes twinkled with mirth and affection.

Br-ring. Br-ring.

Rosie stared at the phone. "What if it's Jerome? I don't know if I'm ready for damage control number one. Or two."

"Pick it up," Pam counseled. "Pretend you're one of those goddesses, the one who's a whiz at handling obnoxious males."

Artemis. She could be merciless to those who offended her. Donning her invisible armor, Rosie picked up the phone. "Rosie Myers," she said crisply. After a beat, she shot Pam a look. "Uh, Mr. Real is out to lunch." She winced as she looked at her wristwatch. "I mean, breakfast. He's at a breakfast meeting." She sucked in her bottom lip as she listened. "I'm, uh, Mr. Real's secretary." Pause. "You'd like to meet with him?" She winced at Pam, who made a pushing motion with her hands. "You think he's pushy?"

Pam mouthed "No!"

"You think he's on target, insightful," Rosie said, repeating the caller's words as she looked at what Pam had scribbled on a piece of paper. "I'm sure he'd like to meet with you, too, but let's push this off for a few weeks." She grinned at Pam. "No?" Her face dropped. In a monotone, she repeated, "It's imperative the two of you meet imminently. Starbucks. Down the block." She slid Pam a forlorn look. "Tomorrow at 11:00 a.m.? I'll need to check his schedule—"

Rosie stared at the receiver. "He hung up," she said disbelievingly. Looking at her friend, she asked, "How did I get into this mess? There's no Mr. Real, just me, the unreal Mr. Real—and I can't show up at Starbucks tomorrow!"

6

THE THRUMMING of insects filled the air. Rosie had always loved that sound. It meant long, hot summer Kansas days. Endless blue skies. Endless thrumming. Endless, jarring thrumming...

Rosie blinked open her eyes and stared at the beige plastic clock on her nightstand. Forget the thrumming. The sound was her alarm *buzzing*. She fumbled for the snooze bar, missed, then finally hit it.

Silence.

She smiled sleepily. She always gave herself four—sometimes five—thumps of the snooze bar before she got up. It was a more gentle way of easing into the day than jumping up at the first buzz. Besides, with seven minutes between thumps, she bought herself an extra thirty or so minutes before she had to get out of the warm, soft bed. Seven more luxurious minutes...

Seven. Her eyes popped open. How many times had she thumped this morning? Three? Four? She stared blearily at the digital clock, trying to piece the lighted red lines into a number. Six-twenty! "I have to meet Paige at seven!"

Jerome had said the meeting was at seven-thirty. But after his deviousness yesterday, she didn't trust him. Not for one minute. Or thirty.

Rosie leaped out of bed, wearing an oversize man's T-shirt—her choice of nighttime apparel because it was comfy and cheaper than women's frilly nighties. "Twenty minutes to drive into work," she muttered. Traffic permitting. Good thing she'd printed off the stats so she could review them at home last night. No need to run to her desk—she could run directly to Paige's office.

Rosie glanced at the clock again—6:22.

"I'll take a birdbath." That'd save five or so minutes in the shower. And she was a whiz dresser—two minutes, tops. Not wearing makeup was a plus. She'd get there on time! No way would Rosie Myers be labeled obsessive-aggressive—or passive-compulsive—or whatever Jerome said Paige called people who were late for meetings.

She bounded to the bathroom in two steps, washed her face, then stared into the bathroom mirror. Her naturally curly hair had taken on a life of its own, sticking out in electrified spirals. "I can't go into Paige's office looking like this! I'll scare her!"

Rosie fumbled madly in a bathroom drawer, shoving aside towels, candy bar wrappers and a few paperbacks until she found a rubber band. "Yes!" She grabbed a brush and pulled it through her hair. The curls mushroomed out, giving Rosie a human Q-Tip look. She grabbed the wiry mass and wrestled a rubber band around it.

She blinked at her reflection. Her hair stuck straight up, like a ponytail that defied gravity. *Don't panic. If you can pretend you're a goddess, you can pretend you know how to make a hairdo.* She grabbed her ponytail, gave it a twist, then tucked the ends into the back of the rubber band. The blob of brown now looked like one of those twisty sweet rolls stuck on top of her head. Rosie groaned. "At least I won't scare Paige, just make her hungry." She raced to her closet.

Minutes later, Rosie frantically zipped her skirt as she

speed-walked through the living room. Grabbing the keys out of the helmet, she momentarily pondered if she should just wear the darn thing to hide her sweet-roll hairdo.

Twenty minutes later, she sped past the *Flamingo,* a tall steel sculpture in downtown Chicago that always reminded Rosie more of an abstract tractor than a bird. The *Real Men* magazine building was only a few blocks away. She glanced at the plastic digital watch face taped to the console.

Six-forty-five! "I can make it!"

Her stomach dropped. *The parking space.* It wasn't her day. "I'll borrow it," she muttered. Why not? Ben had wanted to do that yesterday, when it was *her* day. Besides, the meeting with Paige would be over by seven-thirty or eight, depending when it started, so Rosie would be long gone before that BMW hit the scene.

A black car changed lanes, darting in front of her. She glanced at the license plate.

ILITIG8!

"You—you space stealer!" she yelled at the BMW's rear end. She quickly scanned traffic. If she stepped on it, she could squeeze into the next lane, between that yellow VW and white Audi, and speed through this upcoming intersection. She looked ahead. The green light turned yellow.

"I can win," she said, cutting the wheel. The VW blasted its horn. With a dismissive wave at the driver, Rosie stomped on the gas. Ahead, the light was still yellow. She glanced to her right. A surprised-looking Ben looked back.

Rosie hunched over the steering wheel, as though pressing forward could make the car go faster. "Go-go-go!" she commanded her Neon. It nosed into the intersection as the light flashed red. "Eat my dust!" she yelled, flying through the intersection. Life was good! The space was hers!

Grinning, she glanced into her rearview mirror.

No BMW was stopped back at the intersection.

Honk! Honk!

She looked over. Ben, driving in the right lane alongside her, waved through the driver's window, then shot ahead.

"You—you cheat!" Minor issue that she'd started this race. Rosie jerked the wheel, cut across two lanes of oncoming traffic, and careened down an alley. Accelerating to the end of the alley, she slammed to a stop at Clark Street. Spying an opening in traffic, she turned, and raced toward another alley, a mere block away, that ran behind *Real Men* magazine.

Traffic on Clark, fortunately, was light. She grinned victoriously. The space would be hers! She almost laughed out loud as she turned down the second alley.

Her breath stuck in her throat.

Speeding toward her, from the opposite direction, was the Black Menace, ILITIG8. Rosie gripped the steering wheel. She *had* to win. With a surge of adrenaline, she slammed her foot on the gas pedal, nearly chipping a tooth when the car bounced over the speed bump. The space was directly ahead....

"Yes!" She cut the wheel and eased into the coveted spot. Brakes screeched as the BMW slammed to a stop in the alley. Rosie, the winner, eased to an oh-so-smooth halt between the parking lines. She grabbed the printout of her stats on the seat next to her and jumped out of the car.

Ben jumped out of his car at the same time. He was a good twenty feet away, but she swore she saw his nostrils flare. He wore sweats, again, but this pair was white. And tight. She'd never noticed his body had such a hunky V shape.

"You thief!" the hunk yelled, slamming shut his car door.

Rosie didn't have time for a space showdown. "I'm not stealing!" she yelled. "I—I have a very important meeting."

"And nobody else does?"

"But if I'm late, I'm doomed!"

"Doomed?" He did a mocking double take. "Exaggerating again, are we?" His gaze dropped to her top, pausing where he shouldn't, then back to her eyes. The nerve! He was as bad as Jerome!

"Do you mind?" she said, trying to sound indignant, although that little once-over made her skin tingle. She turned and started to run up the back steps to the building.

"Stop!"

She halted, turned and shot Ben a look. "I'll move the car after the meeting! Promise!"

Ben jogged over, neatly sidestepping the pothole. Reaching her, he said quietly, "Come back down."

"Why?"

"Your—" he glanced at her chest again "—your top is rather...revealing."

Revealing? She looked down and shrieked. She still had on her oversize man's T-shirt nightie! In her panic to quickly dress, she'd thrown on a skirt and forgotten her "top" was still the nightie! The V-neck was halfway to her navel, exposing the mounds of her breasts. Worse, her nipples stuck through the thin cotton fabric like two eraser tips.

She squealed something unintelligible as her motor skills kicked in. Clutching the papers to her chest, she looked frantically into Ben's eyes. "Help," she whispered hoarsely. "I have a meeting with my boss's boss's boss. I can't go in looking like a harlot!"

"You don't look like a harlot." She swore he bit his lip to stop from smiling. "But you do look seriously underdressed." Leading the way, Ben motioned her to a spot behind the brick wall. Once there, he placed himself between her and the alley so she couldn't be seen by any passing traffic. "After stealing my space," he said huskily, "I should let you go in dressed like this."

"I was wrong," Rosie whispered shakily, deciding the best defense was total honesty. "But I'm going to be labeled passive-obsessive if I'm late."

Ben frowned. "Passive—?"

"*If* I'm late. Which I might not be. I don't know if the meeting's at seven or seven-thirty, but knowing that Johnny Depp wanna-be and his blackmailing tactics, it's probably seven."

"Johnny Depp—?"

"*And* I'm only a temporary anyway, so if I pi—I mean upset—my boss's boss's boss, I might as well kiss off any future job openings and take up permanent residence in the gulch—"

"Gulch—?"

"*Especially* after my Persephone and Hera faux—faux—" what was that French word? "—blunders." She gulped a breath. "What time is it?"

He paused, as though waiting to see if she'd really finished her stream of consciousness. But when she didn't say anything else, and kept looking at him expectantly, he checked his wristwatch. "Almost seven."

"Almost? How almost is almost?" She grabbed his wrist and stared at the watch. "I have two minutes! I'm doomed!"

"Shhh." Ben pulled her toward him. She resisted. He pulled again, murmuring, "You don't have to be strong *all* the time, Rosie."

That did it. Fighting tears, she sank against him, too tired to keep it all together. Even if she sprinted up the steps and into Paige's office within the next two milliseconds, Rosie knew she was in no shape to participate at a meeting. She was shaky, teary...all the things strong, competitive Rosie Myers *never* was.

Or was she so competitive? Here she was willfully—okay, maybe a bit exuberantly—succumbing to the warmth of Ben's embrace. Nestling inside the shelter of his arms like some kind of human ship that had finally found a port. Make that a half-dressed human ship with a sweet roll for a masthead. "I have to be strong," she confided weakly to the sweatshirt, her words muffled thanks to her lips being wedged in a soft fold of fabric. Pressed this close, she smelled the fragrance of soap and that killer musk cologne. So close she swore she felt his heartbeats underneath that hard chest, pulsing against her lips.

So close, he'd never notice if she pursed her lips and planted a quick kiss over that heart.

After a quick stolen kiss on the sweatshirt, she huddled closer, relishing her moment of reckless, passionate abandon. And all these years she'd worried about being overly competitive? Maybe she should have worried about being a secret heathen. A wild woman who laughed in the face of fashion—what other woman appeared half-dressed for a power meeting?—and stole kisses from the hearts of men. Literally. Holding her breath, she listened to the throbbing of this particular man's heart. Strong, steady. *Like Ben.*

Belatedly, she realized she'd snaked one leg around

his, holding him in some type of calf-thigh hold. Her arms were wrapped so tightly around him, he had to be wondering if she'd somehow gotten glued on. At least he didn't know she'd kissed his sweatshirt.

She unwrapped her leg, withdrew her arms, and pulled back, putting on her best I'm-together face. "I need to go. My boss's—"

"Boss's boss. Yes, I know." He stepped back and pulled off his sweatshirt, exposing a naked, muscled, hairy chest that could compete with the best hunky covers on *Real Men* magazine. She was trying to remember how to breathe when he handed it to her. "Put this on. It's plain. And white will go with..." He looked at her blue-and-beige striped skirt. "Well, white goes with almost everything. Give me your papers."

She handed them over. If he'd said "Give me all your money," she have given him the six dollars and thirty-five cents in her skirt pocket, too, and offered to rob a bank if that would help. Murmuring her thanks, she accepted the sweatshirt and pulled it over her head. Snaking her arms through the sleeves, she asked, "But what about you? You can't go into work naked."

"Seminaked," he corrected, his voice so velvety deep, her toes wriggled. "I have some clothes in my car, so don't worry, my clients won't see me looking like a barbarian."

Too bad, thought Rosie, adjusting the bottom of the sweatshirt around her midriff.

"Do you often wear your hair like that?"

She stopped her adjusting and met Ben's perplexed gaze. "I know, it looks like a sweet roll." She patted it a little, having no idea if she was helping or hurting. "It was look like this or like a human Q-tip. I opted for the sweet-roll look."

"Oh." His blue eyes glinted. With amusement? "I've heard that let-it-go look is *very* in these days, so don't draw attention to your sweet roll. Pretend it's the look you wanted."

Pretend. How'd he know her hidden talent of pretending?

He took one of her arms and began rolling up the sweatshirt sleeve so it didn't hang halfway to her fingertips. "You have a natural, fresh look, Rosie," he continued, "so pretend the sweatshirt is part of your look, too." He rolled up the other sleeve. "And on you, it *is* a good look."

"You like it?"

The way he looked at her, she *knew* he liked it. But when he murmured, "Like it? I love it," a hot, crazy, out-of-control thrill zigzagged wildly down her spine. *He loves it.* And she loved how he was fussing over her. No man had ever paid this kind of attention to her. Preening her, preparing her, assisting her toward her goal—to be a writer for *Real Men*. And to think she worried about being competitive—here she was, not even lifting a finger.

For a glorious moment, she felt like the most treasured, pampered, precious being on the planet Earth.

"There." He stepped back and looked her over. "You're ready." He glanced at his wristwatch. "And it's only a few minutes after seven. If your boss's boss's boss is mad about a few minutes, then he or she is an obsessive-aggressive clock freak." He grinned. A slow, sexy grin that made her toes wriggle again.

He pointed at the stack of printouts he'd handed back to Rosie. "But if you have a problem, tell them the printer took longer than you'd expected. A small white lie, but it'll show you were preparing for the meeting, not—" he paused "—not getting dressed in the parking lot. Speaking of which, I have a client showing up for an important meeting at eight-thirty, told him he could use the parking space, so do you think...?"

She nodded so vigorously, she felt the sweet roll wobbling. "Eight-thirty. My car will be gone. No problem."

He stepped forward and played with a curl that fell over her forehead. "When you're good, Rosie, you're very, very good. But when you're bad...?"

His touch felt like fire against her skin. But the look in those glistening blue eyes was hotter than his caress. She'd never wanted to be badder in her entire life.

"You're ready," Ben whispered.

"I sure am."

He cocked one eyebrow. "You're not going to make that meeting unless you start walking."

Meeting! "I'm ready," she repeated, infusing her voice with all the professionalism she could muster considering her insides felt like one big white-hot meltdown of bad-girl desire. She pivoted, rounded the brick wall, and trotted up the back stairs. Passing through the glass doors, she glanced back.

Benjamin stood at the bottom of the steps, naked from the waist up. With the sunshine pouring down on him, he looked positively golden. Over-the-top he-man masculine. Her pulse skittered alarmingly as she realized she was getting serious Boom Boom vibes again.

BEN WATCHED Rosie disappear behind the glass doors, stop and flash him a look. Her eyes, big and hazel, were filled with emotion. He read her thanks, her nervousness, and maybe most surprising, a touch of shyness. She might fight to the death over a parking spot, drive like a demon through downtown Chicago, but she had a vulnerable streak. He'd flashed her a thumbs-up.

She'd smiled and disappeared.

And for a long moment he stood there, filled with an ache, a longing, that surprised him. He'd sworn off relationships, hadn't he? Told himself he was moving from Venus to Mars. And yet, he wanted nothing more than to step back in time five minutes and again hold Rosie's body, touch the soft curls of her hair, look into those expressive eyes. And by the way she'd snaked her leg around his and held on, he knew she liked it, too.

He'd felt the spark before with her, but this morning the spark had ignited a desire for more. Heat surged through his veins as he thought of Rosie in that T-shirt, the soft mounds of her breasts exposed. The dark pink of her nipples straining the thin material. He'd seen women in silk and satin, but none had ever looked sexier than Rosie in a man's T-shirt.

He gave his head a shake. Rosie, Rosie. Before, he'd viewed her as a handful, a woman with a serious territorial issue. But now she was...different.

He chuckled at himself. Speaking of different, always professional, always together Benjamin Taylor was standing in the alley behind his office building, stripped to the waist like some kind of barbarian. Which everyone thought lawyers were anyway, but he'd never before actually dressed the part. Now, *that* was different!

He turned, headed toward his car. Writing that letter to Mr. Real had been a good move. Maybe Ben hadn't staked a claim in a "small" space yet, but he'd staked a claim on Benjamin Taylor, taken a step toward becoming a new man. Ben grinned. A new man, all right. In control. Half-stripped. Ready to grab his kayak and camera and head to Africa.

Ready to *conquer* Africa. Like a lion claiming his turf.

"Hey, buddy," yelled a deep, gravelly voice, "what's it with you and this friggin' alley?"

Ben looked up from his reverie. There, in the too familiar yellow truck, sat Dog Breath. Ben stopped in front of the truck. "Yesterday you sucker punched me!" he yelled up at the driver. "But today, I'm ready for you." Ben—part man, part lion—took a fighting stance.

The trucker's jaw fell open. With a shake of his head, he said, "You lawyers are all crazy!"

ROSIE SKIDDED to a stop next to Jerome's desk. "Is she in?"

Jerome, dressed in a white button-down shirt, pinstriped tie and slacks, looked up from his computer. "What's with the hair?"

Pretend it's the look you wanted. "This let-it-go look is very in these days. Is Paige—?"

"And what's that you're wearing? A sweatshirt?" Jerome laughed, the sound more mean-spirited than mirthful. "It's obvious you have a tomboy streak, Rosie, but this is an office, not a playground."

Wouldn't know that the way you behave when Paige is out of the office. Rosie congratulated herself on watching her tongue. Her mother would be proud. Besides, she didn't need to provoke Jerome—he'd already proven he played dirty.

Jerome's haughty attitude suddenly evaporated. He straightened his tie. "Good morning, Paige."

Rosie thought she'd throw up. Jerome could sure turn on the charm when it suited him.

"Good morning, Jerome." Paige stopped next to his desk. "Rosie? I thought our meeting was for seven-thirty."

Rosie plastered on her best professional smile, hoping it compensated for the sweet roll and sweatshirt. "Yes, I...wanted to be on time. So I got here early."

Paige gave Rosie an approving look. "I like that. Punctual." She looked at the papers in Rosie's hands. "And prepared. Good. Let's start that meeting now." Motioning Rosie to follow, Paige headed to her office, her lilac silk suit making soft swishing sounds as she walked.

The meeting didn't take long. Paige sat behind her desk, reviewed the stats, asked a few key questions, then removed her reading glasses and set them aside.

"Metrics look good," she said.

"It's a beginning." After all, Rosie had only been Mr. Real for all of, what, a day?

"A strong beginning. Clear direction. Established expectations. I like that." Paige's gray-blue eyes glanced up, then froze.

Rosie cringed inside. *She's staring at my sweet roll.* "Yes, a strong beginning," Rosie repeated, trying to keep the conversation focused on business. On anything but her hair.

Paige nodded absently, her gaze dropping to Rosie's top. "There's no reason for you to...attend meetings today with any of our clients, is there?"

Meaning, no way Paige wanted Rosie representing *Real Men* magazine dressed like this. "No." An uncomfortableness tightened Rosie's insides as she remembered Starbucks. That Mars guy expected an 11:00 a.m. meeting with Mr. Real, but Paige didn't need to know that. Rosie would figure out something. She'd toyed with sending Seth—but squad-car blue hair?

"Good," Paige said. "And you're steering clear of any goddess references, correct?"

"Yes." *Externally.* Internally, Artemis and Athena had helped Rosie through some tight spots lately, but Paige didn't need to know that, either.

Paige smiled. "Good. Now, one last issue. I know you're busy with the column, but based on the stats, it appears you might be able to squeeze in a quick revision on an article?"

Was she kidding? Revise an article? That was a primo writing assignment! "Sure!"

"It's imperative that it's in a copy editor's hands by ten-thirty this morning." Paige shuffled through a few papers on her desk. "Currently it's being drafted by a writer on Sophia Weston's staff. Let me see...." Paige ran her pink-frosted fingernail down a list. "That's Jane Sharp." Paige looked up. "You know Jane?"

Everybody knew Jane. Cool, efficient. One of the best writers at *Real Men.* And Rosie was being asked to work with Jane? That wasn't just a step out of the gulch—that was a flying leap! But rather than combust right there, Rosie said calmly, "Yes, I know Jane."

"Good. She has to finalize another article, so your help will be a big plus." Paige glanced at her desk clock, a Waterford piece that probably cost more than Rosie's monthly salary. "I need to wrap up this meeting. Let's get together again this time next week, review the new column stats."

"Okay," Rosie said. "Next week. Same time." Seven or seven-thirty? *Don't ask.* She'd just be here early, punctual and prepared.

And looking more professional than a tomboy wearing a sweet-roll hairdo.

HEATHER, the phone cradled under her chin, blinked at Ben. "You're late."

"Had to straighten out a trucker." Actually, the slob had been too chicken to step down from his cab. So Ben had *strolled* to his BMW and driven away. Of course, it had taken time to find a parking spot, so he'd had a long walk back to work before using the exercise club facilities downstairs to shower and dress.

"Trucker?" Heather frowned. "Well, it's eight-thirty."

"Thank you for the time. Tell Carla hello." Ben headed to his office.

"It's not Carla on the phone. It's Mr. Nelson. Your eight-thirty. He's on his cell phone, wondering why he can't use your parking space."

Ben stopped in his tracks. Rosie had sworn she'd move her car! Ben turned to Heather. "Go downstairs and park Mr. Nelson's car for him. This is an extremely important meeting."

"Like I don't know?" She rolled her eyes at Ben. "You seem to forget I don't have a driver's license."

"Can't you just drive a few blocks and park his car?"

"And if I should accidentally crash his Mercedes? Then not only would he be suing that corporation, he'd be suing *you!*" Heather looked at the receiver she was holding. "No, Mr. Nelson, I'm not driving your car." Heather shot Ben a "See?" look. Still listening to Mr. Nelson on the phone, she answered, "Yes, yes, I'll tell him. No, don't do that. Yes." She hung up.

"Tell me what?"

"That he doesn't have the time to find a parking place, come back here and still make it to his next appointment at ten. He's ticked."

"Don't blame him." They were due in court next week—today's meeting had been crucial. Rosie was causing problems for him, again. "What else did he say?"

"When?"

Why did it sometimes seem as though Heather was in a different time zone? "After you said you'd tell me that he had to cancel the meeting, you said 'No, don't do that,' followed by 'Yes.'"

Heather blinked. "Oh. He was muttering something about finding another lawyer to represent him, so I said, 'No, don't do that.'"

"Great," Ben fumed. "Not only is he ticked, he wants to find another lawyer." If he knew where Rosie worked, he'd storm into her office right now and demand she move that green Neon. Hell, he should call a towing service and have that car towed!

He blew out a disgusted breath. Towing wasn't the answer. Staying away from Rosie was. He should have known better than to fall for a pair of big hazel eyes. He'd backstepped in his journey to Mars by toying with Venus. When he saw her again, he'd lay down the law. Literally. Then he'd avoid any future dealings with her, which should be easy after a new space opened up and they didn't have to share that spot any longer.

Ben started toward his office, then stopped. "What was the 'Yes'?"

"In my conversation with Mr. Nelson?"

Time zone lag again. "Yes, with Mr. Nelson."

"He asked if I'd like to have dinner with him."

Ben wondered how much Mr. Nelson liked frozen bagels. "Well, I'll be in my office working for the next few hours. Then I have an eleven o'clock appointment."

"I don't see that in your electronic calendar. Where is it?"

"Mars," Ben murmured, out of earshot.

7

ROSIE SPEED-WALKED into the office kitchen and up to her friend. "Pam, I have thirty minutes to find a man."

They typically met here midmorning to get a drink. For Pam, an herbal tea. For Rosie, a cup of coffee. The kitchen had a refrigerator filled with sodas, cabinets filled with plates and glasses, even a pudgy plastic bear filled with honey sat on the countertop. It was almost like being in someone's home, if you ignored the bulletin board with the sign Real Men Employee News.

"If you need one that bad, Jerome's only a floor away," Pam teased.

The thought of smarmy Jerome gave Rosie the creeps. She shivered, shaking off the bad feeling. "I mean I need a Mr. Real." She checked the wall clock. "It's ten-thirty. I just turned in that revision Paige requested, so I met that deadline. But my next is at eleven, when that guy is expecting Mr. Real to show up at Starbucks."

Chamomile scented the air as Pam dipped a bag into a cup of steaming hot water. "What about Seth?"

"We could always put a hat over that blue hair. But his vocabulary? Please! Mr. Real doesn't say 'cool,' 'chick,' and 'awesome.'"

"Good point." Pam stirred her tea. "Seriously, what about Jerome? He knows the business, has normal-colored hair."

Rosie groaned. "I know you wanted me to do damage

control, but the guy's a bonafide jerk," Rosie said, fidgeting with a salt shaker on the counter. "If I asked him to pretend being Mr. Real, Jerome would probably find a way to get back at me. First, he'd confess he's not Mr. Real, then spill there's no real Mr. Real, but an unreal Mr. Real—a *woman* writing as Mr. Real."

Anxiety rocked through Rosie as she envisioned the fateful scene. "Then the guy, whose entire reason for meeting Mr. Real is to escape Venus and move to Mars, will get furious. He'll call *Real Men* magazine and complain. The complaint will be forwarded to Paige, who told me it's *imperative* the column's tone sound like Mr. Real. And that men who write to Mr. Real are *never* to suspect he's a woman." In frustration, Rosie tugged on the bottom of the sweatshirt. "I'll be fired—the entire reason for getting a journalism degree, for moving to Chicago, down the drain."

"Whoa, girl." Pam blinked. "You're talking faster than you walk!" She put a comforting arm around Rosie. "You're stressing. Think of the positives. You're temporarily—maybe permanently—out of the gulch. You revised an editorial and met your deadline. Now all that's left is this itty-bitty problem on how to make Mr. Real materialize at Starbucks."

"Itty-bitty," Rosie repeated glumly. "Hard to think itty when it's biggie."

"Have I mentioned you're looking thinner?"

The old girlfriend feel-better trick, but it worked every time. Rosie smiled. "How's my hair?" It had started to unravel. Little curls had sprung loose and tumbled down Rosie's neck.

"That sexy, I-don't-care look is very in these days."

"Funny," Rosie said, "that's almost what Ben said

this morning. Except he said that let-it-go look is in these days."

"Ben?"

"The lawyer."

"Did he also call it sexy?"

Rosie felt her face go hot. "No," she said, trying to sound as though that were preposterous. But a little thrill ran a few crazy laps around her stomach as she remembered this morning. How Ben had looked at her, touched her. Did he find her sexy?

"Ben, the lawyer whose sweatshirt you're stretching?"

Rosie, realizing she was still tugging on the shirt, let it go. "Yes, that's the one," she said a bit too casually, adjusting the end of the sweatshirt around her hips. She was liking this sweatshirt a little too much. She'd been taking deep breaths all morning just to catch a whiff of the musky cologne that clung to his clothes.

"Well, here's my advice," Pam said, picking up her cup. "And that's to take *his* advice. Just as let it go works for the hair, let it go will work for Starbucks."

Rosie waited for more. But Pam didn't say anything, just sipped her tea. "Okay, I give up. Let it go. Starbucks. I'm missing a connection."

Pam pointed a finger at Rosie. "Not *it*, honey, *you*. Let *you* go to Starbucks. You pretended you were the man's secretary on the phone yesterday, so, do it again today. Go to Starbucks, say Mr. Real had some crisis and he couldn't make it, and you're there to fill in."

Rosie opened a drawer and grabbed a plastic spoon. In it, she squeezed some honey from the pudgy plastic bear. "This guy won't like some woman meeting him. He's looking for some man-to-man talk."

"Talk about football. Spit. Scratch yourself."

"Very funny."

"Girl, it's better to give him woman-to-man talk than for Mr. Real to be a no-show. And you're right, Jerome's a bonafide jerk. Forget the damage control—I'll think of something else to handle that boy."

"The National Guard?"

"Too tame." Pam winked, then turned serious. "So, you up for doing the Starbucks gig?"

Rosie licked the sweet honey off the spoon, contemplating her friend's advice. "Woman-to-man is better than a no-show," she agreed. Plus, on a deep level, she connected with this guy. He felt he was swimming in a sea of exes. She knew that feeling. Growing up with four older brothers, she'd felt overwhelmed, as though she were swimming in a sea of testosterone. So what if she was the wrong gender? She could lend an ear, listen to this man's gripes.

"Either your tongue is stuck in that honey or you're thinking really hard," Pam said, interrupting Rosie's thoughts.

"Maybe it would work." Rosie helped herself to another spoonful of honey. "I'll bring a handwritten note from Mr. Real."

"Handwritten? Thought everyone sent Mr. Real e-mail."

"Not this guy. He writes his notes. Awful handwriting, but it's kind of classy that he takes the time to pen his thoughts. Old-fashioned. Gentlemanly."

"Sounds like William Clarington. Do you know what this guy looks like?"

"He left a brief voice message saying whoever got there first, should take the seat in the corner, closest to the bookcase, so I'll know him when I see who's sitting there. I agree, though, he does remind me a little of Mr. Real." Rosie reflected on the saying engraved on William's letter opener: Old Men Ought to Be Explorers. "This Mars guy's been married and engaged before, so maybe he's older."

Pam winked. "You got to watch out for those guys. They run away with Boom Boom girls."

Rosie tossed the plastic spoon into the sink, deciding not to confess to her friend she'd had some Boom Boom goddess experiences as of late. "Gotta go—need to write that note from Mr. Real, then scoot down the block to Starbucks."

"You'll be dynamite, whoever that guy is."

Rosie looked at Pam. "Think so?"

"After all that honey, you could sweet-talk Godzilla."

BEN HEADED DOWN the busy downtown Chicago street, his shirt sticking to his skin. Summer in Chicago could get miserably hot and sticky. Didn't help that the sidewalks were more congested than the streets. But on the plus side, he liked having his offices in the Loop—plenty of places to go, to eat, to drink. Like now, meeting Mr. Real at Starbucks was just a short jaunt from the office.

Ben pushed open the door to the coffee house, relishing the onslaught of air-conditioned air. He looked around. Packed. But most people missed those two corner seats behind the cashier, against the bookcase. You'd have to know the seats were there or you'd miss them.

Ben eased his way around scattered tables and chattering people, edged past a line at the cashier and headed to the bookcase.

A woman sat in one of the two seats. She glanced up, started, then smiled.

Ben stopped short. "It's you," he said ominously.

Her smile broadened, as though seeing him was the most wonderful surprise in the world. "Hi!"

"You nearly cost me a client."

"What?"

Those big, innocent hazel eyes couldn't get any wider if she propped them open. Oh, she was good. "Eight-thirty?"

"Eight—?" She blinked rapidly. "Oh! I forgot to move my car at eight-thirty!"

"Oh, really?"

"I'm sorry!" She stood. "I'd—I'd go move it now, but I'm waiting for someone."

Always stealing a space, even at Starbucks. "So am I," Ben said edgily.

"Small world," she said anxiously.

Too small. "Would you mind moving to another chair?" Ben asked. "I have an important meeting."

"So do I."

He shoved his hands in his pockets. Otherwise, he might throttle her. "This morning, you got the parking space because *you* had an important meeting. Seems only fair that you give up this space now for *my* meeting."

Rosie looked mortified. "Wh-what time is your meeting?"

"Eleven."

"Me, too." She bit her lip. "Maybe we could...share these seats until our people arrive?" One look at Ben's face and she stepped to the side. "Bad idea. I've only caused you problems for the past few days whereas you've helped me a lot." She gestured toward her hair, his sweatshirt. "I'll just stand over here and wait for my person." She took another step toward the bakery case. "Just ignore me."

As though he could. "Thanks," Ben murmured, sitting down.

Five minutes passed without any further discussion. As

she watched the crowd for her person, he watched her. That crazy hairdo had fallen apart since earlier. Soft brown curls framed her face, tumbled down her neck. It gave her silhouette a softer border, made her look more feminine. Again, he flashed on his favorite Manet painting, *Portrait of a Woman*.

But watching Rosie reminded him of something else, an old memory from years ago. His little sister, dressed up, standing demurely next to the front door, waiting. She'd been sixteen, wearing a new dress, her long hair curled, pulled back with a barrette. The boy was supposed to pick her up at six. At six-fifteen, Ben had assured his sister the guy was probably running late. At six-thirty, Ben insisted she sit on the couch where he joined her so she wouldn't be sitting alone, waiting.

At six-forty-five, Ben announced that the guy was a loser. And that he, her big brother, would be honored if he could fill in and take his beautiful sister out to dinner.

Watching Rosie waiting, maybe being stood up, unnerved Ben. Okay, so she was a mite strong-willed with a bizarre territorial bent, but Rosie was also refreshingly lovely, intelligent, and despite her bravado tactics, sweet and fragile. *Any man who'd stand her up is a loser.*

Ben stood and tapped Rosie on the shoulder. "Take the seat," he said when she turned to look at him.

She shook her head. "No," she said softly. "I've interfered in your life enough." She turned away.

"I insist." Taking her by the elbow, despite her initial resistance, he guided her to the empty chair.

"So your meeting—?" she said, sitting down.

"He's late."

"So's mine."

"We have a lot in common." He meant it as a joke, but something about it rang true. Although exactly how, he wasn't sure. "I'll get two coffees. Might as well have something to drink while we're waiting."

She reached in her pocket. "Here's some money—"

He waved away the offer as he headed toward the cashier. "Too much sugar and milk, right?"

"Right," she said wryly.

Rosie watched him walk away. He had a self-assured, confident gait, like a solitary creature who was accustomed to making his way in the world. Confidence—she liked that in a man. Her gaze dropped. Great butt—she liked that in a man, too.

She quickly swerved her gaze and stared out the window at the busy street outside. What had she been doing, shamelessly checking out Benjamin Taylor's behind in public? Around him, she lost control—did things she'd never done before. Wrapped her leg around his. Kissed his heart. *It's the Boom Boom goddess again.* She squirmed in her seat. *I'd be better off donning an invisible Athena cloak for this encounter.* Logic-minded Athena never copped a look at a guy's butt.

A few minutes later, Ben arrived with two cups of coffee. "One milkshake," he said, handing one to Rosie. "And one black."

Milkshake. Very funny. She took a sip of the sweet, milky coffee. Delicious. "Meeting one of your clients?" She winced, wishing she could take back the word *client*.

"Forget about it," Ben said. "I didn't lose this morning's client—he threatened it, but didn't mean it. Right now, I'm meeting someone from a local magazine."

"The only local magazine I know of is *Real Men*," she said.

"That's it."

Rosie looked at him in surprise. "*Real Men?*"

"Yes. Its offices are in our building."

Pieces of information, like pieces of a puzzle, started forming a picture in her mind. She and Ben were both meeting someone at the same time, in the same place. He was meeting someone from *Real Men*.

He's Mr. Mars!

She ducked behind her coffee cup, slugging down a mind-altering blast of hot coffee. Her eyes teared as she swallowed the mouthful, and she rapidly sucked in air to cool her mouth.

"Are you all right?" Ben asked, leaning forward.

"I'm—" she sucked in more air "—okay," she rasped.

"Water?"

She nodded vigorously.

He jumped up and headed to a table with napkins, utensils and several water pitchers. Once, on a blind date from hell, she'd accidentally eaten a jungle-hot chili that threatened to meld her tongue to the roof of her mouth. She'd been sucking air then, too, but her date had just stared at her as though she were a fish out of water. She'd had to rush across the restaurant, shoving aside one shocked-looking waiter in the process, and help herself to a pitcher of water. There'd been no glasses, so she'd slugged water right from the pitcher.

"Here," Ben said, handing her a small paper cup.

This time, she'd sip it delicately out of a diminutive cup. "Thank you," she whispered hoarsely.

As she drank the cool liquid, she eyed Ben over the rim of the cup. So *this* was Mr. Mars. She'd guessed, from the letter to Mr. Real, that he'd grown up in a household of needy women, that he still sought those kinds of relationships with the opposite sex. No wonder he'd dressed her this morning, gotten her water. He thought *all* women were needy.

She set the cup on a side table. "I'm not needy."

Ben cocked one eyebrow. "I...never thought that. If anything, you're..." He let his voice trail off.

"I'm what?"

"You're independent."

She waited for more, but Ben said nothing. So either that one word summed up what he thought of her—or he was keeping other thoughts to himself. *Independent*. Did leg-wrapping women come across as independent? Rosie frowned, worrying that Ben viewed her as competitive. Men liked women who wore makeup and teetered around in sleek black high heels, not independent types who couldn't make a hairdo if their lives depended on it. And speed-walked in sensible, scuffed loafers. *I'm just like Eliza Doolittle with soot on her nose.*

"Feeling better?"

Physically, yes. Emotionally, no. But rather than digress into her Eliza Doolittle inferiority complex, she simply nodded.

"So, who are you meeting?"

"A man."

"Any man—or a particular one?"

Was that a twinkle in his eye? Amused at the independent, headstrong girl? Suddenly she wanted to be more than good ol' hardworking, independent Rosie. She wanted to be appealing, sultry, *desirable*. She wanted to be the elegant, sexy Eliza over whom men fawned, who made Professor Higgins jealous. "I'm waiting for a dark, handsome man," Rosie whispered. "Tall." She pulled on a curl that lay against her cheek. Forget Athena. Rosie was going straight for the Boom Boom.

"Let's see. Dark, handsome, tall." Ben looked around the room. "There're several men who fit that description. Have you looked?"

She gave the room a sweeping glance. "Not here."

"You sure? You looked awfully quickly."

"I'm a quick looker."

"Well, I can vouch that you were on time, this time." Ben grinned, that lazy, sexy grin that sent her insides plummeting on a wild roller-coaster ride. If she were his client, she'd never threaten to leave over a silly parking place. She'd never threaten to leave, period.

"So how did your morning meeting go?" he asked.

"Great," she answered breathlessly. She cleared her throat. "I was early. We discussed business. I got a surprise assignment."

"Assignment? What kind?"

"Revising." Oops. Too much. She didn't want him to know she worked at *Real Men* magazine. She had to concoct some story because she obviously worked in the same building. "Revising accounting brochures. You know, numbers and digits and a few words." She took a quick sip of coffee, but carefully this time. She didn't want to do that air-sucking thing again, not if she wanted to be viewed as the elegant Eliza.

"So you work for the accountant in our building?"

"Uh, yes." What if Ben looked for her in that guy's office? "Part-time. I freelance elsewhere in the building, too." That sounded plausible. Plus Ben wouldn't know where to look if he needed to hunt her down. Rosie heaved a breath, wondering what it would take to be hunted down by Benjamin Taylor. She could outrun most guys, but for him, she'd slow down. Way down. Heck, she'd stand in place, claim she had a leg cramp.

They sat in silence for a moment. When Ben looked away, Rosie sneaked a peek at his face. She wanted to watch him, unobserved, catch a glimpse of the Ben who wanted to move to Mars. What kind of man referred to

Mars, the Roman god of war? A man who was bigger than life. Agile. Fierce.

Her gaze traced the straight line of Ben's nose, the sensual curve of his lips. His jaw, except for the swollen patch where he'd been hit, had a strong line. Strong, sensual Ben. Probably had to be if he was swimming in a sea of exes. She felt a stab of jealousy. How many women made up a sea? Hundreds? Thousands?

Ben looked at her. "So you freelance. As a writer?"

"Yes," she snapped.

He paused. "Your mouth still hurt?"

"No. Why?"

"You just looked...a little... So you freelance, huh? Travel much?"

She looked a little what? Jealous? *I've gone over the edge. Jealous over a man who loaned me his sweatshirt.* "Don't travel much," she said, working hard to soften her tone. "But I'd like to."

"Me, too." He glanced around the room, obviously still searching for Mr. Real. If he only knew he was talking to him. Her. "Where would you like to travel?" Ben asked, his blue-eyed gaze landing back on Rosie.

"Lots of places. My favorite all-time movie is *Out of Africa*. As a kid, I'd imagine myself as Isak Dinesen, living in Africa, writing stories."

He stared at her for a long moment, playing his finger along the rim of the coffee cup. "Small world. I also fantasize about Africa."

"Don't tell me you also want to be Isak Dinesen."

He leaned back and laughed, a husky, easy laugh that made her heart swell to twice its size. Big enough to forgive him the sea of women. This man—this Mr. Mars—was light-years from the man who drove ILITIG8.

What was he doing being a lawyer? It was so obvious he wanted to break loose, live a different life.

"I don't have an all-time favorite movie," he continued, "but photography is a hobby of mine. If I had to pick someone, I'd like to be Peter Beard. He took great photos, many in Africa. That's my fantasy. Go to Africa, take pictures of the wildlife, the exotic locale." He shot Rosie a look. "But before I head to Africa, I'd do a pit stop on Mars."

He probably thought that would throw her off, but she knew all about his Mars-Venus thing.

"There're lots of men on Mars," Rosie said slowly, as though she were thinking about Ben's last comment. "Those Venus-Mars books talk about the caves on Mars, how men live in them." Ben was studying her, listening. Of all the moments in her life, this was definitely one when she wanted to watch her tongue. "And how women live on Venus." She wasn't sure exactly *how* they lived, so rather than talk about cold cream and high heels, Rosie continued, "I've often thought that maybe the answer for men and women is to live part-time on each planet so they can better understand each other's worlds." She surprised even herself with that last comment. Competitive Rosie, professing that men and women could *share* each other's worlds?

Ben was staring at her, his blue eyes darkening as though absorbing her words. "Part-time," he finally said. "Sounds a bit...idealistic. Impossible, actually."

She should have watched her tongue. Everything she'd said had just crashed. Changing the subject, she quipped, "Maybe we should call ourselves Isak and Peter."

His sensual lips curved in a half smile. "We'd be quite a combo."

Her heart thumped so hard against her chest, she swore it could be seen through his sweatshirt.

"Baby," said a deep voice.

Rosie stared at Ben. Besides photography, did he also study ventriloquism? "Yes?" she answered breathlessly in her best combo voice.

"No, doll, up here."

Rosie looked up. There stood Jerome, gazing down at her with that I'm-too-cool look in his dark eyes. A lock of dark hair fell over his brow, giving him a sinister edge. Her stomach contracted into a tight ball of angst. She had to get rid of Jerome before he figured out the situation and blew her cover.

"Looks as though your meeting's arrived," Ben said, standing. "Take my seat," he added to Jerome. "My appointment was a no-show." With a nod of his head to Rosie, he walked away.

She wanted to stop Ben. Explain that this jerk was just the office lover boy and not the dark, handsome, tall man she concocted earlier. What had she been thinking, wanting to make Ben jealous? Dumb move! She should follow him. Say something. Remind him they're a combustible combo. Tell him she'd study up on Venus if he'd play Mars. Tell him...tell him...

Too late. Ben was already out the door.

"A GUY WITH BLUE HAIR dropped something off on your desk," Heather informed Ben as he walked back into his office.

Ben halted. "Blue hair?"

Heather tossed back her own flaxen locks. "I thought at first an alien had landed!"

"Impossible," Ben murmured. "There're no parking

spaces available." He walked toward his office. "What time did he drop it off?"

"About an hour ago."

Ben checked his wristwatch. Three o'clock. After Starbucks, he'd headed to lunch with another client, who'd then dragged Ben into yet another meeting. If he'd been expecting an important package, he'd have cut out early. This delivery, then, was unscheduled. Not urgent. Probably briefs or papers referencing another case.

Rounding the desk, he saw a white envelope on his chair. He picked it up. "Mr. Mars" was printed in black ink on the outside. How'd he know the location of my office? Ben wondered, ripping open the envelope. Seemed odd. On second thought, maybe Mr. Real had requested the post office to forward the letter—after all, the post office kept a record of what addresses mapped to the P.O. boxes.

Ben read the letter. "Mr. Mars, A family emergency called me away. My apologies for missing our appointment. I'd hoped we could further discuss your dilemma, brainstorm options. I was wondering if you've picked a vital space. Shared it."

Oddly enough, he had. Wasn't sure if those corner seats at Starbucks were vital, but he'd definitely shared the space...with Rosie.

"And I had wanted to mention something else regarding sharing. In your ocean of women, maybe there's one with whom it's worthwhile to share your time. As I said before, other types of women exist in the world: independent, adventurous, a man's equal. Respectfully yours, Mr. Real"

Ocean of women? Had Ben phrased it like that before?

He sat down, exhausted from the long walk back from that god-awful meeting. Ben undid the top button on his shirt. It wasn't just hot outside, it was broiling. But despite how the day had begun—racing Rosie to the parking space, then ticking off his client who needed to park there—things were improving.

He and Rosie had made amends.

Better yet, he'd gotten to dress her.

And unless she burned off all her memory cells with that slug of hot coffee, she'd promised the space was his tomorrow.

Everything that felt good about the day, Ben realized, had to do with Rosie. He leaned back in his swivel chair and pondered that one for a moment. *Other types of women exist in the world: independent, adventurous, a man's equal.* Could that woman be Rosie Myers, the parking-space wonder?

"Benjamin?" Meredith's head poked in the doorway. Today she wore some kind of wraparound purplish-black number—as though she'd rolled herself in a dismal tablecloth. And, to Ben's horror, she wore matching purple lipstick. Her hair still sported the bird's nest look, but it didn't compare to Rosie's wild and curly hairdo. But then, most women paled when compared to Rosie Myers.

"Where's my square, white toilet, Meredith?"

"Being installed, even as we speak." She flashed him a coy smile. "Your castle shall again be yours. Tonight!"

Yes, indeed, this day was improving.

"And darling?"

"Yes, Meredith."

"I picked out a simple, clear shower door to go with your simple, basic commode."

"Thank you." *Mars rules.*

"Benny?" Heather's head poked in the other side of the door.

"Yes, Heather?"

"Mr. Nelson called to apologize for threatening to find another lawyer. Said his air-conditioning had gone out in the car and the heat got to him. He, like, totally understands about the parking space mishap. Wants to make it up to you."

Had a day ever improved so rapidly? "How?"

"He's taking me out to dinner tonight at this really, really upscale place."

"That's how he's making it up to me? By spending big bucks on *you?*"

Heather looked at Ben as though he didn't get it. "Works for me!"

Behind Meredith and Heather loomed a massive body—at least six-four—topped by a massive head covered with a swarm of dark curls. That had to be the biggest head Ben had ever seen. Like a basketball with hair. The guy's sunburned face compressed into a menacing scowl as he pointed at Ben. "There he is."

Several other massive heads crowded behind Basketball. All those heads and bodies in Ben's doorway blocked out any light from the reception area. Things hadn't looked this dark since that Christmas tree fell on him. Time to put on his best professional demeanor considering his receptionist, who normally greeted guests, could do nothing but stare at the mass of massive men.

"Are you looking for me?" Ben asked.

Basketball, obviously the leader of this scowling group, snarled, "Yeah. We're gonna kill you."

8

"KILL ME? Why? Because I'm a lawyer?" When Basketball curled his hand into a tight ball, Ben feared the guy would say, "All da better."

"'Cause you're trying to have your way with our li'l sister." He shook his fist. "And no man, especially some big-city slicker, takes advantage of our sister."

Meredith and Heather, who'd been standing frozen in their spots, suddenly unthawed. In unison, they revolved toward Ben, looks of shock on their faces.

"Benjamin?" Meredith said, staggering a few steps toward him. Her thick mascaraed eyes batted rapidly. Her purple-glossed lips quivered. "Why young girls?" she whispered. "Why not me?"

She'd done it. Gone over the edge. In her desperate post-Dex state, she was coming on to good ol' former husband Ben. Who would be good ol' almost dead Ben unless he took control of this situation. "Meredith, not now—"

"Benny?" cut in Heather, clomping toward his desk, her blue eyes glazed with questions. "I haven't heard you make one phone call—even send one e-mail—to another woman, yet you've been fooling around with some young thing?" She frowned, which on Heather looked more like a pout. "Are you going through a midlife crisis?"

Midlife—? "Has it occurred to you two," he said, lowering his voice, "that perhaps this isn't the time to talk about my personal life?" He nudged his head toward the men, who stood ten feet behind the women. "In case you haven't noticed," Ben added in a strained whisper, "my *life* is being threatened." He cleared his throat and looked over Super-Ex's heads. "You must be mistaken," he said, speaking loudly. "I'm not involved with anyone." What did they call their female gang counterparts? Sisters? "Especially any...*sister*."

Basketball stepped forward. The floor shook. A corner lamp rattled. "We ain't talking about you being 'involved.' We're talking about you being a jerk!"

"Benjamin," Meredith whispered urgently, leaning over his desk, "how young is this girl?"

Heather was checking her reflection in Ben's polished silver paperweight. "Middle-aged men do crazy stuff like this," she said in an aside to Meredith. "Get into fist fights. Fool around with young things. Next he'll be buying Viagra."

"Viagra?" It was saner to deal with the gang of killer thugs than to attempt further communication with self-absorbed Super-Ex. Ben stood. From this vantage point, he got a better view. Instead of just seeing four ferocious, oversize bodies, now he saw their shoes, too.

Basketball, who was so big he looked like a couch standing on end, wore faded jeans that looked as though he'd hand-wrapped them around his tree-size legs. His short-sleeve, blue work shirt was unbuttoned to his navel, revealing a chest with more wild hair than one of Meredith's bird's nest numbers. Even middle-aged men going through crises didn't wear their shirts *that* open. Then Ben realized the guy's chest was so huge, he couldn't connect the buttons to the button holes.

Behind him, to the left, stood a leaner version of Basketball, which meant instead of being monster-size, he was merely beast-size. But surprisingly, instead of the down-home look, this gang member was upscale. Armani, head to toe. Since when did gang members wear designer clothes?

For that matter, since when did gang members prowl downtown Chicago, harassing lawyers with offices in posh Loop buildings? Maybe this was a new trend. Affluent, urban gangs working out their obsessive-aggressive tendencies.

Another pair of feet stepped forward. Clean, white sneakers. Ben looked up at the third gang member. This man, big like the others, had a gentler expression. He also wore jeans, but unlike Basketball's, these fit. And a white T-shirt with the slogan Mean People Suck. What kind of gang member, out to kill a lawyer, wore a shirt that said *that?*

The fourth member stepped forward. Slacks. Short-sleeve shirt, buttoned. Number Four wasn't tan like the others—maybe this was the indoor gang member? The affluent, urban gang accountant? Maybe he ensured they didn't spend too much on their killing sprees.

They dressed differently, yet something was eerily similar. Besides their massive bulk, they all had brown, curly hair. And except for the one who wore a Mean People Suck T-shirt, they all looked thoroughly ticked off. At Ben.

And he'd wanted to move to Mars? Hell, Mars had moved to him!

"Gentleman," Ben said calmly. Or tried to sound calm. "Surely there's been a mistake." His right eyelid went a little numb as he met their group stare-down. "Meredith and Heather can vouch for me. I haven't dated another woman in years." An image of sitting with Rosie over coffee flashed through his mind. But that was hardly a date. An accidental encounter. A shared space.

Heather put down the paperweight and turned her attention to the Armani member. "That's me," she said, raising her hand. "Heather Krementz."

No vouching. No standing up for her ex-fiancé who was probably living the last moments of his life. Ben closed his eyes. *Please, God, this is a bad dream.* One where he'd open his eyes, discover he was still in his warm bed, waking up to the soothing strains of Bach on his clock radio. With a rush of relief, he'd realize his nightmare was over. Time to get up, feed Max, go to work.

Ben opened his eyes. He was still at work, crammed into his small office with a gang of lawyer killers and Super-Ex. Was it too late to return to Venus, where instead of men threatening his life he'd simply have women redecorating it?

He looked over at Heather, who still had her hand raised, as though looking for someone to call on her. "Heather," Ben said gruffly, "your hand—"

She dropped it with a dramatic flourish, tossing him a peeved look. "Now I can't even raise my hand in your office! I'm not on the phone! And these obviously aren't your clients! Yet, as always, you're concerned I'll embarrass you!"

Ben wished Mr. Nelson had asked her out to an early bird dinner. Real early, like two hours ago.

Basketball narrowed his eyes. "You messin' with her, too? What kind of man are you?"

"I'm a lawyer," Ben said dryly. "And for the record, I'm not messin' with her. She's dating Mr. Nelson."

"Mr. Nelson?" Meredith whined. Her face got that crumpled, poor-me look again. "How come everybody's dating or fooling around when I've just been dumped?'' Those purple lips opened, emitting a mournful wail.

"You poor li'l thing," murmured Basketball, crossing to her. The corner lamp rattled again. Stopping next to Meredith, he put a beefy arm around her shoulders. "There, there," he soothed.

When Meredith dropped her head against the monster-size shoulder, Ben wished she'd worn those chopsticks today. With that rapid head drop, she might have accidentally stabbed Basketball. They'd have had to dial 911, paramedics and police would arrive, and Ben would be out of this mess.

But chopsticks weren't in Meredith's hair. And saving Ben's life was the furthest thing from her mind. In a teary voice, she recounted her woes to a sympathetic Basketball. "I'm...going through...a difficult time. I was in love. He dumped me. He wanted..." Burying her face in his shirt, she sniffled some words.

"What's that, sweetheart?" Basketball dipped his head closer to hear better. "He wanted his ice cream back?"

Ben stiffened, preparing for the big guy's death screams. Great! Chopsticks weren't necessary. Ben edged his hand toward the phone, ready to dial 911.

But Meredith pulled slightly away, her eyes two smudgy black holes of mascara. "Ring," she corrected sweetly. "He wants his *ring* back."

Oh, she was good. It was a different story when a hairy, muscled he-man thought she'd said "ice cream."

Basketball, tugging Meredith closer, glared accusingly at Ben. "Give her back her ring!"

"I did. Ten years ago. She also kept the house, the furniture and the dog." It was bad enough having total strangers want to kill him. Now he had to defend his divorce agreement. He wasn't sure which was worse.

Glancing at his letter opener, Ben wondered how many people he could fend off with it. Maybe he could wield the paperweight in one hand, the opener in the other. Of course, Heather would be upset—it would be difficult to check out her reflection with the paperweight flying around the room.

"We're getting off the subject," interrupted the gang's accountant. "You threatened our Rosie. Tried to invade her space. We're getting a restraining order against you."

Restraining order? Much preferable to death. Ben started to smile with relief when he realized what the guy had said. "Our *Rosie?*" Ben repeated slowly.

"Yeah." Basketball had Meredith enveloped in a protective hug. Those two had blended faster than Baskin and Robbins. "*Our* Rosie."

Couldn't be. Could it? "Is her favorite film *Out of Africa?*"

All four gang members said, "Yeah."

What had she done? Hired some thugs to intimidate him out of sharing that space? Mean guys—well, possibly except for the Mean People Suck one—who also knew her favorite movie? Impossible! But then, affluent, urban gangs probably didn't smoke, drink or take drugs. They went to concerts, art openings, movies. When you interviewed them, you didn't discuss killing tactics, you discussed cultural activities.

Time to take the offensive. "Hey," Ben said, raising both hands, "*she's* the space invader, not me. As a matter of fact, your Rosie didn't just *invade* my space, she's got a *death grip* on it." He flinched. Death grip. As though they needed any hints. Clearing his throat, he continued, "You guys are barking up the wrong lawyer. No one in their right mind would try to invade Rosie."

"No one in their right mind would try to do *what?*"

Rosie stepped into the middle of Ben's office. Her hair tumbled in ringlets around her face. Her full lips were compressed into a thin line of disapproval. Crossing her arms, she stared down the gang. "What is going on?" she asked irritably. "You said you were headed to my place...but I knew better when I saw Dillon's truck still parked at the meter."

Knew better? Knew everything because she'd planned it! "You—" Ben growled, jabbing his index finger at her. "You hired a gang of thugs to threaten me. I've never known a woman who wanted a parking space *that* bad."

She shot him a look. "What are you talking about?"

"Professional urban warfare."

"What?" She gave her head a shake. "Lawyers," she muttered, turning her attention back to the men. "Go. Now. Not only did you embarrass me in front of the managing editor, now you're stalking people in my office building!"

Basketball dropped his arm from around Meredith's shoulders and stepped toward Rosie. Ben watched the corner lamp, hoping it remained intact. "Rosie Posey," Basketball said, looking like a little boy who'd just been chastised. "This jerk wanted to invade you—"

"He's not a jerk!" Rosie insisted. A curl tumbled down the center of her forehead. "And I never said he wanted to invade me, just my space. My parking space!" She leveled all four of them a look, mumbling something about no wonder she grew up competitive—she even had to compete for breathing space around them. Raising her voice, she continued, "You guys have got to get over this overprotective thing! Traveling all the way from *Kansas* to *Chicago* just to protect me! This is worse than the time I got home late and you nearly lynched Orville."

"It was three in the morning," Basketball murmured.

"Men take advantage of good-hearted, beautiful girls," said Mean People Suck.

"You were underage," said No Tan. "Jailbait."

"For all we knew, you were sold into white slavery," added Armani.

Rosie gave them a look of utter disbelief. "How many times have we gone over this? It was 3:00 a.m. because we'd gotten a flat tire." She looked at Mean People Suck. "And if men take advantage of beautiful girls, then I was safe. At best, I'm cute." She looked at No Tan and shook her head. "Jailbait. Only a would-be lawyer would refer to incarceration." And she smirked at Armani. "'Sold' into white slavery. Spoken like a true salesman."

Meredith looked at Basketball, then Rosie. "You're not... dating all these men at once, are you?"

"Dating?" Rosie looked aghast. "They're my brothers!"

Rosie suddenly looked defeated, exhausted. She crossed to the chair with the harp silhouette engraved into its back, and sank onto the seat. Pulling a set of keys from her skirt pocket, she jingled them at her brothers. "Bat, Hoss, you two said you were taking a taxi, but take my car instead. It's parked behind the building. Boxes of books in the back seat, but there's plenty of room for your luggage in the trunk." She looked at Basketball. "You have the directions, right? Write them down for Bat and Hoss, who can follow you and Pal in the truck. When you get to my apartment, make yourselves comfortable. There's some Everything Stew in the fridge."

A look of horror flickered across her brothers' faces. "We'll pick up some burgers," one of them mumbled.

"How will you get home?" asked Basketball.

"My friend Pam—"

"I'll take her," Ben cut in. Super-Ex hadn't defended him, but Rosie had. She wasn't at fault. If anything, she seemed as surprised as he'd been at these four guys invading his office.

"I'd prefer her girlfriend drove her," said Mean People Suck, looking Ben over as though he were a conniving, dishonorable rake who might later claim they'd had a flat tire.

"And I prefer *I* did," Ben insisted. "I'm giving the lady a ride home."

There was a moment's silence as all four brothers scrutinized Ben. "What time will you have her home?" asked No Tan.

Rosie heaved a sigh. "Please. This isn't a date! The man offered me a ride, not a lifetime commitment." Darting a look at Ben, she squirmed in her seat. "I—I only said *date,* because of the previous 3:00 a.m. Orville discussion. I know you don't view me as *date* material." She laughed awkwardly as though that were probably the funniest misconception anyone in the world might have. But her glistening eyes said something else.

That she hoped otherwise?

"I need a ride home!" Heather suddenly said, raising her hand.

"Thought you took the bus," Ben muttered.

Heather swished back her hair with a toss of her head. "Tonight, I need to get home, like, fast."

Like, why? Maybe for her date. Ben paused, waiting for Bat or Pal or Dillon or—what had Rosie called her last brother? Hoss?—to make an offer. None did. "I'll give you a ride," Ben murmured, although after that glistening-eye look from Rosie, the last thing he wanted was third-wheel Heather in his car.

"Not you!" Heather looked at the Armani. "Him."

Rosie frowned. "There's only room for two in my car."

"I'll sit on his lap," Heather offered.

"What about your dinner date?" Ben asked.

"Canceled."

"When?"

"As soon as I make a phone call." Heather clomped double time to the other room.

"I have a car," Meredith said, looking expectantly at Basketball. "I'll give you a ride, then it won't be so crowded in Rosie's Neon."

"But I'm driving a truck," Basketball explained.

"Of course you do," Meredith said huskily. She breathed in and out so deeply, her breasts heaved. "A big man like you would drive a big truck. I've always wanted to ride a big truck myself."

"Well, sure, ma'am. Hoss 'n I would be delighted."

"Maybe later, after we drop off Hoss," Meredith cooed, "you and I can go get an ice cream."

Ben saw the future more clearly than if someone had plunked a crystal ball in front of him. Meredith entering a down-home country phase of decorating. He hoped this evolving romance worked out; otherwise, one day he'd find a bale of hay decorating a corner of his office.

The brothers and Meredith, discussing who was driving whom, migrated out of Ben's office. Heather, hanging up the phone in the other room, clomped after them as they exited the offices of Benjamin Taylor, P.C.

Rosie and Ben were alone.

"Seriously, I can get a ride from Pam," Rosie said.

Ben headed around the desk and sat on its edge, facing her. He studied her. Caught the gleam of interest in her eyes. Caught the flush of her skin. Her body said more than what her lips professed. "Why won't you let me help you?" he asked quietly.

"I'm not needy."

"So you've said." And from her competitive comment, she obviously thought she was that, too. "But accepting a man's kindness isn't being needy. Sometimes being vulnerable is the greatest strength." He knew that one would hit home. "Besides, you owe me one."

"One what?"

"One sweatshirt." He put on his best stern tone. "If I don't take you home, how do I know I'll get my sweatshirt back?"

"My word isn't good enough?"

He cocked an eyebrow.

"Eight-thirty," she murmured. "Hmm, guess my word isn't always binding."

"Then it's settled," Ben said, standing. He held out his hand. She hesitated, then put hers in his. Her hand was small, warm. He liked its soft touch. Liked even better that she continued to hold his hand, even after she stood. He pulled her arm through his, knowing he'd just won a round with the competitive Rosie Myers.

"Good thing you're wearing sensible shoes," he said casually as they walked arm in arm out of his office. "We'll be walking a few blocks because someone took my parking space this morning."

As BEN DROVE along Lake Shore Drive, Rosie stared out the passenger window. In her daily commutes, she never had the chance to play sightseer and check out the lakefront, the Shedd Aquarium, the Adler Planetarium. Better yet, to view it from the air-conditioned front seat of a BMW! She played with the electronic gadgets that adjusted the seat until she found the most comfortable position. Slightly tilted, plenty of leg room.

"Like the air-conditioning?" he asked.

"Love it," Rosie enthused. She'd played with those gadgets too. Adjusted the temperature and the vents until a steady flow of deliciously refrigerated air streamed over her *just* right. She had to occasionally swipe at the curls floating around her face, but she didn't care. It felt good to be away from work, away from her brothers.

Felt *great* to be with Ben.

She hadn't even minded the earlier walk to his car in Chicago's sweltering summer heat. Ben, despite her brother's crazy antics, had been friendly to her. And when they'd reached his car, he'd opened the door for her. *Class*—the guy had oodles of it.

"Music?" he asked.

"Sure." She reached for the console, ready to play with more buttons.

"Uh, no thanks." He pressed something. The delicate notes of a piano played. "Don't mind your being my copilot, but toying with the music is off limits."

Rosie turned away so he wouldn't see her smile. He knew her too well. She'd gleefully take control of every button and gadget in his car if given the opportunity. Closing her eyes, she let herself get lost in the surging piano music. It was emotional, mournful. "What is this song?"

"Beethoven. *Piano Sonata no. 14*. Also called *Moonlight*."

Moonlight. She imagined what it would be like to be in the moonlight with Benjamin Taylor. To watch shadows play across his face. To inhale his musky cologne intermingled with night scents. "I'm impressed," she murmured. With the music *and* her companion.

"So," Ben asked "did you revise that accounting brochure?"

"Huh?" She opened her eyes.

"Your surprise assignment," he explained.

Oh. So much for moonlight and musk. She could blab more about that fictional accounting brochure, make the story sound real, but she was juggling too many stories, and secrets. Like Ben being Mr. Mars. And Rosie being Mr. Real. "Finished that hideous accounting brochure," she said matter-of-factly. "Hated it. Never want to think about it again."

"All right," Ben said slowly, sliding her a sideways glance. "So your brothers drove all the way from Kansas," he said, obviously testing another topic.

This one was easy. She could tell the truth. "Two flew. That was Bat, who wouldn't be caught dead in a truck, especially Dillon's old Ford pickup. And Hoss, who has the bucks to fly spur of the moment. Dillon and Pal drove."

"Hoss? What's that name about?"

"Actually, they're all named after old TV western stars. Marshal Dillon. Bat Masterson. Paladin. And Hoss—he was one of the brothers on *Bonanza*. My brother Hoss was never too wild about his name—got teased a lot as a kid. Resulted in more than a few fistfights. He's now in law school."

"Being a fighter should help him in court." Ben chuckled. "Does that mean there's also a Rosie on one of those shows?"

"By the time I came along, my mom put her foot down. My dad had named the boys, she demanded the right to name her daughter. My dad loved the old TV westerns, but my mom loved old movie classics. She named me after her favorite movie star, Rosalind Russell.''

"Rosalind," Ben repeated slowly, as though tasting each syllable.

"Sometimes my mom called me that. Usually when I was dressed up, you know, for a special occasion." Rosie recalled the night of her senior prom, wearing a floor-length dress her mother had made—pink satin, lace bodice. As she'd walked out the door with her date, her mother had leaned close and whispered, "Rosalind, you're so very pretty."

"So about your four brothers," Ben said, adjusting the volume on the radio. "They often travel hundreds of miles to save you?"

Rosie scrunched lower in her seat. "No." She folded her arms under her breasts. "But I should have known. Ever since I moved to Chicago seven months ago, they call like clockwork every single Saturday morning. Friendly calls, but I know they are checking up on their kid sister."

"I understand. I have a younger sister, too."

"Yes, but do you jump on an airplane and fly across the country just because you think some guy is bothering her?"

"I would, if I truly thought she was being threatened." He glanced at Rosie. "You're the baby of the family, alone in the big city. If you were my sister and I thought you were in trouble, nothing could stop me from getting to you."

Nothing. She imagined Mars, a sword in his hand, fighting to save her. His... "Sister? Is that how you view me?"

"No," he said quickly. He gave her a look that made her heart turn. "I view you as being...precious."

Precious? Her heart went from turning to leaping when he flashed that sexy grin. Precious Rosie leaned back against the leather seat, luxuriating in the word as they drove the rest of the way home.

Fifteen minutes later, they pulled up in front of her apartment. A plain stucco white building, its sole decoration was the narrow strip of green lawn that ran along the cracked sidewalk. A clash of music—rock, country—blared from different windows. A skateboard clattered down the sidewalk as a woman yelled at her son to take out the trash.

"I can get out here," Rosie said, suddenly feeling more than a little embarrassed at her surroundings. Suave, classy Benjamin Taylor probably lived in a sophisticated part of town where people only played classical music and never, never yelled about trash. Not in public, anyway.

"I'll walk you in." Ben cut the motor.

"No, really, I can get out here—"

"No." The word, like a command, stopped Rosie. She looked back at Benjamin, surprised. But her readiness to have a comeback clogged in her throat when she looked into his eyes. They glittered with emotion. Then she realized his hand was on hers, firm, insistent. "Stay here," he whispered urgently, "For just a moment."

"Why?"

"I—I want to look at you. Be with you. For just a moment..."

This was insane, sitting in a sleek black BMW on her street, in front of her tacky apartment building. It was like Professor Higgins's carriage parked in Eliza Doolittle's lower-class neighborhood. But the heat in his voice spread fire to Rosie's heart. At this moment, she didn't feel like the Eliza with soot on her nose. The way Ben looked at her, touched her, she felt like Eliza, the lady. Sophisticated, elegant, *precious*.

"Rosalind," he murmured, "you're so beautiful."

His musky scent swirled around her, teased her, intoxicated her. Raising a trembling hand, she touched a fingertip to his mouth, traced the line of those sensual lips that had fascinated her earlier. When she glanced up, Ben's blue eyes smoldered with desire. He caught her chin with his palm and drew her to him.

Then his mouth was hard on hers, kissing her. And she responded greedily, hungrily, like a woman who'd been without food and water—and now she was sitting down to a feast. She consumed his mouth, his neck, and then arched back, exposing her neck for him to reciprocate. When his lips traced a fiery path along her collarbone, she groaned out loud. She'd lived all her life waiting for this moment, for this passion, for this man to waken the love goddess within her.

Ben pulled her to him. She sank against his hard body, molding herself to him. His plundering lips took hers again and she fought for breath, returning his passion as her blood roared, her heart pounded. Vaguely, she realized her foot was somewhere on the dashboard as they continued to kiss, writhe, devour each other.

Pound. Pound. Pound.

"What's that?" Ben murmured huskily, nuzzling her ear.

"My heart."

Pound. Pound. Pound. Was the car shaking?

Rosie, her eyes still closed, moaned loudly as Ben pulled away. "No," she pleaded, leaning forward, aching for more.

"Mr. Taylor," said a gruff voice, "it's time Rosie came inside."

Rosie's eyes popped open. Her body stiffened in shock.

Outside the BMW stood her four brothers, glaring at her.

9

IT HAD BEEN a five-thump on the snooze bar morning.

Rosie had been tempted to hit the button a sixth time, but she had to get up, get to work. Forget that she'd stayed up half the night listening to her brothers in the other room, snoring like some kind of barbaric barbershop quartet. Forget that she'd stayed up late, pre-snore-a-thon, explaining and reexplaining to them how Ben was really a decent guy, not a heinous pervert.

But she purposely forgot to mention that the next day, now today, was Ben's day to have the space. One comment like that and her brothers would OD on testosterone and start threatening to kill him again.

She crawled out of bed, showered and took extra care to dress properly. No way she was repeating yesterday's act, tearing out of the house in a see-through, low-cut T-shirt. Rosie, who always wore one-piece swimsuits, baggy sweatpants, and sensible loafers, still couldn't believe she'd gone out in public—and almost into Paige's office!—looking primed for a wet T-shirt contest.

"Good thing Bad Boy Jerome didn't see me dressed like that," Rosie muttered, slipping into a pair of loafers. "I'd get another of those 'nice mugs' comments." She eased open her bedroom door and stepped into the tiny living room of her one-bedroom apartment.

It looked like invasion of the body sprawlers. Big, half-dressed masculine bodies everywhere. Dillon lay sprawled across the couch—his body so big, one wouldn't know the couch was covered in tan-and-orange stripes. Bat lay sprawled on top of a sleeping bag, his feet extending several feet beyond the bag bottom. Pal was entwined in some pillows and blankets—more flesh visible than fabric. And Hoss, dressed in a pair of boxer shorts, lay facedown in a beanbag chair. She worried he couldn't breathe until he snorted and rolled over.

And she wondered why she grew up a tomboy? With these guys as her role models, it was a miracle she knew how to put on panty hose.

She tiptoed like a fairy around the bulk of her brothers, then drove like a madwoman all the way to downtown Chicago.

After parking eight blocks from work, Rosie speed-walked like an Olympic hopeful to her office building and nearly sprinted through the editorial department before plunking herself in Mr. Real's desk chair. Panting, she dropped her sack on the floor and glanced at her wristwatch—8:40. Not good.

"A little late, girlfriend." Pam sidled up next to the desk.

"Traffic." Pant. Pant. "Ten blocks." Okay, it had been eight, but it *felt* like ten.

"Don't fret—managers are all in a staff meeting."

When Pam leaned closer, Rosie caught her friend's familiar patchouli scent. "Why were four bulky boys hanging around your desk yesterday?" Pam whispered. "Mr. Real groupies?"

"In a...roundabout way," Rosie said, lifting the framed picture of her family. She pointed at the four men sitting around the table. "My bulky brothers."

"They look different in person," Pam mused, checking out the photo. "Bigger." She leaned back and shot

Rosie a questioning look. "Why're all four here? Family reunion?"

"You might say that." Rosie flicked a switch on the side of Mr. Real's computer. The monitor lighted up as the computer whirred to life. "A surprise family reunion." She'd skip the particulars, like how they traveled a few thousand miles to kill Ben.

"Mr. Real?" Seth called out, crossing to her desk. With his white T-shirt, red suspenders and blue hair, he looked like a walking ad for the Fourth of July. "Another special delivery," he announced, waving an envelope. "It was already at the receptionist's desk when I got into work at seven-thirty. This dude needs some advice, bad."

"Thanks." Rosie accepted the envelope, her insides twisting when she saw the nearly illegible scrawl on the envelope.

"Hey," Seth continued, "saw Mount Rushmore hanging about your desk yesterday." He raised both hands, as though he had nothing to hide. "For the record, I didn't blab to nobody about Mr. Real bein' a chick."

"I know you didn't," Rosie murmured, still looking at the familiar handwriting. Ben had written back, again, to Mr. Real. About what? Itching to know, she was feeling hot and bothered just touching the envelope. Surreptitiously, she lifted the envelope and casually sniffed for any lingering musky masculine scent.

Seth picked up one of the gold paper clips and rolled it between his fingers. "I worried when I saw Mount Rushmore—thought you'd think I'd blabbed. Saw myself in gulchdom for the rest of my life."

Rosie lowered the envelope. "Those were my brothers."

"Surprise family reunion," Pam added.

"Family?" He gave Rosie a once-over. "Lucky you

didn't get the big gene.'' He held up the paper clip. "Can I have this?"

"Sure."

He clipped it to his suspender and started to leave.

"Oh, Seth." When he turned around, Rosie infused her voice with all the professionalism she could muster considering a hint of musk trailed the air and her fingers were leaving sweaty imprints on the envelope. "I might need you to make a special delivery in, say, thirty minutes? You available?"

He nodded his blue head. "For Mr. Real? You bet!" He swaggered away, giving a high five to one of the guys he passed.

Pam glanced at the envelope. "Let me guess. Another handwritten letter from Mr. Bad Penmanship?"

"Mr. Mars."

"The one you called old-fashioned? Gentlemanly?"

Rosie nodded again, feeling her face go hot as she recalled what it had been like in the front seat of Ben's BMW yesterday. He'd been anything but old-fashioned and gentlemanly. He'd been dangerous, hot, fiercely passionate. *He'd been Mars.* And forget Athena and Artemis. She'd been Venus.

"You're blushing, girlfriend," Pam teased. "Guess he looked pretty good when you met up at Starbucks, hmm?"

Pretty good? Wildly, sizzlingly, outrageously hot. "I have a confession," she croaked.

Pam's chocolate-brown eyes widened. "Tell it, girl," she whispered conspiratorially, scooting a little closer.

"I'm being taken over by the goddess Boom Boom."

Pam paused, waiting for more. Blinking, she repeated, "Boom Boom goddess," as though testing each word for its hidden significance. "I give. What're you talking about?"

"Boom Boom was the stripper Mr. Real ran away with."

"So everyone at *Real Men* knows. But what's a Boom Boom goddess?"

Rosie cleared her throat. "I started thinking about how I should be more adventurous, more Boom Boom-like. I used to be a normal, career-driven gulcher. Ever since I tapped into my Boom Boom goddess within, I've been..." *Wanton. Deprived. Ready to writhe and kiss and groan and lick and stick my loafered feet on expensive dashboards in broad daylight.*

Pam held the back of her hand to Rosie's forehead. "You're not running a fever. Stick out your tongue."

"I'm not sick. I'm serious. I've become a different woman while pretending to be a man. I've gotten in touch with my inner Boom Boom."

Pam folded her arms and tilted her head, which made her large gold hoop earrings dangle. "How'd we jump from Starbucks to Boom Boom?" Her eyes lit up as her lips formed an O. "I get it! This Starbucks guy makes you become the Boom Boom goddess!"

Rosie swallowed. "He's more than the Starbucks guy. He's also the guy I stole the mugs from." She glanced at the *Rebel Without a Cause* and *My Fair Lady* coffee mugs.

Pam followed Rosie's gaze. "The lawyer?" she asked, her voice rising in surprise.

"The same."

Pam shot her friend a long look. "Girl," she finally said, elongating the word until it sounded like "giiirrrl." "Your life is getting more complicated than one of those steamy soap operas." She held up her index finger.

"One—he thinks he's writing to his newfound buddy, Mr. Real." She held up two fingers. "Two—he doesn't know it's really you, the mug thief, who's reading his man-to-man words."

Rosie held up three fingers. "Three," she squeaked. "I made mad passionate love with him in the front seat of his BMW while my brothers watched."

Pam jerked back, nearly falling off her perch on the desk. She opened her mouth and emitted a sound like "Ooowee," an even longer string of vowels than "giiirrrl." Then she shook one hand as though Rosie were too hot to handle.

"My brothers weren't too happy," Rosie said glumly.

"But I bet you were!" Pam chortled to herself.

"It was wonderful for all of two minutes." *Wonderful?* That hardly summed up the dizzying, fiery, Boom Boom meltdown lust. "We were like two magnets stuck to each other. Then my brothers started pounding on the car. Made me get out. Yelled at Ben. But he was already used to that after..."

"After?"

"Well, uh, after they'd threatened to kill him earlier."

Pam gave her head a slow shake, her earrings swaying with the movement. "Girl, girl, girl. For a young country thing, you sure got yourself into some big-city boy trouble. Jerome. Mr. Mars. Who's next? Brad Pitt, watch out!" With a saucy laugh, Pam stood and straightened her yellow-print dress. "I got a meeting, or I'd stay to listen to the next segment of 'As the Boom Boom Turns'." As she walked away, Pam said over her shoulder, "If you need someone to double date with, you got my number!"

Date? Rosie frowned. Did two minutes of frantic, feverish making out mean she and Ben were *dating?*

She held up the envelope, feeling frantic and feverish just touching the same envelope he'd touched. She'd never felt like this before. All topsy-turvy, as though her insides were on a nonstop roller coaster ride.

Her hands were shaking so badly, it took her three tries to open the envelope. Finally she pulled loose the letter, and although she tried to suppress it, she sighed audibly when she looked at his god-awful handwriting. It had to be the boldest, most masculine scrawl she'd ever seen.

"Dear Mr. Real, I understand about family emergencies, so no need to apologize. When you didn't show, I had an unexpected encounter where I ended up sharing a space. Definitely a vital space."

She thought she'd swoon right then and there. Vital. Was that how he viewed her? Vital and precious. And beautiful. With a shiver of recollection, she recalled his husky voice and the way he looked at her. *Rosalind, you're so beautiful.*

It had been like a door opening on her sheltered heart, her girl's heart. With an ache that bordered on painful, she'd wanted desperately to shatter everything she'd been taught was right and proper and throw herself into the fire. And then he'd kissed her, burning away her reserve, and she'd greedily responded with the passion of a woman.

Moistening her lips as though she might again taste him, she read on. "And, for the first time, I've met the type of woman you mentioned. She's independent, adventurous, honest."

Rosie held her breath. He'd called her independent before. They'd shared their fantasies of Africa, so he must also view her as adventurous. But honest? Guilt pricked her conscience. Honest, no way. She was reading words—his personal, private words—which he'd never intended for her eyes. Honest? She'd been pretending to be Mr. Real, and writing back as such. If he ever found out... She swallowed back her shame. And her fear. Because if he found out, she knew in her heart she'd lose him. "My only dilemma now is that I'm being stalked by her brothers."

She gasped. Still? She glanced at her family photo. Last night, Rosie had told her brothers, repeatedly, that Ben was a wonderful man. His worse sin was being overterritorial about that parking space, but otherwise he'd always been the perfect gentleman. Okay, except for that frenzied two-minute lovemaking episode, but that had been both of their faults, not Ben's. And after explaining all that, Rosie had made her brothers swear they'd stop their demented bodyguard act.

Were they being as dishonest with her as she was being with Ben?

Fighting a surge of anxiety, Rosie continue reading. "Here I'd wanted to move to Mars, and now I wish I could find my way back to Venus. Too bad there's not a planet halfway between."

So he'd listened to her part-time on Venus, part-time on Mars theory. "No need to write back. Just wanted to thank you for your time, your insights, and wish you well with your family circumstances. Sincerely, Mars."

She glanced at the top of the letter. Yesterday's date. He must have written this last night, after he got home. Why? She thought back to yesterday afternoon after she'd tumbled out of the front seat of the car. Her brothers had threatened strangulation, maiming, and a few other colorful tortures, but Ben—probably accustomed to such threats because he was a lawyer—had remained cool, collected. A true Mars.

After her brothers' grumblings died down, Ben had

insisted he was walking Rosie to her front door because, as he explained, he *always* walked the lady to her door. Classy. Ben had even shaken each brother's hand after she'd gone inside. She'd watched through the glass door.

So why did he write the letter after he got home? Dillon had gone out for hamburgers, but surely he hadn't followed the BMW...had he?

If he had, they'd be up to no good today, either. Frantically, she thought back to the plans her brother had made for today. Dillon was checking out the downtown cow exhibit. Bat was hooking up with some business contacts. Pal was looking for a gym. And Hoss said he needed to catch up on some reading.

Nobody had said anything about *stalking*.

But knowing her brothers, they might still be nursing that overprotective grudge. She grabbed one of Mr. Real's gold paper clips and nervously unbent it as she contemplated her options. If she barged into Ben's office, looking for her stalking brothers, Ben might put two and two together and realize someone other than Mr. Real had read the letter.

The sweatshirt! She glanced down at the bag she'd carried in. Last night, she'd washed it—okay, after sniffing it one last time for that musky scent—then neatly folded it so she could return it to Ben today. Really it was an excuse to see him again. But now that motive had an unexpected urgency—to see if her brothers were skulking where they shouldn't be.

She tossed the mangled paper clip into the trash, grabbed the bag, and speed-walked out of the office.

AT NINE-THIRTY, Ben walked into his office and halted. Heather was sitting on the couch, in a shorter-than-usual shift, her silver-painted toenails peeking out the end of a pair of silver platforms. Normally, he wouldn't have even noticed the toenail or platform color, except her tootsies were propped in Brother Armani's—Bat's—lap.

Br-r-ing. Br-ring.

"Heather," Ben said, "the phone's ringing."

She looked at Ben over her shoulder. "I hurt my foot," she explained, pointing limply at her silver toes. "Pal's answering the phones."

Pal, one snakeskin-booted foot on the receptionist's desk, flashed Ben a thumbs-up as he answered the phone. "Benny Taylor's office."

Ben cringed. He cut Heather a scathing glance, which she missed as she was too busy giggling something in Bat's ear.

"Pal," Ben began, "my name's—"

Pal waved him off. "Heather," he said, holding up the receiver, "it's Carla."

"Ask her to call back," Heather called out. "Tell her I hurt my foot."

Doing what? Clomping too hard? Ben was waiting for Pal to get off the phone so he could explain his name was Benjamin not Benny, when suddenly he heard a familiar voice behind him.

"Benjamin, so delighted you're here!"

Ben pivoted and nearly dropped his briefcase. Meredith, wearing jeans so tight he was amazed she could breathe, much less walk, sashayed into the office with small mincing steps. She wore hanging earrings that looked like miniature wind chimes. And she'd exchanged her high heels for red leather boots, and chopsticks for a cowboy hat. In less than twenty-four hours, she changed from Grieving Geisha to Cheery Country Girl.

And behind her stood Dillon the Basketball, looking like a humongous mountain rising from the cheery countryside. A humongous, hairy mountain as, once again, he obviously couldn't button his shirt.

Meredith smiled broadly, her lips glossed with blood-red lipstick that matched her boots. "Benjamin—" he noticed she wasn't calling him "darling" anymore "—I have some *fabulous* swatches to show you." Holding up a rough-looking square of material, she took a deep breath—or tried to. Obviously the sprayed-on jeans only allowed half breaths. "We're going to re-upholster the couch in denim!" she said exuberantly. "Country is so *in* these days."

We? Ben looked past Meredith at Dillon, who could probably reupholster the Empire State Building without using a ladder. But right now Ben didn't care about that. He and Dillon had some business to clear up.

"Saw your green pickup in my rearview mirror last night. Were you following me?"

"Ben?"

A male voice. From Ben's office? He turned. Hoss was leaning against the doorjamb in Ben's office doorway, holding a legal book. "I've been researching DeMorney versus Lauren, but I can't find any reference to the final judgment. Do you have any additional books I might check out?"

"What do I look like?" Ben snapped. "A library?" He turned back to Dillon to finish their discussion when *another* male voice cut in.

"Special delivery for Mars." It grew eerily quiet as everyone stared at the delivery boy's blue hair. "Somethin' wrong?" he asked, looking around.

"What the hell—?" Dillon stared at Seth's hair.

Seth ran his hand through his short-cropped thatch. "Squad-Car Blue," he announced proudly.

Meredith held up her swatch of material and eyeballed it against Seth's hair.

"No Mars here," chimed in Heather from her couch perch.

"I'll take it." Ben stepped forward and accepted the letter. "Client of mine. Mars." He stuck the letter in his pants pocket.

Dillon, still staring at Seth's head, asked, "How come your brows ain't blue?"

"They'd clash with my eyes," Seth explained, then turned and left.

Dillon gave his head a shake, as though dislodging the alien visit, then stepped forward. The ground shook. Meredith's earrings tinkled. "So what if you seen my pickup in your rearview mirror? It's a free country."

So he was admitting he'd followed Ben last night. Ben had taken on a surly trucker: he sure as hell could take on a surly, hairy brother. He set down his briefcase. "Seeing your pickup in my rearview mirror means you're following me. *That's* what I don't like."

A heavy silence fell over the room.

Br-r-ing. Br-r-ing.

"Benny Taylor's office."

Ben stiffened. He'd taken care of his family and his exes, but no way in hell was he taking care of his exes lawyer-killing boyfriends. "It's Benjamin!" he barked over his shoulder at Pal. "If your goal in life is to be a receptionist, at least answer the phone correctly!"

The silence grew heavier.

Pal cleared his throat. "It's Mr. Nelson. Says he wants to park in your space."

Still glaring at Dillon, Ben snapped, "Tell him to find his own damn space. And if he doesn't like that, tell him to find another damn lawyer."

Pal cleared his throat again. "Mr. Nelson? Uh, Mr. Taylor says to please find another space as he's currently detained and unable to help you."

Ben raised an eyebrow. Pal was good. Ben wondered if he was looking for a job.

"What makes you think I'm following you?" Dillon continued, egging Ben on.

"Correction. *Stalking* me. Especially after we made amends."

Dillon looked puzzled. "Made what?"

A swirl of motion tore into the office. Curls flying. Clothes looking as though the wearer had dressed in front of a wind machine. *Rosie.* Something inside Ben tumbled loose as he looked at her. He recalled tasting her lips. Inhaling the fresh, clean scent of her silky hair. Feeling every curve of her body molded so tightly against him, he hadn't known where he began and she left off.

He tried to hold on to his fury at Dillon, but a greater heat overwhelmed him. The heat of remembering Rosie's passion.

She stumbled to a halt, and stood panting, her gaze traveling around the room. "What's...going...on here?"

Dillon got that sheepish, little boy look again. "I'm, uh, helpin' Meredith reupholster the couch."

"I'm researching," Hoss mumbled, disappearing back into Ben's office.

Pal pointed to the phone. "I'm filling in for the receptionist."

"And I'm supporting her," Bat said with a devilish smile, indicating Heather's feet propped on his lap.

Rosie blew a wayward curl off her flushed face. "You guys!" She sputtered something under her breath. "You're not reupholstering, filling in, researching and supporting. You're *stalking!* Stalking Ben! I explained over and over last night, that—that what you saw in the front seat of Ben's car was just a—a...moment of...liking each other." She said "liking each other" a bit too breathlessly, her hazel eyes darting to Ben.

"Honey," Heather said, limply pointing one silver-tipped finger at Rosie, "your blouse is—"

Rosie's cheeks tinted pink, then red, as she shoved the bottom of her blouse into the waistband of her skirt.

Meredith, who'd been studying the swatch of material as though it contained a hidden message, suddenly snapped to attention. "Liking each other?" She turned so quickly to look at Ben, he again heard that tinkling sound. "Is *she* the young thing you've been fooling around with?"

"She doesn't look like jailbait," Heather commented, the word *bait* ending on a little shriek when Bat tweaked one of her toes.

Super-Ex. They could be caught in the middle of a wind-ripping, earth-shattering tornado, and they'd still be commenting on Ben's personal life. "She's not jailbait," he said tersely. "And we're not *fooling* around."

Rosie, hurt shadowing her face, held up the bag. "Right," she said in a tremulous voice. "We're not fooling around." She laughed, or attempted to, but it came out like a series of choked coughs. She cleared her throat. "By the way, here're your clothes."

The room grew so quiet, Ben could hear the hum of the air-conditioning. Where were those blue-haired interruptions when you needed them?

"Clothes?" barked Dillon, his face redder than Meredith's boots. "When'd he take those off—and why do you have them?"

Before Ben could say something, anything, in his defense, Dillon rushed forward, his fingers gripping a circle of air like a fleshy noose for Ben's neck.

As Dillon's monster-size bulk lumbered toward him, Ben stepped aside. Dillon, a human truck without brakes, careened past and crashed against the receptionist's desk. With a grunt, he pivoted, raised his hands in that noose-grip again and growled menacingly.

"Dillon!" Rosie suddenly yelled, stamping her foot. "You're in a lawyer's office, not a bull pen! If you're so bent to go after a guy who's harassing me, go after Johnny Depp!" Heaving a frustrated sigh, she turned to Ben. "I'm sorry! Maybe if you left me alone with them for a moment, let me talk to them—*again*—I could get this straightened out."

"Johnny Depp?" Meredith whispered feverishly. "He's after you, too?"

Ben, ignoring Meredith, checked his wristwatch. "I need to leave anyway," he said, "I'm meeting someone in ten minutes."

"I don't remember an appointment," Heather said.

"Forgot to tell you." For all her foibles, Heather ran his appointment book like a drill sergeant. Which was great for a receptionist, but bad when he was lying through his teeth, trying to send a secret message to Rosie. He picked up his briefcase. "Yes, yes," he continued, "this is a special meeting regarding a shared space."

Rosie looked confused.

He put on his best bored-lawyer-has-to-go-to-another-meeting look. "Client's Peter Isak. This will be our second meeting. Same place."

Rosie's hazel eyes lighted up. Her lips twisted into a knowing smile.

"Pal," Ben said, glancing at the brother behind the desk, "tell callers I'll be back in a while."

"Yes, Mr. Taylor."

One down, three to go. He headed toward the door, stopped and looked at Meredith. "Can the denim. I want another material. An African print. Something wild. Bold." He grinned cockily to himself as he walked out the door. *Like the new me.*

BEN PUSHED OPEN the door to the coffee house, relishing more than the onslaught of air-conditioned air. He relished the thought of seeing Rosie soon. He could tell by the gleam in her mischievous eyes that she'd picked up the clues. He hadn't said he'd be sitting in "our shared seats," but he knew *she* knew that was what he intended.

Our shared seats.

He almost sounded as though he were ready to live part-time on Venus, part-time on Mars. *Our.* He hadn't used that word when it came to him and a woman since, oh, Heather. And that "our" phase had ended two—three?—years ago. There'd been no woman since, not even a blind date. Not that Super-Ex and others hadn't tried to set him up. He just always declined. Because dating led to more dating, which led to a relationship, which led to Ben playing caretaker—a role he'd always played with women.

Until Rosie.

With her it was different because *she* was different. Spunky. Independent. Honest. Easing his way around people and chairs, he chuckled to himself thinking about Rosie's honesty. Like her beauty, it was refreshing. Direct. Clean. She was the kind of woman you could look in the eyes and trust whatever she said.

That was the kind of bonding he'd pursued by writing to Mr. Real. Yet he'd found that camaraderie—and more—with Rosie. Maybe that was what his best pal,

Matt, had found with that beekeeper. A woman who was your best friend *and* your lover. Part-time on Mars, part-time on Venus. If someone had told him that theory a week ago, he'd have said such a union had one in a million odds.

Funny. Just like the odds must have been for him to find Rosie yesterday in the *exact* spot he was supposed to meet Mr. Real.

Heading toward that exact spot, his high-spirited hopes sank. In one of the seats sat a young man with a pierced nose, sipping coffee while reading the paper. Ben glanced around—there were plenty of other seats. He could always take one of those, flag Rosie over. But the seats they'd shared yesterday had taken on a special meaning. They were their "shared space," a vital space, where they'd shared their dreams.

And, Ben realized with a jolt, where he'd started to fall in love with Rosie Myers.

"Excuse me," Ben said, getting the younger man's attention.

The guy looked up, his spiked, beaded Mohawk reminding Ben of one of Meredith's decorating phases. "Yeah?"

"This might seem an odd request, but can I persuade you to move?"

"Move?" The guy repeated, looking around the room, obviously thinking there were plenty of other seats this older dude could pick.

Ben fished in his pocket and extracted a twenty. "I'll pay you for your seat," he murmured. He'd never tipped a maitre d' for a seat at a restaurant, yet here he was tipping some Generation Xer for a chair at Starbucks.

The guy looked at the twenty-dollar bill, his chair, then back to the money. "You're crazy, man," he muttered.

"Yes." Crazy for a wild-haired, wild-hearted woman named Rosie.

Shaking his Mohawk, the guy stuffed the bill into his back pocket and migrated to another seat.

Ben, triumphant, sat down. He'd wait to get their drinks when Rosie arrived—didn't want to lose this vital space again. Although he'd have paid another twenty—hell forty, fifty, sixty—just to sit here, close to Rosie. To look into those sparkling eyes, to listen to her voice, to imagine awakening that impassioned response in her again...

He stared through the throng of coffee drinkers, and out the windows at the walking pedestrians. He grinned to himself. Venuses in pant suits, dresses. Marses in suits, casual wear.

He bolted upright. Warning alarms clanged in his head. Something big and blue had flashed by. Either it was one of those oversize blue go-cart contraptions the Chicago police scooted around in...or it was one of Rosie's oversize blue-shirted brothers.

His stomach clenched. *Impossible.* She was back at the office, laying down the ground rules. Telling her brothers to cool it. She was...here.

The alarms stopped clanging. His insides turned to liquid as he stared, stunned, at her image. Backlight from the windows outlined her curves in a hazy glow. And her hair—buoyant, curly—framed her heart-shaped face like a dark, glowing halo. He'd never noticed the glints of red in her hair, coaxed to life by a dazzling shaft of sunlight.

"Is that seat taken?" she teased.

Had he ever heard that whiskey edge to her voice? Subtly suggestive, it flooded him with heat. "It's yours," he murmured huskily.

When she stepped toward the seat, he caught another flash of blue outside the window. This was no police go-cart. Unless they were now also covering them with patches of jungle chest hair.

Dillon.

"They followed you," Ben murmured.

She scooted forward to the edge of her seat. "No way! I warned them—"

"Don't look out the window," Ben counseled, not raising his voice one notch. "Just keep looking at me, pretend we're talking."

Ding ding ding.

At first he thought it was those damn internal alarms again, clanging their warning, until he realized it was another sound. From outside, the ubiquitous red trolley, the Loop tour bus, had pulled up in front. Ben had taken his niece and nephew on it last fall during their visit. You could jump on or off the trolley at any one of its many stops downtown, one of which was in front of Starbucks, right now.

"Come on," Ben said, jumping to his feet. He grabbed Rosie's hand and dragged her through the Starbucks crowd, eyeing the window. No flashes of blue and chest hair. Good.

He shoved open the door and stepped into the steamy Chicago heat. "Run!" Ben yelled, tugging Rosie with him. In three giant strides, he reached the trolley door. He jumped to the top step, pulling Rosie onboard.

Ding ding ding.

The doors closed as the trolley pulled from the curb. Ben craned his neck, peering over passengers' heads. Back on the sidewalk, Dillon and Armani shook their fists at the departing trolley.

10

"AND TO OUR RIGHT, ladies and gentleman, my favorite cow, Moovies!" The trolley tour guide gestured broadly out the windows at a piece of art on the street corner, a black-and-white cow inscribed with the word Moovies along its flank, a bucket of popcorn around its neck.

Rosie giggled and nestled closer to Ben, who had his arm around her. They'd spent the past fifty minutes on the trolley tour, listening to the gregarious driver—a stand-up comic wanna-be—point out famous Chicago sites and cows, explaining how the latter was part of Chicago's current fund-raising art event, CowParade, where hundreds of life-size, decorated plaster cows adorned the city.

Warm breezes fluttered through the open window as Ben whispered into Rosie's ear, "Wonder if the Moovies cow ever saw *Out of Africa*?"

She grinned at Ben's whimsy, then gasped when he nuzzled a sensitive patch of skin behind her ear. He murmured things she couldn't quite hear, but his teasing, seductive tone said it all. He knew the effect he was having on her. Powerful. Commanding. And she loved every delicious moment of it.

"We know you love *Out of Africa*," he whispered. "Wonder how you'd look *in* Africa?" She let her mind drift as he continued with the fantasy. "Your body draped in a colorful caftan—" he slipped a finger ever so slightly underneath her collar "—with a low V-neck front."

She shivered with anticipation, imagining the warm breezes swirling in through the windows to be the winds off the Serengeti. How they'd feel against her exposed skin.

"And your hair..." Ben pulled several strands away from her face and fondled them. "You have the hair of a lady—it can be piled high on your head, all curly and tumbling and delicate." He dug his fingers into her hair and playfully tousled it. "Or it can be wild, untamed."

He saw into her. All the layers, the personalities. Just as she pretended to be different goddesses, she *could* also be different women. Something she hadn't dreamed until she'd gotten to know Ben. Different goddesses, yes. Different women? Never. Before, she typically felt like Eliza with soot on her nose. But now, she sometimes felt like the elegant Eliza, a beautiful, desirable woman. And beyond both of those, at the core of her being, she had embraced her truest woman-self. A passionate Rosie—an enthusiastic, primal lover. And, at the same time, a man's equal—his partner, his best friend. All the things she yearned to be with Ben...

He leaned close again, his breath hot with promise, as he continued the African fantasy. "Your skin would be covered with beads of sweat from our treks through the tropical rain forest." One hand caressed her knee, then moved up, teasingly massaging her inner thigh. "And I'd lick off each and every drop."

She had to hook her loafers under the seat in front of them not to jump him right then and there. It was one thing to succumb to unbridled, out-of-control passion in the front seat of a BMW. Quite another in one of the many seats on a packed trolley tour. "We need to stop," she squeaked, glancing around, relieved the passengers were following the scenic tour outside the trolley and not the heated one inside.

Ben leaned back slightly. "But we've just started," he said suggestively. Wind through the trolley tousled his hair as his smoldering blue eyes raked boldly over her.

Every nerve ending in her body was on fire. "You're no lawyer," she whispered feverishly. "You're larger than life. Fierce. Exciting. You're Mars."

He paused and cocked one eyebrow. "What's that about? Because I once said I had to make a pit stop on Mars before going to Africa?"

She nodded, realizing she'd slipped, divulged more than Rosie should.

"Well, I no longer imagine making that trip," he said assuredly. "Instead, I want to live part-time on Mars, part-time on Venus."

Good. Her slip had gone unnoticed. "Maybe a planet...a place...um, somewhere in between."

He frowned. "What?"

Now she'd done it, practically quoted one of his letters to Mr. Real. All this heat—and she didn't mean the summer weather—was mixing her up. Her thoughts were jumping. Her libido was sizzling. She couldn't remember anymore what was Real—and what was un-real. "I mean..." She fanned herself lightly, hoping the movement would distract Ben from what she'd just blurted.

"In between?" he prompted.

So much for fanning. She dropped her hand in her lap, wishing the two of them were back in that African fantasy instead of this suddenly uncomfortable trolley. "You remember," she said lightly, "when I said the answer for men and women is to live part-time on each planet. You know, halfway between?"

Being the woman behind the man, who was really the woman, was messing her up.

"You're right," he finally said, his tone softening. "You said that." He played with a curl that tumbled across her forehead and looked deeply into her eyes.

She stared back, mesmerized. His eyes were like blue flames, burning with emotion. Her insides were on that wild roller-coaster ride again. For safety measures, she hooked the toes of her loafers more securely under the seat in front of her.

"What are you thinking about?" he whispered suggestively.

"My loafers." She squeezed shut her eyes, wishing a strong wind would come up and blow her out the window right now. *Her loafers?* This man had been talking about Africa and caftans and licking all the sweat off her skin— and she's talking about her scuffy, toe-locked loafers?

"Yes, about those loafers," Ben said, his voice low and teasing. "Only a self-assured, sexy woman could wear loafers like you do, Rosie."

Rosie opened her eyes, her heart swelling to twice its size. "Really?"

"Really." He gave her that lethally sexy grin. "Those shoes let you run, be on the move, chasing dreams."

"Like a goddess," she murmured, thinking of Artemis, the huntress whose domain was the wilderness, who loved exploration. Yes, Artemis would definitely have worn loafers.

Ding ding ding.

Ben checked his wristwatch. "It's almost lunchtime." He looked out the window. "We've been gone nearly an hour. Any problem if we took longer? There's an excellent restaurant in that hotel. Shall we?"

"No problem." She could stay late at work, make up

the time. Rosie peered past him at the swank five-star hotel she'd seen plenty of times from the outside. "I'm not really dressed for such a fancy place...."

Grabbing her hand, he pulled her to her feet and gave her that smoldering look times a thousand. "We'll order room service."

ROSIE BUSIED HERSELF checking out the sumptuous bouquet that adorned a corner of the registration desk while Ben checked in. She'd never stared so long at a bird-of-paradise flower in her entire life. It looked exotic with its purple, orange and yellow. Like Africa. Like their fantasies. Like what they'd be doing in mere moments. Her knees were going weak with anticipation when Ben cupped her elbow and escorted her to a bank of elevators. As though this were an everyday, lunchtime sort of thing, they ever so graciously stepped through the opened doors and stood alongside an elderly couple who smiled pleasantly at them.

Rosie tried to smile back, but her lips were quivering.

Then she and Ben exited on the eighteenth floor and walked ever so graciously down the carpeted hallway to their room. Rosie leaned against the wall, too excited, barely trusting herself to stand alone, while Ben inserted the card into the lock.

Then they stepped inside, shut the door, and dropped the ever-so-gracious act.

Ben pressed her against the wall, his body hard against hers. He took her face in his hands and kissed her, long and deep. Then his lips burned their need along her mouth, her hair, her neck. "Rosalind," he murmured. "Oh, Rosalind, you're so beautiful."

She couldn't get enough breath. Gasping, panting, she returned his fervor with her own. It was like writhing in the front seat of his car again, except this time they were vertical, pressed against a wall, frantic with desire. Hands flying, stroking, caressing. Cries of desire. Suppressed passion finally unleashed, like a storm that had hovered in the distance. Finally here, it unleashed its furious, demanding, high-voltage power.

Ben suddenly pulled back, his face flushed. A shaft of his dark-blond hair fell across his brow. "Let's not rush it," he murmured, looking her over as though she were a precious object he wanted to treasure. "Let's take it slow...savor the first time we make love."

First time? That meant more than once. Many times. His words made her quake and swell inside, until she thought she'd explode with rapture.

Pulled by his strong grip, she stepped away from the wall, certain she'd burned her outline into it after all that sizzling passion. Taking a deep, shaky break, she looked around the room for the first time. "It's a palace," she whispered, awestruck. She kicked off her loafers and curled her toes into the thick, plush rug as her gaze traveled over gold-framed paintings, antique furniture and, hanging from the center of the ceiling, a sparkling, multi-tiered crystal chandelier.

"Our first time should be special," Ben murmured, joining her gaze. "Another time, we'll test our African fantasies...."

There he went again. First time. Another time. "Ben," she whispered, "I—I want you so much." Her throat clogged with emotion. She, whose mother always told her to watch her tongue, suddenly couldn't make it work.

He took her in his arms. "I've been selfish. Didn't ask. You're not—?"

She felt a hot flush crawl over her skin. He wondered if she was a virgin. "No." Not technically. "Once before. Years ago." She'd skip over the embarrassing fact it had been eight years. Besides, it had been clumsy, teen-aged, and over before she knew what had really happened.

Nothing like this—making love with the man of her dreams, in a room fit for gods and goddesses.

"We'll take it slow," he repeated, tightening his hold around her. "We'll savor every moment...." And then he kissed her, burning away any of her lingering anxiety. He stopped, with great effort, then stepped back. "Undress for me, Rosie. I want to watch and enjoy the unveiling of your beautiful body."

She'd never undressed in front of *anyone* before. It felt daring, but with Ben, it also felt right, like playing with their earlier fantasies, except this time they could act them out. She undid the top button of her blouse, then the next, her gaze locked with his.

Ben sank back into a high-back chair and crossed his hands behind his head. When he stretched out his legs, she saw his thickened arousal, was aware of the effect she had on him. It filled her with a titillating pleasure, to see how her body excited him. With a self-assuredness that took her by surprise, she unbuttoned the rest of her blouse and tossed it aside. Then did the same with her bra.

The onslaught of cool air puckered her nipples. Instinctively, she covered herself.

"No." Ben stood and crossed to her. "You're too beautiful to be covered." Gently, he took her hands and pulled them away. Then he looked at her breasts, his eyes darkening with desire. He traced a slow, agonizingly sensuous circle around each mound, narrowing the circle until his fingertips brushed across one hardened nipple, then the other. She let her head fall back as she stifled a groan.

Bracing one hand on her back, he unzipped her skirt and let it drop. She stepped out of the pile of clothes and stood before Ben, dressed only in her white cotton underwear. For one excruciatingly unbearable moment, she felt ordinary again. Plain. Country girl Rosie.

"There's nothing sexier than a woman wearing something simple. White." Ben slid his finger along the waistband of her undies, then slipped his hand inside. "Give yourself to me, Rosalind," he murmured, holding her close. "Reveal all your secrets...."

She groaned as he manipulated her expertly, flooding her with heat and need, unleashing desires she hadn't even known she had.

Then he lowered her onto the floor and peeled off her panties. Naked, she lay there on the plush rug, watching as he undressed. Her heart thundered with desire as she inhaled his musky scent, watched him pull off his shirt. She stared at the whorls of hair on his pecs, anticipating how those silky hairs would feel against her skin. How it would be to kiss his bare chest, sense the pulse of his heartbeat with her lips.

Before he took off his pants, he pulled out a wallet and set it on a table near them. And finally, he stood above her naked. She followed the shape of his torso, how it tapered to his molded hips. And in the darkened triangle between his legs, she saw his hardened manhood. Instinctively, she opened her legs, wanting him desperately. Needing his love, his passion, as she'd never wanted a man before.

Then he lowered himself onto her, his hands like flames, burning their path, marking her as his own. He kissed her, whispered his desire for each part of her body. She arched, pressing herself against him, rubbing the fullness of her breasts against his chest, thrilling to his responding groans.

"Now," she begged, unable to hold back.

He reached to his wallet, pulled out a package, then smoothly unrolled the latex over his shaft. She gasped as he entered her slowly, his powerful arousal filling her with a passionate urgency. His tongue eased into her mouth, searching, probing the wetness, then plunging in sync with his slowly building thrusts.

The sensations escalated, wild and sweet and hot. He moaned. A prolonged, guttural sound, like that of a wild animal. She gasped in sweet agony, then stifled a scream of release as her passions, her very soul, skyrocketed with his.

And in the moments afterward, as they lay together, their bodies as one, Rosie realized she'd not only felt beautiful, but transformed. In the culmination of their lovemaking, she'd felt her power. She was no longer poor Eliza or elegant Eliza. And never again would she need to resort to adopting goddess personas.

Rosie was a complete woman.

TWO HOURS LATER, Ben strolled into his office, whistling.

"You were gone a while!" Heather commented, sitting at her desk. Obviously her foot was better.

"No skulking brothers?"

Heather offered a small smile. "They were just doing that for show, you know."

"For show?"

"Stalking you at Starbucks."

Ben had been so caught up in the greatest lovemaking of his life—with the woman who owned his heart, body and soul—he'd momentarily forgotten about Dillon and Bat or Wyatt or whatever that brother's TV cowboy-star name was chasing Ben and Rosie. Although the way Ben felt right now, he could be stalked by a pride of lions, and he'd merely brush them aside.

"They can stalk all they want," Ben said cockily. "Rosie and I are in love."

Heather looked thrilled. "That's exactly what they were hoping!" When Ben flashed her a confused look, she explained, "After you and Rosie left, Meredith and I told them how wonderful, kind and generous you are."

Super-Ex had done that? Extolled Ben's virtues? He grinned. Super-Ex had been super, after all. This was a new twist to the ever evolving world of Benjamin Taylor. "So," he said slowly, trying to connect the dots, "since you convinced the potential lawyer-killing brothers that I'm a good guy, they now stalk for fun only?"

Swiveling in her seat, Heather grinned mischievously. "It didn't take a genius to figure out why Rosie followed so quickly after you left. So they stalked you to Starbucks to make sure you two would keep finding ways to escape together! They saw you jump on that trolley, and pretended to chase you so you'd stay away...and be together longer." She clasped her hands together like a child with a special secret. "Then they came back and told us all about it." Heather giggled. "Meredith and I have been trying to set you up for ages, Benny! Now, finally, you've found someone. Rosie." Heather was so happy, she actually hugged herself. "Meredith has found someone. And I've found someone. Isn't it, like, utterly cool?"

And, to Ben's surprise, he felt the same way. It *was* utterly cool. He liked the idea of Rosie's family wanting them to be together because *he* wanted to be together with Rosie. "I'll be in my office," he said quietly, feeling his insides go liquid again as he thought about the last few hours, and how it had been to make love with Rosie Myers.

Sitting behind his desk, he suddenly remembered the letter in his pocket. Mr. Real! In the trolley escape, then the hotel passion, he'd forgotten all about the letter. There was no longer any urgency to move to Mars. Ben was deliriously happy visiting Venus.

He opened the letter. "Dear Mr. Mars, Glad to hear you shared a vital space. Just as you're Mars, so this woman must be a goddess. One who's, as you said, independent, adventurous, honest."

Yes, Ben had written that before. But he never indicated the woman was a "goddess." Although Rosie had made such a reference on the trolley. Then again while they were making love. "I feel like a goddess." Just a coincidence?

"Part-time on Venus, part-time on Mars is, after all, the way to go. Sincerely, Mr. Real"

Odd. Ben had written, before to Mr. Real, about a planet halfway between, but never about living part-time on Venus, part-time on Mars. That was Rosie's comment, too, when they'd first accidentally met at the coffee shop.

Or was it so accidental?

He had a heavy, sinking sensation, like a stone had been dropped down his gut.

Maybe it *hadn't* been a coincidence that Rosie had been at the coffee shop yesterday. After all, she was there at the *exact* time, in the *exact* place, where he was supposed to meet Mr. Real. And later, what had she said so angrily to her brothers? That they'd embarrassed her in front of the managing editor?

Accounting firms didn't have managing editors...but *Real Men* magazine did.

And it didn't take an accountant to put this two and

two together. Rosie didn't freelance. She worked at *Real Men*.

As Mr. Real.

Ben crumpled the letter and tossed it angrily into the trash can, feeling horribly betrayed, worse, in some way, than Super-Ex had ever made him feel. Rosie had played a game. Deceived him. The honest woman he'd just made love to wasn't so honest after all. But the worst of it was that he'd been taken in by her even while they made love. Had her lovemaking been part of the game?

Emotions raging, he got up and stormed out of the office. He would rattle her until that curl gave it up and he got the truth.

"YOU JOHNNY DEPP?"

"No," Jerome answered irritably, barely looking up from his keyboard, "*Real Men* is a magazine, not a talent agency. Who sent you to me?"

"I did," Pam answered, standing nearby. "Johnny—I mean, Jerome—please meet Dillon Myers, Rosie's brother."

A look of horror passed over Jerome's face as his gaze traveled all the way down, then back up the monster-size man named Dillon. "What's up?" he said, his voice rising.

Dillon reached over, yanked Jerome by the collar of his shirt, lifting him out of his seat. "You."

Jerome grabbed the edge of his desk for support. His face flushing, he coughed, then spoke in a voice that sounded as though he'd been sucking helium. "What the hell?"

Dillon moved his face to within inches of Jerome's. "Don't cuss. And second, don't you ever, ever mess with my li'l sister again."

Paige walked up, halted, and looked at Dillon. "Put down my assistant!"

Dillon, unruffled, kept his hold on Jerome. "He insulted my sister, right Pam? This jerk made rude, sexual innu—innu—"

"Innuendoes," Pam finished.

"I'm calling Security," Paige announced, reaching for the phone on Jerome's desk. At the same time, Dillon picked up the phone and held it above Jerome's head.

Paige paused, then turned her attention to Pam, obviously King Kong's official representative. "What is this about?" she asked sharply.

"This is about your assistant harassing Rosie, implying that if she'd sleep with him, he'd help her get ahead."

"Those are implications," Jerome squeaked, "not facts—"

"Two people in Editorial overheard," Pam interrupted. "Jerome said Rosie had 'nice mugs.' Called her 'baby'. Said he'd help her get another *opportunity* to see you, Ms. Leighton, and that *opportunity*—" Pam waggled her head for emphasis "—had a higher price tag than just *lunch*."

Pam leveled a look at Paige. "Rosie could have hired a lawyer and filed the biggest, nastiest harassment lawsuit this side of the Mississippi. And, after the settlement, walked away with a truckload of *Real Men* money, never having to work again. But not Rosie. She kept her mouth shut." Pam planted her hands on her hips. "But I'm not. I'm standing up for that girl even if nobody else does!"

Rosie speed-walked in and skidded to a stop. "Nobody needs to stand up for me." She quickly checked out the scene. "So the rumors flying around Editorial are true— my brother's found someone new to stalk." She raised her voice authoritatively. "Let him go, Dillon."

"He innuendoed you—"

"Let him go!" As Dillon released Jerome, who fell with a thunk back into his seat, Rosie shot Paige an apologetic look. "I'm sorry your assistant was threatened—"

"Threatened!" Jerome barked, rubbing his throat. "That gorilla tried to strangle me!"

Paige glared at Jerome. "Some serious accusations have been made, Jerome, which you and I will be reviewing with Human Resources—"

"I'm innocent—!"

"You're Mr. Real!" a male voice cut in.

Everyone turned. Horror filled Rosie. There stood Ben, glaring at her with unholy fury. "You lied to me!" he said, pointing at her.

She started to say she was Mr. Real's secretary, but suddenly felt sick to her stomach. She couldn't lie anymore. Didn't want to. Not to the man she'd just bared her soul to. Made love with. Obviously he had guessed she was really Mr. Real. And considering everyone in Editorial knew she'd hightailed it to Paige's office, he could easily have gotten directions to the whereabouts of Rosie, the unreal Mr. Real.

It was almost a relief to shed the facade. "I'm sorry," she whispered.

"Sorry?" He studied her as though seeing her for the first time. "You deceived me! Pretended you were Mr. Real!" He dragged a hand through his hair. "Is that what happened in the hotel room, too? Were you pretending to love me?"

The entire room turned uncomfortably quiet. "The deception," she whispered, "was only temporary."

"Temporary deception? Is that like pleading temporary insanity?"

His raw fury shrank her heart. "You don't understand—"

"Oh, I think I do," he said, biting off the words. "I think *I'm* the one pleading temporary insanity. First, because I actually wrote to Mr. Real!" Ben shook his head, muttering something about it having been caused by Super-Ex. "Worse," he continued, raising his voice, "I believed in you. Believed all that nonsense about living part-time on Mars, part-time on Venus." His eyes blazed, even as she detected a sadness within them. "Was that part of your Venus's-flytrap act?" He narrowed his eyes. "Luring me in," he said ominously, "like meat to the flame?"

"Meat to the—?"

"'Other types of women exist in the world—independent, adventurous, a man's equal,'" he quoted. "My personal letters...I hadn't realized you were *that* competitive, Rosie, that you'd stoop that low."

He was wrong about her—she hadn't used him. And it hadn't been nonsense about living part-time on Mars, part-time on Venus. She'd believed that, wanted it, right down to the very core of her being. And she wanted to say as much. Defend herself. Tell him she loved him...

But maybe he was right about one thing. She'd always worried that her competitiveness, even in relationships, would be her downfall. She'd always had to compete with her brothers—and it became her habit with life, with jobs, with men. She hadn't ever been so fully, painfully aware of that until this very moment. But seeing Ben's fury, his disappointment in her, she knew her competitiveness, her need to get out of the gulch and be Mr. Real, undermined everything they'd shared.

"You're right," she whispered, her voice cracking. She thought about trying to explain everything, but why should he believe anything she said after she'd lied to him?

"And I was wrong," he murmured. Where before his words had been angry, he now sounded distant, almost melancholy. "If I'd thought more, and felt less, I'd have realized I was falling into an old trap. Taking care of you over myself. Something I swore I'd never do again with another woman."

For a long moment, they simply looked into each other's eyes, aware they'd reached an impasse. By the ache in her heart, Rosie suspected she had unwittingly compromised the love of her life with her need to get ahead, a need so desperate she would lie to Ben. She'd made him feel as if he were taking care of her, when the truth was, they were taking care of each other in a way that had to be true love. If only she hadn't deceived him....

He swallowed hard, pain and anger all mixed up in his eyes. "No goddess now, I guess, huh Rosie?"

"Goddess!" Paige, looking more terrifying in her silk ensemble than Artemis in battle armor, took a step toward Rosie. "I'm sorry about what happened with Jerome, but you were warned, Rosie," she said coldly, "that not a *single* goddesslike word should touch that column. And didn't I tell you it was *imperative* our readers *not* know a woman was writing the column? You obviously broke that rule, as well."

Rosie nodded. She was too heartbroken to defend anything anymore.

"Then you understand," Paige continued, straightening, "why you're fired. Please pack up your desk and get out. Now."

Rosie looked up at Ben, but he had already turned and

walked away. He was done with her. As done as Paige. As done as her career.

Of them all, it was losing Ben that hurt her most.

BEN STORMED OUT of the building, the blast of summer heat nothing compared to his fiery mood. Why had Rosie betrayed him? Lied to him? He strode angrily down the sidewalk, not caring where he went, just needing to work off his anger and disappointment.

Minutes later he passed a window. Starbucks. An ache gripped his insides as he imagined those corner seats, remembered that glistening look in Rosie's eyes when he'd shown up, surprising her. It didn't take a shrink to analyze the way she'd looked at him—she'd been thrilled to see him. Excited. Obviously, she didn't know, at that point, that Mars was also Ben. Just as he didn't know Rosie was also Mr. Real.

He halted in his tracks. No deceit there. Their reactions to each other had been *real*. Someone bumped into him. "Hey," a young man griped, "either walk or step aside."

Ben watched the young buck stride away, swinging a briefcase. Typical corporate ladder climber with an expensive haircut, decked out in a power suit. Ben flashed on Rosie yesterday morning with her ladder-to-success power look—sweet-roll hair and oversize, see-through men's cotton T-shirt. If Ben hadn't been there, she'd have been laughed off the top rung.

A pang of realization sliced through him. He stepped to the side, allowing pedestrian traffic to flow past. He'd helped her get dressed for her meeting because he, too, understood competitiveness. Hell, he'd always *had* to be competitive. That's what had gotten him into law school and propelled him to graduate second in his class. He'd sharpened that competitiveness to an art in the courtroom, fighting for his clients.

He dragged a hand through his hair, juxtaposing the image of Rosie greeting him yesterday at Starbucks—a woman thrilled to see him—compared to the woman he just saw in the *Real Men*'s office—a woman horrified at what she'd done, blaming herself for her competitiveness.

Competitiveness was part of being in the working world. Competitiveness was something he, too, was guilty of.

He stood in front of some kind of tourist sports store, its window display crammed with everything from Chicago Bears jerseys to coffee mugs to helmets....

He smiled to himself. Maybe it was time for Ben to give in to his own competitiveness and go after what he really wanted....

POUND POUND POUND.

Rosie jumped, almost dropping her dad's helmet, which she'd started to place into one of the numerous packing boxes scattered around her living room. "Come in!" she yelled.

Pound pound pound.

She stared at the front door. "Dillon? Bat?" No answer. Probably forgot their keys. Well, she might as well greet them now, explain what happened at work, tell them she was joining Dillon in his truck when they headed back to Kansas tomorrow morning.

She opened the door.

It was some guy, wearing a football helmet. Some fund-raising gimmick? "I'm not a Bears fan."

She started to close the door, but the guy wedged his foot between the frame and the door, stopping it from closing.

"I'm not a Bear," he said. "I'm a Mars."

Through the slightly opened door, she looked into those familiar blue eyes. She did her best to give him an impassive so-what look, although her heart was thundering a wild Boom Boom tune in her chest. "I'm not a Mars fan, either," she said shakily. "Please move your foot."

"Food? I'm not hungry." With a slight push of his toe, he nudged open the door.

Yes, he was a Mars all right. Stubborn. Determined. And hard of hearing? A new Mars characteristic. She had enough to do—no time to waste energy competing over her door. With a sigh of resignation, she opened it wide. He stepped inside.

"Didn't know Mars was a football player," she said drolly, wondering where Ben had picked up that helmet.

He looked at the helmet she held. "Didn't know Venus was a veteran. Thought she was a lover, not a fighter." Ignoring her look of surprise, Ben looked around. "Packing?"

"Yes. Country girl's heading back to the farm."

He looked back and frowned. "What about your arm?"

"You know," she said loudly, "you'd hear better if you took off that helmet!"

He grinned, that slow, sexy grin that made her boom-booming heart nearly rip through her chest and soar around the room. "But I'm Mars," he explained. "Have to wear my helmet into battle."

"What battle?"

"To win the woman of my dreams."

"It's too late," she whispered. It would never work. She was too competitive, willing even to deceive a wonderful man. He was a caretaker. They'd spend the rest of their lives either irritating each other or resenting themselves. "I can't do this, Ben. I lied to you. I—"

Ben took off his helmet and set it on the coffee table. "Sorry. Couldn't hear with this thing on." But by the twinkle in his eye, she knew he'd heard every word she'd said. Straightening, he looked at the helmet in her hand. "No need to compete, Rosie. You can put your helmet down, too."

Fighting a grin, she set it in a box.

Emotion illuminated his blue eyes as he dragged his fingers through his hair. He still wore the slacks and shirt he'd worn—then shed—in the hotel room. They looked rumpled. His hair looked wild. She liked the overall effect. Tousled. Heated. A man fighting for his love. *Mars battling for his Venus.*

He took a step toward her, stopping when she held her hand up, toward him. "No, Ben."

"Mars."

She half smiled, then pursed together her lips. "It would never work."

He took another step toward her. "I figured, now that you're temporarily unemployed, we'd go to Africa for two, three weeks."

"Africa—?" She paused. "Kansas. I'm leaving tomorrow."

"Do your brothers know?"

"I'll tell them when they get back from whoever they're currently stalking."

"About that," Ben said under his breath. "Did you know they stalked us to Starbucks as a ploy to bring us together? Heather confessed."

"To bring us together?"

"Seems my exes convinced them I was a good catch." He winked. "Which I am, you know." He pulled an envelope from his shirt pocket and held it up for Rosie to see.

"Another letter for Mr. Real?" she guessed.

"Glad you brought that up," he said, still holding the envelope high. "I reread his, uh, *your* letters. You're a wise woman, Rosie Myers. Caring. Intelligent. Maybe a little self-serving..." He grinned, obviously referring to her suggestions, when she was writing as Mr. Real, that Ben go after an independent, adventurous woman much like herself. "But you changed my life, Rosie. I thought I was caretaking you, but you know what? That's my old history, has nothing to do with what's going on between you and me. All you ever wanted to be was my lover, my friend."

Tears prickled the corners of her eyes. She wanted to say something, but when she opened her mouth, she couldn't find the words.

"And you think you're so competitive," he said, chiding her.

She swiped at the corner of her eye. "I am!"

"But not to your detriment. This had to do with your job. Your deceptions had nothing to do with me. We didn't even know each other then. You're competitive when you should be—at work. Okay, and competitive over that damn parking space, but let's chalk that up to work-related. But with me, my sweet Rosie, you were supportive. Loving."

"When—when was I supportive?"

"Those letters. You cared about my predicament. You offered me friendship." He took another step toward her. Now he was almost toe-to-toe with her. His musky cologne teased the air, tormented her senses.

Ben looked at Rosie's big, sad eyes. That wayward curl was mixed in with the rest of her hair. He reached up, tugged a strand and pulled it gently down the center of her forehead. "That's better," he murmured. He liked that curl in the center of her forehead.

"Want to know what this is?" he asked again, glancing at the envelope.

After a pause, she shrugged. "I give up." Then she grinned. She'd just admitted she didn't always compete.

"Two round-trip tickets to Africa."

She stared at him so long, he wondered if she'd zoned out on him. "Isak and Peter?" he prompted.

Her eyes grew bigger.

"You'll write? I'll take pictures?"

"Is this your way of saying you're sorry for getting me fired?"

He brushed aside her comment. "Oh, that! Paige—that's her name, right?—called me. Said she'd been trying frantically to phone you, but you weren't answering. Said she'd made a *big* mistake firing you. Said your friend Pam—and others—had explained a lot of things to her. Paige also said *People* magazine got hold of your story—wants to do a piece on your Mr. Real stint, titled 'A Rosie by Any Other Name.' Great publicity for you, for *Real Men*. Marketing's thrilled."

"*People* mag—?"

"I told Paige you'd consider the new job offer—as a staff editor at *Real Men*—after we're back from our honeymoon."

"Honeymoon?"

He scooped her into his arms. She fit perfectly in the crook of his embrace. He liked the feel of her silky hair brushing his jaw. Loved those big hazel eyes wide with questions.

Questions he'd answer in a moment.

Holding her, he crossed to the open door and strode

outside onto the balcony. Warm sunlight streamed down on them. A light breeze brought a trace of roses.

"Are you crazy?" Rosie said, squirming a little. But she stopped when she saw her four brothers, plus Pam, standing below on the sidewalk, grinning, looking up at them.

Ben held Rosie so tightly against him, she swore she could feel his heartbeat—and now *it* was boom-booming. "Rosalind Myers," he said loudly, "will you marry me?"

She looked down at her brothers and Pam, their wide smiles saying more than words. They were joyous for Rosie. But not as joyful as she felt. After pretending to be different goddesses, she no longer had to pretend. Venus, love, had really entered her life. Turning to Ben, fighting tears, she said, "Yes, Ben, I'll marry you."

After the cheering and clapping from the street subsided, Ben set her down and cradled her head in his hands. "I figure we can go to the Justice of the Peace, then head to Africa. In a few months, we'll go to Kansas and have a real, down-home wedding. Your mom's already working on the wedding dress."

Rosie imagined her mother leaning close, whispering, "Rosalind, you're so pretty."

"And after Africa," Rosie whispered, "and Kansas, where will we live?"

Ben grinned. "We'll live part-time on Venus, part-time on Mars."

Forget Me? <u>Not</u>
DARLENE GARDNER

HARLEQUIN®

TORONTO • NEW YORK • LONDON
AMSTERDAM • PARIS • SYDNEY • HAMBURG
STOCKHOLM • ATHENS • TOKYO • MILAN • MADRID
PRAGUE • WARSAW • BUDAPEST • AUCKLAND

Dear Reader,

My sister has a friend who dated the same boy from the eighth grade through her senior year in college. I used to wonder why she didn't open her eyes to the masculine possibilities around her. Of course, he could have been her soul mate. But what if he wasn't? What if she met him so young that she only thought she knew what love was?

Those questions inspired me to write this story, my first book for Duets. Amanda has barely looked at another man in ten years of dating until her fiancé gets cold feet and zany, unpredictable Zach swoops into her life. Then she does much more than look.

I hope you fall in love with fun-loving Zach right along with Amanda. I know I did. I also discovered I adore writing romantic comedy.

By the way, my sister's friend has been happily married for a dozen years. And, no, her husband isn't the guy she met in eighth grade!

Happy Reading!

Darlene Gardner

P.S. Readers who are online can write me at darlgardner@aol.com.

To my husband, Kurt, who knows why

1

"YOU'RE BREAKING our engagement six weeks before the wedding?"

The woman's incredulous voice carried over the highback, leather bench seat to where Zach Castelli sat in the next booth. He took a swig of water and located the nearest clock, which was mounted on wooden paneling across the restaurant. His sister was thirty minutes late for their dinner date, which he could have predicted. Marlee wouldn't be Marlee if she could keep track of dates and times. He sighed. Without his sister to occupy him, it was going to be nearly impossible to avoid overhearing the death knell of a relationship.

"It's six and a half weeks, not six," a cultured, carefully modulated male voice replied. "I thought it would be better to tell you now than to wait until the wedding invitations were mailed."

"I mailed the invitations two days ago."

The woman had lowered her voice considerably, but Zach still heard her clearly. The acoustics in this restaurant, he thought idly, were better than those at the rock concert he'd attended at the Miami Arena the other night. Whatever twinge of guilt he might have felt for listening to words not meant for his ears vanished in curiosity about why the man had waited so long to end the relationship.

"Nevertheless, it's best that we cancel the wedding sooner, rather than later. It's early enough that you should be able to recover most of the deposit money. I'd wager that the Coral Springs Country Club will refund the deposit for the hall. You know how much in demand the club is for these types of functions. They'll be able to book the place without any trouble. You might even be able to return your wedding dress, considering that you haven't worn it."

"Reid, will you stop talking about money?"

The woman was clearly distressed, but she was making an obvious effort to keep her composure. Her voice was lower in pitch than most female voices he had heard, causing Zach to think of textured satin. He wrinkled his nose. Where had that thought come from? Before he could think of an answer, the woman spoke again. "You just told me that you no longer want to marry me. I deserve an explanation."

Zach nodded in agreement, and couldn't stop himself from leaning out of his booth and looking over his shoulder in the hope of glimpsing the occupants in the next one. Only Reid was visible, and he fit Zach's mental image to perfection. He wore an impeccably tailored dark suit over a white shirt and a silk tie in a muted pattern. His dark hair was precision cut, and he had the bland good looks of a man who spent his time in the office rather than under the sun. Reid looked like the kind of jerk who would value money over romance.

"Of course you deserve an explanation, Amanda."

So her name was Amanda, Zach thought. From the sound of her voice and her name, she was probably as cool and cultured as her companion. He took another drink of water.

"You, better than anyone, know how many hours I've been putting in at the law firm. It's imperative that I make a good first impression, so the firm's demands on my time are not negotiable. This simply isn't the best time to take on the added responsibility of marriage."

"You make our relationship sound so..." She seemed to be groping for a word.

"Unromantic," Zach supplied under his breath.

"...oppressive," she finished.

"Oh, come now, Amanda. That's a little harsh, don't you think? I'm trying to say that relationships take time, and I don't have that time to give. You don't either, for that matter. You're a highly independent woman. Your job consumes most of your time, and your mother takes up the rest. I don't think this marriage is in your best interest, either."

"Don't you turn the tables on me, Reid Carrigan," she said softly, with a composure Zach admired.

Reid was trying to shift the blame for the broken engagement from his shoulders to hers, and she was having none of it. Good for her.

"I was doing nothing of the sort," he said with a stilted voice. He obviously hadn't enjoyed being put in his place. "I was simply stating that this isn't the right time for either of us to marry."

"When will be the right time? In case you haven't been keeping track, we've been going together for ten years."

Ten years! Zach leaned out of the booth for another quick glance at Reid Carrigan, who appeared to be in his mid-twenties. If the woman were the same age, that meant they had been dating since high school. Zach shook his head. He'd recently turned thirty, and he could barely remember the names of the girls he'd dated in high school.

"I rather think there won't be a right time," Reid said.

She didn't answer for a long time, and Zach was rooting for her to hold on to her dignity in the face of Reid's callousness. Amanda wasn't some woman this Reid character had wooed and hastily decided to wed. This was somebody he had known for a decade.

When Amanda spoke, it was in an unwavering voice.

"So this is it? You're saying that those ten years no longer mean anything?"

"Of course they mean something. I'll treasure each and every one of those years. You've been a major part of my life, Amanda. Letting you go is the hardest thing I've ever done, but I feel strongly that it's the right course of action for both of us."

Silence descended over the table, and Zach wondered why Amanda had wasted ten years on somebody as self-serving and sanctimonious as Reid. He wouldn't spend ten minutes with the guy, even if it were only across a pool table. Conversation buzzed around him, but Zach tuned it out, listening closely for Reid's next comment.

"Could I have the ring?"

"Excuse me?"

"Grandmother Carrigan's ring. It's a family heirloom, and since you're no longer going to be part of the family..."

"Just take your precious ring," Amanda retorted, and Zach pictured her wrenching it from her finger and flinging it at him. In actuality, she was probably handing it over with the most civil of manners, but Zach fervently hoped not. He disliked Reid more with each overheard syllable.

"I appreciate that, Amanda. My fondest wish is to see my bride wearing this ring one day."

Whatever reply Amanda, who had been going to be his bride up until about twenty minutes ago, would have made was cut off by the arrival of a waitress wearing a tight miniskirt. She set a pair of menus on their table and, oblivious to the tension radiating from her customers, proceeded to recite the specials of the day before leaving them to decide on their culinary choices.

Zach leaned back in his seat, a little ashamed for having eavesdropped. He typically didn't waste time on self-recriminations, but he couldn't remember ever having listened in on a private conversation. In this case, the only way he could have avoided it was by leaving the restaurant. He looked at the clock again. Since it was obvious that Marlee wasn't going to show, that's probably what he should do.

"What are you going to order?" Reid's voice again drifted over the back of the booth.

"Do you honestly expect me to have dinner with you after you just broke our engagement?" Amanda was talking again, and Zach was listening. He couldn't help himself.

"I suppose I do see your point." Reid paused. "Shall we leave then?"

"You can leave," she said, putting emphasis on the pronoun. "I'd like to be alone."

"Be reasonable, Amanda. How will you get home?"

"I'm a highly independent woman, remember? I can manage to call myself a taxi."

"But..."

"Just get out of here, Reid." Her soft voice shook slightly. In the next moment, Reid left the booth and strode out of the restaurant, his head high and his posture erect, as though he hadn't just engineered the clumsiest, most dispassionate breakup in the history of relationships. Zach was tempted to follow him and shake him by the fancy lapels of his suit jacket.

"Sir, are you ready to order yet?" The same waitress who had been serving Reid and Amanda stood alongside Zach's table, smiling at him. She was petite with a cherubic face framed by a profusion of dark, curly hair, and Zach thought she was maybe eighteen years old.

"Actually, since it looks like I've been stood up, I'm going to get going," he said, throwing a few bills on the table.

Marlee had heard about this restaurant, which was located on a busy commercial street in the heart of Fort Lauderdale, from one of her customers. The decor was a combination of rich, polished wood and green, leafy plants. The dishes listed on the menu contained ingredients such as tofu, bean sprouts and baby carrots. It was definitely not Zach's kind of place. "Sorry to take up a table."

"It was no problem," the waitress said, slanting him another flirtatious smile before she picked up the bills and walked away. He stood, a little amused by her attentiveness. He would have walked out of the restaurant if he hadn't heard a sniffle.

The sound was so soft that at first he wasn't sure he had identified it correctly. He stopped and listened. There it was again. There was no way around it. The second sound was undeniably a sniffle.

Aw, hell. Amanda whatever-her-last-name-was seemed to be crying.

Zach was a lot of things, but cold-hearted wasn't one of them. He couldn't stand it when a woman cried. It made him want to do something, anything, to stem the liquid flow.

Here goes, he thought, before his brain kicked in with all the reasons he should change his decision. He pasted on a smile, pivoted, walked a few steps and slid into the booth across from a woman who didn't look anything at all like he'd pictured.

She had thick red-gold hair that she'd attempted to tame by gathering it into a chignon, but tendrils of it had escaped and softened the effect. Her face was a pale oval with a smattering of freckles that had been almost entirely camouflaged by makeup. Her quivering mouth was wide and full, her lashes surprisingly dark and thick. Her eyes, when she looked at him, were green and confused.

"Hello, Amanda," he said, and this time his smile was

genuine. She was the most appealing woman he had seen in a long time.

Amanda Baldwin lifted her chin and encountered the wildest shirt she had ever seen. It was shot through with color and looked like an artist had taken a blank canvas and thrown paint at it. Above the shirt was a sun-bronzed face that contained the bluest, sunniest eyes and whitest teeth she had ever seen. He had a high, wide forehead, a dimple in his right cheek and a slight cleft in his chin. An unruly mop of brown hair with golden highlights completed an attractive package, one she was sure she had never seen before. Except that he had called her by name.

"Do I know you?" She blinked a few times to dry the tears that had pooled in her eyes. One of them escaped and slid down her cheek. She wiped it away, horrified that this man had caught her crying. She never cried. Not only was it undignified, but a waste of time where Reid was concerned.

"The name is Castelli," he said, extending one of his hands. She stared at it, noting that it was attached to an arm that was as sun-kissed as his face. The arm, muscular and long, was sprinkled with tiny, golden hairs. "Zach Castelli."

"Do I know you?" she repeated, trying not to be amused at an introduction that had been stolen straight out of a James Bond film.

He grinned, tipping his head to the side with boyish charm, not at all insulted that she had ignored the hand he offered. If he'd perfected that look as a child, Amanda would bet his mother had never yelled at him for sticking his hand in the cookie jar.

"You know me now. I just introduced myself."

His answer was as cheeky as his smile. Amanda temporarily forgot her misery as she stared at him open-mouthed.

"Look, Mr. Castinelli..."

"It's Castelli. But you can call me Zach. Everybody does."

"Mr. Castelli," she began again, but he interrupted again.

"Zach."

"Okay, then, Zach," she conceded, exasperated. "I was about to order dinner..."

He picked up one of the menus on the table and opened it. "Good. I haven't ordered yet either. Have you ever eaten here before? Maybe you can recommend something, as long as it doesn't have sprouts. I don't think I can make myself eat a sprout."

She stared at him, wide-eyed with fury. Was the man dense or was he deliberately ignoring what she had just said? "Mr. Castelli..."

"Zach." He peered at her from over the menu, his blue eyes twinkling. That convinced her that it was time to speak bluntly.

"Zach, I'm not in the mood for company. I'd prefer it if you'd leave."

"I don't believe that," he said, setting down the menu. "Nobody likes to eat alone. Take me, for example. I was supposed to meet my sister Marlee here. She's wonderful, even if people do find her a bit bizarre. That's probably because she's a body painter. Anyway, Marlee's great when it comes to the big picture. But she tends to forget details, like the time and place she was going to meet her brother for dinner. So that's why I'm alone. When I saw that you were alone, I thought why should we both be alone when we could be together?"

"You're deliberately misunder..." Amanda's voice trailed off before she could finish her thought as something belatedly registered in her mind. "Your sister paints people's bodies?"

He nodded, set down his menu and rested his elbows on the table, his chin on his knuckles. "Uh-huh. She has a little storefront on Hollywood Beach. She'll paint anything you want. A flower, a butterfly, a snake, a lion. She uses this special ink that wears off after a couple of washings. I'll take you there and you can see for yourself, maybe even get yourself painted."

"I'm not the sort of woman who gets her body painted," Amanda said, realizing that their conversation was growing more absurd by the minute. "And what do you mean you'll take..."

"I think a butterfly would look pretty right there," he interrupted, reaching across the table and touching the hollow of her throat. Since she was wearing a tailored business suit, the scoop-necked, cream blouse under it provided practically the only exposed area of skin.

His finger lingered for a moment, infusing the skin with warmth, before he removed it. Amanda reasoned that she hadn't swatted away his hand because she was shocked by his boldness. She didn't realize that her fingers now covered the spot he had touched.

"Are you ready to order?"

The question came from the waitress who had recited a litany of specials to Amanda and Reid in what seemed a lifetime ago. She was grinning, her dark eyes moving from Zach to Amanda until they settled on Zach. He smiled back at her.

"I see you decided to stay for dinner after all," she said.

"Yes. Amanda here has been kind enough to allow me to join her."

His comment caused Amanda to realize that she hadn't agreed to anything of the sort. Before she could say so, he ordered a glass of draft beer along with a sproutless chicken dish. Since Amanda had yet to open a menu, it was easiest to say that she'd have what Zach was having when the waitress asked for her selection.

The waitress took the menus and walked away, leaving Amanda a bit bewildered. Zach's eyes hadn't left her face, and there was an amused glint in them.

"I just agreed to have dinner with you, didn't I?" she asked, still not sure how it had happened.

"You did," he confirmed.

Amanda found herself thinking that there couldn't be any harm in sharing a meal with him. It was certainly preferable to sitting here alone, trying to figure out what had gone wrong between her and Reid. How could she mourn what might have been when she was with a man wearing a shirt as ridiculous as Zach's?

"That's some shirt."

"Do you like it?" He seemed to assume that she did. "My nephew picked it out. He's four. He told his dad—that's my brother Clay—that it reminded him of me."

"Is that a good thing?" she asked warily.

"Of course it is, Amanda."

His use of her name brought up another issue, one that she had nearly forgotten amid the swirl of talk about body painters, inedible sprouts and psychedelic designs.

"You still haven't told me how you know my name."

The corners of his mouth drooped, diluting his smile. His eyes shifted, and he paused a few seconds too long before he answered. "It was a lucky guess. You look like an Amanda."

"You're a lousy liar."

He sighed dramatically. "Tell me about it. You'd think that, after all these years, I'd learn not even to try. I bet your second-grade teacher didn't figure out that you were the one who put the frog into her desk drawer. All because I couldn't look her straight in the eye when she asked me if I did it."

"I didn't put a frog in my second-grade teacher's desk drawer."

"Well, then, you should have. The look on her face when that sucker jumped out was worth all those hours clapping erasers."

Amanda frowned. How had they started talking about frogs? Hadn't she been questioning him about how he knew her name? This man Zach wasn't good at lying, but he was an expert at distraction. "We're getting off the subject. You were going to tell me how you knew my name was Amanda."

"I was?"

She nodded solemnly, and he finally shrugged in resignation.

"Okay. I heard Reid call you by name."

"You know Reid?" she asked, shocked. Zach's mouth twitched, his eyes shifted, his smile faded. Amanda had just met him, but even she could tell that another lie was coming.

"Well, yes. He and I are, er, cousins. Distant cousins, which is probably why he never told you about me."

She shook her head slowly, amazed and a little amused that anyone could lie that poorly. Then the probable truth occurred to her, and she no longer found him so humorous.

"You were eavesdropping," she accused.

He winced. "No, I wasn't eavesdropping. That would mean that I wanted to listen to what you were saying, and I didn't. I tried not to hear. I almost put my hands over my ears."

"I can't believe this. That was a private conversation, not to mention one of the most humiliating experiences of my life. How could you possibly eavesdrop on something so personal?"

"I told you. I wasn't eavesdropping. And if it was such a private conversation, Reid should have picked a private place to have it." He paused and stroked his chin. "Then again, he probably thought it was easier to break up with you in a public place so you wouldn't create a scene."

"A scene?" Amanda's voice rose, and a few of the diners at adjacent tables glanced at her. She lowered her tone. "I've never created a scene in my life."

"I didn't think that you had, which means that I'm giving you more of the benefit of the doubt than Reid did. If your engagement wasn't already broken, I'd be suggesting that you break it. Reid seems to have ice where his heart should be."

Pain stabbed at Amanda. But she was surprised that she had forgotten about it. Since Zach Castelli had slid into the booth, she hadn't spared Reid and her broken engagement more than a passing thought. The harsh reality was that not only wasn't she getting married next month, but a ten-year relationship was over.

"He *was* cold about the whole thing, wasn't he?" she asked reflectively, and Zach nodded.

"You're well rid of him."

"Oh, I am?" Again the pain faded as she considered the outrageous man in the equally outrageous shirt. Now he was dispensing advice on her love life!

"Yes, you are. What I'm trying to understand is why it took you ten years to figure it out."

"Figure what out?"

"That you're well rid of him."

"But I didn't say that I was. You did."

"And I'm right."

He smiled, and she had a crazy urge to smile back. But it was ridiculous, considering that he was making disparaging remarks about a man she had known and loved forever. A man, she reminded herself, who had canceled their long-awaited wedding as though it were inconsequential.

The waitress chose that moment to arrive with cool bottles of brew and steaming plates of food. "I made sure the chef held the sprouts," she told Zach.

Zach picked up a fork in one hand and a knife in the other and held them upright on the table. "Excellent," he drawled, stretching the syllables. This time Amanda couldn't prevent the smile from creeping onto her face.

When the waitress retreated, Zach took a bite and chewed thoughtfully. "Not bad, although it doesn't compare to a juicy burger."

"Chicken is much better for you."

He finished another bite before he replied, and she found that she enjoyed watching him eat. She hadn't been conscious of it until this moment, but Zach Castelli was quite something to look at. He had a strong jawline, and a tiny Adam's apple that retreated and advanced as he chewed. His tan was so deep that it accentuated his blue eyes.

"I bet Reid doesn't eat hamburgers."

"Reid's a vegetarian."

"Aha!" he said, pointing his fork at her triumphantly. "I always say that you can't trust a man who won't ingest red meat. It's positively un-American."

Her smile made another appearance, and she held up a hand. She was starting to fall into the ebb and flow of their preposterous conversation. "I know what you're going to say. That it should have taken me less than ten years to figure that one out, too."

"Ten years is a long time," Zach said. "How old were you when you started going out with the guy anyway? Nine?"

"I was sixteen. A sophomore in high school," she said, indignant that he thought her a teenager, until she noticed the teasing glint in his eyes. They really were the most incredible shade of blue. "Reid took me on my first date."

"Surely you've had other boyfriends," Zach said, as though it were a given. Amanda shook her head, and he stopped eating. He was staring at her as though she were an alien life-form. "You can't be saying that Reid is the only man you've ever dated."

"He's the only man I've ever wanted to date."

"You went to college, didn't you?"

"I have an MBA from UM," she replied, a shortcut way of saying she had a master's degree in business administration from the University of Miami.

"College is full of available single men. You must have dated a few of them."

"Reid went to UM, too," Amanda said. "By then, we were already going steady."

The word seemed terribly outdated and juvenile when she spoke it. At noticing Zach's widened eyes, Amanda frowned. She'd never thought it the least bit strange that Reid had been the only man in her life, but she realized how it must seem to somebody like Zach. He probably changed women as often as he changed shoes.

"I'm not like other women you know," she said, not bothering to question why she wanted to make him understand. "Once I found what I wanted, I stopped looking."

"But how do you know what you want until you've tried a few samples?" Zach asked, looking contemplative. "Take candy, for example. Let's say you bite into a piece of dark chocolate. Chances are you'll think it's delicious. But then, suppose that you get adventurous and sample some milk chocolate. It practically melts in your mouth. In comparison, it's far better than dark chocolate. Finally, imagine that you take a taste of premium milk chocolate. It's creamier, richer and smoother than run-of-the-mill milk chocolate. The very best of all."

She scowled at him, even though he made maddening sense. If you could stretch your brain enough to equate men with chocolate...she searched for a hole in his argument and found one.

"Not everybody likes milk chocolate better than dark chocolate," she said triumphantly. Her dinner had become secondary to their conversation, but he'd been eating steadily. She waited for him to finish chewing.

"My point exactly." He shook his index finger at her. "If you don't try both, you'll never know which you prefer."

"This is ridiculous," Amanda muttered under her breath. She wasn't sure when she'd had a more ludicrous conversation. Never, she decided. She took a swig of beer and wrinkled her nose at the bitter taste that flooded her mouth. He laughed, and she found herself likening the rich, smooth sound to premium milk chocolate. She chastised herself.

"If you don't like beer, why did you order it?"

"That's it?" Amanda arched her brows. "You're going to ask me a straightforward question without hidden meaning, instead of implying that Reid is like a bottle of bitter beer?"

His laugh grew deeper, richer. His eyes crinkled at the corners with much-used laugh lines. "You said it, not me."

"But I was joking." Her tone was plaintive.

"Okay, then. Here's a simple question. What are you doing with that MBA of yours?"

She blinked, momentarily nonplussed, because it was a simple question. She'd been expecting him to exercise his uncanny knack to scramble her brains. "I'm a systems analyst."

He held up a hand and waved it slightly, a corner of his mouth lifting self-deprecatingly. "Sorry. I'm at a loss. I don't know what that means."

"It means I work with computers. A lot of what a systems analyst does involves improving current computer operations."

"Do you mean you're a computer repairman?"

"No." Amanda shook her head. "Maybe you'll understand better if I tell you what I'm doing now. The company I work for, Systems for the Twenty-First Century, is putting in a new computer system at the *Fort Lauderdale Times* newspaper. I'm part of a team that's getting the system running and helping to teach the employees how to use it."

"And that takes up too much of your time?"

"It does not." The scowl she slanted him was intended partly for Reid, who had made the charge, and partly for Zach, who had obviously overheard it. "I seldom work more than nine hours a day, which is reasonable, considering I usually break for lunch."

"So it's your mother who takes up too much of your time?"

"She most certainly does not." Amanda's tone was indignant, even though Reid's assessment had some validity. She phoned her mother daily and visited frequently, more so lately because her mother had been helping to plan the wedding.

"Isn't that what Reid said?"

"Since when are you on Reid's side?"

"Let's get something straight." The twinkle had gone out of his eyes, and they looked straight into hers. "I wouldn't be on Reid's side if we were both playing on the same team for the Stanley Cup."

"What's the Stanley Cup?"

"It's like the World Series of ice hockey."

"And the World Series is a football thing?"

He chuckled. "It's a baseball thing. Don't you know anything about sports?"

"I don't have time for sports."

"Is that because you spend so much of it with your mother?"

"You wouldn't understand," Amanda said, absently picking up her beer glass and taking another swallow. Again, she grimaced.

"Why wouldn't I?"

"You're not an only child. You meet your sister for dinners. Your brother's little boy gives you shirts. I bet your mother and father gather the whole family together in a house that has pictures by Norman Rockwell hanging from the walls."

"My mother's dead," Zach said quietly, and Amanda's eyes instantly filled with compassion.

"I'm sorry. That was incredibly insensitive of me." Before Amanda opened her mouth again, she knew she was going to confide her entire family story. She didn't have a clue as to why. "My father's dead, too. He died in a car wreck when I wasn't much more than a baby. That's why I worry about my mother. I hate to admit this, but she'd be better off if she married again. She has a dependent personality, and I'm the only one around to take care of her. But I'm starting to think that one-man women run in my family. I don't think Mother's been on a date since Dad died."

"Have you tried to fix her up?"

"Repeatedly," Amanda said with resignation. "Although I don't think she realizes it. I'll occasionally have someone her age over to my place for dinner and invite her, but it never goes further than that. I think she thinks I have an affinity for developing friendships with men in their fifties."

Zach laughed, and the sound reverberated through Amanda. It was unaffected and joyous, not at all like Reid's restrained laughter. Her fiancé, make that ex-fiancé, acted as though he thought laughter undignified. She immediately felt guilty for comparing the two men, especially since Reid had come out unfavorably. He no longer deserved her loyalty, but it would take longer than a night to break the bond she had had with him.

"I know what you mean, but my father caught on to Marlee, Clay and me a long time ago. He would get so mad when we introduced him to some eligible lady that we haven't tried it in years."

"He doesn't date, either?"

"No. Although some of the ladies in the neighborhood have tried to rope him in." Zach reached into his back pocket, pulled out a wallet and flipped to a photo of an older version of himself. The man's hair was graying and character lines were etched into his face, but he had the same blue eyes and the same winning smile as Zach. "That's my papa."

"You keep a picture of your father in your wallet?"

"And my sister, brother, niece and nephew. Why shouldn't I? I love them." His voice didn't hold a trace of embarrassment at the declaration. He closed his wallet and returned it to his pocket. "Besides, who else am I going to have pictures of? I'm not married, thank God, so I don't have kids of my own."

"Do you find marriage objectionable?" Amanda asked, picking up on his editorial comment. For some reason, it irked her.

He shrugged. "Guilty as charged."

"What's wrong with marriage?"

"Nothing..." one of his eyebrows rose "...if you want to end up divorced."

"That's a cynical comment," Amanda said irritably. "Not everybody gets divorced."

"You're right. Some people just live unhappily ever after."

"You can't possibly be saying you believe there are no happy marriages."

"Sure, there are happy marriages," Zach said easily,

"but having one is about as likely as a snowstorm in Fort Lauderdale. Speaking strictly for myself, I thrive on warm weather."

She raised her eyebrows. "So you're never getting married?"

"That's right."

"What if you fall in love?"

"I won't," he said with confidence. "The women I date know that right off the bat. Anyone who wants a serious relationship doesn't want me."

Why that irritated her, Amanda didn't know.

"Does your family have the same views on marriage as you do?" she asked.

"Hardly." Zach smiled broadly. "Papa hates it when I talk this way. He and my mother were happily married for twenty-five years, and old Paul thinks marriage is a natural state."

"Paul." Her voice was incredulous. "Your father's name is Paul?"

"What's so strange about that?"

"My mother's first name is Pauline."

His eyes lit up. "Hey, that gives me an idea. Papa's family is Italian, and he's a killer cook. Most Sundays he has the whole clan over for dinner. Why don't you and your mother come this Sunday? Papa never minds a few more around the table. I'll just tell him I made some new friends."

"I don't think so…"

"Why not? You were just complaining that your mother never dates. And her name's Pauline while my papa's name is Paul. Don't you think that's a sign that they'll hit it off? If you come along, he'll never suspect a thing."

Amanda was about to refuse more strenuously when a thought struck her. "Why would you want to fix our parents up when you feel the way you do about marriage?"

"What does marriage have to do with our parents? Just because you date somebody doesn't mean you have to marry them. I'm all for Papa meeting a nice lady and having a good time."

"But inviting us over for dinner? It's so...impulsive."

"What's wrong with being impulsive." He shrugged, his brow crinkling.

"Plenty," Amanda retorted. "You can't just go through life saying whatever comes into your mind and doing whatever you please."

"Why not?"

"Because." Amanda stared at him, and not a single reason occurred to her, although she knew there must be plenty. "Because you just can't, that's why. Take this family dinner, for example. You can't go around inviting strangers to family dinners."

"You're not a stranger."

"Yes, I am. You don't even know my last name."

"What is it?"

"Baldwin," she said.

He grinned. "I know it now."

"But you don't know much more about me than my name. We're two strangers who happen to be having dinner together. When we're through eating, our relationship will end."

He was finished with his meal, and he gestured to her full plate. "Speaking of dinner, you better eat yours."

"I'm not very hungry," she said, realizing he had changed the subject again. He really was the most exasperating man.

"If you don't eat some of that, you're going to regret it."

"Why?" she asked, looking at him as though he were speaking another language. Half the time she couldn't follow his train of thought.

"Because you're going to need the energy. I'm taking you dancing."

"I haven't gone dancing in years," Amanda protested.

He smiled, and she tried to think of another man in her acquaintance who had a dimple. Reid certainly didn't.

"That's why I want to take you."

2

THE MUSIC THRUMMED an incessant beat that Zach's body echoed as he watched Amanda on the crowded dance floor. She looked like a different woman than she had at the restaurant. About an hour into their dance-a-thon, her red-gold hair had come partially loose and she'd taken out the rest of the pins to let it cascade past her shoulders.

She'd also removed her suit jacket, revealing a simple, short-sleeved blouse that he suspected was silk. Combined with the mid-length navy skirt, she should have looked staid, but he'd never seen a woman appear so sexy in a blouse and a skirt.

Her body wasn't the stuff of typical male fantasies, but it was exactly the type that he preferred. She was on the tall side, he'd guess about five-feet-eight, with small, high breasts and a slender waist. Her hips flared nicely into what he thought was her best feature—slender legs that seemed to go on forever, despite her sensible, low-heeled shoes. He envisioned her legs wrapped around his waist, and his jeans tightened uncomfortably.

When in the name of displaced chivalry had this happened?

This wasn't what he'd intended when he made the impulsive decision to join her in her booth. He hadn't even known what she looked like then. He'd heard her muffled sobs, and all he'd wanted was to cheer her up. He certainly hadn't harbored any motive of getting into her bed.

If he acted on his impulses, which he usually did, bed

is exactly where he suspected they'd end up. If they did, he'd open himself up to charges that he'd been intending to sleep with her all along. That he'd taken advantage of a woman who had just been jilted by her fiancé. That he'd caught her on the rebound.

She gave him an innocent, trusting smile, and a fresh wave of desire washed over him. He tried to will the wanting away as he watched her, but it was impossible. She'd claimed that she wasn't much of a dancer, but her innate grace served her well on the dance floor. With every sway of her body, every turn of her hips, Zach wanted her more.

He gritted his teeth, because this time he wasn't going to surrender to his impulses. Even if it killed him. He'd only known Amanda Baldwin for a few hours, but already her opinion mattered. And he most definitely didn't want her to think of him as a man on the make.

"Enjoying yourself?" he asked near her ear when the song ended.

His warm breath sent delicious pinpricks along her skin.

"Immensely," she replied, surprised that it was true. Whatever instinct that had possessed her to agree to come dancing with him must have been the right one. She supposed, under the circumstances, it would have been perfectly understandable if she'd refused to come with him. But he'd offered to drive her home and said all he wanted in return was more of her company.

"Good," he said.

The lead singer announced that the band was taking a break, and the less-raucous strains of a recorded melody filled the club. For the first time in an hour, Amanda could hear the buzz of conversation instead of the overpowering beat of the music. The place was a throwback to the discos of yesteryear with chrome, steel, mirrors and overhead lights, but it had the reputation for playing the best dance music in the city. She wouldn't have thought it was Zach's kind of place.

"Do you come here often?" she asked.

"Not unless you consider 'once' often," he answered, and she immediately understood that they were at the Dancing Flamingo for her benefit. The place was so overblown, the logo so ridiculous that it was impossible to become introspective and feel sorry for oneself. Even the painting on the front of the building was designed to elicit a smile. A hot-pink flamingo balanced crazily on one leg, its wings akimbo, as though shaking its stuff to an irresistible beat.

Zach took her hand to steer her through the crowd to the table they'd been sharing, and her skin tingled where it came into contact with his. Zach's hand was hard and slightly callused, unlike the feel of Reid's soft grip when he held her hand. But Zach wasn't holding her hand, she reminded herself. He was simply making sure they didn't get separated in the crowd.

"I'm surprised you can dance like that," Zach said when they were back at the table, which miraculously hadn't been claimed. Amanda had tossed her suit jacket across it to indicate it was occupied, but clothing wasn't usually a deterrent to foot-weary dancers. She gratefully sipped the non-alcoholic drink that she'd ordered before the last set, not caring that it had gotten warm. He took a swig of beer.

"Dance like what?" she asked, eyeing him suspiciously.

He laughed. "Don't get defensive. That was a compliment. I meant that I was surprised that you danced so well."

"I took ballet and modern dance lessons when I was a little girl, but it's been so long since I've danced that I'd forgotten how much I enjoy it," Amanda confided. She was unwilling to enter a discussion about why she never went dancing with Reid. Zach would surely imply that their relationship had been stale and boring. "I'm going to have to make a habit of saying yes whenever a good-looking man asks me out dancing."

His eyebrows rose inquiringly, and he looked inordinately pleased. "So you think I'm good-looking?"

"Stop fishing for compliments," she scolded, surprised at what she'd admitted. Oh, well, there was no use denying it now. "I just said that I did."

He grinned again, making no secret that her assessment meant something to him. It was nothing but the unvarnished truth. He had the healthy look of a man who spent a lot of time outdoors. His wholesome appearance, though, was bedeviled by a sinfully sexy mouth and those sparkling blue eyes.

But it wasn't just his face that she liked. He had an athlete's body, with wide shoulders tapering to a small waist and legs that looked powerful beneath the denim of his jeans. She'd paid attention when they were dancing and she was especially partial to his rear end, which was decidedly more round than Reid's. Zach wasn't as tall as Reid, probably a shade under six feet, but he carried himself with such poise that he appeared taller.

"For the record, then, I think *you're* dazzling," he said, startling her out of her inspection.

"And I think you're a silver-tongued devil," she shot back to cover her confusion at his lavish compliment. It was probably a line, one that a more experienced woman would immediately discount, but she found herself wanting to believe him.

He threw back his head and laughed, a throaty chuckle that gave her yet another thing to like about him. She liked a lot about him, she admitted to herself. How many other men would be nice enough to spend an evening cheering up a rather boring woman who had just been jilted by her fiancé?

"Would you like to dance with the devil?"

She hadn't until that moment realized that the band had finished its break. Dancing with him was heavenly. While other men gyrated, jerked and stamped, he moved smoothly and naturally. Amanda had caught more than one woman staring at him admiringly while they danced. He extended his hand across the table and she put hers in it, smiling into his eyes while she silently acquiesced.

"Amanda!"

A startled voice she instantly recognized sounded somewhere behind her left shoulder, and her hand tightened around Zach's. Amanda turned and her stomach flopped at the sight of the slight, blond man closing in on them.

"Hello, Martin," she said. With his condescending air and self-righteous manner, Martin Kimball had never been one of her favorite people. It had taken an effort to be civil to him throughout the years, and she'd only done so because he was Reid's best friend.

"I saw you on the dance floor, but I thought my eyes were playing tricks on me. And now I find out that it really was you." His eyes shifted to Zach and strayed downward to their still-linked hands. Belatedly, Amanda realized how the scene must look to Martin. She started to pull her hand from Zach's, then changed her mind. She had absolutely nothing to feel guilty about.

"Yes, it really is me." She gave him a thin smile. "Martin, this is Zach Castelli. Zach, Martin Kimball."

She expected the two men to shake after she made the obligatory introduction, but Zach merely nodded, keeping the fingers of his right hand firmly entwined with hers. She was absurdly glad of the contact. It made her feel as though he'd sensed that she didn't care for Martin and that he was on her side.

"Zach, are you a friend of Reid's?" Martin asked smoothly, an artificial smile on his face. Since he traveled in the same social circles as Reid, Amanda suspected he knew perfectly well that the two men weren't friends.

"Nope," Zach said, smiling. "Can't say that I am."

"You do know that Reid is Amanda's fiancé."

Amanda almost laughed aloud at Martin's haughty declaration. Martin was probably more outraged than Reid would have been if he had come upon her in a similar situation.

"I wouldn't be too sure about that," Zach said in the same cheerful tone with which he'd answered the last question.

"I'm quite sure..."

"Martin, Reid and I are no longer engaged," Amanda said, interrupting his indignant statement, her voice steady.

"What? But that's impossible. I received your wedding invitation in this afternoon's mail."

"It just happened," Amanda said, surprised that Reid hadn't confided in his friend about the imminent breakup. More often than not, Martin was his sounding board.

"When did it happen?" Martin asked suspiciously.

"It doesn't matter when it happened, just that it has," Zach said, sounding for all the world like he was her new boyfriend. "Now if you'll excuse us, Martin, Amanda and I were just about to dance."

He didn't wait for Martin to reply, but rose and pulled Amanda to her feet and led her to the dance floor. Martin stared after them open-mouthed. The first slow dance of the evening was playing, and Zach pulled her into his arms. Amanda's heartbeat quickened, but she told herself it was in reaction to Martin's inquisition. It couldn't have anything to do with the delicious way one of her breasts was pressed against the solid expanse of Zach's chest. Or the intimate touch of his thigh against hers.

"I take it that was a friend of Reid's," Zach said, holding her upper body slightly away from his so he could look into her face. Reality intruded on their dance.

"His best friend," she said, making a face. "As soon as Martin can get to a phone, Reid will know that I was at a dance club holding hands with some strange man in a wild shirt."

"Strange man? I'm not sure I like the sound of that," he teased. He asked the next question in the same, light tone. "Does it bother you that Reid will know you've been with me?"

"Bother me? Why should it?" she retorted. "It's not as though we're still engaged."

In answer he smiled and drew her closer, but the magic of a moment ago was gone. She held herself stiffly, picturing Martin on the edge of the dance floor, staring at them with a reproachful gaze. She didn't exactly feel as though she were cheating on Reid, but Martin's obvious disapproval caused her to reassess what she was doing with Zach. She barely knew the man, and here she was cradled in his arms, the length of her body pressed intimately against his.

"It does bother you," Zach said after a minute, drawing back and gazing down at her face to find the truth.

She averted her eyes, then brought them back to his. She wouldn't have pegged him as a perceptive man, but now that he'd guessed what she was thinking, there was no point in lying.

"Maybe a little. It's going to take a while before I can stop thinking of myself as Reid Carrigan's girlfriend."

An emotion she could have sworn was disappointment flickered across Zach's face, and she glanced away. When she looked at him again, it was gone, as if she had imagined it.

"Would you mind terribly if we left?" Amanda asked.

"Not at all."

This time he didn't reach for her hand as they retrieved her suit jacket and threaded their way through the crowd to the exit. Amanda kept her eyes trained on Zach's back as he forged a path, unwilling to let her gaze swing around the room and again meet Martin Kimball's critical stare or to dip lower to reexamine Zach's lovely rear.

The night air was cool when they walked out the door, befitting a February night in South Florida. Zach gazed up at the cloudless sky. Only the brightest stars were visible. The rest were obliterated by the lights of the city. He wished that he and Amanda were alone where only starlight illuminated the night, so she could experience a million stars glittering overhead like scattered fairy dust.

Cars sped by, but the soft whir of tires sounded like little more than whispering after the clamorous interior of the nightclub. Amanda had the look of a deer caught in the headlights of an approaching car. Zach wanted to gather her against his side, but he quashed his instinct to do so.

Running into that friend of Reid's had somehow changed things, and he needed to proceed slowly if he wanted to make any progress with her. A soft, slightly salty breeze blew through her heavy mass of red-gold hair, and she turned her face toward the gust of air. The streetlights illuminated her skin, which was flushed from dancing and tantalizingly touchable. Zach definitely wanted to make progress, he decided.

"Where to?" he asked, as he held open the passenger door of his car. He drove a rakish blue MGA convertible that he and his brother Clay had rescued from a salvage yard. They had restored the British-made car to its present condition, despite repeated warnings that they were wasting their time. They'd succeeded, but only to a point. The car was like a high-spirited racehorse. It looked lovely, but only ran when it wanted to.

"I think you'd better take me home," she said in a small voice. Zach shut the passenger door and got into the driver's seat before turning to her. She kept her eyes straight ahead, although there wasn't anything to see except the other cars in the parking lot.

"Spoken like a woman who doesn't want to go."

"Don't be ridiculous." She cut a glance at him, then looked away again. "Why wouldn't I want to go home?"

"Maybe you just think you should want to go home. The same way you thought you should want to leave the dance club even though you were having a good time."

"I really hate the way you do that." She sounded irritated.

"Do what?"

"Act like you can read my mind."

"I'm not reading your mind. I'm reading your expressions and your tone of voice. And it just seems to me that you're not ready to go home."

"And where do I want to go, Mr. Know-It-All? Keep in mind that it's nearly midnight, and I have to be at work early tomorrow morning."

"I think you'd rather go for a walk on the beach. With me."

"You're wrong," Amanda said quickly, too quickly. "I want to go home."

Zach sighed, because he didn't want the evening to end. In her precarious mental state, he sensed that Amanda was like the sand on the nearby beach. If he let her slip through his fingers, he might never hold her again. "Don't you ever give in to your impulses?"

She really looked at him then, for the first time since they'd left the nightclub. Her face was a pale oval, and her green eyes were troubled. "I'm here with you, aren't I?"

"That's only because I shanghaied you from the restaurant. You never would have sat down in my booth and invited yourself to have dinner with me."

"That's because, unlike you, I don't believe in giving in to my impulses."

"It figures," he said softly.

"What is that supposed to mean?"

"Promise you won't get angry if I tell you?"

"Why should I promise? You're going to tell me anyway. Aren't you the impulsive one who says whatever comes to mind?"

He shrugged. "Okay. I think you're afraid to give in to your impulses, because then you might find out that an orderly life with someone like Reid isn't what you want at all."

"So now reading my mind isn't enough. Now you're psychoanalyzing me. After you've known me for, what, a few hours?"

"You promised you wouldn't get angry."

"I didn't promise," she snapped. "And who said I was angry? Why are we sitting here in the dark anyway? I thought you were going to take me home."

Disappointment stabbed at Zach, because he'd been trying to get her to prolong the evening. He'd sensed that she was angry at herself and her nonsensical reaction to Martin Kimball's disapproval, and he'd pushed too hard. So much for his skills of persuasion. "You haven't told me where you live."

"I live in a townhouse in Plantation about seven miles west of here."

"I could have predicted that."

"Predicted what?" said Amanda in an exasperated voice.

"Forget it," he said, before his penchant for saying what was on his mind got him into even deeper trouble.

"I don't want to forget it."

He shrugged. "Okay. I just meant that I could have predicted that you'd live among the concrete and shopping malls of western Broward County instead of by the ocean."

"Some of us don't go to the ocean." Her voice held an edge.

"That was my point."

"Some of us lead busy lives, with responsibilities and commitments that don't leave time for frivolities such as walking in the sand or swimming in the ocean."

"The same way some of us make sure we don't give in to our impulses?"

"Has anybody ever told you how infuriating you are?"

"If they had, I wouldn't admit it to you." He switched on the ignition and pulled the starter switch. The little car's engine rumbled to life. "Now, how about giving me some directions to your place?"

Fifteen minutes later, as they approached the gated community that contained her townhouse, Amanda was still stewing over the things he'd said in the parking lot. So she wasn't impulsive. As though that were a positive quality.

They hadn't talked at all during the drive, because it would have involved shouting through the wind tunnel that swirled through the little car. It hadn't occurred to Amanda to insist that Zach raise the roof until they were well underway, and by then she was enjoying the unfettered feel of the wind in her face. She would have enjoyed it more if the words "predictable" and "impulsive," which he claimed she wasn't, hadn't been blowing through the car along with the wind.

She probably looked a wreck, she thought, combing her fingers through her hair as the gate attendant recognized her and waved them through with a speculative look. He's wondering what I'm doing with a man who isn't Reid, Amanda thought, unsure of the answer herself.

She studied Zach, who looked even better now that the wind had gotten hold of him. Over the course of the night, she'd grown used to his multicolored shirt, so that it no longer seemed so outrageous. His cheeks were reddened from the slight chill in the air, and his hair was deliciously mussed, the way it probably looked when he got out of bed. Amanda reproached herself. He turned and looked at her expectantly, as though waiting for an answer to a question.

"What?" she blurted.

He looked amused. "You don't have to bite my head off. I just asked which of these places is yours?"

"You did?" she asked, flustered that she hadn't heard him the first time. They were driving through the maze of whitewashed two-story townhouses that were carefully accentuated with tall palm trees, beds of impatiens and splashes of greenery. She'd always thought that the complex was a pretty place, but now she was seeing it through Zach's eyes, and it looked artificial.

She told him where her unit was and leaned back in her seat as he drove halfway around the darkened complex and pulled into a parking spot. Almost all of the lights in the windows of the adjoining townhouses were off, reminding her that the next morning was a work day. Unlike her, the sleeping neighbors were preparing for it. And Zach had said that she wasn't impulsive. Worse, that she was predictable.

She meant to tell him not to bother to walk her to her townhouse, but he quickly got out of the car and opened the passenger door. She was careful not to touch him as she preceded him up the short sidewalk. A pair of steps led to the door, and she climbed one so that she was at eye level when she turned to face him. He had such beautiful eyes, she thought. So blue. So sexy. She blinked, trying to restore her common sense.

"Thank you for driving me home," she said, and immediately realized that her acknowledgment was incomplete. If not for Zach, she would have spent a miserable evening at home crying over her broken engagement. She might still do that tomorrow, but at the moment she seemed numb at the prospect of having lost Reid, as though Zach had injected that part of her heart with something to protect her from the pain. The other part, though, was thumping so loudly she thought he might hear it. "And thank you for sharing dinner with me and taking me dancing. I really had a...good time."

"Was that so hard?"

"Was what so hard?"

"Was that really so hard to admit? That you had a good time with me?"

"Of course not. Why would you ask that?"

"Maybe it was the way you wrenched the words out of your mouth." His eyebrows rose, and she noticed that they were perfectly shaped and thick. "Like you would never have predicted that you could have a good time with someone like me."

"Would you quit saying that I'm predictable!"

Amanda didn't analyze why the word made her so angry. His face was just inches from hers. So close that she could detect the faint stubble that had begun to appear on his lower face. So close that she could see that his lashes were long and thick. So close that he made her want to do something unpredictable. The things he had said at the restaurant about the different flavors of chocolate swirled through her head, and she wondered what he tasted like.

Before she could think about the consequences, she closed the small gap between them and noticed the way his eyes widened and then darkened in the instant before she pressed her lips to his. He tasted like warm breath and wind, she thought, like man and desire, better and more addictive than the finest candy.

Aw, hell, Zach thought, as she molded her mouth to his, easily igniting the passion he had been struggling against. A part of his brain reiterated the silent warning that she would think poorly of him after this, but she tasted so sweet that he was no longer listening to his brain. It went against his nature not to act when he saw something he wanted, and he'd wanted her more with each passing moment. He couldn't worry about tomorrow at the expense of tonight.

Her mouth moved tentatively against his and her hands rested lightly on his shoulders, revealing that she'd seldom played the aggressor. Her innocence flamed a fire low in his groin, and he opened his mouth, inviting her to deepen the kiss. She had incredibly soft lips, and at first she was content to press tiny kisses against his mouth. But then the tip of her tongue flickered forward to touch his, and he was lost.

His own tongue advanced, tangling with hers as his arms drew her against his body. The way her lower body initially retreated, but then shifted to press against the hard evidence that he wanted her, increased his ardor. Had he ever desired a woman this much, this soon? If he had, he couldn't remember when.

He pushed his fingers through the thick hair he had been wanting to touch all night, deepening the kiss as he did so. She was so soft, so pliant. He ran his tongue over her teeth and the slick roof of her mouth until he wasn't sure if the soft guttural sounds he heard came from him or from her.

Then he felt something contradictory to what had been happening between them: the flats of her palms pushing against his shoulders. The pressure was half hearted, as though she weren't sure whether to commit to the gesture, but he gathered his resolve and drew back.

"We...have...to...stop," she rasped, and he knew without a doubt that she was as affected by what had just happened as he.

He almost told her that he could have predicted that, but for once he held his tongue, because he didn't want to give her an excuse to replace desire with anger. He disentangled his fingers from her hair, all the while keeping his eyes on hers.

Amanda looked away, uncomfortable with the desire she saw in his face, and she reached trembling fingers into the small handbag that hung over her shoulder. It took an inordinate amount of rummaging before her hand fastened on her key. She climbed the last step and inserted it into the lock, relieved that she'd been able to do so on the first try. The door swung open, inviting her inside to escape this strange and unfamiliar passion that flowed through her.

She turned back to Zach, intending to say a firm goodnight before she shut the door on the temptation he presented, but he'd also climbed one step. Again they were at eye level, and she would have been blind if she hadn't seen the naked passion on his face.

Nobody had ever looked at her that way. Until this moment, the sort of palpable desire that she read on his face would have been as unwelcome as a flame escaping from a fireplace. But if he could read her expression as easily as he'd read her mind all night, she knew he saw a reflection of what he was feeling.

She cleared her throat.

"Good night, Zach," she said, her voice an unfamiliar croak. It seemed an eternity before he answered.

"G'night."

They stared at each other, neither moving for interminable seconds, until Amanda could stand it no longer. It was as though an invisible magnetic force charged the air between them. She stopped resisting it and reached across the chasm separating them to brush his cheek with her fingers. He captured them, bringing them to his lips.

Afterward, she wasn't sure whether he had pushed her inside her townhouse or whether she had pulled him. She'd never know who shut the door or how they came to be kissing inside the darkened foyer. She only knew that, even though the lengths of their bodies were touching, she wanted to be closer to him. And that she had never been so out of control in her life.

"This is crazy," she murmured against his mouth, but her words were swallowed in his kiss. His tongue slid into her mouth, and she moaned, wanting to experience more of him. A coil of heat had begun deep inside her, beating a tattoo in tempo with her ardor. One of his hands slid up her rib cage and inside her suit jacket to cup her breast through the thin fabric of her blouse. Immediately her nipples tightened and her flesh swelled.

She'd never undressed a man before, but that didn't stop her from tugging Zach's shirt free of his jeans and unfastening the buttons, so she could explore the muscle-hardened skin under the material. When the shirt fell to the floor, Amanda admired the pectoral muscles sprinkled with an ideal amount of soft chest hairs. She couldn't suppress an unexpected giggle. Zach, who had been about to resume trailing delicious kisses along her throat, looked at her quizzically.

"What's funny?" he asked, but she couldn't speak coherently with his hands on her breasts. Certainly not clearly enough to convey that she'd been wondering what he would look like without that ridiculous shirt all evening. "Were you laughing at my shirt?"

"Yes," she admitted, but her giggles turned into whimpers of pleasure when he rubbed the pads of his fingers over her nipples. She'd been picturing him in a different shirt, of course, not in bare skin so beautiful that it could never be enhanced by clothing. "You look...better... without one."

"Why don't you see how I feel?"

She hesitated, but her desire to touch him overcame her shyness. Tentatively, she ran her hands over warm skin that was dusted by hair, reveling in the solid feel of him. When she pressed an open-mouthed kiss to his chest, he made a sound deep in his throat and again became the aggressor. Her suit jacket and blouse followed his shirt to the floor until her upper body was covered only by a lacy bra at odds with her practical clothing.

She held her breath as he worked the front fastener of her bra, and a thread of sanity wove its way into her brain. She, who'd only ever kissed Reid before tonight, was allowing Zach Castelli unthinkable privileges. She circled one of his wrists with her hand, intending to draw it away from her body, but then his fingers trembled.

That simple act of vulnerability weakened her resolve, making her want him with an intensity that was impossible to deny. His eyes flicked questioningly to hers, but the answer in them was clear. Her bra dropped away, and her skin was so heated she didn't even feel the slight chill in the air. When his warm, wet mouth fastened on her breast, her legs gave way. Together, she and Zach sank to the floor.

She was only dimly aware of the cool tile against her legs and the stucco wall pressed against her bare back as he suckled, and the pulse inside her grew more insistent. One of his hands pushed up her skirt, resting tantalizingly on her hip before slowly inching around until it reached the juncture between her thighs. He rubbed softly against the material of her pantyhose and underwear, and she knew that she was already wet with desire.

"Where's your bedroom?" he asked, and only then was she aware of their uncomfortable position. She was sprawled on the floor, and he was leaning over her, half covering her body with his. She drew a shaky breath.

"It's upstairs," she said, surprised that she could talk. "First room on the right."

The invitation was implied in her answer, and Zach didn't wait for a more formal one, immediately rising and scooping her into his arms. Before she could protest that she was too heavy, he strode up the stairs as though he were used to carrying one hundred and twenty-five pounds.

He stopped at the threshold of her bedroom to switch on the light, revealing the pretty pink-and-white bedspread and matching wallpaper border that rimmed the room. The decor was the epitome of femininity, down to the ornate whitewashed makeup table and fancy filigreed mirror. A streak of possessiveness hit Zach, and he couldn't stand the thought of her having brought another man to this room.

"I wish I were the first," he said softly, and she knew instinctively to what he referred.

"In this room, you are," she murmured against his throat, too shy to bring her eyes to his face. "I've never brought another man here."

Zach wasn't naive enough to think that she hadn't been intimate with Reid during their ten-year relationship, but he was absurdly glad that she had never allowed Reid to make love to her in her bedroom. That single fact seemed significant, although he'd have to examine why later. For now, he couldn't focus on anything except the lovely woman in his arms and the effect she was having on him.

He laid her gently on the bed, fearing that she had changed her mind during the walk up the stairs. He had desperately wanted to take her on the bare, cold tile of the foyer, but a sixth sense had warned him that Amanda would be dismayed at not being able to control herself. So he had carried her up the stairs, giving her time to reconsider what he himself wanted more than his next breath.

Her eyes, however, were still bright with passion, the nipples on her small, firm breasts still hard with desire, granting him silent permission to continue where they had left off. He joined her on the bed, taking his time while he peeled off the rest of her clothing, stopping frequently to fondle and kiss her, until she was naked.

"You're so lovely," he said, unable to resist touching her, from the curve of her throat to her pretty arched feet with toenails painted pink. His hands traced the length of her long, smooth legs to her delicately swelling hips to the juncture of her thighs. He touched her there, finding her slick and welcoming.

Then she was tugging at his jeans, and her desire further inflamed his. He rolled away from her, stripping off the remainder of his clothes, and rejoined her so that the length of his naked body was pressed against hers.

She made a series of small noises in the back of her throat as they kissed with lips and tongues and, Zach thought, minds. When her hand came between their bodies to stroke him, he thought he would lose control.

"You don't know what you're doing to me," he said, barely managing to contain himself.

"Good," Amanda murmured, dimly aware that she had never before acted so boldly.

"Good?"

"You're doing..." he parted her legs "...the same thing..." the tip of him pressed against the center of her "...to me."

She could stand the wait no longer. Before he thrust into her, she elevated her hips, enveloping him in her hot tightness. She closed her eyes and it seemed as though the psychedelic swirls of his shirt were imprinted on the backs of her eyelids. Reid had been her only previous lover, and she had thought that sex with him was pleasant, the sensations it evoked fairly uniform. She vaguely wondered why having this man inside her was bliss. Then he began to move and she could think no more.

She wrapped her legs around his waist, binding them together even more tightly, and moved with him in such perfect unison that it belied the fact that this was their first time together. She'd always believed that because of its private nature, lovemaking should be completed in silence. But the moans of pleasure that now filled the room came from her, and she didn't try to restrain them.

A few of her female friends had described what it felt like to lose yourself in a man, but, until this moment, Amanda had thought they were exaggerating. An intense pleasure like she had never known steadily grew within her until it burst into a million pieces, making her feel like a butterfly that had finally emerged from a cocoon.

Then something incredible happened. Zach drove into her a final time, and the eruption that signaled his release echoed in her a new wave of spasms and clamors that rocked her world.

When she could finally move, she wrapped her arms around Zach, unwilling to return to reality. Her body was pleasantly spent, her nerve endings still tingled. In minutes, even before Zach had disengaged his body completely from hers, she started to fall into a deep, dreamless sleep. The last thing she wanted was to analyze the moment or to think about the fact that she had been engaged to another man before the evening had begun.

3

THE BEDSIDE TELEPHONE emitted a shrill ring, interrupting a languorous dream in which a handsome man, who looked a lot like Zach Castelli, offered Amanda a selection of fine chocolates. She was about to ask if she could have him instead of the candy when the phone blared. She groaned, reached for the receiver and cradled it against her shoulder.

"Hello," she said sleepily, her eyes not yet open.

"Amanda, where have you been?"

Reid Carrigan's strident voice carried over the line, bringing Amanda instantly awake and aware of the warm hand covering her bare breast. Her nipple immediately hardened. She turned, and Zach Castelli, the owner of the hand, opened his beautiful blue eyes and smiled lazily. Last night's events returned with a rush, and it felt like her entire body was blushing. She sat up, banging the back of her head against the headboard, and scooted away from his touch. Frantically, she gathered the bedsheets around her nakedness.

"I've been sleeping, Reid," she said, and then became upset with herself for calling him by name. She didn't want Zach to know who she was talking to, but now it was too late. Dim sunlight filtered through the mini blinds on her window and cast thin streaks of light on the bed. Her head throbbed from where she'd banged it against the headboard. "What time is it?"

"Seven o'clock. Are you going to tell me where you were last night?" His voice was so loud that Amanda was sure that Zach could hear every word. Again. She half turned away from him, cradling the receiver closer to her ear, wondering how on earth she had gotten herself into this situation. "Martin called me last night and said he saw you at the Dancing Flamingo with another man. I tried phoning you until midnight, and then I left a message for you to call me."

"I didn't check my machine when I got in," Amanda said, blushing as she remembered that there had been other things on her mind. Her body was pleasantly sore, attesting to what those things were. She hazarded a glance over her shoulder at Zach, who was propped on one elbow, unashamedly listening in on her conversation. She shot him a censuring look, but he merely smiled, his dimple creasing. She again turned away from him.

"Who is this man? Martin said he was wearing an abominable shirt and holding your hand."

His questions finally penetrated her brain, which was still fuzzy with sleep, calling to mind the scene at the restaurant. Considering the things that Reid had said last night, this interrogation didn't make a bit of sense.

"Wait a minute," she said, with more force behind her voice now that she had shaken off her grogginess. "You don't have the right to ask me any questions. Didn't you break up with me last night? I could have sworn I heard you say that the wedding was off."

Behind her, she heard three soft claps. Applause. As though she needed Zach's approval for how she handled her fiancé. Make that ex-fiancé.

"We've been together for ten years, Amanda. Last night was an aberration, a moment of panic. If I had thought it through, I never would have said the things I did. Surely you didn't take me seriously."

"I always take you seriously, Reid," she whispered. "You didn't sound like you were in the throes of panic."

"Why are you whispering? Is somebody there with you?"

"You know me better than that," Amanda said, as shame licked at her body like wildfire gone out of control. She'd never been the kind of woman to take a stranger to bed, but that didn't explain the presence of Zach Castelli nestled among her pink and white sheets. She could still feel the imprint of Zach's body on hers as they surrendered to the mindless pleasure that their passion had brought.

"Then who was this man, and what were you doing with him last night?"

"Listen, Reid, I can't handle this right now," Amanda said, and at least that much was true. She couldn't have a coherent conversation with a man who had been her fiancé until last night, while another man lay naked in her bed listening to every word. His eavesdropping had gotten them into this situation in the first place. "I have to get ready for work."

"I'll pick you up for lunch, and we'll discuss it."

"I'm too busy today to go out to lunch."

"Then dinner. I can be at your office at six o'clock."

"I'm not going to dinner with you, Reid. You can't expect to break our engagement one night and pick up where you left off the next."

"You can't be saying that you want our engagement to stay broken?" His voice was incredulous.

"What I'm saying is that I don't want to go to dinner with you. I don't want to see you. I need time to think about all of this."

Before he could protest further, Amanda pressed the off button on her portable phone, glaring at it as though it embodied Reid.

"Meet me for dinner instead?"

"What?" Amanda whirled to face Zach, forgetting to hold on to the sheet that was covering her. It dipped, revealing one of her breasts. His eyes dropped, his small smile telling her he took pleasure in the sight, and she hastily covered herself again.

"I've already seen you without your clothes on, you know. If you ask me, I think it's a shame to hide anything so beautiful," he said casually, and she colored. Darn this infernal blushing.

"I didn't ask you," she snapped, refusing to be sidetracked. After listening to Reid issuing orders, she didn't need Zach telling her what to do. Even if he looked incredible in the morning with tousled hair, sleepy eyes, stubble on his chin and a sculptured chest that she ached to touch. What is the matter with me? she thought. She took her anger out on him. "And I don't need you telling me who I should or shouldn't have dinner with."

"I wasn't telling you. I was asking if you'd have dinner with me." Her anger bounced off him as easily as a Ping-Pong ball from a paddle. "I know a place on the beach that serves oversize hamburgers and great pizza. There isn't a sprout on the menu."

Amanda gaped at him because he was acting completely natural, as though he woke up in her bed every morning. The covers were bunched around his waist, covering his sex but leaving the rest of him exposed. His chest was as bronzed as the rest of him, which meant he probably spent a lot of time outdoors without a shirt. The golden hairs that dusted the planes and valleys of his chest were repeated on the long, muscular leg that peeked out of the sheets. He had the body of Adonis, and merely looking at him made her want him all over again. Adonis grinned as though he knew what was on her mind.

"Aren't you going to put that phone down?"

She colored again, damning the redhead's tendency toward blushing, and slammed the portable phone's receiver onto the cradle. She hadn't even realized she was still holding it.

"This is insane." She shook her head and closed her eyes.

"What's insane?"

"You. Here. In my bed." She put one hand on her forehead, careful to keep the bedclothes covering her with the other. Her head throbbed. "I don't do this sort of thing."

"I know. You told me," he said, his eyes dancing. She remembered her foolish revelation that she'd never invited another man into her bedroom. On the infrequent occasions that she and Reid had been intimate, they'd stayed at his place. They hadn't been intimate at all for months, because she'd gotten the notion that their honeymoon night would be more special after a long period of abstinence.

And now she'd been to bed with a man she hadn't even known existed until last night. Worse, she'd wanted him so desperately that she'd forgotten the elementary principles of her life. She'd even forgotten the warnings against having unprotected sex with a stranger. Horrified, she realized that the thought of birth control hadn't even crossed her mind.

"I meant I don't go to bed with strangers."

"I thought we established last night that I'm not a stranger," he said, deliberately misunderstanding her. "But if that still bothers you, go ahead and ask me anything at all."

"That's not the point," she retorted, biting her bottom lip until it hurt. "My God, we didn't even use protection. For all I know, you could have a terrible disease."

"I don't have a disease," Zach said quickly, but he looked contrite. "But you're right. We should have protected you. We would have if things hadn't happened so fast. And we will. Next time."

"The fact that you think there will be a next time means

you're entirely missing the point," Amanda rejoined, dismayed.

He blew out a breath. "Then maybe you should tell me what the point is."

"The point," she said succinctly, "is that I don't go to bed with men I barely know."

"So go to dinner with me tonight, and get to know me better."

She shook her head, marveling at his good-natured responses. Didn't he realize that she was trying to brush him off? "I can't go to dinner with you. I can't do anything at all with you. I'm engaged."

For the first time that morning, his smile faded. She'd wanted him to take her seriously, but she was instantly struck with the crazy notion that she wanted his smile back.

"I distinctly remember you becoming disengaged last night," he said.

"Reid's having second thoughts."

"You are, too. I heard you on the phone just now. You didn't sound like a woman about to walk down the aisle when you told him you didn't want to see him. Besides, if you're so sure you want to marry Reid, what are you doing in bed with me?"

Amanda abruptly got out of bed, almost tripping over the frilly quilt she dragged with her. She glared at Zach, wishing she could claim that she'd had too much to drink the night before. But she'd barely touched her beer at the restaurant and had switched to ginger ale afterward. Her headache had nothing to do with a hangover. "That's what I've been wondering ever since I woke up. This is all your fault, you know."

Zach briefly raised his eyes to the ceiling because he had expected this. Even as they'd been intimate the night before, he'd realized on some level that he wouldn't wake up to a warm, willing woman. He hadn't counted on the call from Reid to confuse the matter further.

"I wouldn't use the word fault. There wasn't anything wrong with what we did last night."

"Of course it was wrong," she responded, her expression pained. "I don't live my life like you, doing whatever I feel like doing on the spur of the moment."

"You should try it sometime," he drawled. "You might like it. You did last night."

"Don't start that again. That's why we're in this predicament. Because you don't even try to control your impulses."

Zach stroked his chin, dimly noting that he needed a shave. "If I remember correctly, you kissed me first last night."

"That's your fault too. If you hadn't kept telling me how predictable I was, I never would have done that." She stopped to form her thoughts. "Besides, you didn't have to kiss me back. You knew that I had just broken up with my fiancé. You didn't have to take advantage of me."

"I didn't take anything from you that you didn't want to give," Zach said softly, and Amanda's face crumpled and her lips quivered. In an instant, Zach was out of bed and striding across the bedroom, unashamed of his nudity as he gathered her stiff form to him.

"Aw, honey, don't cry," he murmured into her hair, which was a mass of sweet-smelling strawberry tangles. She relaxed against him for an instant, and his heart softened even though another part of him was already growing hard. "It's never wrong to do what your heart tells you to do."

"I don't want you to comfort me," she said, pushing against his chest and retreating a few steps. She was careful not to look anywhere but at his face. "We're going to have to forget this whole thing ever happened."

He raised skeptical eyebrows. "Are you kidding? Didn't you feel what happened between us last night? You can't believe that either of us will be able to forget it. All I'd have to do to remind you is kiss you again."

She stared at his lips, which were full and moist and inimitably kissable, and only a conscious effort of will prevented her from tasting them again. She concentrated on refuting him as she backed a few steps nearer to the refuge of her bathroom. Her eyes took in his arousal, and an answering need leaped in her traitorous body.

"You're totally out of line to say things like that to me," she said, her voice biting to counteract the craving that was growing inside her. "And you're crazy if you expect me to fall into bed with you whenever you get an urge."

"I didn't say that..."

"Look, last night was a mistake that I'm not going to repeat. I'm not going to change the way I live my life because of a single night. I'm going to take a shower, and when I come out of the bathroom I want you gone."

"Is that what you really want, Amanda, or what you think you should want?"

The question hung suspended between them, and Zach thought that both of them knew the answer. But then she straightened to her full height, and looked him imperiously in the eyes.

"Goodbye, Zach. Just forget about me."

The bathroom door shut before he could reply. He stood for a moment staring at the closed door before he gathered his clothing strewn throughout her house. He knew that forgetting about Amanda Baldwin would be even more difficult than convincing her she didn't want to forget about him.

He'd be able to forget her eventually, of course, but only after their affair had run its natural course. In the meantime, there wasn't any reason to deprive themselves of such exquisite sexual chemistry. Zach's agile brain went to work plotting ways to ensure that their sensuous interlude wouldn't be a one-time aberration.

AMANDA'S HEAD THROBBED, and the area behind her eyes ached as she gazed at the computer screen, trying to focus on explaining the principles of the high-tech operating system to the small group of journalists gathered around her. The problem was that she couldn't concentrate on much at all except that she had made incredible, implausible love with Zach Castelli.

"Think of your computer screen as a notebook," Amanda said, dredging up one of her standard teaching analogies. "The frames on the screen are the pages. When you're using a notebook, you flip from one page to the next. With the computer, clicking the mouse while positioned on the desired page brings it to the front of the screen."

Complete silence greeted her remark, which was reflected in the newsroom around her. The quiet had surprised her when she'd first come to the *Fort Lauderdale Times* to implement the new computer system. Like most people, she had imagined a newspaper to be a loud, bustling place.

This newsroom, with its wide-spaced desks and multi-windowed perimeter, looked more like an insurance office than the home of a hundred town criers. During the day, the noise level didn't get any louder than the soft tapping of computer keys combined with the low buzz of conversation.

"Any questions?" she asked, gazing into the faces around her.

"I have one," said Celia Lewis, a petite, attractive woman with whom Amanda had become friendly during her six months at the newspaper. "Who's the lucky woman getting that pretty bunch of flowers headed this way?"

Her comment caused everybody in Amanda's small group to turn toward a deliveryman. He was carrying an enormous bunch of small-petaled blue flowers with yellow eyes that immediately tipped Amanda off to the sender and recipient of the gift.

"Anybody here Amanda Baldwin?"

"She is." Celia indicated Amanda and affected disappointment. "Some women get all the luck. Here she is set to get married in a month, and her fiancé is still sending her flowers. They sure are pretty little things. What kind are they anyway?"

"Forget-me-nots," Amanda said in a low voice, before the deliveryman could answer. He set the fragrant flowers beside her and handed her the card, but she didn't have to look at it to know that the flowers weren't from Reid.

"Somebody has a colorful way of getting his point across," the deliveryman said, smiling. He was a pudgy man with a cheerful, round face who was perhaps in his mid-forties. The speculative way he studied her made Amanda feel exposed, as though he and everybody else in the room knew what she'd done last night. She glanced at the clock, relieved to see that it was a few minutes before noon.

"I think now would be a good time to break for lunch," she said. "It's just about twelve o'clock."

Mavis Harris, a middle-aged woman with artificially enhanced blond hair, waggled her dark eyebrows. "Sounds like the perfect time to call your fella and thank him for those flowers."

"Just don't tell my fiancée about this," said a slender, dark-haired man in his twenties whose name eluded Amanda. "I stopped sending her flowers the instant she agreed to go out with me for the second time."

The knowledge that it wasn't "her fella" who had sent the flowers burned in Amanda's brain as the group dispersed. She fingered the card, reluctant to open it. Confirmation of what she already suspected would make the gift, and the sentiment behind it, real. Realizing that she was only postponing the inevitable, Amanda drew the card out of the small envelope. Two words were written on it.

You're unforgettable.

She immediately stuffed the card inside the envelope, but the words were imprinted on her brain. *You're unforgettable.* She'd told Zach just this morning to forget her, and he'd countered by sending a bouquet of forget-me-nots and a card proclaiming her unforgettable. It was a touching, romantic gesture, the kind a lover might make, but Amanda didn't want Zach as a lover. At the very least, she didn't think she should want him.

"What's the matter? Did you and Reid have a fight?"

Amanda jumped, startled by Celia's voice. She'd thought the other woman had departed with the rest of the group.

"They're not from Reid," Amanda said.

"They're not?" Celia immediately lowered herself into the chair adjacent to Amanda's and spun it around. Her face was alive with curiosity. "Pray tell, girl. If they're not from Reid, who are they from?"

Amanda shook her head. "Nobody important," she lied. "Just a man I met last night."

"Wait a minute. You met a man last night who today is sending you a bunch of flowers, forget-me-nots no less, and you say it's not important. My rear end it's not important. Who is this man, and what's he do for a living?"

Amanda stared at Celia blankly because she didn't know the answer to the last question. She had slept with a man whom she knew precious little about. She hadn't even asked what he did for a living. For all she knew, he could be a dogcatcher or a florist's deliveryman or a diplomat. She thought of Zach's mop of hair and frowned. He definitely wasn't a diplomat.

"Don't tell me you don't know his name," Celia said, reading the confusion on Amanda's face.

"Of course I know his name. It's Zach Castelli." Her voice lowered. "I just don't know what he does for a living."

"Why, Amanda Baldwin, I never would have guessed you had a side like this."

"I don't have a side like this. That's what I kept trying to tell Zach."

"Zach. A nice, strong name. Does he look as good as he sounds?"

"Better," Amanda admitted reluctantly. "He has this wonderful tan and these incredible sapphire-blue eyes and, uh, well you know."

"Are you trying to say he has a body that would melt butter?"

Amanda nodded at the apt analogy, although she wouldn't have put it so colorfully.

"Come on, tell me the rest. I can't stand the suspense. I'm dying to know what a nice engaged lady like you was doing with this Zach last night?"

Celia didn't intend her question literally, but that's how it sounded, and Amanda colored all the way to the roots of her red hair. Although she trusted Celia not to repeat anything she said, she regretted discussing Zach. She hadn't been able to make sense of what happened, so she surely couldn't explain it to anybody else. But Celia, like all the good reporters Amanda knew, wouldn't let go of a subject once she'd delved into it.

"I wasn't engaged last night."

"What?" Celia exclaimed, and immediately picked up Amanda's left hand, revealing that her ring finger was bare. "What happened?"

"Reid broke the engagement off last night," Amanda said, trying to use a matter-of-fact tone. "This morning, he tried to patch things up. In between, I met Zach."

"You must certainly have made a good impression on this Zach, considering that big bunch of flowers sitting on your desk. Are you going to call and thank him?"

Amanda slowly shook her head. "I don't have his phone number."

"Ever heard of a phone book, girl?"

"You don't understand. I've been seeing Reid for ten years. I've never even looked at another man in a romantic way. I know he did an unforgivable thing, but chances are that I'm going to forgive him and go ahead and marry him. If I call Zach, it'll just muddle things. He'll get the wrong idea and think I want to see him again."

"Do you want to see him again?"

Amanda hesitated slightly, but it was long enough to reveal to both herself and Celia that she wasn't sure of the answer. "Of course I don't want to see him again. I just want to let the whole thing die."

Celia snorted. "Fat chance."

"What do you mean by that?"

"A man who sends a woman a bouquet of forget-me-nots the morning after they meet is not going to just let the whole thing die. You can mark my words on that."

By SUNDAY AFTERNOON, as she drove to her mother's house for her customary visit, Amanda was wondering whether Celia's assessment had been correct. She'd expected Zach to be on the other end of every ringing telephone in the newsroom after the florist's delivery, repeating his offer of dinner. Not that she would have accepted.

She'd meant it when she told him to forget her. Chances were she'd eventually do exactly what she'd told Celia: forgive Reid and marry him. That didn't leave room in her life for Zach.

Still, she had to admit to a twinge of disappointment that Zach had given up so easily. The upshot was that two men had asked her to dinner for Friday night, and she'd spent that evening and the next one alone. Reid hadn't stopped phoning, but she'd finally convinced him that she needed time apart to think. Zach, on the other hand, hadn't given her another chance to accept his invitation.

Not that I would have accepted, she told herself again, as she pulled into her mother's driveway. Even if he had changed her entire concept of lovemaking with his heady kisses and heavenly hands. She switched off the ignition and sat behind the wheel of the car for a full minute, while her mind fought with her body's memories. She simply would not waste another moment thinking about Zach Castelli, no matter how skilled a lover he was. For all she knew about him, and that was precious little, he slept with a different woman every night.

She got out of the car, her steps purposeful as she approached the entrance to her mother's two-bedroom house. It was flanked by a pair of palm trees that nicely complemented the cream-colored stucco walls and burnished tile roof. A few years before, Amanda had convinced her mother to move to this sparkling new suburb of western Broward County that boasted immaculate landscaping and dashes of color provided by strategically placed flower beds.

Amanda had emphasized the positives of the move, but the truth was that her mother could no longer afford the mortgage payment on the large house in which Amanda had grown up. The proceeds from the sale had eased her mother's money problems, but Amanda feared they would soon begin again. Mother, she knew, had no fear.

Before Amanda could ring the doorbell, her mother appeared in the doorway, a welcoming smile on her still-youthful face. Mother had grown up in a more formal time and always dressed well, no matter the occasion, but Amanda was surprised that she was clad in a particularly becoming dress of cornflower blue that she usually reserved for church.

"Hello, Mother." Amanda bent to kiss her on her soft cheek. Even in heels, her mother was only a few inches over five feet tall, and Amanda sometimes wondered how they could share the same genes. Her mother had stopped coloring her hair five years ago, and the gray strands framed a face that looked little like Amanda's. Thin, high cheekbones highlighted pretty brown eyes and skin that tanned rather than burned.

"I'm so glad you got here a few minutes early, dear." Her mother clasped her hands and drew her inside. Amanda started to say that she had arrived at the same time she always did, but her mother didn't give her a chance. "I've been dying to show you what I bought."

"What you bought?" Amanda repeated.

"The nicest woman was here yesterday selling them, and after twenty minutes of listening to her I didn't see how I'd lived without one." Her mother chattered as she walked briskly to her kitchen.

Amanda followed behind while a familiar sense of dread filled her.

"It's a water softener," her mother said triumphantly, indicating the white plastic contraption hooked to her kitchen faucet.

"You mean a water purifier, don't you?"

Her mother looked confused for a moment. "No, no. A water softener. That nice lady told me all about the hard water we have out here in the suburbs and how everything tastes so much better with one of these softeners. Here, let me get you a glass."

Sighing inwardly, Amanda watched her mother bustle around the kitchen. She knew from experience that denouncing her latest purchase wouldn't do any good. She was the sort of woman who inspired dances of joy in salespeople when she opened the door to their establishments.

"It's good," Amanda said, drinking water that tasted exactly the same as it always did. She sat down at the kitchen table, idly wondering when her mother would offer her some of the chocolate cake that sat cooling on a baker's rack. Her mother joined her, carrying a large glass of newly softened water.

"I think it tastes divine." She drank deeply and smiled at Amanda. Something about the smile made Amanda vaguely uneasy. "Did you and Reid have a good time last night?"

Amanda had a standing Saturday night date with Reid that stretched as far back into the years as her Sunday afternoon visit with her mother. Every Sunday, her mother asked whether they'd had a good time the night before. An innocent question, to be sure. Except today it didn't sound quite so innocent.

"Actually," Amanda said slowly, "Reid and I didn't see each other last night."

To Amanda's growing unease, her mother seemed not the slightest bit surprised. She simply nodded and waited, a slight smile curving her lips. Amanda wet hers nervously, debating how much to tell her mother. "Reid and I have decided to spend some time apart."

"I already figured that out, dear," her mother said, even though Amanda had never spent time apart from Reid in the ten years they'd been dating. "Oh, you should know that the vocalist who was supposed to sing at your wedding called today. I thought it best to tell her we didn't need her anymore."

"You did?" Amanda's voice squeaked in surprise. "But why? I didn't say the wedding was off."

"You didn't have to, dear," her mother said, reaching for Amanda's left hand. She rubbed her index finger over the bare spot where Amanda's engagement ring had been. "You'll cancel the wedding sooner or later, if you haven't done so already. I knew it as soon as I got the phone call."

"The phone call? Do you mean Reid called you?"

Her mother laughed and let go of her hand. "Reid barely talks to me when we're in the same room. I can't imagine he'd have anything to say to me on the phone."

"Then who—"

"Oh, dear, look at the time. It's almost two o'clock." Her mother got quickly to her feet and rummaged through one of the kitchen drawers. Within seconds, she pulled out a cake dish. "I hope this cake has cooled enough. I can't wait any longer to transfer it to the dish. Are you bringing anything, dear?"

"Bringing anything?" Amanda furrowed her brow. Her mother was making less sense by the minute. "I hadn't realized you wanted me to bring something."

"I'm sure they don't expect us to bring anything, but a bottle of wine would have been nice. Or maybe some sparkling water. You never can assume a family that sounds as nice as Zach's drinks alcohol."

"Zach?" The inside of Amanda's head rang like a fire station after an alarm had been tripped. "How do you know Zach?"

She was so busy settling her cake into the dish that she didn't look at Amanda. "I don't actually know him, dear, but I did talk to him on the phone yesterday. He's such a nice young man with such perfect manners. He assumed I knew you had accepted the dinner invitation for both of us, and I didn't want to hurt his feelings by saying I didn't.''

Only part of her mother's prattle registered upon Amanda. "Zach is the one who called you?"

"When he couldn't reach you, he thought about trying me. He said it was a good thing my name was the feminine version of his father's. That way he remembered it straight off, and got my number from directory assistance. Isn't that funny? That his father's name is Paul while mine's Pauline?"

Amanda remembered that she and Zach had thought so when they'd discovered the coincidence, but she also recalled that she hadn't given him a definitive answer to his invitation to have dinner with his family. Amanda certainly hadn't agreed.

"Anyway," her mother continued, oblivious to Amanda's distress, "he tried to explain where his father lives, but you know how hopeless I am with directions. He said you hadn't been there either, so we finally agreed that he would pick us up here at two o'clock and take us there. His family dines early on Sundays, you know."

As if on cue, the doorbell chimed and Amanda seethed. If Zach Castelli thought for one minute that she was going to be railroaded into spending time with him just because her mother was gullible, there was something seriously wrong with his brain.

"That must be Zach now." Her mother wiped her hands on a kitchen towel. Her eyes sparkled. "I have to admit that I'm looking forward to this. He's quite charming, this Zach. I can't help wondering if his father's the same way."

"His father?" Amanda asked, so surprised she stopped seething. She couldn't remember the last time that her mother had expressed interest in meeting a man. "Zach did mention that his father was a widower, didn't he?"

"Yes, he did." Incredibly, her mother's complexion colored and she smoothed the skirt of her dress. "How do I look?"

"You look lovely, Mother." Amanda's temper rose again as she silently acknowledged that she wasn't going to disappoint her mother by refusing to have dinner with Zach's family. But that didn't mean she had to like it. "But your lipstick needs touching up. Why don't you check the mirror while I get the door?"

Amanda waited until her mother had headed off in the direction of the bathroom before she walked to the front door, her strides long and angry.

4

WITH WORDS OF ANGER simmering on her lips, Amanda flung open the door and saw checks. Hundreds of checks in eye-popping colors. Lime green, hot pink, lemon yellow. They were all represented on his shirt. The display was so blinding that it struck her dumb, and her angry tirade died a quick death.

"Hi there, beautiful," Zach said, displaying his dimple with a grin as sunny as the sky. "Dare I hope that you're imagining how I'd look without this shirt, too?"

Amanda's tongue grew thick in her mouth, and her brain couldn't make it work. Tongue-tied! She was actually tongue-tied! It wasn't supposed to happen this way. *He* was supposed to apologize for turning her world upside down and assuming she wanted to keep hanging by her toes.

Instead, he'd unnerved her by alluding to a remark she'd unthinkingly made during the most reckless night of her life. Worse, he'd actually managed to make her picture just how flawless his chest was under that kaleidoscopic shirt.

"Don't call me beautiful," she snapped, although that hadn't been on her agenda of things to tell him. His casual compliment was the very least of his crimes.

"Why not?" His brows lifted merrily. "I call 'em like I see 'em, and you, Amanda Baldwin, are beautiful. That green shirt you're wearing goes wonderfully with your eyes. But you'd look even better if your mouth wasn't hanging open. Didn't anyone ever tell you that you can catch flies that way?"

Zach leaned forward and covered her open mouth with his in a brief, sweet kiss. Her lips softened in welcome before she could quell her response, but by then he was already drawing back. This time, his grin was knowing, which was enough to unleash the anger that had been momentarily paralyzed by his blinding shirt.

"How dare you pretend that—"

"Amanda?" Her mother's sweet, high-pitched voice drifted into Amanda's consciousness, cutting off her words. In the next instant, she circled her daughter's waist with her arm. Amanda was still standing in the doorway, so she popped her head around Amanda's shoulder. "Amanda, is this your new young man?"

"He's not my—"

"I'm Zach Castelli, Mrs. Baldwin," Zach interrupted, sticking out a hand. "I can certainly see where Amanda gets those beautiful high cheekbones. It runs in the family."

Her mother glowed, and Amanda fumed. Leave it to Zach to zero in on the sole feature that she shared with her mother and turn it to his advantage. Her mother responded to flattery the same as most women, but she adored it when anybody complimented Amanda. Zach had managed to do both in one sentence.

"Amanda didn't tell me how charming you were. Or how handsome." Her mother, obviously, was not as affected by shirt blindness as Amanda had been. She poked her daughter in the ribs with her elbow. "Don't you think he's handsome, dear?"

Zach cocked one eyebrow, and mischief shone in his eyes. Amanda thought the entire man should be outlawed, because his appearance was definitely an unfair advantage.

Not only were his features handsome enough to stop her heart, but his body was perfect. Below the preposterous shirt, he wore a pair of shorts that left long, well-muscled lengths of tan legs bare.

"Well, dear, don't you?" her mother asked, and Amanda blushed when she realized that Zach's grin had grown to the size of the Everglades. What was the matter with her? For a woman who had decided she wasn't going to let him touch her again, she was sending out all the wrong signals.

"Yes," she said, her tone as snappish as an alligator that hadn't eaten in months. This marked the second time that she'd told him just how attractive she found him.

"I'm so looking forward to meeting your family, Zach," her mother continued, seemingly oblivious to her daughter's distress. "I had just been thinking that I needed to get out more, and then you called with your dinner invitation. It was such a nice surprise. Just give me a minute to find my keys and get my chocolate cake, and I'll be right out."

"I'll wait until the moon comes up if you're bringing chocolate cake." Zach glanced at Amanda, looking like an imp. "I like chocolate almost as much as Amanda does, Mrs. Baldwin."

"That sounds so formal. Call me Pauline."

"Pauline, then." He favored her mother with a smile that could have melted ice in winter. As soon as her mother retreated into the house, Amanda stepped forward and jabbed her index finger into Zach's chest.

"I never said I would have dinner with your family, and you know it," she muttered under her breath.

"The way I remember it, you never said you wouldn't." He grinned like a Cheshire cat. "Besides, Pauline wants to come."

"Why do you think I'm coming?" she asked rhetorically, not expecting an answer. She should have known to expect the unexpected from Zach.

"I think you're coming because, deep down, you know you and I will have a good time together no matter what we do."

"Of all the conceited, preposterous, ridiculous assumptions," she sputtered, jabbing him anew with her finger for every adjective she uttered.

"There I go again." He feigned self-disgust she knew he didn't feel. "I should have known I'd get in trouble with you if I said what I thought. And, honey, I can think of a lot of things I'd rather have you do to me than scold."

Zach wrapped the fingers of one of his hands around the digit that was still pressed to his chest, brought it to his lips and kissed the tip of it. She yanked it free, ignoring the queer way he'd made her tingle all over merely by kissing her fingertip. She put her hands on her hips.

"Stop making sexual insinuations," she said. It was a toss-up whether she was more furious at him for making them or at herself for responding to them.

"Do you always have to think the worst of me?" He playfully pulled a strand of her hair and shook his head from side to side. "I wasn't talking about sex at all. I was tactfully suggesting that what I'd like to have you do is thank me for the flowers."

Unwelcome guilt caused Amanda to lower her eyes to the sidewalk, her argument with him temporarily forgotten. She had been brought up much too well to ignore a gift, especially when it had been such a lovely one.

"Thank you for the flowers." She knew the words sounded as though they had been wrenched from her. She lifted her chin, a defiant glint in her eyes. "But I didn't want them."

"No, no, no." Zach shook his head, but his smile hadn't faded. "When you attach a 'but' to a thank you, it ruins the effect. You're just supposed to say thank you."

"Thank you for what?" Pauline walked out of the

house, triumphantly jingling her keys. Zach immediately took the cake pan from her so she could lock the door.

"Amanda was thanking me for the flowers I sent her at work," Zach supplied, before Amanda could answer.

"You sent Amanda flowers at work? How lovely." Pauline smiled broadly and sent Amanda what seemed to be a look of approval. Amanda turned away and rolled her eyes.

"They weren't big flowers," she muttered. Her mother and Zach both looked at her curiously before proceeding down the sidewalk. Zach actually patted her on the shoulder, as though he were comforting her. She jerked out of his range and led the way to the parking lot.

"Mother gets carsick unless she sits in the front seat, so I'll take the back," she tossed over her shoulder, determined to control her own destiny.

She scanned the parking lot for his MGA until she realized that car had only two seats. Zach passed her, and her eyes immediately dropped to his delectable rear end. Horrified at herself, she looked away.

Her mother linked an arm through hers, propelling her forward as surely as if she had been caught by an ocean undertow. Zach stopped at an oversize station wagon in a silvery color.

"You know that ad campaign with the line, 'This is not your father's Oldsmobile?'" he asked as he unlocked the passenger-side door, referring to the company's well-touted redesign. "Well, this *is* my father's Oldsmobile. A 1965 model, to be exact."

"Ooh, look, dear. It has a bench seat. Now you won't have to sit in the back." Her mother sounded excited at the prospect of riding in the car, which was strange, because she typically adored only what was shiny and new. That definitely didn't include this car. "Go on in and sit in the middle. That way, we won't have to crane our necks when we talk to you."

"Why don't you get in the middle, Mother?" Amanda asked quickly.

"Oh, no, dear. You know that I like a window seat. Even when I take an airplane ride, I have to sit by the window. The view's so much prettier from there, don't you think?"

Amanda thought she heard Zach chuckle, and she sent him a vicious glare. He probably thought that she was afraid to sit next to him because of his potent charm. Well, she'd show him that she wasn't afraid.

Five minutes later, Amanda held herself rigidly, careful that no part of her body touched Zach. Still, his presence was overpowering. His shampoo mingled with the warm, clean smell that came off his skin, and the scent was so heady that she had a childish urge to hold her breath. She glanced at his bare legs, remembered how the hair-roughened texture of his skin felt, and clenched her fingers into a fist.

The corner of his mouth curved upward, as though he knew what she was thinking. But that was impossible. He was paying attention to the highway, where cars whizzed by as though the old Oldsmobile were standing still.

"This baby will only go forty miles an hour. I would have come in my car, Pauline, but then Amanda would have had to sit on my lap." He slanted Amanda a devilish look. She scowled.

"Zach's car only has two seats," Amanda explained, determined not to react to his teasing. She inched closer to her mother.

"Don't you find that impractical, Zach?" Pauline asked.

He laughed, as deep and chocolate smooth as she remembered. When she breathed, his clean male scent smelled even better than the chocolate cake balanced on her mother's lap. "I'm not a practical person. If you don't believe me, just ask Amanda."

"I hadn't realized you and Amanda knew each other so well." Amanda's chest filled with dread. She recognized her mother's tone only too well, and what it usually foretold was an inquisition. Amanda could have easily deflected the questions if she and her mother had been alone, but who knew what Zach would say.

"We don't know each other well at all." Amanda struck first with a harmless, generic denial.

"That's right," Zach said. "But I have to tell you, Pauline, that I intend to get to know your daughter much better."

"That's good news." Her mother leaned around a horrified Amanda so she could peer at Zach. The space between her eyebrows got smaller. "Has Amanda told you everything about herself?"

He took his attention from the road to smile at her mother. At the same time, he gently caressed Amanda's left thigh through the thin linen of her slacks, removing his hand the instant before she would have slapped it away. "Do you mean has she told me about Reid?"

Pauline's eyes widened. "Why, yes! That's exactly what I mean."

He looked back at the road. "Since he's no longer in the picture, I'm not going to let him worry me. Amanda's dating me now."

"Since when?" Amanda asked in utter amazement. Sure, she'd slept with Zach, but she didn't intend to date him. It was as though neither Zach nor her mother had heard her.

"How nice. Reid's never been quite right for Amanda, so you're wise not to worry about him," her mother piped up, shocking Amanda.

She and Reid had been together for so long that she

thought her mother considered him part of the family, even if she had never asked Reid to use her first name.

"Especially now that the wedding's off," Zach added, and Amanda wondered where she could get her hands on boiling oil.

"I wouldn't put it that way exactly..." Amanda said.

"But that's the bottom line," Zach interrupted.

If her mother hadn't been in the car, Amanda would have gladly hit him. As it was, arguing with Zach about whether she was getting married or whether they were dating wouldn't serve any constructive purpose. Especially since *her* mother seemed to be on *his* side. She had to content herself with silent seething.

After a moment, her mother leaned forward so she could see Zach's profile. She was smiling, as though the subject of Reid was of so little importance that it was already forgotten.

"I'm afraid I don't know much about you, Zach," Pauline said, managing to imply that Amanda had been remiss in not filling her in.

As though Amanda knew anything about him herself.

"What do you do for a living?"

Amanda's ears perked up. This, of course, was a question she should have asked before she went to bed with him. She rubbed her forehead. There were a lot of questions she should have asked before they'd become intimate, the number one being, "What am I doing?"

"I'm a fisherman," he replied cheerfully.

Amanda shut her eyes. Great. He was a fisherman. Somebody who got a length of line, cast it into the water and pulled out his dinner. Great. Just great.

She let the conversation swirl around and over her the rest of the trip. If she didn't say anything, there was always the slight possibility that she wouldn't get herself involved any deeper with Zach Castelli. The *very* slight possibility.

ZACH'S FATHER LIVED in a one-story ranch house with a white stucco exterior and a cornucopia of plant life in a neighborhood with plenty of shade, about a mile from Hollywood Beach. Paul Castelli's yard was the shadiest of all. Palm trees in various shapes and sizes were interspersed with fruit trees, leafy green bushes and flowers in every color of the spectrum. Zach stood on the small front porch as Amanda and her mother surveyed the property.

"Don't tell him I told you this," he said with a conspiratorial wink, "but we've long suspected that Papa must have lived in the jungle in a previous life. Either that, or he's been watching too many Tarzan movies."

Her mother laughed aloud, but Amanda suppressed her smile. She was determined to prove Zach wrong. She was not going to have a good time. She was not going to take pleasure in his company.

Zach opened the door, allowing them to precede him into the house. Amanda trailed her mother, and Zach guided her through the door with a hand on the small of her back. She quickened her step to get away from him, and stumbled over the threshold, defeating the purpose. His arm immediately encircled her waist, and an interested pair of young eyes assessed them.

"Is this your latest girlfriend, Uncle Zach?"

A beautiful, dark-haired girl of about nine years old was standing just inside the doorway, her hazel eyes trained on Amanda. She had on a baseball cap turned backward, black sweat shorts, a red T-shirt and miniature, growling, panther faces painted on each cheek.

"She's a girl, and she's my friend. So, yeah, I guess you could say she's my girlfriend." Zach's logic was skewed, but he made it sound so reasonable that Amanda couldn't argue.

The little girl shrugged, obviously untroubled by the thought of her beloved uncle with a new woman. It was probably because he never stuck with one long enough to warrant the girl's jealousy, Amanda thought.

"Just don't kiss him in front of me," she told Amanda sternly. "I can't stand that mushy stuff."

Laughter filled the room, and Amanda gradually became aware that the little girl wasn't the only one staring at her. She, Zach and her mother stood just inside a charmingly cluttered living room which opened up into a dining room filled with curious Castellis.

"Sport," Zach said, addressing the little girl, "would you take the cake from Mrs. Baldwin and put it in the kitchen?"

She obeyed wordlessly, dipping a finger in the icing and licking it when she thought no one was looking.

Without taking his arm from around Amanda, Zach propelled Amanda forward. He hooked Pauline's elbow with his free hand. "Everybody, this is Pauline Baldwin and her daughter Amanda. Now pay attention, ladies, because I don't think I can get through this round of introductions twice.

"The distinguished gray-haired gentleman is my father Paul, the handsome guy beside him is my brother Clay, and the luminous lady with the long hair, my sister Marlee." He took a breath and looked at the little girl with the tiny panthers on her cheeks as she returned from the kitchen. "This is Mia, who has a slapshot that all the boys would die for. Those panthers, by the way, represent her favorite ice hockey team. And that woman over there is her lovely mother Maria."

As Amanda's gaze swung from one Castelli to the next, her eyes widened. All of them, with the notable exception of Zach, were adorned with paint. An eagle soared on Paul Castelli's left forearm, and a flag flew across Clay's right. Maria sported psychedelic designs on the visible portions of her legs, and Marlee had a warrior with a fierce face flanked by some unintelligible printing smack in the middle of her forehead. Belatedly, Amanda remembered Marlee's profession.

"You didn't prepare them, did you, Zach?" The question came from Clay. With his sandy hair and gray eyes, he was a less vibrant version of his brother. "You let them walk into Papa's house without revealing the family secret."

"Oh, stop it, Clay. You're acting like they've never seen body painting before." Marlee disengaged herself from the group to walk toward the trio in the living room. She was tall and thin with dark hair that was parted in the middle and extended to her waist. Her flowing, print dress and round granny glasses looked straight out of the flower-child era. Amanda squinted. Up close, she still couldn't make out the printing on Marlee's forehead.

"It's supposed to say *Charge!*," Marlee explained, "but I was looking at the mirror when I painted it, and I forgot that the mirror gives you a reverse image on printing."

Zach whooped with laughter, and Marlee shot him an irritated glance before returning her attention to Amanda and her mother. "Big brother here is the only one in the family who won't let me paint him. I think it's because he thinks my designs will clash with those abominable shirts he wears."

"You're just jealous," Zach said blithely. He removed his arm from Amanda, grabbed a colorful swatch of checkered shirt and grinned. "Because you can't reproduce designs as spectacular as these on the human skin."

Marlee tried to look stern, but the corners of her mouth twitched until her smile broke free. Amanda watched in amazement. Was it possible that Zach had the ability to discombobulate all females, even the ones who were related to him?

"The two of you will have to let me paint you sometime," Marlee said, taking in Amanda and Pauline with her comment.

"I don't think—" Amanda began.

"I'd love that, dear." Her mother leaned forward. "Do you think you could paint something on my lower leg that's similar to that warrior on your forehead?"

Before Amanda had time to puzzle over her mother's bizarre request, a small boy with a shock of black hair emerged from a hallway and sprinted across the floor at warp speed. The three women flanking Zach parted like the Red Sea.

"Uncle Zach! Uncle Zach!"

The boy threw his arms, which were painted with multiple flying superheroes, around Zach's legs. Zach picked up his nephew and whirled him around once, eliciting peals of laughter from the boy.

"We call this little guy Scooter," Zach said, laughing along with his nephew, "because he scoots from one place to the next."

"Make me fly! Make me fly!" the little boy cried.

Zach cut a glance at Amanda. "Watch carefully and see Zach Castelli, the bestower of impossible dreams, transform a small, earthbound boy into a magical flying hero."

He hooked an arm under the little boy's chest and pressed down on his back with his free hand. Scooter made his legs as stiff as boards and stretched out his arms as though they were wings. Zach circled the living room, dipping and elevating the boy as he went.

"Faster than a teenager in his daddy's car, more powerful than a kid with a slingshot, able to leap deep mud puddles in a single bound. Look, in his uncle's arms. It's a missile, it's a rocket. No, it's Super Scooter." Zach made his voice deep and rich, like an old-time radio announcer. "Yes, it's Super Scooter. Lovable nephew from another neighborhood, with sweetness and intelligence far beyond those of ordinary little boys."

This time, Amanda couldn't contain the laughter that bubbled from her lips. The entire family was laughing, and Scooter wore a look of pure joy rivaled only by the glow on Zach's face. There was love here, Amanda thought. Love and laughter.

"Welcome to the madhouse." Amanda had been so focused on Zach's antics that she hadn't seen Paul Castelli approach. "Come into the dining room and pull up a chair. Whatever you do, don't just sit there silently. If you can't get a word in, interrupt. It's the only way to be heard in this family."

Zach's father had the same blue eyes and engaging manner as his son. Even though he wore a perfectly normal shirt in a solid color, Amanda instantly saw that his personality was much too overpowering to appeal to her sweet, naive mother. So much for the Paul-Pauline matchmade destiny.

"It was very nice of you to let Zach invite us to dinner, Mr. Castelli," Amanda said.

"Paul! I want you to call me Paul." He shifted his attention to Pauline, and his slow smile was reminiscent of the best of his son's. "Of course, your mother can call me anything she wants. As long as it's flattering."

"I can think of a few things I'd like to call you already." Pauline actually giggled, and she looked at Paul from under her lashes. Amanda's eyes rounded. Her mother, the same mother who had barely acknowledged the smiles of the half-dozen men Amanda had tried to fix her up with, was actually playing the flirt!

"Why don't you come with me and tell me about them?" Paul put out his hand, and Pauline let him take hers. They walked away from Amanda, their eyes locked on each other as though they were the stars of a sappy romantic movie.

"Is something the matter? You look like I could knock you over with a feather," asked Zach, suddenly appearing at Amanda's side.

If you don't stop whispering in my ear, Amanda thought, you could knock me over with a breath. She thrust the unwelcome thought away and turned her ear out of breathing range.

"It's working." She indicated their parents with a nod. They were sitting next to each other at the dining room table, their gray heads pressed intimately together. Her mother's face flushed at something Paul said, and he covered her hand with his.

"Of course it's working." Zach sounded as though he'd never doubted it. "They're not named Paul and Pauline for nothing."

She smiled up at him, and his eyes crinkled before he kissed the tip of her nose. Amanda tried to mind, but the atmosphere in the house was so inviting and Zach's expression so guileless, she found that she couldn't.

An hour later, after they'd devoured two pans of his father's chicken lasagna with pesto sauce and as many loaves of crusty bread, Zach watched Amanda interact with his family. She'd finagled it so they weren't sitting next to each other, but she'd stolen enough glances at him when she thought he wasn't looking that he wasn't worried. Amanda didn't want to admit it, but their sexual chemistry was potent enough to ignite bricks.

"So how did you meet Zach, Amanda?" Maria, the softest spoken member of the group, asked the question when the table had lapsed into a rare moment of silence.

"I, um, we, uh, met in a restaurant." Amanda looked at Zach, her eyes begging for help.

"At a restaurant, dear?" Pauline tilted her head curiously. "How ever could you meet a man at a restaurant?"

"Simple." Zach smiled at Amanda, and her shoulders sagged in relief that he had come to the rescue. "She was alone in a booth. I sat down and invited myself to dinner. She told me to get away from her. I wouldn't go. And voilà! Here we are."

"How romantic," Maria said, sighing. Her voice was dreamy. "Why can't I meet a man like that?"

Zach was watching Amanda, so he caught her flabbergasted expression before she tried to disguise it.

"I know what it sounds like, but Maria really isn't announcing to the family that she plans to cheat on my brother," Zach explained. "She's Clay's *ex*-wife."

Maria covered her mouth and giggled. "I'm sorry. I didn't realize you didn't know. I suppose it seems like Clay and I are married. But, believe me, we get along much better divorced than we ever did married."

"Hallelujah!" Clay said. "Ain't that the truth?"

Only Zach realized that Amanda's shock didn't abate with the explanation. She obviously held marriage in high regard, which was yet another reason for him to continue pursuing her. She needed somebody to keep her away from snobbish, unfeeling Reid Carrigan or she might do something incredibly stupid. Like forgive him and marry him.

A little while later, after they'd eaten Pauline's scrumptious chocolate cake, Pauline insisted on helping Paul with the dishes. They shooed everybody else away, and it didn't take a genius to figure out they wanted to be alone. Clay, Maria and Marlee retreated to the backyard to check on the children, while Zach followed Amanda into the living room. He plopped himself next to her on the sofa.

"Enjoying yourself?"

"I wouldn't tell you if I were," she said, giving him a taste of his own rhetoric. She didn't smile, but her mood had softened considerably since the drive over. The change suited her. Her red-gold hair spilled over her shoulders, complementing the creaminess of her skin and highlighting her beauty. His body hardened, and he shifted in his seat.

"Tell me what you think of my family, then." He thought his voice contained only a touch of desire-induced hoarseness.

"Your family is wonderful," she said without reservation, the truth shining out of her green eyes.

One of the corners of his mouth lifted. "More or less wonderful than I am?"

"More." She didn't hesitate before delivering the answer. "Definitely more. As a matter of fact, I don't happen to think you're wonderful at all."

"You don't?" He gave his best shot at looking injured. "Maybe I should bring Mia and Scooter over here to convince you otherwise. I happen to be their favorite uncle."

"And I happen to know that Maria is an only child. That means you're their only uncle."

"Their *favorite* only uncle."

She laughed, and her mirth spilled into her eyes and made them sparkle. He was overwhelmed with an urge to touch her, so he reached out, tucked a lock of strawberry hair behind her ear and let his fingers linger in the long, silky strands. Her laughter instantly faded.

"What are you doing?"

"I'm playing with your hair, silly."

Her enchanting green eyes filled with exasperation. "You can't just reach out and touch me whenever you feel like it."

"Why not?" he asked, touching her cheek with the back of his hand. He rubbed gently against her soft skin. "Remember, I'm a man who follows my impulses."

"I think this impulsiveness thing of yours is an excuse for doing whatever you feel like doing." Her voice was steeped in displeasure, but she didn't try to remove his hand from her face.

"Isn't that the point of being impulsive?" His eyes danced, and he leaned forward, intent on kissing her. He heard the quick intake of her breath, saw the slight darkening of her eyes and knew that she was going to let him.

"I said *no kissing.*"

Mia stood a foot from them, and the tiny panthers on her cheeks seemed to be roaring at them in disapproval. Zach's hand dropped from Amanda's cheek, and he gave his niece a good-natured grin. "You have rotten timing, sport."

"You're not supposed to be kissing in Grandpapa's living room," she scolded, wagging her finger. She addressed Zach. "Grandpapa asked me to tell you that his shower door is off the hinges again. He says you're the only one who can fix it. And the Frisbee's stuck up in the tree, and Dad says nobody else is crazy enough to climb up there and get it."

"I'm sure he meant crazy in a good way," Zach said. He got up and cast a reluctant gaze back at Amanda. Her cheeks were flushed, and he would have dearly loved to finish what he had started. Ah, well. There was always later. "I'll be back."

"That's what I'm afraid of," Amanda whispered, as she watched him go. Now that she knew he was a fisherman, his deep tan and sun-lightened hair made sense. She should have figured that he wasn't the type of man to stay confined in an office. He had an untamed quality to go along with his broad shoulders, lean hips and long legs. God, he was breathtaking. But he was more than that. It was evident in the jaunty way he walked, with a little bounce in his step that made him even more attractive. There was a joy inside him that was contagious.

"He's gorgeous, isn't he?"

Marlee spoke from just inside the front door, and Amanda's traitorous skin reddened. She'd been so busy running her eyes over Zach that she hadn't noticed the other woman enter the house. She stammered something unintelligible. Marlee perched herself on the coffee table, and the warrior painted on her forehead seemed to be staring Amanda down.

"Gorgeous and tender and funny and completely carefree." Marlee paused and adjusted her granny glasses. "Don't let him break your heart, Amanda."

"Zach's not going to break my heart," Amanda denied quickly, puzzled at the concern in Marlee's eyes. They were blue, like Zach's. "Why would you say such a thing?"

"Zach would never deliberately hurt anyone, but you don't look quite as free and easy as the other women he's dated. You look like you take your life, and your men, seriously. If you do that with Zach, you'll get hurt."

Something twinged deep inside Amanda, and in any other instance she would have identified it as pain. But her pain, she reminded herself, wasn't over Zach. "You have the wrong impression, Marlee. I just broke off a very long relationship with another man. Zach and I aren't even dating."

"You're not?" Marlee looked skeptical.

"We're not," Amanda said forcefully.

"Well, then, bully for you. I just assumed that, well, considering the way you look at him..."

"What way do I look at him?"

"Like you're hungry for him," Marlee answered, and Amanda bit her bottom lip so hard that it hurt. Marlee was mistaken. She had to be.

"I look at him because he's easy on the eyes, that's all. You were right before. He's not the kind of man that I need."

"I can understand that." Marlee nodded wisely. "Take myself, for instance. I could never date a man like Zach."

"What's wrong with him?" Amanda asked, then pressed her lips together. She was supposed to understand what was wrong with him.

"Zach's never committed to a woman in his life. I need a man who's going to be there for me." Her words were so passionate that Amanda grew curious. With her flower-child aura, Marlee looked like a woman who would embrace free love.

"Have you ever found a man like that?"

"Three of them." Marlee's shrug was wry. "Unfortunately, they seemed a whole lot more committed to me before I married them than afterward."

"You've been married three times?"

"Married and divorced three times," she said, grimacing. "Serial marriage seems to run in the family. Maria is Clay's second ex-wife."

That meant that Clay and Marlee had five bad marriages between them. The number was staggering. "Is that why Zach is so against marriage?"

"The state of unhappily-ever-after? That's what he calls it, you know. I suppose that's part of it, but I think it goes deeper than that. Zach has a problem making a commitment. To anything."

"Come again?"

"Because of what he does, he can travel all over the country. He jumps from job to job and from place to place. He has a house at the beach, but it's vacant most of the year. And I've never seen him with the same woman more than twice." Marlee frowned. "Maybe I shouldn't be telling you all this."

"Telling her what?" Zach came into the room, wearing his usual smile.

"All your deep, dark secrets, big brother."

He grimaced dramatically. "Oh, no. Don't tell me you told her about the time you were holding a séance and I leaped from behind the couch dressed like a figure from the netherworld?"

"I didn't tell her about the time you put black spray paint in my aerosol deodorant can, either. You were incorrigible, Zach," Marlee said, but her eyes were affectionate as she gazed at her grinning brother. "You still are."

Incorrigible and so engaging that charm was practically seeping out of his pores, Amanda thought. She composed herself, careful not to be taken completely in by his charm. As long as she kept up her guard and was careful not to be alone with him, she could handle this strange, churning feeling he roused in her.

All she had to do was get through the next hour and the chaperoned drive home. After he dropped her off at her mother's house, she wouldn't have to see him again.

"Get off that couch, girl. The kids need some more players for their Frisbee game." Zach reached for Amanda's hand before she could tell him she was hopeless at throwing anything. He pulled her to her feet so she was standing just inches from him, leaned close and whispered. "By the way, my father just told me he's driving your mother home. Isn't that great?"

He wiggled his eyebrows suggestively. "There's a side benefit, too. On the drive home, it'll be just you and me, kid."

5

ZACH PULLED THE MGA to a stoplight, oblivious to the stares of admiration the little convertible was receiving from his fellow motorists. All his attention was on Amanda, who had yet to say a word since they'd left his father's house.

"All right, let's have it," he said.

"Let's have what?" She'd finally spoken, but she still wouldn't look at him.

"The reason you're acting like this. You were having a ball at the house. You even caught a Frisbee." He tactfully neglected to point out that it was the only one she'd caught out of the few dozen thrown her way. "Then the instant we got into the car, you clammed up. There's got to be a reason."

She didn't answer, which caused the traffic noise around them to seem inordinately loud. Somewhere in the distance, an ambulance siren wailed and tires screeched.

"Are you worried about your mother?" The more he thought about that, the more sense it made. Hadn't Amanda said that Pauline hadn't dated since her husband's death? "Because if you are, don't. I can vouch for my father. I know it seemed like he couldn't wait to get her alone, but he's a gentleman through and through. If you're worried, I'll even phone the house and tell him to behave himself."

He could tell by the tight set of her lips that she hadn't taken his offer seriously, although he'd meant what he said.

"I'm not worried about my mother," she said.

He thought hard. "Then are you still angry at me for telling your mother we were dating?"

Fresh outrage swept over her face as she turned to confront him, and Zach grimaced. "Oops. You'd forgotten about that, hadn't you? Well, now that I've brought it up, we might as well talk about it. Since your wedding's off, I don't see any reason for us not to date."

"Haven't you been listening to me? I haven't yet decided whether the wedding is off!"

"Come on, Amanda. You're not the kind of woman who dates two men at the same time, especially if you're married to one of them."

"But I'm not dating you!"

Car horns blared, drawing Zach's attention from her defiant face to the traffic signal. It was a damnable time for the light to turn green, especially since the MGA was first in line. He put the car in gear, and stepped on the gas.

The wind made it impossible for him to say what he'd intended, which was that Reid Carrigan was as wrong for her as rain on a Fourth of July parade. It had taken him all of ten minutes to determine that. She'd spent ten long years with the guy and still didn't see it.

The interstate was just ahead, but all it offered was an uninviting path back to Amanda's safe, snug little life in Plantation. Once he deposited her there, he feared she'd tell him that she didn't want to see him again. He spied a familiar turnoff to the right, and impulsively took it.

"This isn't the way to my place," Amanda shouted, but he merely pointed to his ear and mouthed the words *I can't hear you.*

Zach had barely pulled the MGA into a space in the parking lot at his destination when Amanda whirled on him. "What do you think you're doing?"

He shrugged, and indicated the scene in front of them. They were outside a vast go-kart track that twisted around an open field like a monstrous, slithering snake. He tried a smile. "I thought you might enjoy a spin in a go-kart."

"A spin in a go-kart?" She was beyond incredulity, and he thought she looked kind of cute with her eyes wide and her mouth open. "Are you nuts? We were having an argument about the way you keep insisting I'm not marrying Reid!"

"You're not going to marry him," he said, ignoring the fact that she was trying valiantly to interrupt him. "You can't want to marry a man who treated you as badly as he did at that restaurant. When you start thinking clearly, you'll realize that."

"That's the problem! I can't think clearly when I'm around you!"

From the way she colored, she clearly hadn't meant to reveal that. But Zach wasn't so sure the revelation was a good thing. He frowned. "Maybe a spin around the track will clear your head."

"You're impossible!"

"Actually, where you're concerned, I'm quite possible."

"That's not what I meant, and you know it. You can't just arbitrarily decide that I'm not going to marry Reid."

"There's nothing arbitrary about it. You aren't going to marry him. Which brings up another point. Since you've already sent out the wedding invitations, shouldn't you send out cancellation notices? I'll help you do it."

"What do you mean you'll help...wait a minute, how do you know that I've already sent out the wedding invitations?" No sooner had she asked the angry question than she smacked her forehead. "How could I have forgotten? You heard me say so at the restaurant when you were eavesdropping!"

Since they'd established days ago that he didn't have a good defense to that charge, he decided to leave it alone. He grinned. "So how about that spin around the track?"

He had the impression she was counting to ten under her breath. "I'm not going to drive a go-kart."

"C'mon. Let's get out of the car. You might change your mind once you get an up-close-and-personal look at the track."

"I'm not going to change my mind," she retorted, "and I'm not going to get out of the car until we set some rules."

"Some rules?" His voice was wary. "I don't like the sound of this."

She squared her shoulders and lifted her chin. He would have told her that her hair was so wind-blown it looked vaguely like scattered hay, but he thought that would only make her angrier. "Rule number one is that you can't touch or kiss me anymore."

He thought for a moment. "If you get to make a rule, I get to make one too. Here's mine. You can touch and kiss me anytime you want."

She blew out a breath, and pinched her brow together. "Aren't you ever serious?"

"I was being serious." He held up his fingers in the time-honored pledge. "Scout's honor. I won't mind at all if you kiss me. In fact, I encourage it."

"Rule number two," she continued as if she hadn't heard him. "After tonight, you have to promise to leave me alone. No more flowers. No more showing up to take me to dinners I didn't agree to."

"I bet the kids in your neighborhood never let you invent any games when you were growing up."

"What? What are you talking about now?"

"The kid who invents the game makes up the rules. And, honey, I've gotta tell you, you're one heck of a dreadful rule maker. I thought your first rule was bad, not to mention possibly harmful to my health, but your second rule takes the grand prize for all-time rotten rule." He shook his head. "It's so atrocious that I don't think I can follow it."

"Zach?" Her eyes and voice were imploring, but he thought she probably didn't even know what she was asking for. He hopped out of the car, walked around to the passenger side and opened the door.

"C'mon. Let's not talk about this right now. It's depressing me, and I'm in the mood for a go-kart ride. Just get out of the car, Amanda. Please?"

"Oh, if I must," she said finally, just when he'd decided that she was going to dig in the heels of her sensible shoes and refuse. "But I'm not riding. And that's my final word on the subject."

Minutes later, after Zach had bought his ticket to ride, they approached a noisy track where workers in red jackets and hats stood among three rows of gaily bedecked go-karts. They were painted an array of bright colors and wore typical race-car labels. About fifteen people—Amanda mentally referred to them as victims—waited their turn.

"Wait in line with me and keep me company?" Zach asked, so cheerfully that nobody would have guessed they'd been arguing a few minutes ago. Then again, few others probably had Zach's penchant for eavesdropping.

She nodded, trying valiantly to keep her anger alive. It faded just a little when she realized that, aside from a few lanky teenage boys, they were the tallest ones in line.

"Do you realize that this line is full of children?" Her voice was louder than normal, because the din was so great.

"You're right," Zach replied. Around them, the adolescents in the line kept up a stream of excited chatter. "That just goes to show you how much fun it is. Kids wouldn't come here if it wasn't."

"Do you come here often?" She sounded suspicious, and he let out a deep, resonant laugh that evaporated the rest of her anger. Darn it. It was so hard to stay mad at the man.

"I usually come here with Mia or Scooter. They're not old enough to drive a kart by themselves yet, but they have two-seat karts that are almost as much fun." His eyes gleamed. "But I have been here by myself before. I don't happen to believe that children are the only ones who can have fun."

Amanda bristled. "Are you trying to say that I don't have any fun?"

"You said that." He put his palm out to divorce himself from the statement. "Don't blame it on me."

"Because you're wrong. I do have fun."

"So that's why you refuse to get on a go-kart," he said under his breath. She was standing so close to him that, despite the track noises, she heard his comment.

Her temper, which until a few days ago had been typically serene, ignited again. "Don't you dare say that you could have predicted before we got here that I wouldn't get on a go-kart!"

"Okay," he agreed readily, "I won't."

"Because it's not going to work this time. You can't get me to do what you want me to do by saying that you could have predicted that I wouldn't do it just so I will."

They had moved through the line quickly, and only one person stood between them and the rows of go-karts.

"You think I'm afraid to ride, don't you?" Amanda asked, recklessly now because the probability of her having to get in one of the little cars was slight. "Well, you're wrong. I'm not. I'd get in that kart and prove it to you right now if you had bought another ticket."

The boy in front of them settled himself into a gleaming yellow go-kart, bringing Amanda and Zach to the front of the line. Amanda had an odd premonition as Zach grinned and reached into his back pocket. When he withdrew his hand, he held up not one, but two, tickets.

Everything happened quickly after that. Amanda's mouth dropped open at the same time one of the workers took the tickets and indicated a pair of go-karts. The lead kart was cherry-red, and Zach urged Amanda forward with a hand on her back until she ducked under the roll bar and climbed inside the contraption. He pulled the seatbelt across her body and fastened it.

Panic flared in her breast, and her eyes were wild when they met Zach's. "How do you drive one of these things?"

"Put the pedal to the metal and go."

Zach, the fiend, actually looked as though he was enjoying her hysteria. It would serve him right if she did what she felt like doing, which was standing up in the kart and screaming like a banshee. He gave her a quick thumbs-up signal and retreated to the kart behind hers, which was painted a metallic green.

Suddenly, Amanda couldn't get enough air, and her heart hammered wildly in her chest. The riders who had started before them were already whipping their karts expertly around the crowded track, but Amanda had no experience at this sort of thing. Her eyes fastened on a sign near the starting area. It said, Ride At Your Own Risk.

One of the workers rapped the back of her kart with his hand, signaling that she should go. She took minor consolation in the fact that the wildly winding track was lined with double rows of sheared tires and long lengths of rubber.

Closing her eyes, she gripped the steering wheel and took Zach's advice. She pressed down on the pedal with all her might. The kart jerked forward, her survival instincts kicked in and her eyelids popped open. Double rows of lights illuminated the snaking, blacktopped course and momentarily blinded her.

Her eyes adjusted to the artificial glow before she had driven twenty yards, which was just in time to identify the track's first hairpin turn. She took it with her heart in her throat. Her palms were clammy, but she managed to hold onto the vibrating steering wheel as the kart whipped around the turn.

Then she was flying, her hair flowing behind her and the wind wilder than it had ever felt in Zach's convertible. She took the second turn at the same frantic clip, but this time her heart had dipped back into her chest.

Take that, Zach Castelli.

On the straightaway, she dared a glance over her shoulder and spotted Zach's shiny green kart a few lengths behind her. A latent competitive streak kicked in with a vengeance.

I'll show him, she thought as she zoomed around another curve. *There's no way that he's going to pass me.*

The course was laid out even crazier than it had appeared at the starting area, and Amanda focused all her thoughts and energy on navigating it. She heard herself screaming as she whizzed through a particularly perilous turn, but she kept going, propelled by the knowledge that Zach was behind her.

She passed a white kart driven by a preteen boy on a long straightaway and took a yellow kart on the following curve. Her spirits soared as high as a helium balloon, and she actually whooped aloud. She streaked through the rest of the course in a blur of cherry-red metal and screeching tires until only two treacherous curves remained before the finish line.

The nose of Zach's green kart was visible in her peripheral vision, and she turned her steering wheel so that the body of her go-kart blocked his passing lane. She maneuvered the first turn, saw that Zach was positioning his kart to pass her on the straightaway and yanked her steering wheel again.

"You can't pass me, Castelli," she yelled, uncaring that he couldn't hear her. It felt good just to say it.

By the time she hit the final turn, there was no earthly way he could overtake her. Her little vehicle, the one that had made her quake before the ride, flashed under the finish line a full car length ahead of Zach's. She eased up on the pedal and raised both arms in victory.

She'd no sooner gotten out of the kart than Zach was beside her, picking her up and spinning her around as she laughed in triumph. She raised her glimmering eyes to his, and he kissed her full on the lips. Her arms snaked around his neck and she kissed him back, tasting wind and exhilaration and man. She would have kept on kissing him if one of the red-jacketed workers hadn't tapped her on the shoulder.

"You two are gonna have to do that somewhere else." He was smiling and shouting to be heard above the noise. Amanda giggled. She actually giggled, every bit as giddily as her mother had when she'd met Paul Castelli. Her laughing eyes met Zach's, and he grabbed her hand. Her fingers closed around his.

"You were a little hellcat," he said, when they were far enough away from the track that their ears no longer rang from the loud whine of go-kart motors. "Where'd you learn to four-wheel drift like that?"

"What does that mean?" She was still giddy from her victory, and there was a little bounce in her step that matched his.

"It means what you did with the kart when you got to the turns. How you let your rear wheels kick out and then snapped them straight with the steering wheel."

"I didn't do that," Amanda confessed, shaking her head in bemusement. "I only did what you told me to do."

"What I told you to do?"

"Uh-huh. You told me to put the pedal to the metal and go. That's what I did."

They had reached the parking lot, and he stopped walking. When he clasped her shoulders and turned her to face him, his eyes were as round as the steering wheel on the go-kart. "That was just an expression of speech. I didn't know you'd take it literally."

"Well, I did." Feeling inordinately pleased with herself, she lightly flicked him on the chest with her fingertips. "And it worked, didn't it? You couldn't catch me."

"That's because you had a head start. And, there at the end, you deliberately blocked my way when I would have passed you."

"Oh, pooh. That's sour grapes, and you know it," she teased. She titled her head back and kissed him lightly, and very briefly, on the lips. "I beat you, fair and square. Say it, Zach. Say Amanda beat Zach."

"Amanda beat Zach," he complied readily. They were standing between two cars in the parking lot, and his face was in shadows. The overhead street lamp gave off just enough light that Amanda could pinpoint the second his smile faded and the teasing glint disappeared from his eyes. "It's funny, but I don't feel much like a loser right now."

She knew he was going to kiss her just as surely as she knew that she had time to move out of kissing range. The crazy thing was that she didn't want to elude him.

His kiss was soft, so soft and tender that she felt unbelievably cherished. He seemed to draw the breath from her mouth and blow it back inside, filling her with an intangible something that had been missing her entire life.

He kissed every inch of her lips, from one corner of her mouth to the other. When his tongue touched hers, she gasped, drawing it deeper inside her mouth. The feel of it, wet and warm against hers, was so erotic that liquid heat pooled in the very center of her.

Her nipples hardened and her fingers tangled in the long, silky hair at the nape of his neck. She rubbed her breasts sensuously against him, feeling just as wild as his checkered shirt. Her lower body came into contact with the hard length of him, and she wanted him right then and there.

He drew his mouth from hers, and she moaned in protest. But then he firmly, determinedly, put distance between the lengths of their bodies before he leaned his forehead against hers.

"I hate to be the one to point this out, honey, but we're in a parking lot."

In a parking lot. The fuzziness at the corners of Amanda's brain abated, and embarrassment swept over her. She had been wantonly kissing Zach in a parking lot where anyone could have happened upon them. Worse, it was the very last thing she had intended to happen.

"We broke my first rule," she lamented.

"It was a bad rule, anyway, and you know it. Not to mention completely unenforceable," he said, lightly massaging her shoulders. She couldn't think clearly with him touching her, with his forehead against hers, so she stepped out of his reach.

"But I made it for a reason, Zach." In the space of a few moments, she had gone from incredibly aroused to incredibly confused. The embers of desire still glowed inside her, adding to her bewilderment. "Think about this from my point of view. It's possible that I'm at the end of a ten-year relationship. I'm not ready to start another one."

"But that's why I'm perfect for you. I'm not about serious relationships or commitment or any of those things. I'm about having a good time. Period. I'm not going to ask you to marry me. I'm not even going to ask you to live with me. All I'm asking is that we have a good time together for as long as it lasts."

His logic was off-kilter. Nothing was as simple as he made it sound. Life was full of twists and turns and downright surprises. Such as Zach Castelli, oozing irresistible charm, slipping into a restaurant booth across from her and upsetting the delicate balance of her life.

"I don't know, Zach." She looked down at the ground as though it would give her the answer, but all she saw was pavement. "I don't know if I can have a casual relationship."

"Take it from me, a casual relationship is the best kind of relationship. Both people are upfront about what they want, and nobody gets hurt."

He tipped her chin up with one of his fingers, and Amanda saw that he really believed the words he was spouting. But there was nothing casual about the way her skin tingled where his fingers touched her or the way her body still clamored for his. He smiled, and his dimple was so prominent that even the darkness couldn't cloak it.

"Well, what do you say?"

Amanda swallowed the words of agreement that were tapping against the back of her lips.

"I say that you should drive me to my mother's house so I can pick up my car and that we shouldn't see each other after that."

"That's an impulsive decision."

"So what if it is?" Her back went ramrod straight.

"You're not impulsive, Amanda. You like to consider things from all angles, think them through, turn them around and look them over. I'm afraid that I'm not going to be able to accept your decision until you give it some more thought."

"Some more thought," she parroted. "Of all the narcissistic—"

"Now don't start with the names, Amanda." He sounded completely unaffected by her outrage. "I'm just letting you be true to your nature. C'mon. I'll do what you said and give you a ride to your mother's house. It's getting late. I'm sure that practical mind of yours is telling you that you need your sleep because you have to work tomorrow."

He turned and walked toward his car, leaving Amanda stewing. A trio of teenagers walked from the direction of the go-kart track, and one of them pointed at Amanda and said something she couldn't make out. They all giggled, and she imagined they were discussing the amorous display that she and Zach had put on.

That was his fault, too, she thought as she followed Zach to his car. If he hadn't tricked her into taking that wild ride, none of this would have happened.

She ignored the little voice that told her that the kiss had been worth every exasperating moment.

THE INSTANT AMANDA GOT HOME from work the following Friday, she kicked off her shoes and sank into the paisley-print sofa in her immaculate living room. Her pantyhose felt confining, so she peeled them off, crumpled them into a ball and flung them across the room. They unfurled and floated harmlessly to the floor. The next time she threw something, she'd have to pick a material more substantial than nylon.

It had been a thoroughly rotten week. After days of procrastinating, she'd finally told Reid halfway through it what she'd known in her heart since he'd asked for his grandmother's ring back. The wedding was off. Irrevocably off.

He hadn't taken it well, but she had steeled herself against his pleas for her to reconsider. She'd loved Reid for a long time, but he had harbored doubts before she even knew hers existed. She supposed she should be grateful those doubts had cropped up before the wedding rather than after.

So now what was she going to do with the rest of her life?

She'd had forever-after mapped out as recently as two weeks ago. A March wedding to Reid, followed by a Hawaiian honeymoon and then life as a lawyer's wife in a stunning new house in Miami Beach. She and Reid had even agreed that they should wait no longer than three years to have children.

Those dreams, which had taken ten years to build, had crumbled in seconds. Now Amanda was adrift, and she didn't even have her mother available to listen to her fears. She'd told her the breakup with Reid was definite in a hurried phone call, but she hadn't talked to her since because her mother had spent every day of the past week with Paul Castelli. Amanda didn't even want to think about where she was spending her nights.

The single thing that had gone right this past week was that Zach had taken her decision to stop seeing him seriously. She refused to analyze why that didn't improve her spirits.

The doorbell chimed. Amanda shut her eyes and wished she could shut out the world as easily. The gatekeeper phoned residents for guest approval, so it couldn't be anybody who didn't live in her townhouse complex.

It was probably that irritating little man next door who was running for president of the townhouse association. She padded to the door on bare feet and put the chain in place. If she talked to him through just a sliver of daylight, he'd have less chance of gaining entry. She opened the door a crack.

Twinkling blue eyes smiled into hers. Zach tilted his head, trying to see through the crack.

"Is that you in there, beautiful?" His voice was playful.

She could see vivid shards of orange, red and yellow and presumed they were on his shirt. "If you don't open the door soon, I'm going to get a crick in my neck."

The rush of joy that swept through Amanda was so powerful, and so confusing, that she staggered. She hadn't wanted Zach to seek her out. She'd even told him to stay away. But, now that he was here, she yearned to throw her arms around him and pull him inside. Which was exactly why she kept the chain in place.

"What are you doing here?"

"I was in the neighborhood and thought I'd drop by and say hello." His voice was light, teasing.

"You weren't in the neighborhood, Zach. Remember, you don't like concrete and shopping malls. Just go away. You shouldn't have gotten past the guard at the gatehouse in the first place."

"Okay. But first I've really got to use your bathroom," he said, gritting his teeth dramatically. "I've gotta go really bad. C'mon, Amanda. Have a heart and open the door. The guard didn't think I was all that menacing. You shouldn't either."

"Are you telling the truth?" she asked suspiciously.

"Sure, I am. I'm a terrible liar. You said so yourself. Please, Amanda. Please open the door."

"Oh, all right. But make it quick," she groused, closing the door so she could unfasten the chain. The dynamic lightning bolts crisscrossing his shirt didn't even make her blink when she threw open the door because she'd become used to his flamboyant clothing. She thought the shirts even suited him.

Zach smiled, dropped a light kiss on her forehead and walked past her, making a beeline for the kitchen. She closed the door and hurried after him, baffled by the brown-paper grocery bag that he set on her counter.

"Let's see what I have here." He reached into the bag

like a magician with a magic hat. "A six-pack of beer for me, although don't worry about me getting smashed: I don't plan to drink all of it tonight. And a four-pack of wine coolers for you, since we both know how you feel about bitter beer. Finally, two great big gooey strombolis. One has pepperoni, and one doesn't. I'll eat either, so you get to choose which one you want."

"What are you doing here, Zach?" Amanda ignored his offerings, although the scent of the food was making her empty stomach growl. Even if it were cholesterol-laden and artery-clogging. "Why did you bring all this stuff?"

"Because we have work to do," he said, as though it were the most logical answer in the world. "Everybody knows your brain power diminishes when there's no fuel in your stomach."

"As though strombolis are brain food."

"I eat them, and there's nothing wrong with my brain."

Amanda could have disputed that, but something important occurred to her. So important that she decided to ignore his latest nonsensical comment about their having work to do. She narrowed her eyes.

"Wait a minute. Don't you have to use my bathroom?"

"Nope."

"Nope?" She was flabbergasted. She'd also been had. Zach Castelli had talked his way inside her townhouse as effortlessly as he had maneuvered his way into her life. "Do you mean you were lying? But how could you have been lying? You're an atrocious liar. Your mouth twitches, your eyes shift, your smile fades. None of that happened."

"That's because I wasn't lying." He held up his hands, which had the second and third fingers folded over each other. "I had my fingers crossed behind my back."

"You had your fingers crossed behind your back?"

"Yep. I crossed those babies right before you opened the door, just in case you were going to be difficult about letting me inside. I even put down the grocery bag to do it. Anybody over the age of three knows that it isn't really a lie if you cross your fingers."

"But you have to be in your late twenties at least," she pointed out, thinking that it was hard to argue with lunacy.

"I'm thirty," he said cheerfully, and turned his attention to her kitchen drawers. He started yanking them open. "Knowing you, I bet you'll want a knife and fork to eat that stromboli. So are you going to tell me which one contains the silverware or should I just guess? We can't get started until we eat."

"Get started on what?"

"Our work."

"What work?" She wasn't sure whether he was making less sense than usual or whether she was still reeling from the fact that he thought crossed fingers negated a lie.

"I brought some envelopes and stationery. The thick, cream-colored kind. I almost bought some with purple and orange streaks, but I didn't think you'd appreciate that. If you give me a list, I'll address the envelopes. You can write the notes."

"What notes?"

He sent her an exasperated look, as if she should know what he was talking about. "The ones telling your intended guests that the wedding is off."

Amanda's indignation shriveled like a cashmere sweater that had been thrown into the dryer. Her expression softened. She should be furious at Zach for railroading his way into her townhouse, but there was something incredibly sweet about his offer to help her send out notices for a canceled wedding.

"How do you know that my wedding is off?"

He stopped rummaging through her kitchen drawers and raised his eyes. For once, they weren't twinkling. His dimple wasn't even showing. "It *is* off, isn't it?"

She was tempted to tell him she was still vacillating about whether to marry Reid, but she could have sworn he was holding his breath. As though her answer really mattered. Lying wasn't an option, Amanda knew, even if she did cross her fingers.

"Yes," she said, "it's off."

His slow smile was as warm as the Florida sunshine. The warmth seeped through the upper layer of her skin and penetrated the defenses she had erected against him.

"Second drawer on the right," she said.

His smile widened, highlighting his dimple, as he pulled open the indicated drawer and drew out the silverware. They both knew that she had just invited him to stay for dinner.

Thirty minutes later, Amanda put down her fork in surrender. She and Zach were seated at her kitchen table with the remnants of their strombolis on their plates. Amanda had eaten so much that she was glad that the summer-weight leggings she'd changed into had an elasticized waist. Her wine cooler, a refreshing strawberry concoction, was half empty.

"That's it. I give up. I can't possibly eat another bite."

"Not even if I feed it to you?" A juicy piece of pepperoni peeked out of Zach's stromboli. He speared it with his fork and held it in front of her, as though he were Adam offering Eve a bite of apple.

"That's not fair." Amanda's eyes fastened on the pepperoni, and she licked her lips. "I love pepperoni."

"Then why didn't you take the stromboli with the pepperoni?"

"Oh, let's see." She pretended to think. "Because it had about a thousand more calories than the other one, which I would say had about a thousand calories itself."

"You're exaggerating." He wiggled the pepperoni

temptingly. "Besides, if you're worried about the calories, I can think of something we can do to burn them off."

She glowered at him, and he burst out laughing. "You should see your face, Amanda. I only meant that you needed your strength for all the notes you're going to write."

"You didn't mean that at all."

"All right, maybe I didn't. But you can't blame a guy for trying. C'mon, I know you want this." His brows rose, and she thought that he probably knew she wanted him, too.

She opened her mouth, and he inserted the food. Her eyes met his while she chewed, and she savored both the spicy taste of the pepperoni and the warm glow in his eyes. She damned herself for finding him so attractive. His flashy shirts would have overshadowed any other man, but not Zach. Never mind his classic high forehead, boyish mop of hair and his dimple. His dazzling smile alone was enough to make her heart flutter in a way that it never had when she was with Reid.

A thought struck her, and she voiced it before thinking, à la Zach Castelli. "This is surreal, being here with you instead of with Reid."

"Does breaking up with him hurt very much?" He almost whispered the question, and Amanda considered it.

If anyone had told her a few months ago that she and Reid wouldn't be spending the rest of their lives together, she wouldn't have believed it. Now that it had happened, she could hardly believe her reaction.

"What hurts is that I no longer know what I'm going to do with the rest of my life," she said truthfully. "The odd part is that breaking up with Reid hardly hurts at all. It did at first, of course, when you met me at the restaurant. But not now."

"What I don't understand is why you spent ten years with him."

Ten years. Amanda thought back, and the memories blurred one into another. They left a vaguely pleasant impression, but she was stunned to realize there wasn't a single vivid memory she would cherish over the years to come. Already, in the short time she'd known Zach, she had a storehouse of memories.

"I guess it was inertia," she mused. "I started going out with him when I was sixteen, and I never stopped. One year blended into the next until he became a habit."

"But he's such a jerk."

"He's not a jerk," she denied. "He's intelligent, for starters. He's also obliging and undemanding. Unlike somebody else I know."

"Let's see if I've got this right. Intelligent, obliging and undemanding. Just the character traits every woman wants in the man she's going to marry." At her dark look, he put up a hand in apology. "Sorry, I shouldn't have said that."

"No, you shouldn't have. I don't see anything wrong with having an intelligent, obliging, undemanding husband."

"If Reid was so wonderful, suppose you explain why you like me better." Zach summoned the grin that was never far from his lips.

He was toying with her again. Amanda understood that, but it didn't make the knowledge any more palatable. He'd thrown her off balance again, and she had to right herself by whatever means possible.

Once, just once, she'd like to turn Zach topsy-turvy and see how he liked it. She thought of Zach in the parking lot at the go-kart track, earnestly informing her that he wasn't about commitment. That all he was about was having a good time. A devilish idea struck her, and she didn't even try to extinguish it. It was time she got back at Zach.

"I'm not sure if I do like you better," she lied, "but I certainly couldn't go ahead with my wedding to Reid considering that I might be pregnant."

"Pregnant?" Zach uttered the single word. Then his gorgeous mouth dropped open, those incredible blue eyes widened and his smooth skin paled beneath his tan.

For the first time since Amanda had met him, Zach Castelli was speechless.

6

"WE HAD UNPROTECTED SEX, Zach. Surely you realize that pregnancy is one of the consequences of unprotected sex."

"But..."

Zach, who prided himself on being loquacious and imperturbable, was unsure if he could complete a sentence. His throat seemed to close, and he wasn't even sure if he could speak. His skin was clammy, and he felt overheated. He wondered if Amanda's air conditioner had shut off. He tried again to speak.

"If..."

Again, he couldn't make his mouth and brain work in unison. She was gazing at him with steady green eyes, and he had the odd feeling that she was enjoying his discomfort. But that couldn't be. There was nothing to relish about the possibility that she might be pregnant. He cleared his throat and tried again.

"But aren't you on the birth-control pill?" This time he managed to speak, but he sounded like somebody else, somebody with panic swelling his throat.

She shook her head, her eyes wide and innocent. "Whatever gave you that idea?"

"Afterward, you said something about being afraid I might have a disease. You didn't say anything about being afraid you might become pregnant."

"I thought that was implied."

"Was implied?" he asked, and then realized that he had picked up one of her habits, which was repeating the last few words of the previous sentence. For the first time, he wondered why he hadn't thought to use birth control.

He always carried condoms in his wallet, but they hadn't even occurred to him the night he and Amanda had been intimate. That was curious, because he'd never forgotten before. In fact, he'd been so determined never to become deeply involved with anyone that he'd insisted on using condoms, even if the woman claimed she was on birth control. Which Amanda had not.

"What's the matter, Zach?" Again, her expression was as innocent as undisturbed snow the morning after it had fallen. "Don't you like children?"

"Of course I..." He stopped speaking, unsure of what to say. He'd always loved children, but he'd never pictured himself as a father. Because, according to his moral code, being a father meant being a husband. And he never could be that.

"Oh, don't worry, Zach. If I am pregnant, I won't insist that you marry me. Or that you help me raise our baby. It doesn't need to have anything to do with you."

"What do you mean it wouldn't have anything to do with me?" Zach's confusion instantly turned to incredulity, and he realized in amazement that he had raised his voice. What's more, he sounded angry. He closed his eyes and massaged his temples. He never got angry.

"Zach?" Even in his agitated state, Zach picked up on the concern in Amanda's voice. He wasn't yet ready to open his eyes, so he kept them closed. "Zach, would you look at me? I'm sorry. I shouldn't have done this."

He had no idea what she was talking about, and he didn't have the strength to ask her to explain.

"Zach, listen to me. I'm not pregnant. I just said that I might be because around you it seems like I can't tell up from down. I wanted you to know what that felt like. For once, I wanted to see you speechless. But it wasn't nearly as much fun as I imagined it would be."

"Are you trying to tell me," he asked slowly, "that you are on the pill?"

"Well, no," Amanda answered.

"Then there is a possibility that you're pregnant?"

Amanda bit her lip, and her green eyes looked troubled. "You're not listening to me, Zach. I'm not pregnant. It was the absolute safest time of my cycle."

"Then there's no possibility that you are pregnant?"

"I guess anything's possible, but..."

"When will you know for sure?"

"I already know for sure." She pursed her lips.

"You just said that anything's possible," he pointed out.

"It's infinitesimally possible. Unlikely. Improbable. *Remote*. Now can we drop the subject?"

"When will you know for sure?"

"Oh, for Pete's sake, Zach. You're like a pit bull that's gotten hold of a bone. I'll be one hundred percent positive in a week or so. Now, can we let it go?"

"I suppose so," Zach said, as some of the feeling oozed back into his limbs. He suspected that he wouldn't feel entirely relieved until she was entirely sure. But it wasn't like him to dwell on something that might never happen, even if it was a momentous something.

Today, he reminded himself, the topic wasn't a possible unplanned pregnancy. It was a canceled wedding. He stood and started to clear the table.

"You don't have to do that," she protested.

"My mother taught me that I did have to do this. You just sit there and relax." He dumped the remnants of the food into the trash and rinsed the plates before putting them in the dishwasher. "It was pretty evident early on that I couldn't cook worth a lick, but I can clear dishes with the best of them."

She watched him as he worked, and her recent annoyance with him faded. There was something incredibly sexy about Zach in the kitchen. Especially her kitchen, because her white cabinets were trimmed in cotton-candy pink and she'd hung white wallpaper decorated with delicate rose flowers. Zach's clothing clashed wildly with the decor, but he still looked as though he belonged.

"Have you thought about what you're going to write?" He returned to the table with an armful of supplies, and she looked at him blankly. Her mind was still on the ridiculous notion she'd just had of Zach belonging. As though he could ever be hers. As though she even wanted him to be.

"Write? Write what?"

He deposited his bounty on the table, and she saw it was the stationery and envelopes he had referred to earlier. He tweaked her nose. "If you send the notes out blank, it might be too hard for people to figure out that the wedding's off."

"Of course." Amanda covered her confusion with brisk efficiency as she rose. "I'll get a couple of pens and the invitation list. There are about one hundred names and addresses on it. You can work from that."

"So what are you going to write?" Zach asked when she returned to the kitchen. She sat down, handed him the invitation list and a pen and opened a thick, hardback book. She immediately turned to the index.

"I don't know yet. I need to check this book first."

"What is it? The book of life?"

She cut her eyes at him. "It's a book on wedding etiquette."

"You actually bought a book on wedding etiquette?"

"I didn't. Reid did. But I thought it was a good idea. We wanted to make sure we did everything—"

"By the book," he interrupted, and she scowled at him.

He looked as though he was trying hard not to laugh, and she expected him to ask why Reid hadn't checked the entry on the polite way to break up.

"Here's something on the wording of the notes you're supposed to send out," Amanda said, after she'd flipped through the pages. "You're simply supposed to announce that the marriage will not take place."

"So how, exactly, are you going to say that?"

She closed the book with a thump and looked at him, shaking her head. "Why do you have to know the exact wording?"

"I'm looking out for your interests. You have to be careful not to put in words like 'postponed' or 'delayed.' That might give people the wrong impression."

"The wrong impression?" He was irritating her again. She didn't know how he managed it so effortlessly. "Maybe it wouldn't be the wrong impression. Maybe I'll forgive Reid and still marry him at some later date."

"That's not what Pauline said. She said that you told *intelligent, obliging, undemanding* Reid that it was over with a capital O. She was real happy about it. She said that it was about time you opened your eyes and noticed there were other men in the world." He grinned. "Men like me."

"My mother said that?" She sent him a sharp look, and he nodded happily. "Wait a minute. When did you see my mother?"

"This morning. I know you think I'm omniscient, but I'm not. The truth is that Pauline told me your wedding was off before I came over here."

"This morning?"

"Uh-huh," he continued. "I stopped by my father's house on the way to work, and there she was."

"Do you mean she spent the night there?" Amanda was horrified. "That can't be. Your father probably invited her to breakfast, and she must have gotten up early this morning to drive there."

"It was six o'clock in the morning, and she was wearing my father's bathrobe," Zach informed her dryly, and Amanda's world tipped a little further off center.

"Pauline is past the age of consent," Zach said gently. "And, judging by the way she and Papa were acting, I'd say this was a positive development. I don't think Pauline would appreciate your acting as though somebody just died."

Amanda looked down at the paper in front of her and deliberately picked up a pen. The image of her naive, sweet-faced mother in Paul Castelli's bathrobe was too much for her brain to process.

She absolutely refused to discuss her jumbled feelings with Zach. If she did, he'd probably take the opportunity to talk about how natural sex was. He might even reiterate his good-time-guy speech and say that sex didn't actually have to mean anything. She scribbled furiously on the surprisingly tasteful stationery Zach had picked out.

"So what are you writing?"

Amanda sighed. He had returned to their earlier topic, and she realized he wouldn't let go of it until she answered his question. She read from the card she had just finished.

"Amanda Baldwin and Reid Carrigan regret to inform you that their marriage will not take place." She raised her eyes from the card. "Satisfied?"

"Get rid of that 'regret to inform you' part. I think a better way to state it would be: Amanda Baldwin is delighted to inform you that she is not, nor ever will be, marrying supercilious, sanctimonious Reid Carrigan."

The bait was dangling in front of her, like a worm on the end of a line that Zach had cast into the sea, but Amanda refused to take it. She couldn't afford to keep losing her temper. She couldn't think straight when she was angry, and she needed all her mental faculties around Zach.

"I didn't know fishermen knew such big words," she said.

He grinned. "And I didn't know it bothered you that I'm a fisherman."

"Why would it bother me?" Amanda retorted, denying the allegation a shade too quickly. The hard truth was that she'd always imagined the man for her would be a college graduate with a good job. She frowned because that didn't make sense. This was Zach, the good-time guy. Mr. I'm-Not-About-Commitment. "It doesn't matter to me in the slightest what you do for a living. Why should it?"

"You tell me." He put his elbows on the table and his chin in his hands.

"I just told you it didn't matter," she said, her voice rising. "Now can we get back to work? You're the one who wanted to do this tonight, and so far you haven't addressed a single envelope."

He pinned her with his blue gaze, and she couldn't meet his eyes for more than a second. She picked up another piece of stationery and wrote, reproducing her first note.

"Okay," he said, "maybe I'll imagine I'm Arnold Schwarzenegger while I'm writing."

"Arnold Schwarzenegger?"

"Don't you go to the movies? He was the Terminator." He imitated the actor's Austrian accent. "Let's terminate this wedding."

TWO HOURS LATER, Zach flexed and unflexed his fingers as he considered the stacks of stuffed envelopes atop the kitchen table. He frowned a little when he glimpsed the address on the top one. It was supposed to say Mr. and Mrs. Todd Sloan, but Todd looked like Toad and Sloan looked like Slime.

He quickly flipped the envelope over before Amanda could say that she didn't know anybody named Toad Slime. If she noticed how atrocious his penmanship was, she might even insist on addressing the envelopes over. That wouldn't be good. Zach wanted Reid Carrigan out of her life and her thoughts as quickly as possible.

"Arnold had better watch out for competition for the title role if they decide to make another Terminator movie," Zach said. "You and me, we can terminate with the best of them."

"Don't they use guns in those movies?" Amanda asked.

"Ah, but the pen is mightier than the gun."

"Isn't the expression the pen is mightier than the *sword?*"

"Yeah, but the expression's dated. If Baron Lytton had written that play today instead of more than a hundred fifty years ago, he'd probably substitute gun for sword." Zach screwed up his forehead. "On second thought, he might say the pen is mightier than the stealth bomber."

Amanda's eyebrows shot up. "You know where the expression 'the pen is mightier than the sword' comes from? I'm impressed."

"I know a lot of things," Zach said, rising and retrieving the brown-paper grocery bag from the kitchen counter. He used a swiping motion to transfer the envelopes from the table to the bag. "Such as the post office won't deliver these letters without stamps. I'll get some and mail them tomorrow."

Amanda smiled at him and leaned back in the kitchen chair, extending her arms over her head. The movement stretched the fabric of her cotton shirt and called attention to her chest, which made him wonder why some men preferred women with large breasts. Hers were perfect. Just the right size to fit into his hands.

The thought blasted him with warmth, as though somebody had just opened the oven door and let the heat escape. He glanced at Amanda's oven, but the door was firmly closed.

"You don't have to buy one hundred stamps," she said, stretching her arms even higher. The temperature in the room rose further. "Helping me address the envelopes was more than enough."

"Believe me," Zach said, slightly breathless, "thirty-three dollars is not too much to pay to have Reid out of your life."

Amanda stopped stretching, and Zach wasn't sure whether to be relieved or to grab her hands and extend them over her head again. Her green eyes were piercing when they looked up at him, and the recessed lighting in her kitchen ceiling illuminated her freckles.

"Why do you care so much, Zach? You said yourself that you're not going to stick around for long, so why should it matter to you if I let Reid back into my life?"

Why *did* it matter? Her question made Zach pause in his envelope gathering, because it was one he hadn't asked himself. He only knew that the thought of Amanda with Reid was enough to make him want to hit something. Preferably Reid's face.

"I like you." Zach thought she'd be able to tell exactly how much if she looked a little lower. The material of his jeans was suddenly way too tight. "I don't want to see the people I like get hurt, and Reid will hurt you."

"Meaning that you won't?"

Zach sighed and sat down. This thing with Amanda was growing more complicated with every tick of the clock. He reached across the table and took one of her hands in his, noticing how small and delicate it was. He slid his thumb back and forth against the smooth skin of her palm.

"I like women too much to hurt them. I tell the women

I date up front what I want out of the relationship, and that eliminates the possibility that anybody will get hurt.''

Amanda couldn't think straight with his thumb sliding over her palm, so she snatched her hand from his. If she owned the universe, she would have bet the stars that not all of the women who'd drifted through Zach's life had escaped unhurt. His expression was so earnest that she would have offered a side bet, risking the moon, that he didn't know that.

"What do you want from me?" she asked, praying she wasn't one of those vulnerable women whom Zach could unwittingly hurt.

"You." All of the teasing was gone from Zach's eyes, and they blazed with unconcealed passion. "I want you."

"You mean," Amanda said, her voice cracking and her heart thudding, "that you want sex?"

He smiled crookedly. "I mean that I want what we had the other night. I thought that was pretty terrific. Didn't you?"

She pursed her lips because she already suspected that what they'd shared had been more than sex. At least it had been for her. He was looking at her with those damnable blue eyes, waiting for her answer, and it was suddenly too much to take. She pushed herself away from the table and rose, turning her back on him and walking a few steps.

"Am I on the wrong track here?" Zach prodded. Even if she hadn't heard the scrape of the chair on the kitchen floor, she would have known he had followed her. The heady, clean smell that came off his skin made her want to turn toward it. Toward him. "Didn't you think the other night was pretty terrific?"

"Yes, but..."

"No. No buts." One of his hands cupped her neck, rubbing the sensitive skin at her nape. She shivered, but it wasn't from the cold. She was much, much too warm. "In my experience, I've found that a *but* can ruin a perfectly good sentence."

"But," Amanda repeated. Zach used his other hand to slowly spin her into his arms, and placed his fingers on her lips. She wondered if he could feel them trembling.

"Shh," he said. "I'd rather you blast me with four-letter words than hear that heinous three-letter monster again."

They were so close that she could feel his breath. Heat pooled between her legs and pulsed with an urgent beat. If she could have spoken, she would have told him that she had forgotten what she was going to say.

Amanda moved forward at the same instant that Zach did, bringing her breasts up hard against his chest, making them swell and ache. She tilted her chin, and his mouth was on hers, hot and hard and heavenly. She parted her lips, asking for more and receiving all he had to give.

His tongue plundered the sensitive roof of her mouth and wantonly circled hers while his hips ground against hers in a motion so sensuous that she thought she had stopped breathing. Her knees buckled just as they had the first night they'd kissed in the foyer. Just as the knees of passion-drunk heroines collapsed in the old, romantic movies she liked to watch.

But this was different, because while her knees buckled from passion, her soul swelled with need. This was different, because this was Zach. Zach, who had entered her life with the force of a sledgehammer and bulldozed his way into her heart.

She clutched at his shoulders to keep from falling, and he was so in tune with her that he understood even that. He caught her under the legs, swept her off the floor and carried her into the living room, kissing her as he walked.

"I don't know about you, honey," he said as he deposited her gently, reverently on the sofa, "but I can't make it all the way to your bedroom."

He pulled at her soft cotton overshirt, easily turning it inside out and tugging it over her head. Then his mouth was teasing her nipples through the lacy material of her bra. She was vaguely aware that his fingers shook as he worked to unfasten the front clasp of the garment.

Her breasts spilled free and something sweet and liquid splashed inside of her, flooding her with a sensation as new as it was wonderful. Zach pulled off her leggings and panties in one fluid motion, and covered her body with fluttery kisses that she felt in even the tiniest pores of her skin.

She'd only known him for little more than a week, but her body responded to his as though it had been attuned for an eternity. As though he were a part of her that she hadn't even known was missing until she'd found him. The part that made her complete.

He started to join her where she lay stretched on the sofa, but he was fully clothed and she didn't want that. She reached for his shirt with both hands and pulled it open, popping some of the buttons and baring a chest so dazzling she had to close her eyes for a minute to steady her nerves.

He smiled, probably because he knew that she really did like him better without his zany shirts. Her fingers moved to the button that fastened his jeans, and he took the cue, slipping out of his remaining clothing until he was as naked as she was.

There. That was how she liked him best.

"You're beautiful," she whispered, and she didn't realize that she had said the words aloud until he replied.

"Not half as beautiful as you are." His eyes ran over her with such ardent admiration that her shyness wilted before it could bloom.

She wished he'd say more, that words might give her a window into his thoughts, but he was a silent lover. Silent and serious, while the every-day Zach was just the opposite.

She forgot her disappointment a moment later when his beautiful mouth moved from her swollen breasts to her quivering stomach and lower, lower, until his tongue parted her with exquisite tenderness. Her instinctive embarrassment fled as flames licked at her body, and she saw jagged lightning bolts in red, orange and yellow. They surged through her, making her convulse in euphoria.

She opened her eyes and reached for Zach, tugging him up over her sweat-slick stomach and aching breasts. She half expected him to still be wearing his shirt, but the lightning bolts had been inside of her rather than imprinted on his shirt.

She kissed him, tasting her essence. There was an empty place inside her that needed to be filled, and only Zach could fill it. She reached between their bodies, finding him hot and hard, and stroked. He gasped against her mouth, and all she wanted was Zach. Zach inside her, Zach spilling his seed into her. He was nudging her willing legs apart when that last thought registered on her brain.

"Zach," she said, and the word sounded strained. He pulled back slightly and looked at her with passion-drugged eyes. "Protection?"

He groaned, detached himself from her, reached for his jeans, removed his wallet and plucked out a foil packet. In record time, he was sheathed, his body once more covering hers.

"Hurry," she whispered against his mouth, opening her legs and lifting her hips. "Oh, Zach, please hurry."

He sank into her with one smooth, fiery stroke, and the heat within her flared again. Bolder. Brighter. More brilliant. He was still for just a moment, but then he started to move. Before exquisite sensations rendered her mindless, Amanda was able to muster a few last coherent thoughts.

Zach was wrong. This wasn't nearly as uncomplicated as having sex. She'd had sex with Reid, although she hadn't known until now that was all it had been. She and Zach were making love. Earth-shattering, mind-blowing love.

Zach thrust into her over and over, and she rose to meet him as her heart slammed against his. Again and again. But it wasn't enough.

It would never be enough.

SLOWLY, VERY SLOWLY, Zach came back down to earth. His tremors subsided. His pulse slowed. His skin cooled. He grinned.

"I remembered right, didn't I? We are pretty terrific together."

He was still lying on top of her, still inside of her. Considering what they'd just done, it was a little strange that she blushed. Strange, but nice. At least she wasn't looking at him in horror as she had the morning after the last time they'd enjoyed each other. Her eyes, he thought, even contained a little tenderness.

"Yes," she agreed, "we are."

He smoothed the hair back from her face, enjoying the well-kissed way her lips looked and the rosy flush that clung to her skin. "See? We just proved my point about uncommitted sex being the best kind of sex."

Her eyes widened, then darkened, and Zach didn't have time to brace himself for what happened next. She rolled to the side at the same time that her right hand braced against his shoulder. Then she shoved.

He spun off the sofa in an unceremonious, naked heap. By the time he hit the floor, he wasn't sure what hurt worse: his ego or the entire right side of his body.

"Hey," he protested, lifting himself on one elbow. He rubbed his aching hip and thought he'd probably have rug burn tomorrow. "What'd you do that for?"

Amanda had scrambled to a sitting position and was already pulling her oversize, inside-out T-shirt over her glorious, naked breasts and flat stomach. Pangs of remorse and loss hit him until he remembered that he was peeved at her.

"That was for not letting me finish my sentence before this happened."

He blew out a breath and sat up. "You don't mean the sentence with the *but* in it?"

"Exactly," she said, tugging on her panties and leggings. "I was about to say that I don't believe in having sex without a commitment."

"You've already had uncommitted sex with me twice," he pointed out, trying to understand how her mind worked. She scowled, and he figured it was an exercise in futility.

"I didn't have sex with you because I wanted to!"

His eyebrows rose. She was getting harder to understand by the sentence. "The woman I just had sex with definitely wanted to have sex with me. So, unless you have an evil twin who only appears when you're about to get naked, I'd have to disagree with that one."

She pursed her lips and veins bulged at her temples, which led Zach to believe she was clenching her teeth. Since her jaw seemed locked, he aired his thoughts. "And don't try to tell me that having uncommitted sex with me isn't better than having committed sex with Reid, because I won't believe it."

He expected her to blast him with more nonsensical garbage but, instead, the fight seemed to drain from her. Her shoulders slumped. Her head bowed.

"You're right, of course," she said, looking everywhere but at him. "I can't say that, because it wouldn't be true. I shouldn't even be angry at you, because this isn't your fault. It's mine."

"I thought we got it straight the last time this happened that fault isn't a word that belongs in bed with us."

"That's the problem, Zach," she said, and this time she did look at him. Her green eyes were troubled. "We didn't get anything straight the last time. I certainly didn't make it clear that I don't believe in having sex without a commitment."

"But you don't want a commitment," he protested. "You had a ten-year commitment with Reid, and look where that landed you."

Her mouth twisted, and she ran a hand over her forehead. She looked as confused as he felt. "That doesn't change the fact that I believe people who have sex should be committed to each other."

"It doesn't change the fact that you want me, either."

The sentence hung in the air between them until she reached down and picked up his shirt. The colorful lightning bolts looked incongruous in her hands, because her face was as serious as a shroud. She handed the bundle to him.

"I'm not a child. I know I can't always have what I want."

"You're wrong," he said, shaking his head for emphasis. "You *can* have me."

"I'm right," she countered, "but that doesn't mean that I'm not glad I met you. You taught me something that I would have been hard-pressed to learn by myself. You taught me to open my eyes and look at the possibilities around me. Before I met you, I only looked at Reid."

Her voice was so sad that something broke inside of him. The problem was that he suspected she was the only one who could fix it. "You sound like you're saying goodbye."

"I am." Amanda's smile was melancholy. "You were going to say it in a few weeks yourself. I'm just saying it first."

"But I don't want to say goodbye yet."

"I don't want to get up in the morning when my alarm clock rings, but I do." Amanda rose and walked to the foot of the steps. Even though her shirt was inside out and her hair was disheveled, she looked regal. Like a queen kicking the king out of her life. "I can't be what you want me to be, Zach. So would you just get dressed and leave?"

She walked up the stairs, and Zach was torn. He wanted to race up the stairs and convince her anew that they belonged together. At least, he thought, they belonged in bed together. He grimaced. Since he was pretty sure she already knew that, there wasn't much point in following her. Unless he had something else to say. Which he didn't.

She was right. He wanted uncommitted sex, and she wanted to make love with someone with whom she had a commitment. That wasn't him. That could never be him.

So Amanda could never be his. Unless, of course, she was pregnant. Which she emphatically claimed that she wasn't, no thanks to him and his recent penchant for forgetting just how much he didn't want to get a woman pregnant.

Zach sighed heavily and dressed the rest of the way before he picked up the grocery bag full of wedding cancellation notices and silently let himself out the front door.

7

"I SEE THAT THIS PLACE survived without me for a week. What I want to know is, how?"

Amanda looked up from her glowing computer terminal to see Celia Lewis, her petite figure resplendent in a scarlet dress that had a hemline six inches above the knee. Amanda's face automatically creased in a smile of welcome, one of the first she'd managed since saying goodbye to Zach nearly a week before.

"Hi, Celia. How was your sister's wedding?"

"Depressing," said Celia, dropping into the seat next to Amanda's. "All that white lace. All that sappy music. All those gooey eyes. It was enough to make me sick."

"Why? I think it sounds kind of sweet."

"I'll tell you why." Celia put her hands on her hips as though Amanda should have been able to guess the reason. "Cupid has something against me, girl. He's aiming his little bow and letting arrows fly everywhere I go, and not one of them is hitting anybody who looks at me."

Amanda chortled, which only gained her another reproachful look from Celia.

"Don't laugh," Celia said. "It's true. The only person interested in me is mailroom Joe, and he's spooky enough to scare the stuffing out of Stephen King. But I'm depressing myself, so let's change the subject. What's the status on your engagement?"

"Hopelessly, irreparably broken," Amanda said, and again she was amazed at how little that fact hurt.

"I'd say that I was sorry, but I'm not," Celia said, and Amanda wondered if anyone in her life besides Reid actually liked Reid. "I bet you aren't sorry either."

That was the problem with having friends who were journalists, Amanda thought. They delved and pried until they'd unearthed all your secrets.

"If the glum face isn't because of Reid, it must be because of Mr. Forgets-You-Not. Spill it, girl."

"There's nothing to spill," Amanda said. She tried to keep her voice carefully neutral, so Celia wouldn't guess that losing Zach, only days after meeting him, hurt far worse than losing Reid after ten years of dating. "It's over."

"Over? I thought he had eyes like sapphires and a body that could melt butter. How could it be over?"

"He's not for me, Celia." Amanda paused, trying to put her thoughts into words. "He treats life like a joy ride, and he doesn't take a single thing seriously. He thinks commitment is a four-letter word."

"So what?" Celia screwed up her pretty face. "You had commitment, and look where it got you. Why don't you just relax and have some fun and games?"

"Because I'm not the fun-and-games type. If I'm sleeping with somebody, I want it to mean something. It's not enough that bombs burst and rockets soar if it doesn't mean anything."

Celia considered her. "So bombs burst and rockets soared?"

"That's not the point." Amanda was embarrassed and exasperated at the same time. Celia didn't seem to grasp what she was trying to say any more than Zach had. "Besides, things wouldn't work out between us even if he did want a commitment. He doesn't have a real job."

"You're saying that he pretends to have a job?"

"No. I'm saying that he fishes."

"What kind of fishing does he do?" Celia asked, peering at her. "Is he a commercial fisherman? Or does he take tourists on deep-sea charters? Does he have his own operation or does he work for somebody else?"

Celia kept firing the questions, but Amanda didn't have an answer to a single one of them. She realized with a jolt that was because she hadn't asked. She'd slept with Zach twice, and last week had even imagined that she might be falling in love with him, but she didn't know him.

And that made her behavior all the more foolish.

The phone on her desk rang, saving Amanda from Celia's questions. She reached for the receiver, but Celia covered her hand before she could pick it up.

"If that's Mr. Forgets-You-Not, I think you should give him another shot. If bombs are bursting and rockets are soaring when you're in bed, he's going to have a hell of a time leaving you alone in it."

After delivering her cryptic comment, Celia removed her hand from Amanda's and walked away, hips swaying saucily beneath her scarlet dress. Amanda almost called her back to tell her that she didn't want to give Zach another chance, but Celia wouldn't believe her. She wasn't sure whether she believed herself.

Amanda picked up the phone before it could ring for the fourth time and murmured a greeting.

"Amanda, dear, is that you?"

"Yes, it's me, Mother," Amanda answered while something akin to pain clenched her insides. Had she honestly believed that Zach would phone her a full week after she'd shoved him off her sofa and out of her life? Did she even want him to?

"I'm sorry to bother you at work, dear."

"It's no problem, Mother. I have a minute." Amanda forced her thoughts away from Zach. "I've been trying to reach you, but all I get is your answering machine."

"I know I've been difficult to reach, dear. This last week has been such a whirlwind. That's one of the reasons I'm calling."

"Don't tell me you're going to cancel our Sunday afternoon together again?" Amanda's question was close to a wail, because she'd been planning to talk some sense into her mother.

"I was hoping you wouldn't be too upset, dear. I mentioned to Paul how much I love Barry Manilow's singing, and wouldn't you know it? Barry just happens to be in town this weekend! Paul managed to get tickets to a matinee performance Sunday, and I said I would go..." she paused "...that is, if it's okay with you."

"Of course it's okay with me," Amanda said, even though it wasn't.

"I knew that you'd understand, dear. But actually, that wasn't why I was calling. I wanted to know if you could meet for lunch tomorrow?"

"Lunch?" Amanda's spirits perked up. This would be a golden chance to warn her hopelessly naive mother about whirlwind courtships. "I'd love to."

"I know of this darling place near the beach—"

"Hollywood Beach?"

"Of course Hollywood Beach, dear," she said, and proceeded to provide directions, while Amanda wondered how much time, if any, her mother was spending in her own home. Less than two weeks ago, she seldom ventured out of her neighborhood. Now it sounded as though she had made Paul Castelli's world her own. "Would noon be okay?"

"Noon would be fine," Amanda said. After all, she didn't have anything else to do tomorrow. Except to try again to convince herself that her righteousness was better company than Zach. "Just fine."

"Are you okay, dear? You sound a little down."

"I'm fine."

"Does this have anything to do with Zach?" Her voice was sharp with perception, a word that Amanda didn't normally associate with her mother. "Did the two of you have an argument?"

"Of course not," Amanda said, thinking that her verbal sparring battles with Zach couldn't be called arguments. It took two to argue, and Zach wasn't willing to enter into a serious exchange. "We just decided not to see each other anymore."

"Really?" Her mother's tone was disbelieving. "That's not the impression I got from Zach, but I'm sure the two of you will straighten things out when he comes back from his business trip tomorrow."

"His business trip?" Amanda asked, instead of correcting her mother's misconception about her relationship with Zach. "What business trip? Fishermen don't go on business trips."

"He's much more than a fisherman, dear," Mother said. "He writes articles for magazines devoted to the outdoors, and he does consulting work for resorts and travel agents. Why, he's talking to some developer in North Carolina about a job even as we speak. Didn't he tell you all this?"

"No," Amanda murmured, feeling like a fool. She should have known that Zach was more than what he appeared to be. He used words like supercilious and sanctimonious, for goodness' sake. He knew that Baron Lytton thought the pen was mightier than the sword. How could she have been so blind?

"Ask him about himself, dear. Everybody knows that men just love to talk when the subject is themselves."

Amanda almost laughed. Zach, it seemed, loved to talk about everything but himself.

A vague nausea settled over Amanda after she'd hung up the phone. She wasn't going to talk to Zach again, but how could she avoid talking about him tomorrow when her mother's luncheon conversation was sure to revolve around his father?

Of more immediate concern, however, was how to make herself stop thinking about Zach today.

AT PRECISELY TWELVE O'CLOCK the next day, Amanda approached the restaurant that her mother had specified with the certainty that she had written down the wrong directions. Her mother, who preferred chrome and polish over all things old and wooden, couldn't possibly have intended for them to lunch here.

Le Bowl was an open-air establishment hugging the Intracoastal Waterway that was cooled only by sea breezes. The entire place was situated on planking that had seen better days. Wooden tables shaded by thatched umbrellas were positioned so close to the intracoastal that diners seemed to be in perpetual danger of falling in the drink.

Most notably, the place was decorated with kitchen and bathroom fixtures. A yellowed washbasin here, a porcelain tub there. Rusted faucets, careworn kitchen sinks and old shower stalls all came together to form a bizarre ambiance. It dawned on Amanda that the name, Le Bowl, probably referred to washbowl.

A tinkling filled the air, and Amanda slowly raised her eyes to find the source. Wind chimes made from suspended spoons, knives and forks hung above her head and at various spots throughout the restaurant. Again, she thought that she must have the wrong restaurant.

Then she spotted her mother smiling and waving under one of the thatched umbrellas. The fact that Paul Castelli was sitting next to her made the irrational seem a little more logical. She made her lips smile, but knew her eyes didn't follow suit.

"Over here, dear," her mother called, rising halfway out

of her seat and revealing a flowing dress not unlike the one Marlee Castelli had worn at the family dinner. It wasn't unattractive, but the swirling fabric was completely out of character for a woman who had always preferred linen and lace.

"Good to see you, Amanda," said Paul Castelli, looking handsome and vigorous in chinos and a collarless white shirt. He stood and clasped her hand in both of his. His blue eyes were so like his son's that Amanda felt a pang in the region of her heart.

"Hello, Mr. Castelli."

"Paul," he corrected, his voice booming. "I want you to call me Paul."

She nodded in acknowledgment. His presence was so overpowering, and so reminiscent of Zach, that Amanda wondered why it hadn't occurred to her that he would be at this lunch. Her mother and Zach's father had behaved like Siamese twins since they'd met, so she shouldn't have expected them to separate on her account.

Paul and Pauline sat on one side of the square table, their chairs nestled together and their hands linked. Her mother kicked up one of her legs, and what Amanda saw was almost enough to pitch her backward into the intracoastal.

A tribe of ferocious-looking Indian faces, complete with war paint, decorated her leg. They wore headdresses on their long, raven-colored hair and scowls on their lips.

"Doesn't Marlee do fabulous work, dear?" her mother asked, lowering her leg and smiling at Amanda. Paul smiled at her mother, even though she wasn't addressing him. Amanda noticed that a matching pair of the Indians graced each of his forearms.

Amanda murmured something that could have passed for agreement, but she couldn't quite summon another smile. She was too busy wondering whether she had been transported into the movie *Invasion of the Body Snatchers*. It certainly seemed as though a pod person had swooped down from outer space and invaded her mother's body.

"Isn't this a darling little place?" Her mother was practically gushing. Behind her, a waitress threw some leftover food into the water and huge catfish eagerly devoured it. "Paul hates to eat out, but he makes an exception for Le Bowl. He wanted to have the two of you over for lunch, but I wouldn't hear of it. I didn't want him worrying about serving food when what we have to tell you is so important."

"The two of us?" Amanda picked out the portion of her mother's chatter that made the least sense.

"Your mother and I have something to tell you," Paul said, tearing his eyes from Pauline just long enough to complete his sentence, "but we need to wait until Zach gets here."

"Zach?" Alarms clanged in Amanda's body, far more raucous than the wind-aided silverware that clinked overhead. She pinned her mother with a glare. "You didn't tell me that Zach was coming."

"That's because I didn't know until last night." Her mother looked completely unconcerned, as though they were discussing something an innocuous as the weather. "Paul and I meant to tell him yesterday, when we told Clay and Marlee, but he didn't get back from his business trip until late. So Paul invited him to lunch so we could tell you together."

"Tell us what?" Amanda asked, but neither Paul nor her mother paid any attention to her.

"There's Zach now," Paul said, and Pauline went into her grin-and-wave routine.

Amanda's back was facing the entrance to the restaurant, so she had time to brace herself before she turned. It didn't help. The air whooshed out of her lungs just the same, and her gaze was as thirsty as a marathoner who hadn't drunk a drop in twenty-six miles. Her heart beat as though she had run twice that far.

His wind-tousled hair looked even more sun streaked than it had a week ago, and his shorts exposed those long, muscular legs. His shirt, which was tame by Zach's standards, but still a shocking shade of lime green, billowed around the chest that looked so beautiful bare. Sunglasses shaded his eyes, but a slow grin spread across his face.

Gazing across the restaurant at Amanda, Zach could no more have stopped himself from grinning than the wind from blowing.

Damn, but it was good to see her. She was wearing another of her prim outfits—tan slacks paired with a black, short-sleeved turtleneck shirt—but she looked far more beautiful than any of the scantily clad women on the beach.

He'd tried telling himself during the past week that he hadn't missed her, but one look blew that theory—and his good intentions to leave her alone—into the intracoastal.

Besides, it was too soon to say goodbye. She may not even know for certain yet that she wasn't carrying his child. He didn't want Amanda to be pregnant, but it was his obligation to stick beside her until she was sure that she wasn't.

He walked eagerly across the restaurant, passing washbasins and faucets along the way.

"Good to see you, Papa," he said when he reached the table, clasping his father on the shoulder. Paul Castelli looked so radiant that the smile Zach sent Pauline was extra bright. "You're looking as lovely as ever, Pauline."

He had saved the best for last. Sitting down next to Amanda, he turned to face her. She looked delectable, her freckles peeking through her makeup and her hair a windblown strawberry tangle. Her wide, full mouth was slightly parted. And irresistible.

He leaned forward, fastening his mouth on hers in a kiss sweeter than the nectar of the gods. Then he drew back and grinned. "Hi, beautiful."

Her eyes widened and she seemed about to say something that Zach suspected wouldn't be entirely flattering, but then Pauline, dear Pauline, interrupted. He took the opportunity to slip an arm around Amanda's shoulders.

"I'm so glad the two of you have patched up your differences," she said, beaming at them. "I was just telling Paul while we were sitting here waiting for you what a cute couple you make. Don't you think they make a cute couple, Paul?"

"The cutest," he said, and Zach felt Amanda's muscles tense under his fingers. A memory of her shoving him off the sofa flashed in his mind. Since he was sitting next to the water, he withdrew his arm.

"Of course," Paul continued, "I can think of another pretty terrific couple sitting right here at this table."

Pauline giggled, and Zach thought the sound was sweet. Kind of like the tinkling of wind chimes. He raised his eyes and saw the silverware, most of which was rusted, dancing in the breeze.

"That sort of brings up the reason we asked you to meet us," Pauline said, glancing at Paul, who nodded, as though encouraging her to proceed.

Amanda was studiously avoiding looking at Zach, but he sensed that she had gone rigid with anticipation.

"We've decided," Pauline said, her voice filled with glee, "to live together."

Genuine pleasure filled Zach. Pauline was like a magic potion that had revived his father's soul. He hadn't seen him look this happy since before his mother's death six years ago. "That's great. Just great."

"You've decided to what?"

The question came from Amanda, who was staring at

the couple as though a sea monster had just jumped out of the intracoastal and was looming behind them. Zach examined her profile. Her skin was pale, and her lips white underneath her lipstick. On second thought, maybe he had kissed all the lipstick off.

His chest swelled with concern, and he reached for her limp hand. He grew even more worried when she let him take it.

"Paul and I are going to live together," Pauline repeated.

Amanda squeezed Zach's hand until his turned white, and he thought she probably didn't know she was doing it. "But you haven't even known each other for two weeks!" she said. "Don't you think this is a little rash?"

"Rash?" Pauline shook her head and sent Paul a tender look. "I've been waiting half my life for someone like Paul to come along. Now that he has, I don't want to waste another minute without him."

"Then I think you should go for it no matter what anybody says," Zach said earnestly. Amanda yanked her hand from his as though she'd been scalded. *Oops*. So much for consoling Amanda.

"Thanks, son," his father said, so heartily that Zach felt a little better. "I know how this must seem to you, Amanda, but to us it makes sense any way we look at it."

"Then maybe," Amanda said, drawing out each syllable, "you could explain it to me."

Zach didn't dare take her hand again.

"Pauline showed me her bank book, and she can't really afford that house where she's living. It's draining her dry. Since she's been spending all her time with me anyway, it makes sense to sell it and move in with me."

"But what if it doesn't work out between you?" Amanda cried.

"It'll work out, dear," Pauline said, her brown eyes earnest, "because we love each other."

"Yes. We love each other," Paul agreed.

A lump formed in Zach's throat. Against all odds, his father seemed to have found happiness with a woman twice in the same lifetime.

"Then why don't you just get married?" Amanda asked.

"We couldn't do that, dear," Pauline said, and her smile never faltered. "We've only known each other for two weeks."

THE LUNCH PASSED in a swirl of conversation and food, but Zach thought that Amanda got through it on autopilot. She seemed in too much distress to order, so he'd done it for her. He'd bypassed the juicy cheeseburger he'd chosen for himself and requested a luncheon portion of trout almondine for her.

She hadn't eaten more than a few bites, or contributed any more to the conversation than was absolutely necessary. By the time his father had spirited Pauline away, Zach was seriously worried.

He followed Amanda into the parking lot, noticing that the steps she took were no more animated than a robot's. Before she could reach her car, he grabbed her hand. The green eyes that met his had more flash than they had at any time during lunch.

"What do you think you're doing?"

"Have you ever seen the movie *Shanghai Surprise?*"

Confusion clouded her eyes, and she shook her head.

"Neither have I," Zach confessed, "but I imagine it started something like this. By grabbing your hand so you can't get in your car, I thought I'd shanghai you."

"Let go of me, Zach." Her voice was tired, dispirited.

"No." Zach shook his head, lending emphasis to the

word. This battle was too important to lose. "You're in too much shock to drive."

"Why shouldn't I be in shock?" she asked, but didn't protest when he tugged on her hand and led her across the street. "Did you get a look at my mother? Did you see her flower-child dress? The Indians on her leg? Did you see the way she was looking at your father? It was like she was in the grip of a cult."

"The cult of the Castellis?" Zach asked, and couldn't stop from smiling. She glared at him, and he pressed his lips together. He wasn't sure whether he should be glad she'd found her voice or not.

"And you! You didn't help at all! I didn't hear you telling our parents that it was insane of them to live together after knowing each other for only two weeks."

"Maybe I don't think it is insane," he said, pulling her toward the cement walkway that stretched the length of the beach. They joined an eclectic bunch of walkers that included long-haired teenage boys with earrings, children who skipped and giggled and blue-haired ladies in velour sweat suits.

"Of course you think it's insane," Amanda said. "You're the one who doesn't believe in commitment."

"Wrong. It's not that I don't believe in commitment. *I* just can't quite manage it. Besides, I wouldn't dream of telling anybody else how to live their lives."

"And you think that's what I did?" She sounded angry, an emotion at odds with the setting. To the right of them, a wide white beach dotted with sunbathers on colorful beach towels stretched to the calming blue of the ocean. A warm breeze rustled the fronds of the palm trees, and there wasn't a cloud in the azure sky.

"The way I see it, I'm not going to win any points with you by answering that question." He gave her hand a jaunty swing, figuring that maybe if he pretended she wasn't arguing with him she would stop. "So I'll take the fifth."

"Speaking of points," she reminded him, "you lost a couple of thousand when you kissed me and let our parents think we were still seeing each other."

He tilted his head. "Didn't you like it when I kissed you?"

"Well, yes. I mean no." She exhaled loudly. "That's not the point. We decided to break things off, and you deliberately misled our parents into thinking we were still seeing each other."

"Don't twist things around, Amanda. *You* decided to break things off with *me*. I didn't agree."

He abruptly switched directions, cutting across the cement walkway so abruptly that they narrowly avoided being hit by a Goliath on Rollerblades. The Goliath shook a fist. Zach grinned and waved.

By the time Amanda had recovered her equilibrium, she noticed that they were standing in front of a small beach house sandwiched between a pair of two-story buildings that had been divided into efficiency apartments.

The little whitewashed beach house had blue-and-white awnings that shaded louvered windows opened to allow in the ocean breeze. A white wicker rocking chair beckoned invitingly from the small porch, which was littered with sand.

"What is this place?" she asked suspiciously.

Zach fished a key out of his pocket, unlocked the door and swung it open. "This is my place," he said.

She stared at him. Somehow, he'd completely disarmed her again. One minute she had been enduring a surreal lunch with a mother gone mad, and the next she was standing in front of a house on Hollywood Beach that belonged to Zach. Worse, she was actually considering going into it.

"Well, are you coming in?" Zach asked.

"Why should I come in?"

"To change out of those clothes, silly. You can't spend the day at the beach dressed like that."

"I didn't say that I'd spend the day at the beach with you."

"You didn't say that you wouldn't, either," he pointed out.

The sun glinted off his dimple, giving new meaning to the term sunny smile. He was impossible, maddening and thoroughly, utterly irresistible. She took a few steps forward, then stopped and narrowed her eyes.

"I'm not wearing one of your shirts," she warned.

He threw back his head and laughed, so she added another qualifier. "And I'm not wearing any castoffs from the legion of girlfriends you've *cast off*."

He instantly sobered, which caused his delectable dimple to disappear. Darn it! Why did she say things to wipe out his dazzling smile?

"I've already told you that I don't treat people like that," he said. "Besides, the only women's clothes I have belong to Marlee. Her shop's on the beach, so she keeps some bathing suits here. She won't mind if you wear one. Now, are you coming in?"

"Yes," Amanda snapped, not sure whether she was angry at him for maneuvering her to the threshold of his beach house or at herself for willingly accompanying him. "I'm coming in."

Minutes later, Amanda twisted her body so she could survey the back side of Marlee's tie-dye bikini in the bathroom mirror. She tugged, trying to cover some of the flesh that was left exposed beneath the bathing suit, but only managed to uncover the skin atop it.

Frowning, she surrendered to futility and pulled on the purple fishnet cover-up that came with the set. Triangles of pale flesh peeked through the holes, stripping the garment of its name. It didn't cover much of anything.

Taking a final look in the mirror and slipping on a pair of thong sandals that were only a size too big, she squared her shoulders and emerged from the bathroom. Zach was sitting on the overstuffed sofa, his feet propped up on an attractive coffee table made of sun-bleached wood. He let out a low whistle.

"That getup sure looks better on you than it does on Marlee."

Amanda blushed. "That's because Marlee's your sister."

"No." He shook his head solemnly, and his eyes bore into hers. "That's because you're wearing it."

Telling herself he probably dispatched compliments as easily as he gave out Halloween candy to children, she surveyed him. He was still wearing the eye-popping lime-green shirt, but he had changed into bathing trunks. They were conservative. And navy blue.

"Why doesn't your suit have candy-cane stripes or leopard spots?"

He shrugged. "All of my suits are solid colors. My pants and shorts, too. They'd clash with my shirts if they weren't."

"They wouldn't clash with that shirt. That's the first time I've seen you wear something that doesn't have an outlandish pattern."

"Oh, this." Zach gave his shirt a solemn perusal. "That's because this is one of my mourning shirts."

"Mourning shirt?" Amanda repeated, thinking he looked as much like a mourner as a circus clown. "What are you mourning?"

His eyes turned serious. "A week without you."

"Stop it," Amanda said, because she wanted to believe

him. Dear God, she ached with wanting to believe him. "You're going to make me forget that I'm angry at you."

"Are you angry about the same old things or is this something new?"

"Something new." She crossed the tile floor and sank into a yellow canvas director's chair across from him. Nothing in his house matched, but it went together all the same. The sun shone through the louvered windows, almost blinding her. She squinted and arranged her so-called cover-up for optimum coverage. "Why didn't you tell me what you really do for a living?"

"I did tell you. I'm a fisherman."

"You're more than a fisherman. My mother says that you're a fishing consultant, but you never told me that."

"That's because," he said, "you never asked."

She bit her lip because he had a point. Stretching the matter even further, she hadn't asked because she hadn't wanted to know that he was not ambitious. But was that what she would have discovered?

"I don't know much about you at all," she said, even though that wasn't entirely true. She knew that he was kind to women who had just been dumped by their fiancés. She knew that he was thoughtful and good-hearted and that he loved his family with a rare passion. And she knew that, no matter how hard she tried, she couldn't resist him.

"So ask. I'll tell you anything you want to know."

"What do you do for a living?"

"I fish," he quipped, and she was just about to get angry again when he continued. "But you're right. It's more complicated than that. The way it usually works is that a travel agency or a resort developer pays me to investigate the fishing potential of a particular area. I scout the place and report back to my client. Most of the time, the client asks me to stay on and develop a structured program for guests who are into fishing."

"What about the magazine articles?"

"You know about those too?" He shrugged, and the sun shone through the blinds and glinted off his hair until it looked gilded. "I regularly contribute to a number of magazines. When I'm on assignment for a client, I take photos and write articles. Sometimes, a magazine sends me on location with the sole purpose of getting an article out of me."

His true occupation was so different, and so much more impressive, from what Amanda had imagined that she couldn't help but be peeved by her gullibility.

"I bet you even have a college degree," she said sulkily.

"A bachelor of science degree in geology from the University of Florida, although it hasn't done me much good. I thought studying the earth and all her wonders would be exciting, but it didn't take me long to realize I liked the gathering part but not the studying part. I can't tolerate being behind a desk—or a microscope—for longer than it takes to write an article."

"So you fish?"

"Yeah," he agreed. "So I fish. All over the United States and parts of South America and the Caribbean. Most of the jobs only last a few months. It satisfies my wanderlust."

His legs were still stretched before him on the coffee table, and his hands were locked behind his neck. All around him were thriving plants that gave his little house, with its comfortable mix of furniture, life. The plants and the house had a look of permanency that Zach didn't.

"Then you're just renting this house?"

"No. It's all mine. I bought it a couple years ago. If I'm away from my family for more than six months, I get an uncontrollable itch that doesn't go away until I return. It made sense to have a place to come to."

"You mean a place to leave?"

"That, too," he agreed.

"Is that why you were out of town job hunting last week?" Amanda asked. A sixth sense had kicked in, and she dreaded the answer. She didn't know what she wanted from Zach, but she didn't want him to leave. "Is your wanderlust acting up again?"

"Actually," Zach said slowly, and she had the impression he was watching for her reaction, "this isn't something I initiated. A former client is building a resort near the Outer Banks in North Carolina, and he wants to gear it toward people who enjoy the outdoors. He wants me in on the ground floor."

"For how long?"

"He says a year."

Amanda tried to swallow. Couldn't. "Did you take the job?"

"Not yet. I've been setting up a fishing camp for a company in Fort Lauderdale, but I'm just about through. I need something else, but I told my friend that I wanted to think about his offer. That's longer by half than any job I've ever had before."

Hope flamed in Amanda that he wouldn't take the job, but she ruthlessly extinguished it because this particular job wasn't the issue. If Zach passed on this opportunity, he'd no doubt take the next one. Either way, he'd be leaving soon.

But what had she expected? He'd told her that he wasn't about commitment, that all he was about was having a good time. If he couldn't commit to a job for more than a few months at a time, he'd certainly never commit to her.

She didn't want him to, of course. She needed someone stable and secure: the anti-Zach. But she didn't want him to leave either. And, there was no doubt about it, he was going to leave.

Her wisest move would be to run away from him and

never look back, because looking back would just make her want to run toward him.

The muscles in Amanda's thighs bunched, preparing for flight, but she didn't move.

Zach got up from the sofa with a lazy grace that exuded sex appeal, walked toward her and extended a hand. She tried to practice mental imagery, picturing a cage of steel around her heart that Zach couldn't penetrate. But then he smiled, flashing his dimple, and the steel melted like butter in the sun.

"That's enough serious talk," Zach said. "It's warm and sunny, and we're at the beach. Let's go have some fun."

Amanda returned his smile and took the hand that he offered.

8

As tentatively as a newborn colt, Amanda took a step. Her legs wobbled, and she looked about as steady as a drunken sailor. She giggled, and Zach's arm came instantly around her. She smelled of the cocoa butter he had insisted she lather her skin with hours before. The cocoa butter she hadn't allowed him to lather on her. He frowned in remembered frustration.

"Do your legs always feel like this when you get off Rollerblades?" she asked, grinning up at him.

"Only if you've never been on them before. Your muscles aren't used to it."

"Neither is my rear end," she said, and Zach wished she'd ask him to rub where it hurt. Hell, he hurt. He hadn't fallen like she had, but his body ached after an hour of watching her try to learn how to rollerblade.

She hadn't been particularly graceful, but that hadn't mattered. Her attempts to prevent herself from falling had given him all sorts of tantalizing glances. A flash of thigh. A glimpse of cleavage. Extended looks at long, lithe legs.

He hoped she hadn't meant what she said the other night about eschewing sex without commitment because he was becoming increasingly committed to having sex with her. Soon.

"Thanks for teaching me how to skate, Zach." Her expression was all innocence and candor, and he felt like a heel.

She'd told him that she wasn't going to be intimate with

him any longer, and she probably expected him to believe her. It wasn't that unreasonable a request, when he thought about it. She'd been honest and straightforward, qualities he treasured and tried to implement in his life.

Come to think of it, he wasn't supposed to have an ulterior motive for talking her into this day of fun and sun at the beach. He was supposed to be taking her mind off the shock of learning that their parents planned to shack up.

Yet here he was, outside the cheerful shop that had rented her the Rollerblades, lusting after her. He thanked providence that he had rejected a previous girlfriend's suggestion that he buy a men's bikini fashioned out of Lycra or else she'd surely guess what he was thinking.

He was positively reprehensible.

"Zach?" Amanda asked. "Didn't you hear me? I asked where we're going next."

She had? Considering that all he'd heard were the recriminations in his head, that was news to him. She'd recovered her land legs, so he slipped his arm from her shoulders and captured her hand.

As they joined the throng of walkers, a twenty-something in a thong bikini offered him a sultry-voiced hello, but he was too preoccupied to do more than nod.

"You're wearing me out, beautiful," he told Amanda, and for once his effortless teasing was anything but. He was working at it. "Wasn't rollerblading and throwing around the Frisbee on the beach enough for you?"

"You're not wearing out, Zach," she said.

Even the sound of her voice saying his name gave him a thrill. What was wrong with him?

"I was there when we played Frisbee, remember? You made some spectacular sprinting catches."

"That's because you didn't throw anything in the general vicinity of where I was standing," Zach said.

"So my aim was a little off," Amanda said. "You've got to admit that I'm doing better. I caught two this time."

"Yeah, you're a regular Carlton Fisk."

"Carlton who?"

"I should've figured you hadn't heard of him. How about Johnny Bench?" Zach asked, naming another famous baseball catcher of the past. She shook her head, and he gave up.

"I suppose they're sports stars of some sort," she said. "I already told you I wasn't into sports. But judging by the way you ran after my Frisbees on the beach, I bet you've been playing since you were a kid. What were you, Zach? Quarterback of the baseball team? A pitcher for the football team?"

"It's quarterback of the football team, and pitcher of the baseball team," he corrected, horrified at her ignorance. Then she grinned, and he belatedly realized that she'd known that all along. "You're teasing me, aren't you?"

"You know us women—always striving for equality," she said, and he had to laugh. "So, tell me, what kind of teams did you play on?"

"I didn't."

"Really?" Amanda looked skeptical. "Why not? I can't believe that you weren't good enough."

"I wasn't dedicated enough," he admitted, which he supposed was another way of saying that even as a teenager he hadn't been able to make a commitment. Not even to an athletic team.

"Hey, Zach!"

At the sound of his name, Zach looked up just in time to see a volleyball flying his way. He dropped Amanda's hand, and caught the ball easily. The bare-chested boy in his late teens who had thrown it stood about twenty yards from them in the sand. Next to him was a volleyball net and three other players.

"You playing today, Zach?" Donny Aldrich, the blond, shouted. Zach flung the ball back at him before answering.

"Nah," he said, indicating Amanda. He experienced a jolt of pride. "Why should I hang out with you guys when I can hang out with her instead?"

Even from the walkway, the flash of Donny's white teeth was visible. "Bobby around today?" asked another of the youths.

"Not today, Corey. Tomorrow."

"Who's Bobby?" Amanda asked, as the distance between them and the four-man volleyball game increased.

"My little brother."

"Your little brother? I thought that Clay was your only brother."

"Clay's my only blood brother. I belong to the Broward County chapter of the Big Brothers program. You know the one. You sign up, and they assign you a boy to spend some time with."

"But isn't a cornerstone of that program stability?" She was looking at him as though she found it impossible to associate the word stable with him. "How can you be a Big Brother when you can't stay in one place?"

"I got Clay to agree to do it with me," Zach answered, frowning. "Since the three of us spend our time together, it won't be too hard on Bobby when I leave."

"And you spend your time playing volleyball?"

"Sometimes," he said, and then made himself smile. Her comment about his lack of stability still resounded in his head, and the smile took an effort. "And sometimes we ride go-karts or rollerblade or swim in the ocean. But volleyball is definitely our favorite thing to do."

"You can keep up with those kids we just saw? They couldn't have been out of their teens."

"They aren't," Zach said, "but I do okay."

"Then you must have one heck of an exercise routine. I mean, look at you. You're in great shape."

"Oh, really?" He squeezed her hand and wiggled his eyebrows à la Groucho Marx. "So you think I'm in great shape, do you?"

"You're shameless," Amanda scolded, but she seemed more amused than angry. "It's not enough for me to compliment you once. No. You try to make me say it again."

"Will you say it again?"

"No way!"

He laughed. "For the record, I don't have a regular exercise routine. I do what feels good whenever I think it would feel good."

Which was yet another way of saying that he couldn't commit, not to an athletic team nor to Bobby nor to a regular workout. He looked down at Amanda, and his eyes drifted to her flat belly, which was partially visible through the fishnet cover-up.

For one crazy moment, he thought of his baby growing inside her and wished that it were so. Because, if she were pregnant, he could prove to himself, and to her, that he could make a commitment.

Zach immediately discounted the thought. Yeah, right. Who was he fooling? He'd probably run if she were pregnant, and that would only prove that nobody—not Amanda, and certainly not a tiny, innocent baby—could count on him.

"So where are we going now?" she asked again, and this time he did hear her. He mentally ran through a list of destinations, trying to think of the one that would be the least depressing. He was depressed enough already.

"The little shop of horrors," he said dramatically, affecting the voice of Count Dracula, "where you'll see bizarre drawings and painted ladies, not to mention an odd long-haired lass who draws some scary lines."

"Oh, good," Amanda said, "I've been wanting to see Marlee's shop."

Marlee Castelli's shop was located on a section of beach that hadn't yet been revitalized. While much of the beach boasted sparkling storefronts and new buildings painted in tropical hues of turquoise, green and pale pink, this section was comfortably worn.

It wasn't difficult to pick out Marlee's business. Paintings of dragons, butterflies, beer bottles and flowers graced the sturdy Plexiglas that fronted the beach. Above the door was a sign that read, The Painted Lady.

Zach opened the door, and Amanda preceded him into a one-room shop that was as cozy as it was peculiar. The wall was covered with paintings, which represented samples of designs customers could have inked onto their bodies.

A young girl, her green spiked hair cut into a mohawk and her midriff bared, was lying on a table. Marlee bent over her, a pen in her hand, butterflies floating up her arm, the tip of her tongue thrust over her lower lip as she concentrated.

"Be with you in a few," she called, her attention never wavering from the stomach she was painting. To the prone girl in front of her, she said, "Would you try to stop giggling? I'm putting the finishing touches on now."

"I can't help it," the girl said, her uneven gasps revealing that she was trying to suppress her laughs. "It tickles."

"Just one more minute," Marlee demanded in a voice that would have earned her instant silence had she been a kindergarten teacher. "There. I'm done."

The instant Marlee issued her proclamation, the girl sat up, affording Amanda and Zach a look at the painting on her stomach. It was of a teenage boy, his hair cut and dyed in the same manner as the girl's, his lips slightly parted.

Marlee looked up and spotted them. She was wearing a flowing, flowery dress similar to the one that Amanda's mother had worn at Le Bowl. Her long, dark hair was caught in a clasp at her nape. She pushed her granny glasses back up her nose and smiled.

"Hey," she said, her face lighting up. "To what do I owe this pleasure?"

Zach walked across the shop and dropped a casual kiss on his sister's brow. "I wanted to show Amanda how the painted half lives."

"Show her, Tisha," Marlee demanded of the girl, who immediately sent her stomach into quivering movements that made it seem as though the painted boy was laughing.

"Hey, cool," Tisha said, looking down at her stomach. "It works. Wait'll I show the gang."

"Be sure you tell them who painted the laughing boy," Marlee said, getting in a plug for her store. "Here's the photo back."

"Sure will, Marlee." The girl took the photo and withdrew a couple of bills from inside her halter top before exiting the shop on black-booted feet.

"That was nice work," Amanda said, "but I'd be a little more careful of what I put on my skin."

"And what beautiful skin it is," Zach said, cupping her cheek. She leaned into his touch, and her stomach fluttered like the wings of one of the butterflies painted on Marlee's shop window. "Amanda insisted on covering some of it, so we borrowed your bathing suit, Mar. I told her you wouldn't mind."

"Of course I don't mind," Marlee said. "But I thought you two weren't dating."

Amanda turned, breaking Zach's contact with her cheek.

The sensual haze in which he had enveloped her was slower to dissipate.

"We're not dating," she said, and waited for Zach to contradict her. When he didn't, her disappointment was so thick that it tasted bitter in her mouth.

"This isn't a date," he said. "This is the aftermath of Papa's and Pauline's luncheon announcement at Le Bowl."

"So they sprang the living-together news on you, too? They told Clay and me last night. Isn't it terrific? It's hard enough to find happiness in this world. If they've found it with each other, great."

"I agree," Zach said, hoisting himself up on a counter and dangling his long, tanned, well-muscled legs.

"How about you, Amanda?" Marlee asked, and Amanda guiltily tore her attention from Zach's legs. "What do you think?"

"I think they're being rash," she answered honestly.

"Maybe, but rash can be fun. If you didn't think so, you wouldn't be *not* dating my brother." Her eyes twinkled. "Why don't you be a little rash now? Pick out something in the shop, and I'll paint you for free."

"Oh, but I couldn't—"

"Why couldn't you?" Zach asked, and Amanda considered her reasons. She couldn't have her body painted because it didn't fit her self-image. She was conservative, reserved and oh-so-proper. Adjectives, she realized, that applied to the pre-Zach Amanda. Not the Amanda who was standing in a body-painting shop in a tie-dye bikini.

"I guess there's no good reason why I couldn't," she said, surprising herself.

"Oh, this I've got to see," Zach said, sounding gleeful.

"I'm not going to chicken out, if that's what you mean." Amanda was affronted.

Zach shook his head. "I didn't mean that. I meant this

I've got to see. I've been trying to get you to take that cover-up off all day. If Marlee's going to paint you, it has to come off."

"I'm not getting your face painted on my belly." Amanda tried to wither him with a glare, but the effect was diluted because she wasn't actually angry. "I was thinking more on the lines of a flower on my shoulder."

"Make it a forget-me-not, Mar," Zach told his sister, and Amanda's heart constricted even though his tone was lighthearted.

He couldn't know that months from now, even years from now, the flower would forever conjure an image of him. Because, no matter how far away his wanderlust took him, she already knew that it would never be far enough to allow her to forget him.

THE SUN HAD SET hours before, but the beach wasn't yet ready to sleep. The crowd that had frolicked and sunbathed in the bright light of day had donned sweatshirts and lightweight jackets while continuing to enjoy the beach's charms.

Dressed once again in the clothes she had worn to lunch, Amanda held hands with Zach as they strolled in the surf. Her pant legs were rolled up to her knees, and her shoes dangled from her free hand. The forget-me-not that Marlee had inked onto her shoulder was covered by her shirt and the white windbreaker Marlee had lent her.

Zach kicked at the water with his bare foot, and droplets sprayed in a rainbow-shaped arch in front of them. They glistened for an instant against the night sky before disappearing back into the sea.

Just like Zach would disappear when he took his next job. Amanda wondered if it would be a few weeks from now or just a few days. She pulled her hand from his, trying to harden her heart against him. They'd had a wonderful day together, but it was nearly over. Just as their relationship was nearly over.

She was aware of him walking beside her, tall, broad and impossibly sexy. She'd been aware of him all day, just as she'd been aware that she couldn't have him and shouldn't even want him. But she did.

"Thanks for today, Zach," she said, refusing to dwell on her disappointment. There would be plenty of time to do that when he wasn't around to witness it. "It seems like you're always trying to cheer me up."

"Trying?" he asked, and she heard the teasing note in his voice. He caught at her hand again, and she didn't have the willpower to pull away a second time. "I thought I succeeded."

"You did," she conceded. "I still think the cult of the Castellis has my mother in its grip, but I guess I'll get used to her living with your father."

"You have to," Zach pointed out. "You could try to make her stay in her own room in her own house, but I don't think she'll listen. She's a little too old to ground."

"Don't tell me you're getting tactful on me, Zach. That sounded suspiciously like a nice way to say I should mind my own business."

"You should," he answered, and she smiled. Zach, it seemed, could only take tact so far. A few days ago, that fact might have set her off like a firecracker. Today, she accepted it, because he was right.

"Thank you for helping me to realize it," she said.

He leaned over to drop a soft kiss on her brow.

Although the water lapping at their ankles was cool and a chilly breeze blew off the ocean, Amanda felt heat where his lips brushed and heat where his hand touched hers. It radiated up her arm, across her chest and straight to her heart, and she knew she had to do something to cool it.

"You've been a good friend."

"Friend?" He said the word as though he'd never heard it before. He tugged at her hand, causing her to stop. They were virtually alone, yards removed from the people who strolled on cement past the open-air restaurants and T-shirt shops. "Is that how you think of me? As a friend?"

"That's how I'm trying to think of you. That's how I want you to think of me."

He took the shoes that dangled from her left hand and, along with the sandals in his right, threw them onto the dry portion of the sand. Then he turned her shoulders so that she was facing him. The moonlight shone on his face, illuminating it until he looked golden.

He took the hand that was clasped in his and brought it to his chest. He wasn't wearing a jacket, and she could feel the rapid beat of his heart beneath one of the yellow-and-red swirls that decorated the clean shirt he had changed into.

"My heart wouldn't be beating this quickly if I thought of you as a friend," he said, and he transferred their joined hands to her chest. She felt her own heart speeding like a runaway train. "And your heart wouldn't be racing, either."

For an instant, neither of them moved. But then Zach's head dipped, and Amanda raised her lips and drew forward as though propelled by a force stronger than the tide.

It didn't matter that she'd lived her entire adult life thinking that she wanted stability in the form of Reid Carrigan, because she'd been wrong. This was what she wanted. This wild passion that erupted so effortlessly whenever Zach touched her.

They were pressed against each other, but Amanda didn't think they were close enough. Not with the barrier of their clothing, not while they stood on a public beach, not while their time together was running out.

At the thought of Zach leaving, a vestige of logic

wormed its way into her muddled brain. It gave her the strength to push at his shoulders and to draw back from him. She was still shaken from his kiss, so she clung to his shoulders as she looked into his eyes. His were glazed with passion and desire.

"Come home with me, Amanda," he said thickly, and it sounded like a plea from the heart. But, even with her senses swimming, she knew that she was indulging in wishful thinking. He was more likely asking because of another part of his anatomy.

"No," she said, retreating a few steps from him on trembling legs. She shook her head. "No. I meant it when I said I didn't believe in sex without commitment."

"Ah, hell, Amanda." Zach ran a hand through his hair, frustration stamped on his features and in the rigid way he was standing. "I want you, and you want me. Isn't that enough?"

"No. It's not enough. Not when you're making plans to leave. I won't be a one-night stand."

He swore, surprising her. He rubbed his lower face with his hand, and it was obvious that he had surprised himself too. "I'm sorry. I didn't mean to swear, but you have to know that I don't think of you as a one-night stand."

"A two-night stand or a three-night stand then."

"No," he said vehemently. "I think of you as an incredibly sexy, desirable woman who I want to be with."

"Until you leave, that is."

"Until," Zach said, "we're sure you're not pregnant."

Nothing he could have said would have angered her more. He was perfectly willing to leave her, but he'd stick around if there were a pregnancy to consider. It was downright insulting. And, considering the circumstances, nonsensical.

"Don't start that again," she warned. "I told you I wasn't pregnant."

"You also told me that you weren't one hundred percent sure of that."

"I said I was ninety-nine percent sure."

"That's not one hundred."

"You're impossible," Amanda said, stalking away from him to pluck her shoes off the beach. She tossed her next words over her shoulder. "So let me get this straight. You're saying that you're not leaving Florida until I'm one hundred percent sure I'm not pregnant?"

"Yeah." Zach's voice came from behind her. "That's what I'm saying."

His insistence on being honorable for the sake of a baby, which was almost surely non-existent, incensed her. So did the fact that he had managed to insert a sliver of doubt into her mind about whether she was pregnant.

As though she wanted to be pregnant with the baby of a man who wouldn't stick around unless she were expecting.

"Hey, where are you going?" Zach yelled as she turned away from him. The sand slowed her progress, but she tromped determinedly on.

"Home," she shouted back without turning. "And don't you dare try to follow me."

9

"ARE YOU SURE this is the right thing to do, Uncle Zach?"

Mia's voice was skeptical as she skipped alongside Zach from the parking lot to the front door of Amanda's townhouse. The sun was rapidly setting, and the glare was blinding as the golden orb prepared to settle beyond the horizon. The light made the miniature panthers on Mia's cheeks look like they were about to leap off her face.

"Sure, I'm sure." Zach plucked her backward baseball cap off her head, turned it around and resettled it. "When have I ever made a wrong move?"

Mia flipped her baseball cap back around. "How about last year when you told Mom that you were taking me to see a Disney movie and instead we ended up watching *Independence Day?* Boy, was she ever mad at you."

"That's because I got the times mixed up, smart aleck. And how was I supposed to know the movie was about the destruction of the planet? Judging by that title, I thought it was about the Fourth of July." He made his voice stern. "And you didn't help any, you know. Keeping a body count like that and then telling her what it was."

"But that proves you don't always do the right thing. So how do you know this is the right thing?"

"I just know. Amanda will be happy to see us, you'll see," Zach said, although Mia's constant questions were starting to make him doubt himself. He'd given Amanda three days to cool down, three days to miss him as much as he'd missed her.

He supposed apologizing would have been simpler than waiting her out, but the hell of it was he wasn't even sure what he had done wrong. One minute, they'd been on the verge of another sexual romp. And the next, she was yelling at him and stomping away through the sand.

The best he could figure, it had something to do with pregnancy. She was probably angry that he hadn't taken the proper precautions to protect her the first time they'd been intimate. Maybe she was even angry about the second time, when she'd had to bring up the subject herself.

Either way, Zach had learned by his mistake. He'd even formulated a plan. He wasn't going to mention pregnancy again. If she were pregnant, he reasoned that he was going to find out about it sooner or later anyway.

Fortified by his plan, he rang the doorbell.

"You're sure she's going to be happy to see us?" Mia asked again, and he thought she sounded like a woman-in-training.

"Of course I'm sure, sport," Zach answered just as the door cracked open. He'd been getting ready to summon a smile, but at the sight of Amanda one spread naturally across his face.

She didn't have the chain engaged this time, and the door was cracked open just wide enough for him to get a good view. She looked delightful. She'd pulled her fiery hair back from her pretty face, and her freckles popped out from fair skin scrubbed free of makeup. "Hey there, beautiful."

"Go away, Zach," she all but hissed. "And don't you dare try to say that you need to use the bathroom because I won't believe you this time."

"See? We drove all this way for nothin'. I told you this was the wrong thing to do," exclaimed Mia as she stood beside him, her small hands perched on her hips.

"Mia?" Amanda's voice contained shock as she let the

door fall open the rest of the way. Amanda was dressed in an old University of Miami T-shirt and faded blue jeans that clung to her slim figure the way Zach wanted to. Pink nail polish adorned the toenails of her bare feet. "I didn't see you standing there."

"He wouldn't listen to me," Mia said, jerking an accusing finger at Zach. "I told him that you didn't seem all that interested in ice hockey, but he kept saying you'd want to go."

"Go? Go where?"

"To the hockey game," Zach said, quickly sizing up the situation. Amanda was still angry at him, but she was much too polite to slam the door in the face of a nine-year-old child. Just in case, he braced a hand against said door. "I had an extra ticket, and I figured you might want to come."

"And of course it never occurred to you to pick up the phone and ask me if I wanted to come?"

"Sure it did," Zach said. "But I didn't think I'd like the answer, so here we are."

Amanda drew a full ration of air into her lungs, and Zach realized she was trying hard not to lose her temper. He wondered if Mia would agree to come along and run interference every time he and Amanda had an argument.

"If you didn't think you'd like the answer," Amanda said through her teeth, "why come at all?"

He grinned, enjoying the way the color had seeped into her cheeks. Her green eyes were as captivating as a cat's, but considerably more animated. Had it only been three days since he'd seen her last? It seemed like three weeks.

"I was hoping Mia and I could talk you into going with us. Hockey's just about Mia's favorite thing in the world. She thinks anybody who hasn't seen a game is deprived. Don't you, Mia?"

"I don't even know what deprived means," Mia answered.

"It means she's been missing out," Zach said. An idea struck him, and he leaned down, as though confiding in Mia. "Amanda's missed out on a lot of things. She spent ten years with this boring guy who didn't take her anywhere fun, and it had a bad effect on her. It gave her a mild form of this disease called agoraphobia, which makes her afraid to go out in public."

Mia's eyes grew as round as hockey pucks as she turned to Amanda. "Is that true, Amanda? Are you really afraid to go to a hockey game?"

It took Amanda a few moments to fight what Zach felt sure was a fresh surge of anger before she finally composed herself enough to answer. "Of course it's not true!"

"Then get a sweatshirt, and let's go. Our seats are close to the ice, and it gets pretty cold down there," Zach said, before she could add anything else, such as that ice would go up in flames the day she'd consent to go anywhere with him.

"Hurry, Amanda," Mia pleaded, and Zach couldn't have scripted it better. "If you don't, we'll miss the face-off."

Amanda tore her furious eyes from Zach to look at Mia blankly. "The what?"

"The start of the game," Mia explained.

Zach's eyes twinkled now that he had nearly succeeded in getting what he wanted. "Hurry, Amanda," he added. "You know Papa's Olds won't go above forty."

"Okay. Okay. I'll go," Amanda groused. "But I am not sitting in the middle this time."

"Fine," Zach said quickly, before she could change her mind. As long as she agreed to come, he wouldn't mind if she sat on the roof. He wanted to be with her, pure and simple, despite her senseless no-sex directive. He thought he could live by her rules because this had nothing to do with sex.

She turned to retrieve her belongings inside her townhouse, and he noticed the way the material of her jeans hugged her delectable bottom. For a moment, he felt dizzy.

Maybe insisting that his desire to be with her had *nothing* to do with sex was carrying things a bit too far.

THE GROWLING PANTHER in the center of the ice at the arena matched the miniature cats painted on Mia's cheeks. Since the forget-me-not on Amanda's shoulder had only lasted forty-eight hours, Amanda figured that Marlee must repaint new panthers whenever the old ones faded. She wistfully touched the shoulder that had been adorned by the forget-me-not, thinking that she'd like to pay Marlee another visit soon.

She was taken aback by the stray thought. Hadn't she told Zach less than a month ago that she wasn't the sort of woman who got her body painted? She blew out a breath. Until tonight, she wasn't the sort of woman who went to hockey games either.

She glanced down at her attire. A month ago she wouldn't have dreamed of going out in public in a pair of old blue jeans and a T-shirt. Tonight, with Mia urging her to hurry, she hadn't given her appearance much thought. She'd shoved her feet into some tennis shoes and grabbed her purse and a sweater. She didn't even have on any makeup, aside from a hurried coating of lipstick.

"These seats are great, Uncle Zach," Mia said enthusiastically, as they settled into seats four rows back from the perimeter of glass surrounding the ice. Amanda gave a silent sigh of resignation when Zach took the seat between herself and Mia. She'd gotten her way during the drive to Miami, but she should have figured she couldn't pass the entire evening without sitting next to him.

His left shoulder brushed hers, causing goose bumps to break out on her arm. She jerked away from him, and her right shoulder immediately collided with a soft mass of flesh. Amanda turned, intending to apologize, and almost screamed.

Her seatmate's face was a larger replica of the panthers on Mia's cheeks, and it was growling at her. She relaxed slightly, but only slightly, when she realized it was a mask.

"Pardon me," she murmured dutifully, but the masked woman didn't pay any attention.

The woman jumped to her feet, and hollered even though the game hadn't started yet. "Ice 'em, Panthers," the woman yelled to no one in particular, in a voice that could shatter eardrums.

Amanda inched away from her, bringing her shoulder back into contact with Zach's.

Everywhere their bodies touched, hers tingled, making it difficult for her to remember why she'd been so angry at him. He'd kissed her senseless and made her feel desirable, hadn't he? He'd claimed responsibility for the baby she was relatively sure they hadn't conceived, hadn't he?

He'd also walk away and not look back if she weren't pregnant. Amanda felt miserable. Considering that Zach had always been honest about his lack of intentions toward her, she shouldn't even be angry at him for that.

"I like the way you look in jeans," Zach whispered in her ear, deflecting the anger, inflaming the desire. Even though it was cool seated so near the ice, she felt uncomfortably hot. "There isn't another woman in this building who looks as good as you do."

Her pulse quickened at the compliment. She renewed her effort to remember why she was angry at him. That wasn't easy considering that his shirt of the day was a starry depiction of the solar system. Planets revolved around his broad chest and flat stomach.

"Agoraphobia," she muttered under her breath. "I can't believe you told Mia I suffered from agoraphobia. And, speaking of Mia, how could you use her to get in my door?"

"Mia loves me. She didn't mind helping." Dimple flashing, Zach took her hand and brought it to his mouth. At the soft, moist touch of his lips on her skin, heat shot from the back of her palm to the very center of her being. "And, as for the agoraphobia, it got you here, didn't it?"

"Hey," Mia objected loudly. Amanda shakily took back her hand while the little girl leaned forward in her seat and regarded them both with impatience. "If you're going to sit here beside me, you've got to remember the no-kissing rule."

"You're as bad a rule-maker as Amanda," Zach said, giving his niece's hair an indulgent pull. "Considering we're in public, I might go along with the no-kissing nonsense for the length of the game. But I'm not making any promises about afterward."

"I guess I can live with that," Mia said as she screwed up her mouth and dropped back in her seat before adding, "as long as I'm not around to see it."

"Get it out of your mind right now, Zach." Amanda figured she needed to set him straight, but to do so without Mia hearing she had to whisper in his ear. The sensation of being so close to him, with her lips almost touching his earlobe, made her lightheaded. "I'm not kissing you after the game. I didn't even want to come with you in the first place."

"Sure you did," Zach said, cupping her cheek. She knew she should turn away from his touch, but his palm felt so blissful against her flushed cheek that her muscles were temporarily immobilized. "The only reason you came to this game with me is because you wanted to."

His words effectively broke her daze. "I came because you tricked me!"

Zach shook his head, and his voice was so low that only

she could hear. "Stop fighting it, Amanda. You came because you wanted to, just like you let me into your townhouse the other day because you wanted me there. Just like you spent the day at the beach with me because you wanted to be with me."

The beginning strains of the national anthem prevented him from continuing the logical conclusion to his argument, which was she'd let him into her bed because she wanted him there. He got to his feet and reached for her hand, and she let him take it. *Because she wanted him to.*

Damn. She was holding his hand, reveling in the feel of his work-roughened skin against hers, because she wanted to hold his hand. Still, she couldn't let him have the last word, not when she'd made such a production about not wanting to come to the hockey game.

"I bet," she said when the national anthem was over, "that you wouldn't come with me if I showed up unannounced at your door and said we were going to the symphony."

He looked at her, widened his gorgeous eyes and squeezed her hand. "Sure I would. You should have told me that you wanted to go to the symphony."

"It's going to start," Mia said excitedly, as stick-wielding men in helmets took their positions on the ice. They were wearing so much protective padding that Amanda wondered why they didn't topple over.

She wouldn't have much chance of understanding the game while she was distracted by Zach's hand-holding, so she withdrew her hand from his and folded it onto her lap. A man in a zebra-striped shirt that Zach would have thought too tame to wear dropped a black disk onto the ice, and players skated haphazardly in every direction.

Amanda grimaced. She wouldn't be able to follow the action even by giving the game her full attention.

"You might enjoy the game better if you picked out a

player to cheer for," Zach said, as though sensing her confusion. "That way you could focus on one player and appreciate what he does in the game."

The player closest to them had long, flowing dark hair, which had made him stand out from the rest of the players during the warm-up. Amanda nodded in his direction. "I think I'll watch that one with the long hair. He's kind of cute."

"He's not even a Panther!" Mia, who had been listening to them, was indignant. "He's wearing black and gold, which makes him a bad guy. The good guys are the ones in the red and blue."

Zach peered at Amanda. "You think he's *cute?* He can't possibly be your type. He has really long hair, and a big, beefy face besides."

"What?" Amanda said, slanting him a look filled with incomprehension. "I think he has a cute face. And, besides, how do you know he's not my type? I'm branching out. Weren't you the one who told me that I should reach out and taste the chocolate?"

"Yeah, but I thought you understood I was the one giving out samples!"

Mia wasn't any happier with her than Zach. "Just don't embarrass me by cheering for him, all right?" she said before sitting back in her seat and crossing her arms over her chest.

The game passed in an incomprehensible whirl as the men fought for control of the disk—Mia called it a puck—that slid and skittered up and down the ice.

Zach was right, however. Focusing on the cutie with the strange name she couldn't pronounce helped. He epitomized grace and strength, and she began to appreciate the controlled skill with which the players moved on the frozen surface.

She'd never understand the fans, however. When the

home team scored, they rose en masse to utter a deafening roar. Most of them, including Zach and Mia, raised both arms overhead. And all of them seemed to enjoy it when one player bashed into another.

"Hockey fans sure are a bloodthirsty lot, aren't they?"

"Violence is part of the game," Zach said, and he grinned at her.

She felt a little woozy, and she wondered when her attraction to him had escalated so far that he didn't even have to touch her to get a response.

No more than a minute later, the long-haired cutie stole the puck and streaked down the ice. A Panther was hot in pursuit, but it was evident that he wasn't going to catch up. So he reached out a stick, hooked the cutie's ankles and pulled him down to the ice with a loud splat.

"Hey," Amanda yelled indignantly.

The cutie, full of what Amanda thought was righteous anger, came up swinging. The Panther threw down his stick, ripped off his gloves and flew at the cutie like the wild animal that had lent the team its name.

"Hey! You stay away from him!" Amanda screamed, leaping to her feet and pointing. The Panther, of course, kept attacking. The cutie got in a right uppercut, then a left.

"Punch him! Get him!" Amanda yelled, bouncing on the balls of her feet and mimicking the motions of a prizefighter.

"Oh, brother." Mia's exclamation was so loud even Amanda heard it over the roar in her ears. "She's embarrassing me, Uncle Zach."

LESS THAN AN HOUR after the game ended, with Mia safely deposited at home, Paul Castelli ushered Zach and Amanda into the cozy interior of a house that didn't look quite as cluttered as it had during her last visit. Amanda thought of her mother's ultra-tidy home in Plantation and concluded that this was the compromise when disorder met order.

"Thanks for letting me park the MGA here and use your car, Papa," Zach said. "I filled it up with gas on the way home."

"You didn't have to do that, son," Paul said, then grinned. "But I'm glad you did. How was the hockey game?"

"We had a great time." Zach's ever-present grin was teasing as he regarded Amanda. "But next time, I'm taking Amanda to a boxing match."

Paul laughed, as richly and smoothly as his son. His blue eyes crinkled at the corners, and it wasn't difficult to see why her mother had fallen for him. Not when he was an older version of his son. "So you liked the hockey fights, did you, Amanda?"

"Not exactly," she said, coloring.

"She sure did," Zach contradicted, while his arm came around her. Amanda briefly considered knocking it away, but the warmth of his body felt good after the chill of the night. "She was yelling and jabbing at the air as though she were Muhammad Ali."

"What's this about Muhammad Ali?" Amanda's mother appeared from the back of the house dressed in an oversize plaid bathrobe that undoubtedly belonged to Paul Castelli. Her gray hair was mussed, and Amanda hoped it was because she hadn't brushed it lately. Paul smiled at Pauline as though she were Aphrodite emerging from the sea. He took her hand and kissed it. "Was Ali at the game?"

This was the first time that Amanda had seen concrete proof that her mother was living with Zach's father, and for a moment she felt as though her air supply had been cut off. Zach gave her shoulder a comforting rub, and she started to breathe again.

"No, he wasn't," Zach answered, "but Amanda did a great impression of him."

"Oh, how exciting. She used to put on the most marvelous one-girl plays when she was a little girl." She frowned. "I haven't seen her act in such a long time."

"I wasn't..." Amanda started to refute what Zach had said, but then she caught the twinkle in his eyes. He was teasing. Again. Her eyes twinkled back, and then she looked at her mother. "I might take up acting again. Or maybe shadowboxing."

"That's wonderful, dear," her mother said. She smiled at Paul, as though she couldn't help herself, and then looked back at Amanda and Zach. "Can I get the two of you something to drink?"

"Nothing for me, Pauline," Zach said, still lightly massaging Amanda's shoulder. "We're not staying long. I just wanted to bring back the car and point out that one of the turn-signal bulbs is burned out."

"Which one?" Paul finally tore his gaze from Pauline.

"It's one of the bulbs on the right side of the car," Zach said. "If you have a spare, I'll change it for you."

"I think I have one in the garage," Paul said, dropping a soft kiss on Pauline's upturned lips. Zach didn't kiss Amanda, but his eyes were warm when they looked at her. She smiled at him.

"We'll only be a couple of minutes," Zach said, returning the smile. She watched him walk out of the house with his sexy, long-limbed walk, his father at his side.

"I hope you're still not upset about Paul and I living together," her mother said, when they were alone.

Amanda prepared to reassure her mother, but the words wouldn't come. She might have been able to muster a denial if her mother hadn't been dressed in Paul's bathrobe, but she wasn't even sure about that. She sighed and crossed the room to the sofa. She dropped down into it, and her mother followed suit.

"I don't want to be upset," Amanda said, running a hand through her hair, "but I can't seem to help it."

"Oh, honey." Instead of becoming angry, her mother took one of Amanda's hands in both of hers, a gesture that Amanda couldn't help but link with Paul Castelli. "Let me explain something to you. Something I should have explained a long time ago."

She paused, and blinked a few times. Moisture glistened in her brown eyes.

"Your father died when you were just a year old, so you can't possibly remember this. But I loved him like the flowers love the sun." She gave a watery smile. "Aside from you, he was my world. My life. My everything."

"Mother, you don't have to tell me this."

"But that's just the point, dear. I do. I do, or you won't understand." She tightened her grip on Amanda's hand. "For a long time after your father died, I was dead inside. Eventually, I revived a little, but I was certain I would live the rest of my life without a man's love. I couldn't imagine loving anybody like I loved your father."

"Is that why you pretended that you didn't realize I was trying to fix you up with those men I invited for dinner?" Amanda asked with sudden insight.

"They seemed like nice men, and I couldn't bear hurting their feelings," she said. "But I didn't want to date them. I didn't want to date anybody. Until I met Paul."

Amanda grew still. She had a premonition that her mother was about to say something important. Maybe even something life-changing.

"When I met Paul, it didn't take me long to realize that I was getting a second chance. All those years without your father, I had been merely existing. But here...here was love. And suddenly, life was radiant again."

"Are you trying to say you fell in love with Paul at first sight?" Amanda asked.

"Not at first sight. No." Her mother shook her head. "But I know better than most people that you can't take happiness for granted. That you have to embrace it because you never know how long it will last. Before the day was over, I had found something so special with Paul that I couldn't let it go. Something like you've found with Zach."

"Zach?" Amanda's eyebrows shot up, and her heartbeat quickened. "What does Zach have to do with this?"

Her mother smiled. "Everything, dear. If you hadn't fallen in love with Zach, I wouldn't have found Paul."

"But I'm not in love with Zach," Amanda denied reflexively, even though a little voice inside her protested that she was lying. She tried to silence the voice with logic. "How could I be in love with Zach when three weeks ago I was in love with Reid?"

"You were never in love with Reid, dear," her mother said, shaking her head. "Haven't you figured that out yet?"

"But, I..." Amanda started to deny her mother's words, but then stopped. If she had been in love with Reid, getting over him wouldn't have been so effortless. Or so painless.

"You're in love with Zach, dear. I think you have been from the first night you met him."

"But... but..." Amanda sputtered, trying valiantly to collect her thoughts. "But I always thought that the females in our family were one-man women."

"There's something else I never told you, dear. I was afraid to because you were always such a sensible child and never one to act on impulse." Her mother smiled conspiratorially. "I'm afraid that we Baldwins aren't one-man women so much as we are quick workers. I only knew your father for one month before I married him."

ZACH WONDERED at Amanda's silence as they walked an arm's length apart to the front door of her townhouse. She'd been fairly chatty at the hockey game and afterward, but she'd seemed pensive since he'd left her inside his father's house with Pauline. Pensive and remote.

"Are you still upset about your mother and my father?" he asked, hoping that's all it was. He didn't think he could stand it if she went into her I-can't-see-you-anymore routine again.

She didn't answer until they'd reached the two steps leading to her door. She climbed the first one, just as she had the first night they'd met, and looked at him. Their eyes, and their mouths, were level.

"She says they love each other." Zach watched her lips as she talked. They looked more luscious than milk chocolate. And kissable. Eminently kissable. "She lived for so long without a man's love that I can't be upset. Not when she's so happy."

"It's me, then, isn't it?" Zach jammed his hands into his pockets so he'd be less tempted to touch her. He leaned backward on his heels so his mouth wouldn't come forward. The fragrant scent of her strawberry shampoo had been teasing his nostrils all night, and now it combined with the smell of orange blossoms that wafted in the night air.

"Listen, Amanda. I'm sorry about whatever I said at the beach that made you so angry. I've been racking my brain, and I can't figure out what it was. But that doesn't mean I'm not sorry about it."

She stared at him, her eyes huge in her beautiful face.

He jerked his fingers through his hair. "I know I'm making a mess of this apology, but just be patient with me. I heard what you said about sex without commitment, and I can live with that. Don't get me wrong, I don't like it. But

I can live with it." He sighed. "Not that I want to live with it—"

"Zach?"

"Yeah?" he asked, grateful that she'd interrupted him.

"Aren't you going to tell me that I'm predictable?"

His eyes widened as he remembered how angry she'd gotten the last time he said that. "I'm trying to apologize here. Not make you angry again. So why would I say that you're predictable?"

"Because then I might do something unpredictable." She wet her lips, and for a moment he couldn't breath.

"You're..." he whispered huskily, afraid to trust his instincts on what she was offering "...so predictable."

She grinned then, a grin that rivaled the best ones he had given her. Then she reached out, grabbed him by the planet Saturn on his shirt and pulled him to her.

The kiss was different than the others they had shared because it was as reverent as it was passionate. He closed his eyes and let the sensations flow through him and into her. He tried to tell her with his mouth that she was more, much more, than a fling. If that's all she had been, his body wouldn't be growing rock hard even as his heart softened. He wouldn't feel as though he needed her kisses as much as his lungs needed air.

When she broke off the kiss to unlock the door, he knew what he had to say even though everything inside him rebelled.

"I still can't give you a commitment," he said. He glanced into the darkness of the night because he couldn't stand to look into her face and see the rejection written there.

"I know," she whispered back, and his eyes fastened on hers. They were glowing with an emotion he didn't dare try to identify. "But I don't care anymore."

She grabbed his hand and pulled him inside.

10

CELIA LEWIS STAGGERED into the women's restroom at the *Fort Lauderdale Times* and headed for Amanda, who was at the mirror applying lipstick the color of red wine. The back of Celia's hand pressed against her forehead as if she were staving off a swoon.

"There is a man out in the hall who is to die for," Celia said, her voice lilting dramatically. "Lord have mercy, I do love a man in a tuxedo."

Amanda smiled at her friend's antics and unhurriedly finished putting on her lipstick. For a moment, she'd thought Celia was describing Zach. But he wasn't due to pick her up for another ten minutes, and she was quite sure he wouldn't show up wearing a tuxedo.

"Speaking of looking fine, look at you," Celia said. Amanda regarded her reflection in the mirror. She'd pulled her hair back into an elegant French twist, and she was wearing a clingy black dress that flared around her thighs and was held up by spaghetti straps. Sheer black hose and high-heeled pumps completed the ensemble. "I would have noticed if you'd worn that to work. When did you transform yourself?"

"Just now. I changed in there." Amanda indicated an alcove off the restroom and then smoothed her skirt. "I had to work late tonight, but Zach didn't want to cancel our date. Do you really think I look okay? He's supposed to meet me here any minute."

"Do you mean that hunk out there is Mr. Forgets-You-Not?"

"Is the hunk wearing a white shirt under his tuxedo?"

Celia nodded.

"Then trust me. It's not Zach. He'll be wearing banana yellow or neon green. Now, how do I look?"

"Like you want to be ravished." Celia noted the effect of her comment and positioned her fists on her hips. "Suppose you tell me what's going on. The last I heard, you didn't want to have fun and play games with Mr. Forgets-You-Not."

"I changed my mind," Amanda said, thinking that love had changed it for her. Since the hockey game three nights ago, she and Zach had spent every non-working hour together. She didn't want to admit how deep her feelings ran, so she tried for flippancy. "Maybe I am the fun-and-games type, after all."

Celia chuckled while she checked her makeup in the mirror. "I know I am, girl. Believe it or not, I have a date too. A blind date. But a date. I've gotta go. If I go now, I might even get another long look at the hunk in the tuxedo."

Amanda smiled, but the smile faded as soon as the door closed behind Celia. Even the thought of Zach planning their first arranged date couldn't completely cheer her because this date was destined to be their last.

Her mother had been wrong when she claimed that you never knew how long happiness would last. Amanda knew because Zach had put a deadline on theirs. It was up tonight, when she informed him that he was free to take the job in North Carolina.

"Stop it, Amanda," she told her sad-eyed reflection in the mirror. "You've had three glorious days with him. You knew going in that there wouldn't be many more. Just stop it, and enjoy this last night with him."

She squared her shoulders, picked up her purse and the bag containing her clothes and walked out of the restroom.

She wasn't going to tell him her news until the night was over.

The man in the tuxedo had his back to her, and Amanda's first thought was that he had a long-legged, broad-shouldered physique that rivaled Zach's. Her second was that he couldn't possibly be as good-looking as Zach. Then he turned.

She blinked once. Then twice. Then another time.

The tuxedo-clad hunk, the one Celia had said was to die for, was her own sapphire-eyed, dimpled Zach. He grinned and let out a low whistle as his appreciative gaze took in her appearance.

"Why didn't I think of this date thing before tonight? You look spectacular."

At any other time, his praise would have warmed Amanda to her toes. Tonight, she was too busy squinting at him in surprise. "Is that a white shirt you're wearing?"

"I'm not sure," he said. "I'm color-blind."

"You're color-blind?" Amanda's mouth dropped open. "Gosh, I should have figured it out before now! That's why you're always wearing those crazy shirts with all those mismatching colors!"

Zach let out a hoot of laughter. "Amanda," he said, "I'm not color-blind."

"You're not?"

"No." The corners of his mouth were still twitching with amusement. She tried to glare at him, but couldn't manage it.

"You're a devil," she said.

"Then give the devil his due," he said, "because I have quite a night planned for you."

Her expression softened, and she hooked her arm into the crook of his elbow. He bent down to kiss her upturned lips. For a moment, their mouths clung. She savored the moment, tucking it into the storehouse of memories that would be all she'd have left of him after tonight.

MORE THAN three hours later, Zach speared a piece of triple-chocolate cake off the dessert plate he was sharing with Amanda and popped it into his mouth. Her fork was suspended in mid-air, and her assessing eyes ran over his face as he chewed.

"What's wrong?" He wiped at the corner of his mouth. "Do I have a big gob of something on my face?"

She shook her head and smiled. He loved it when she smiled at him. Her green eyes gleamed with something tender that reached out and filled him with warmth. He smiled back.

"No gobs," she said. "I was just trying to figure you out. Was I dreaming tonight or did you actually take me to the symphony and then to a restaurant where you had reservations?"

"You have to have reservations to get into this place." Zach indicated the crowd of well-dressed people who still waited at the front of the elegant restaurant. "And I thought you wanted to go to the symphony. You said as much at the hockey game."

"I did want to go. I just didn't think anybody as impulsive as you would arrange an evening like this."

"I wanted to show you how cultured I can be," Zach countered. "I didn't want you to think that I spend all my time guzzling beer, watching ball games and having fun."

"So you're saying that going to the symphony's not any fun?"

He grinned, remembering the way she had buried her face against his shoulder in a valiant attempt to smother her helpless laughter during a particularly solemn movement of Beethoven's Fifth. "I thought it was pretty much fun tonight."

"That's because you kept likening the performers to their instruments!" she exclaimed.

"It wasn't my fault that skinny, flat-chested woman looked like her flute. And I wasn't the one who told the bulkiest man on stage to take up the bass cello," he said as he leaned back in his seat. "Admit it. You had fun tonight."

Her lips quivered with remembered amusement. "I had fun tonight," Amanda said dutifully, and brought some sinfully rich chocolate cake to her mouth. She savored the taste as she chewed. "I think I've finally learned to appreciate the merits of premium chocolate."

Zach was still thinking about Amanda's comment thirty minutes later as he pulled his MGA into the parking lot outside the *Fort Lauderdale Times* newspaper. She'd meant that she'd learned to appreciate him, and that elated him.

Because of the lateness of the hour, only a few cars remained in the parking lot. He pulled alongside hers, put his into park and left the engine idling. He reached across the seat to fondle the soft skin at the nape of her neck and felt her shiver. He smiled.

"Your place or mine?"

When she stiffened, his fingers stilled. The wind blowing through the convertible was cool, and he had a sudden premonition of disaster. It hit with a vengeance when she spoke.

"I think we should sleep apart tonight, Zach."

It was a testament to Zach's powers of denial that he hadn't seen this coming. She'd had bouts of melancholy between the laughter tonight, but he thought they'd vanish if he ignored them. He tried to make his voice light. "Who said anything about sleeping? I feel a lot of things when I'm around you, Amanda, but sleepy isn't one of them."

"Don't." The word sounded like a plea.

"Don't what?"

"Don't make this harder than it has to be."

"Since I don't know what you're talking about," he said, fearing that he did, "I can't make any promises."

"I'm not pregnant, Zach."

"What?" His heart stopped in mid-beat. He'd kept his word to himself, and he hadn't mentioned pregnancy since the night she'd gotten so angry with him on the beach. That didn't mean he hadn't thought about her belly swelling with his child.

"You heard me. I'm not pregnant," she repeated, and he waited for the rush of relief to wash over him. Instead, he went numb. His throat felt dry. Bone dry.

"So," she continued, not looking at him, "you can take that job in North Carolina."

Zach licked his lips. The only time he had thought about the job in the past week was the day before when he'd listened to a message on his answering machine asking for his decision. He'd ignored the message and promptly forgot about the job offer.

"What does your not being pregnant have to do with me taking that job?"

She sighed, and she sounded miserable. Just like he felt. "You said you'd stay until we were sure I wasn't pregnant. We're sure. There's no reason for you to stick around anymore."

"That doesn't mean," Zach said uneasily, "that we have to end things tonight."

"Yes. It does. It has to end, Zach. Right here. Right now. We've both known all along that it has to end. Please don't make it any harder on me than it already is by postponing it."

Zach opened his mouth to protest, but then closed it. He didn't want her to leave him, but he couldn't give her any reason to stay with him. What could he say? That the man who'd never committed to anything in his life had suddenly seen the light?

Pain flowed through him as if there was an open wound in his heart.

"Can I at least kiss you goodbye?" he asked.

Her eyes were sorrowful when she finally turned toward him, and fresh pain assailed him because he knew he was responsible for the sorrow. He also knew that he couldn't take it away. He reached for her anyway, because he couldn't help himself, knowing he hadn't been able to since the first time he'd seen her.

As their mouths met, he imagined that the valves holding his heart in place were intertwining with those surrounding hers. He drank in the taste of her, knowing that he'd never forget it.

Finally, she wrenched her lips from his. Moisture glistened on her cheeks, and he wasn't sure if it was from her tears or his. She gazed at him with eyes reflecting passion and sorrow, before jerking open the car door. He sat stunned as she fumbled in her purse for her keys and opened her car door. A moment later, he watched the red taillights of her car as she drove out of his life. Then she was gone.

Gone, like the pregnancy that never was. Gone, like the gladness in his heart.

11

ZACH SWIPED at the low-hanging branch of a black olive tree as he walked up the sidewalk through the jungle his father called a yard. The cool blue sky was bright and cloudless, but Paul Castelli's yard was shaded by short, fat areca palm trees and bougainvillea growing out of control.

The ambiance was so overpowering, and so familiar, that Zach's heart hurt. He hated saying his goodbyes in person, which was why he'd been more than sixty miles up the road when he'd gotten the SOS over his cellular phone.

His father's shower door had come off the hinges again, and he asked if Zach could fix it before he left town. Zach, who'd had the phone service at his beach house disconnected days before, didn't bother to point out that he'd already left town.

Fueled by the certainty that his father would spend the next six months taking baths, Zach had executed a neat U-turn.

An hour later, he was in Paul Castelli's front yard. He called a greeting through the screen door and let himself into the house. Pauline was reading the newspaper in the living room, and she looked up long enough to glare at him.

"Hey, Pauline," he said, and that apparently was enough to cause her to set the newspaper down and stalk out of the room. He stared after her, puzzled.

He found his father in the bathroom unsuccessfully struggling with the broken shower door. "I can't ever fix this blasted thing," he griped, swiping at the sweat on his brow. "Thanks for coming to do it for me."

"You know I don't mind," Zach said, "but it might make more sense if you'd let me buy you a new door."

"We've been over this before, son. It's not broken. Just temporarily out of order. I'm just glad you hadn't left for North Carolina yet." Something in Zach's expression must have given him away. "You had left already, hadn't you?"

"Don't worry about it. I hadn't gotten far." Zach waved aside his father's apology before he could make one. Then he jiggled the pieces of the shower door.

"What's with Pauline?" he asked as he worked. The door was well and truly stuck. "She acted like I was persona non grata."

"You know the saying, 'Hell hath no fury like a woman scorned?'...well, I think they should change it to, 'Hell hath no fury like the mother of a woman scorned.'"

"I didn't scorn Amanda!"

"Pauline thinks that you did."

Zach muttered an oath. "C'mon, Papa. This is me you're talking to. I wouldn't hurt anybody, least of all Amanda."

"Then why," he asked softly, "are you leaving her?"

Zach sighed because he'd been struggling with the same question for days. For the first time in his life, he wasn't eager to start his next assignment. For the first time in his life, he hadn't wanted to leave. "Because it's what I do, Papa. I leave. You know that. Everybody who knows me knows that."

"Maybe it's time to ask yourself why you leave."

"You know why." Zach was annoyed that his father, who knew his deficiencies so well, would make him voice them. "I can't commit. I never could. Not to anyone. Not to anything."

"Malarkey."

"Malarkey?"

"Yes, malarkey. You're here, aren't you? You turned your car around and came back because I needed you. What do you call that if not commitment?"

"I call it love," Zach said.

"Exactly."

That said, Paul Castelli clapped his son on the shoulder and left him alone in the bathroom. For long minutes, Zach stared blindly at the white tile on the wall, digesting what his father had just said.

Could his father be right? Could he have fooled himself all these years into thinking he couldn't make a commitment when he had been committed to love all along?

He was a man who had never loved anyone except his family. He'd certainly never loved a woman. Until now.

Until Amanda.

Could that be why he hadn't been relieved when she'd told him there was no baby? Why he'd kept forgetting to ensure there wouldn't be? Why he hadn't wanted to leave?

Zach ran out of the bathroom and down the hall, nearly plowing into Pauline in the process. He put out his hands to steady her. She glared at him.

"Sorry," he said, "but I need to get to a phone."

He wasn't aware of Pauline following him into the living room, or of her watching him as he punched in the number, but she must have because she was regarding him warily as he listened to the endless unanswered rings. For once, he was phoning ahead and Amanda didn't even have her answering machine turned on.

"If you were calling Amanda," Pauline said after he hung up, "she's not home."

"Where is she?" Zach knew he sounded desperate, like a man gone mad, but he couldn't help himself. He'd just realized he could have what his parents had, what his father had with Pauline, and he didn't want to wait any longer.

"Humph," she said, and would have turned away if he

hadn't gripped her arm. Her gaze was unfriendly. "Why do you want to know? You're leaving, aren't you?"

"No," Zach said vehemently, surprising her, surprising himself. He lowered his voice. "No. I'm not leaving this time."

A slow, brilliant smile spread across Pauline's face. "She's having lunch with Marlee at a restaurant in Fort Lauderdale. I'm not sure of the name, but Marlee says it serves great vegetarian dishes with lots of sprouts."

Sprouts. Zach almost laughed aloud because he knew where they were. He kissed Pauline full on the lips, and headed out the door, with a smile as bright as the pattern on his shirt.

MEETING HERE FOR LUNCH had been a very bad idea. Amanda gazed around the familiar restaurant, taking in the dramatic contrast of green plants and dark, burnished wood, before bringing her attention back to Marlee. Through the shield of her granny glasses, Marlee's eyes were blue. Like Zach's.

Because she couldn't help herself, Amanda pictured him sliding into the booth and sending her one of those dimpled smiles. *And then what would he do?* she asked herself crossly. *Ask you to marry him? Mr. I'm-Not-About-Commitment? Yeah, right.*

"The next time we have lunch," Amanda said, smiling wanly at Marlee, "can we have it someplace else?"

"Someplace else?" For a moment, Marlee looked blank. Then she grimaced. "Oh, no. This is where you two met, isn't it? I'm such an idiot. Here I am trying to cheer you up, and I'm depressing you. We can go somewhere else."

"We've already ordered, Marlee. Don't worry about it. I shouldn't even have mentioned it. I'll be fine." The words were no sooner out of her mouth than Amanda knew they weren't true. How could she be fine when Zach was gone? She knew, with a quiet and desperate certainty that she was going to spend the rest of her life yearning for what she couldn't have.

Marlee reached across the table and patted one of Amanda's hands. Adorning it was the first of a trail of forget-me-nots that extended up her arm. Marlee had painted them the day before and then wanted to cheer her up by inviting her to lunch.

"Men are such jerks," Marlee said.

"Zach's not a jerk. Remember what you told me the first time we met? That he was tender and funny and completely carefree? You were right. He is. It's not his fault I fell in love with him."

"It is too his fault. I swear, Amanda, if he weren't my brother, I'd…" Marlee broke off in mid-sentence, and she seemed to be looking past Amanda.

"You'd what?" Amanda asked.

A queer look came into Marlee's eyes. "I'd…I'd go to the restroom."

"What?"

"Excuse me." Marlee scooted to the edge of the bench seat and stood up. She grabbed her purse and slung it over her shoulder. "I hope I'm doing the right thing."

What she said didn't make sense. When you had to go, you had to go. Because Marlee was a Castelli, Amanda nodded anyway. Then she leaned back against the highback leather bench-seat and closed her eyes. A few tears seeped out of them.

"Hello, Amanda."

The voice was deep, rich and unmistakably Zach's. Amanda didn't for one second think the voice was real. She'd simply flashed back to the first night they'd met, to the moment she'd been sniffling over Reid's defection. An eon ago, before she'd realized the true meaning of love.

"Amanda?"

She knew he wasn't there, but she opened her eyes anyway. And saw the same wild, paint-spattered shirt that she'd seen that night. Her eyes lifted to his cleft chin, luscious mouth and straight nose, his sapphire eyes and high forehead. The features came together to form the face she loved. The face of the man who had made her love him. And then left her. Her defenses rose.

"What are you doing here?" she asked, swiping at the tears.

"The name is Castelli. Zach Castelli." He extended one of his hands just as he had that first night, and the intonation in his voice, again, was pure James Bond.

"What are you doing?" she repeated, ignoring his hand.

He grinned, looking boyish and handsome and dear. She knew from Marlee that he was leaving for North Carolina today, so he was probably here to say goodbye. How was she going to resist him when all she wanted was to throw herself in his arms and beg him not to leave?

"I'm starting over," he said.

"Starting over?" Amanda blinked, then shook her head. She couldn't let him see how badly she was hurt. "As usual, Zach, you're not making sense. And I'm not in the mood to try to figure out what you're talking about. Besides, I'm having lunch with Marlee. She'll be back any minute."

"No, she won't."

"Of course she will. She just went to the restroom."

He shook his head. "She went to the parking lot. I asked her to. I was standing behind you, just about even with the next booth, when she saw me."

"You were eavesdropping again!" Amanda's mouth dropped open while she frantically tried to remember what she'd said before Marlee excused herself. Oh, God. She had said that she loved him.

"Yep, I was eavesdropping." His smile was good-natured. "I didn't plan on it, but then I realized the two of you were talking about me."

"Look at you. You're not even ashamed of it." She regarded him fearfully out of the corner of her eye. "How much did you hear?"

"Let's just say that it's not true that eavesdroppers only hear bad things about themselves."

"That's just great," Amanda said bitterly. "You do realize that I didn't mean it?"

"Oh, no. I heard you. You can't take it back."

"There goes my pride," Amanda said, dropping her head. "Just get out of here, Zach. The embarrassment of a stranger listening to your fiancé dump you is nothing compared to the humiliation of the man you love overhearing a declaration of unrequited love."

"Who says I don't love you back?"

Amanda's head snapped up. Her heart thumped painfully in her chest, and her eyes were wary. "What?"

"Who says I don't love you back?"

"I heard what you said, Zach," Amanda said, exasperated. "I was asking what you meant."

"I mean," he said slowly, clearly, "that I love you."

Amanda nodded gravely, realizing that she'd known that on some level for the past week. Nobody could act the way Zach had acted without being in love.

"Okay. I can accept that. Now will you leave?"

"Leave?" It was his turn to look confused. And adorable. And irresistible. "Why should I leave?"

"Because," she said succinctly, trying to resist him, "as you're so fond of telling me, you're not about commitment. I am, Zach. I can't put my life on hold until you finish your job in North Carolina and come back here. I can't be with a man who will never ask me to marry him."

Zach took a breath. "Will you marry me?"

"What did you say?" Amanda bit her lip.

"You're not making this easy on me, Amanda. I just asked you to marry me."

"But you call marriage the state of unhappily ever after."

"The only way I'm going to live unhappily ever after," Zach said slowly, his eyes never leaving hers, "is if I live without you."

Her eyes teared. "You want to marry me?"

"More than anything in the world." He reached across the table and gripped her hands, covering one of the forget-me-nots, and he looked almost desperate for her to believe him. "If you say yes, I'll stop traveling all over the country. I have enough money saved that I can start a charter fishing business right here in Florida.

"You'll see, Amanda. I'll commit. To the business. To you. To children. I was a fool when I said those things about commitment. My father helped me see that today. I'm committed to my family. I'm committed to love. I'm committed to you."

"Oh, Zach," Amanda said, her heart swelling. "You never had to convince me that you could make a commitment. You only had to convince yourself."

"Then you'll marry me?"

She wanted to shout her acceptance, but instead she pretended to think. "I've only known you for a month, Zach. Don't you think accepting a marriage proposal after a month would be too impulsive?"

Zach's grin, the one she loved, spread across his face. "I think," he said, playing along, "that you're about the most predictable woman I've ever met."

"Then, yes, I'll marry you," she said, and smiled back at the man who'd turned her world upside down.

The view, she thought, was much better from here.

ROMANTIC FANTASIES COME ALIVE WITH

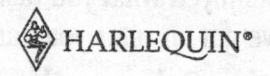

HARLEQUIN®

INTIMACIES

Harlequin is turning up the heat with this seductive collection!

Experience the passion as the heroes and heroines explore their deepest desires, their innermost secrets. Get lost in these tantalizing stories that will leave you wanting more!

Available in November at your favorite retail outlet:

OUT OF CONTROL by Candace Schuler
NIGHT RHYTHMS by Elda Minger
SCANDALIZED! by Lori Foster
PRIVATE FANTASIES by Janelle Denison

Visit us at www.eHarlequin.com

PHINT1

If you enjoyed what you just read,
then we've got an offer you can't resist!

Take 2 bestselling love stories FREE!
Plus get a FREE surprise gift!

Clip this page and mail it to Harlequin Reader Service®

IN U.S.A.	IN CANADA
3010 Walden Ave.	P.O. Box 609
P.O. Box 1867	Fort Erie, Ontario
Buffalo, N.Y. 14240-1867	L2A 5X3

YES! Please send me 2 free Harlequin Duets™ novels and my free surprise gift. Then send me 2 brand-new novels every month, which I will receive months before they're available in stores. In the U.S.A., bill me at the bargain price of $5.14 plus 50¢ delivery per book and applicable sales tax, if any*. In Canada, bill me at the bargain price of $6.14 plus 50¢ delivery per book and applicable taxes**. That's the complete price—what a great deal! I understand that accepting the 2 free books and gift places me under no obligation ever to buy any books. I can always return a shipment and cancel at any time. Even if I never buy another book from Harlequin, the 2 free books and gift are mine to keep forever.

So why not take us up on our invitation. You'll be glad you did!

111 HEN C24W
311 HEN C24X

Name	(PLEASE PRINT)	
Address	Apt.#	
City	State/Prov.	Zip/Postal Code

* Terms and prices subject to change without notice. Sales tax applicable in N.Y.
** Canadian residents will be charged applicable provincial taxes and GST.
All orders subject to approval. Offer limited to one per household.
® and ™ are registered trademarks of Harlequin Enterprises Limited.

DUETS00

Your Romantic Books—find them at

www.eHarlequin.com

Visit the *Author's Alcove*

- Find the most complete information anywhere on your favorite author.
- Try your hand in the Writing Round Robin— contribute a chapter to an online book in the making.

Enter the *Reading Room*

- Experience an interactive novel—help determine the fate of a story being created now by one of your favorite authors.
- Join one of our reading groups and discuss your favorite book.

Drop into *Shop eHarlequin*

- Find the latest releases—read an excerpt or write a review for this month's Harlequin top sellers.
- Try out our amazing search feature—tell us your favorite theme, setting or time period and we'll find a book that's perfect for you.

All this and more available at

www.eHarlequin.com
on Women.com Networks

HEYRB1

You're not going to believe this offer!

In October and November 2000, buy any two Harlequin or Silhouette books and save $10.00 off future purchases, or buy any three and save $20.00 off future purchases!

Just fill out this form and attach 2 proofs of purchase (cash register receipts) from October and November 2000 books and Harlequin will send you a coupon booklet worth a total savings of $10.00 off future purchases of Harlequin and Silhouette books in 2001. Send us 3 proofs of purchase and we will send you a coupon booklet worth a total savings of $20.00 off future purchases.

Saving money has never been this easy.

I accept your offer! Please send me a coupon booklet:

Name: _____

Address: _____ City: _____

State/Prov.: _____ Zip/Postal Code: _____

Optional Survey!

In a typical month, how many Harlequin or Silhouette books would you buy <u>new</u> at retail stores?

☐ Less than 1   ☐ 1   ☐ 2   ☐ 3 to 4   ☐ 5+

Which of the following statements best describes how you <u>buy</u> Harlequin or Silhouette books? Choose one answer only that <u>best</u> describes you.

☐ I am a regular buyer and reader
☐ I am a regular reader but buy only occasionally
☐ I only buy and read for specific times of the year, e.g. vacations
☐ I subscribe through Reader Service but also buy at retail stores
☐ I mainly borrow and buy only occasionally
☐ I am an occasional buyer and reader

Which of the following statements best describes how you <u>choose</u> the Harlequin and Silhouette series books you buy <u>new</u> at retail stores? By "series," we mean books within a particular line, such as *Harlequin PRESENTS* or *Silhouette SPECIAL EDITION*. Choose one answer only that <u>best</u> describes you.

☐ I only buy books from my favorite series
☐ I generally buy books from my favorite series but also buy books from other series on occasion
☐ I buy some books from my favorite series but also buy from many other series regularly
☐ I buy all types of books depending on my mood and what I find interesting and have no favorite series

---

Please send this form, along with your cash register receipts as proofs of purchase, to:
In the U.S.: Harlequin Books, P.O. Box 9057, Buffalo, NY 14269
In Canada: Harlequin Books, P.O. Box 622, Fort Erie, Ontario L2A 5X3
(Allow 4-6 weeks for delivery) Offer expires December 31, 2000.

PHQ4002

MAITLAND MATERNITY

Where the luckiest babies are born!

Join Harlequin® and Silhouette® for a special 12-book series about the world-renowned Maitland Maternity Clinic, owned and operated by the prominent Maitland family of Austin, Texas, where romances are born, secrets are revealed...and bundles of joy are delivered!

Look for

MAITLAND MATERNITY

titles at your favorite retail outlet, starting in August 2000

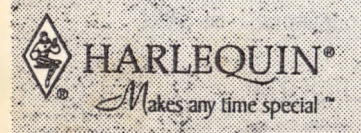

HARLEQUIN®
Makes any time special™

***Silhouette*®**
Where love comes alive™

Visit us at www.eHarlequin.com

CELEBRATE VALENTINE'S DAY WITH HARLEQUIN®'S LATEST TITLE— *Stolen Memories*

Available in trade-size format, this collector's edition contains three full-length novels by *New York Times* bestselling authors Jayne Ann Krentz and Tess Gerritsen, along with national bestselling author Stella Cameron.

TEST OF TIME by Jayne Ann Krentz—
He married for the best reason.... She married for the only reason.... Did they stand a chance at making the only reason the real reason to share a lifetime?

THIEF OF HEARTS by Tess Gerritsen—
Their distrust of each other was only as strong as their desire. And Jordan began to fear that Diana was more than just a thief of hearts.

MOONTIDE by Stella Cameron—
For Andrew, Greer's return is a miracle. It had broken his heart to let her go. Now fate has brought them back together. And he won't lose her again...

Make this Valentine's Day one to remember!

Look for this exciting collector's edition on sale January 2001 at your favorite retail outlet.

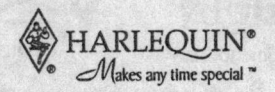

HARLEQUIN®
Makes any time special ™

Visit us at www.eHarlequin.com

PHSM